the
MERCY
DIALOGUES

a novel

PHILIP
KENNEY

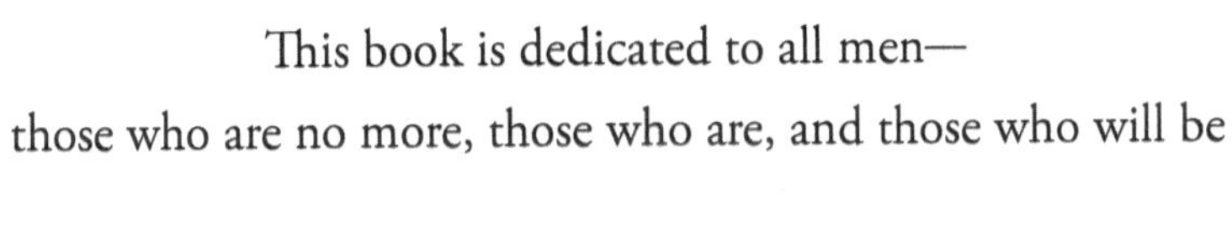

This book is dedicated to all men—
those who are no more, those who are, and those who will be

Autumn evening—
it's no light thing
being born a man.

Kobayashi Issa (1763-1827)

PART ONE

WHAT WAS BROKEN IS SHATTERED

At the end of my suffering
there was a door.
Hear me out: that which you call death
I remember.

—Louise Glück, *The Wild Iris*

Chapter 1

In the chill of a late august morning, Dr. David Chase, still wearing his surgical blues, paused on the stairway outside his home and cast a glance toward the west hills of Portland. There, a long, swollen bank of smoke stretching the length of the ridge loomed over the city like a medieval army of dread preparing to storm down the west slope and engulf the City of Roses.

Had he turned and looked to the east, he would have seen the sunrise turn an ominous blood orange as though the sky too was ablaze and trying to warn him of the dreadful event in the making. But he did not. He turned his back on the hundreds of miles of fire and smoke racing up the coast of the Pacific from California to Oregon, pillaging groves of redwoods in the Golden State and devouring Sitka spruce that cover the coastal hills of Oregon.

Dr. David Chase turned away from the smoke storm that would soon occupy Portland and bring anxiety and dread to its people. He walked into his house, closed the door, and thought nothing of the devastation to the forests or the suffering soon to envelop his neighbors, their eyes burning and lungs filled with ash. The fire and smoke did not touch him because before noon, his life as he had known it ended on a sidewalk holding the broken body of Emily, his only child. Emily suffered a gruesome death. She died in her father's arms, and the mind of David Chase, held together for years by rigid bands of fear, shattered into a thousand pieces of rock while what little there was of his soul drifted away toward the smoke and ash.

. . .

It is said only a daughter can open a man's heart. Only a daughter can locate the hidden chamber that makes men tremble. Emily sensed the truth of her father's life: that love is the villain. She knew what he could not face, that his heart was barricaded. It opened on occasion, but only for an instant, and it closed fast as a door slammed shut by a draft of wind. Emily's mother, Claire, was the first to realize that his heart was more than muscle and though hardened, built with blocks of loneliness. But it was the stealth love of Emily that found the cracks in her father's deadened interior; it was the exuberance and unbounded joy of her being that found its way inside and began undoing his blockade.

Otherwise, only the quickened pulse for the curve of a woman interrupted the mechanics of his life. Most of his hours were spent at an operating table under bright lights, removing one heart and replacing it with another. One heart, taken from the dead, given to the living. Warm hearts that resume the rhythms of living, of day and night, of loving and hating. The beat that starts and stops once in a lifetime.

On occasion he wondered what he might find if he carved open his own chest. An empty cage? A piece of dried fruit? These wonderings were brief, and Dr. David Chase went about his business of cracking open chests, tunneling through arteries, and chasing women, one after another. In the gaps, he tried but failed to rid his mind of the sight of blood.

Until the end. Until all the light that can be seen left his world and the blood of his daughter's life spilled over his chest, through the cloth of his shirt, and into his skin, becoming his. Emily left this world as she had entered it, bathed in blood. As she left her mangled body, a whispered prayer for her father passed through her lips—a prayer that would haunt David Chase throughout the darkened days to come.

"Daddy . . . love . . ."

Chapter 2

Hour no. 1

David Chase stands alone outside an office door. The door dares him to enter as he paces in the hallway. He is a tall pole, wooden and stiff in his movements, unable to be still. In a moment he will sit face-to-face with someone and speak for the first time in nearly three years.

The door opens, slowly, then wide. There is a figure. The figure is a blur. It says something from underwater. Then it moves aside.

David Chase moves past the door, past the figure, into a room. The door closes. The room is a perfect square. A box. The figure is a body now. It motions to something, a chair with wooden arms. By a window.

David Chase drops into the chair and crumbles.

The other body lowers into a chair. It is leather. And brown, like chocolate. The body speaks. A voice moves toward David Chase; it circles him like smoke.

Welcome, Dr. Chase, I am Dr. Ed Jones. Please make yourself comfortable. Your friend and attorney Keith Stone informed me that you would be coming for therapy. I understand you have suffered a terrible loss, and you are struggling to get your life back. My sympathies go out to you. I have also been informed that you once saw Dr. Smith, but he has retired from practice. It seems most unfortunate, considering the circumstances, that you need to begin with someone new. But I trust

*we can get to know one another and establish a working relationship to
help you through this ordeal and reclaim your life.*

How can I be of help, Dr. Chase?

Dr. Chase? Dr. Chase, I'm here.

David Chase looks to the door, but the door is a wall now, a
faceless barrier barring a way out. He closes his eyes, and his head
drops to his chest. It takes a few moments for him to speak, and when
he does, his voice is barely audible and drenched in defeat. "No."

*You're not able to talk just yet? I understand. I can wait. Please
take your time.*

"No. Nothing." His voice raises a decibel.

Nothing, I see. Maybe you're telling me that nothing will help you.

"No help."

Are you trying to tell me you don't deserve my help? Is that right?

"Dead."

*Dead? Perhaps you feel numb. I can imagine you're in shock, terrible
shock, Dr. Chase. You've suffered a horrific trauma.*

David Chase stands. He walks to the door and back to the
chair, muttering to himself. He sits and stands again. This time he
turns around, and with his back to the figure in the chocolate chair
he says, "Him." When he turns around his face has disappeared.

The man in the chocolate chair shifts his weight to one side.
His brow furrows as he struggles to understand what David Chase
is trying to tell him. A strange disturbance grows in his stomach as
he begins to sense David Chase is not a person, but a collection of
shattered selves. He clears his throat.

*Him? I don't understand, Dr. Chase. Are you telling me someone
else is dead? Dr. Chase, who is dead?*

Dr. Jones says the words, but a great confusion has taken over his mind.

"He should be."

I see. You are alive and you think that's not right, you don't deserve to be.

"Everyone but him."

Others are dead and you are not. Why should you be dead?

The room leans toward the man who should be dead.

"Wretched, should be dead."

What have you done that you deserve to die?

"Too wretched to die."

The one too wretched to die turns to the door abruptly.

The door opens and closes on a tomb.

The figure in the chocolate chair stares at the trail of ghosts that follow in the wake of David Chase. He shudders and rubs his face, trying to break the spell. The tomb is silent.

Chapter 3

Dr. Robert Bergstrom, the evening's attending physician on the emergency room floor of Emanuel Hospital and the person in the hospital most resembling a friend in the narrow life of David Chase, sat in his office outside the operating room with a stack of reports waiting for his review. But he was unable to work, staring at the cold plaster wall, worrying about the operation underway to save Claire, the wife of David Chase, and her baby. His agitation only increased wondering about the whereabouts of David Chase, who could not be found anywhere in the building.

"Dr. Chase, please report to Emergency. Dr. Chase, to Emergency."

For the third time in fifteen minutes the voice on the PA system blared its demand. Each time the urgent plea sent a surge of anxiety through Robert Bergstrom's body. It was after midnight when Claire had begun hemorrhaging and was taken by ambulance to the hospital. She was eight months into a high-risk pregnancy and was immediately rushed into surgery for a C-section delivery and attempt to save her life and the life of her baby.

Robert knew David was on call and had probably not received the message about Claire's condition. Yet that didn't add up because the hospital staff was competent enough at communicating with the medical teams and should have located him. Robert's anxiety was turning to agitation when he realized where David Chase would be unreachable. With a start, he pushed back his chair and leapt to his feet, but before he took a step, the door flew open and Claire's brother Andrew burst into the room.

"Where the fuck is that bastard? Where the fuck is he? My sister's in there dying and her fucking husband is nowhere to be found. Fuck him, he's probably out fucking a dog."

"You go back and be near Claire, Andrew. I'll find him, go on."

Robert Bergstrom left his office and raced to the elevator. As he ran down the hallway, he saw the look on Andrew's face in his mind's eye. He had seen that look in the eyes of hundreds throughout his career. The desperate look of those about to step into a world no longer inhabited by family and love. Robert entered the elevator and hit the button for the fifth floor, where the old cardiac operating rooms waited to be updated.

■ ■ ■

The sounds of a woman flooding and breaking into rivers of delight filled the vacant hallway and echoed off the no-longer-sterile walls as Robert left the elevator. The song of pleasure and a light coming from Room 4 toward the end of the hallway told him where to find David. At the door, Robert Bergstrom hesitated, brought short by a propriety that acted on him despite the moment's urgency. In that hesitation he looked through a window in the door and saw brown legs high over David's shoulders and a pink, candy stripe dress layered back on the operating table. He saw the blues of David's surgical gown bent over the body moving like foothills shaken by a quaking earth.

For a second Robert Bergstrom envied David Chase. Then he crashed through the door and shouted at David with all the contempt he'd concealed from his friend for years. "Damn you, David, Claire's in trouble, get the fuck down to ER!" David's pink candy shrieked at the intrusion, not realizing she was only a few gasping breaths away from being discarded.

David had spent weeks priming her for this moment. Seducing with intermittent flattery, difficult-to-come-by flashes of his crystal blue eyes, and the occasional light touch to her forearm. He was always careful not to make too much of it, but to slowly develop in a woman the feeling of possibility and the fantasy that she might be different from the others. The hunt was as routine as the daily surgical procedures he performed. It required only the patience needed to lure in a fish on the line. It required even less of him to turn and abandon his women. He simply pulled up his surgical pants and followed Robert out the door.

"Claire's here?"

"Jesus, David, what the fuck? What kind of man are you? This is the worst." Robert Bergstrom picked up his pace and tightened every muscle he could to restrain the impulse to bloody the face of the man he now wished he'd never befriended. "Yes, she's here, in ER. She began cramping and bleeding around midnight. Martha called the ambulance, but by the time she got here she was in bad shape."

David Chase stared straight ahead, his face blank as a chalkboard.

"Claire is in there bleeding to death and you're fucking some teenager."

"She's hemorrhaging?"

"You cold prick. When I left, they had the bleeding under control, but it doesn't look good. What a bastard."

Without another word they walked the narrow hallway. The lights in the corridor flickered as they passed. In the elevator, they stood shoulder to shoulder in an ominous silence. The tension in the enclosed space shrank the elevator to the size of a telephone booth. Each wanted to flee, to run. Robert Bergstrom watched the floor numbers change and cursed the elevator for not going faster. David Chase gazed at the braille writing above the selection board and felt an urge to rub his fingers over the rounded nubs. Neither of them thought about the young woman trying to gather herself to walk the long corridor of her humiliation.

At the operating room David Chase forced his way through the door past the nurses. Narrowed eyes riveted him with scorn. But David saw only Claire, her legs spread, blood everywhere, her empty body still as the dark. When he reached her, the faintest light remained in the brown eyes of the woman who had brought him in from the cold. He could not tell if the slight shimmer in her eyes and hint of a smile meant she recognized him or if becoming a mother had brought happiness to her final breath.

And then, her eyes went blank. The light left her like the last sliver of the sun going into the ocean. As she left, David Chase heard the cry of the wild. He turned to see his daughter in the hands of Dr. Jefferies, slathered head to toe in the blood of her mother. Forever coated with her mother's sacrifice and love, Emily took her first breath of air from this world informed by the union of life and death.

She cried as some sing. As a bird might in early April, the sound was one of joy, not pain. The room stilled, listening. The strangely pleasant song of her hello captured the breath of attending doctors and nurses alike. It banished the contempt they held for David Chase so that when Dr. Jefferies handed the newborn to her father, and when they saw Claire's blood coat his hands and arms, and when they saw him, for the first time anyone could recall, moved to tears, his face overcome by awe, they forgot their bitterness, forgave life for its cruelty, and joined him to gather around Claire to allow her soul's departing glance to be of the beautiful, ruby red child her body had made and given to the world.

Chapter 4

Hour #2

The door is closed. On either side, a man waits. One is a barren, burnt field. The other is a lake containing images that swim. The door opens and the charred ruins of a person walk toward the other. The smell of water is lost to David Chase. The door closes and they sit, six feet apart.

Hello, Dr. Chase. Welcome back. Where would you like to begin today?

The silence is heavy, dense as a child's fear.

"No."

No? No, you don't want me—

"No. Nothing."

You don't want anything. You don't want to be—

"Nothing. I am nothing. Nothing."

Nothing but wretched.

Dr. Jones feels the return of the disturbance in his stomach. His head turns to the window and the morning light.

"Not even that."

Dr. Chase, can you . . .

"Stop! I am not a doctor."

What name would you like me to use?

"Don't."

You'd prefer I not use your name?

"I am no one."

Will you tell me what it's like for you, this wretchedness?

"Why?"

I'd like to know what you're experiencing.

"You want to get inside."

Yes, I want to get to know you, you're right.

"I have no inside."

You feel wretched.

"No. I am wretched."

You are wretched, no inside, only wretched, nothing else.

"Nothing."

The room begins to squirm. There is a ripple on the surface of the lake. David's eyes are fixed to the far corner of the room. Dr. Jones remembers a nightmare from his childhood. His eyes want to close.

You're telling me you are nothing but wretched, there is no you left, only this terrible badness. You seem to feel you deserve nothing, no help, no empathy, nothing—

"No. I deserve this."

Tell me why you don't deserve to be here.

"I told you, I'm here because I'm too wretched to not."

Yes, you're right, you did tell me.

"You don't want to believe it."

You may be right. It could be that I'm feeling a very small bit of what you feel, that what has occurred and what you are living with is too horrible, too devastating, to get near. Yes, I think you're right—too horrible to feel. I shouldn't try to rush you.

"Not living. Dead. Nothing."

Not living, dead, nothing. I understand now how important that is. I'm wrong to try to alter that. That is yours to decide, and yours only.

The lake is still. The room looks to the burnt field and exhales. David Chase feels nothing, but his eyelids blink twice, and those eyes, prisoners of horror, turn ever so slowly from the corner of the room toward the window. They lower and come to a rest on the shore of the lake.

Chapter 5

David Chase never saw his brother-in-law coming. Andrew Nelson's furious fist to the jaw sent him tumbling headfirst to the unforgiving concrete. The impact made a terrible crushing sound— the crunch of a head-on collision at an intersection. David fell and landed on his side. His head hit the floor and he lay there on his stomach unconscious like a dead man in a murder mystery. Andrew stood over David outside the ER operating room like Ali over Liston, shaking his fist and releasing years of repressed rage. His face was red, his fists were clenched, and spit flew from his teeth. He managed to kick the disgraced doctor in the crotch before the orderlies dragged him away yelling, "Fuck you, David Chase, fuck you, you bastard, you killed my sister, you're gonna pay for this, you son of a bitch."

The blow to his head sent David's mind into delirium. Bizarre, fragmented images of Claire hung in the air, floating like disembodied figures. Her face assumed a range of expressions from the sublime to the grotesque, from Rembrandt to Picasso. They flashed on and off in his mind, one strange portrait after another, before morphing into an image of her face as he knew it. The image grew larger and larger until it filled the room and then silently blew into pieces which fell like a soft rain to the cement floor, where each slowly disappeared like raindrops on a hot sidewalk.

He woke with a start and rolled onto his side crying for her. Robert knelt by his broken friend and held his arms. David Chase grabbed him and cried his name and then hers, desperate for a look that would signal it was all a terrible dream—that the blood was not real, that Claire was holding the baby right now, that she had not vanished into the cold, sterile floor, that he had not failed her once again. But Robert gave him no such affirmation. He shook his head when David cried Claire's name and pleaded for word of her ongoing life. When those words were not forthcoming, the frantic hope emptied from his eyes and he collapsed back onto the floor, staring into the bright light of the truth.

Chapter 6

Hour #5

There is no door. Only walls that meet, and divide. No outside. An inside that must not be. That is not. The body is there again, but it is no more real than a slice of a forgotten dream that drifts by and evaporates.

Tell me why you come to therapy, Dr. Chase.

"What?"

I'm curious why you come to see me.

"I don't."

You don't come of your own choosing?

"I'm not here. You keep talking to me as if I were a real person, as if I am here. You insist on me being Dr. David Chase. That is your mistake."

The walls buckle and moan.

You tell me you're not here, but you are. You're sitting in that chair. Somehow you arrive at the door at the right hour on the right day. I hear your voice and you hear mine. Tell me, where are you if you aren't here?

"It should be obvious. I am dead."

But why? I know your friend, Keith Stone, suggested you come to therapy, but why? Why do you think you are here? What do you want? Why do you show up?

"You don't listen. You want me to be something. Someone.

Why do you want that so badly? Why don't you just accept that I am gone?"

Gone is not dead.

"Dead and gone. Dead and gone."

Then why did your friend beg you to come to therapy? And why do you? Something in you is not dead, I feel it. And something in you is hiding, not gone. Terrified, not dead.

"You're pushing."

It is true. He is pushing again. He is ashamed of wanting to break something. Wanting to break into what must not be entered. Dr. Jones pauses and exhales for the first time in the hour.

I am pushing. I am. We could sit here for years and agree that you are dead but that would, I think, be a disservice to you. I have an idea of the massive loss you have suffered and the pain, the unimaginable pain that you live with, that you try to extinguish—

"No pain. Everything dead."

Everyone and everything is dead. No life survived. It's all dead, and it can't touch you. It can't hurt you ever again.

"No pain."

Yes, no pain. No hurt. No love.

"No."

No?

"No love. Love kills."

I see. Love kills. You believe your love killed someone. Who did you kill?

"I told you."

Tell me again, who did you kill?

"It doesn't matter."

You're sure you killed someone, and you feel . . . no, you have sentenced yourself to damnation.

"I don't have to."

Yes, I see, you're right, you don't have to because there is no mercy for what you have done. There is only death.

"No heart."

You have no heart— is that why you are wretched and deserve no mercy?

"Never."

You're telling me you never had a heart?

"I eat people, women, I eat women—she was right."

The ceiling cringes. Dr. Jones looks to the window for air. For something living. He finds it hard to breathe.

Your mother said something, she told you . . . she said you were killing her, she saw you as bad, as eating her alive.

"She knew."

And you believed her. Of course, you believed your mother. What happened? Tell me about her. Something bad happened, didn't it? What was it? I have the feeling you've been carrying this secret for a long time, David. I think it's eating you up.

"Tulips. There were tulips on her dress."

The air in the room turns humid. It recognizes the scent of tragedy leaking in through the windowpane. Dr. Jones sees the tulips, but not the blood.

Chapter 7

David's mother had her first psychotic break on the morning of his third birthday. It was a cold day in January. The snow was deep and drifted against the fence surrounding their house. His mother put on her swimsuit and bathing cap, humming to herself, and paid no attention to her little boy while he watched. She emptied her cup of coffee and dried her lips. From the kitchen, she walked to the front door and into winter's grip with nothing on her feet but nail polish. She paused on the front steps, gazed into the blinding white, spread her arms wide, and gave a shriek that frightened a band of crows from the wires.

In sync with their flight, she ran, gasping and whooping, and dove headfirst into the bank of snow mounded against the fence. She lay there kicking and rolling in her white dream. David stood on the front steps, watching. Shivering, and wearing nothing but pajamas, he ran after her, imitating her cry and the freedom of her limbs, and jumped feet first onto her snow-covered breasts. "Mommy, Mommy." He yelled her name again and again, loud enough for all the neighbors to hear. But his mother did not see him running to her. Startled by his landing, she screamed, and when she did, dry snow fell from the branches above them.

She screamed again, throwing him off her body into a foot of snow. When he freed himself and stood, he saw her running down the street away from home. Her body moved differently than it had when she'd run from the house. It zigged and zagged across the street and back, and as it did, she yelled at the top of what was left of her lungs, "That thing tried to kill me! That thing wants to eat me! Help, somebody, help me." She disappeared around the corner as her voice trailed back to a shaking, bewildered boy. He did not see her for six months.

■ ■ ■

When he was six, she ran away again. This time was different. He watched her carefully pack her bag full of dresses, pants, and blouses. She packed a second bag with her hairbrush, toothbrush, makeup, and a few bottles of pills. He stood there and said nothing. His mother stared at a photo on the wall, as if trying to remember something important.

"Where are you going, Mommy?" he asked.

But she didn't answer. She kept staring at the picture on the wall.

"Mommy, are you all right?"

She turned and looked at him. Her eyes had already left. And then she said something he didn't understand at all.

"Tell your father it's his turn." A smug smile passed over her face as she bent over to pick up her bags.

The little boy followed her to the bedroom door. "How will I get to school?"

With her back and frozen shoulder blades turned toward him, his mother walked from the room, leaving only one word behind.

"Swim."

Chapter 8

Hour #9

There is no exit. No floor, only falling. The room cannot hold him. Dr. Jones cannot hold him. David Chase is falling backwards, through a black hollow of fear.

"He killed everyone."

Who did he kill?

"Everyone."

People he loved?

"No love. He didn't love."

He couldn't love, could he? Maybe he wanted to, but he couldn't.

"Good people, good . . ."

These people mattered to him. They mattered enough to condemn himself when things turned bad.

"He is bad. That's all."

He blames himself for everything that happened. He sent himself into exile, never to return.

"That is the only thing he deserves."

His punishment seems just. That is the only way he can live with himself, isn't it? By not living. A life sentence of not being.

"No life."

Right, no life, no person—stare at the prison wall, shit, walk in perpetual darkness—the perfect sentence. No pardon. Solitary confinement.

"A pardon would be unforgivable."

Who did he kill? Who did he eat?

Dr. Jones is pale now. Both men are cold. The room shivers.

"There was blood. So much."

There was blood, too much blood. You remember the blood— you can't forget it.

"Blood . . . on her cheek . . . on the tulips."

Your mother's dress. What does he remember?

Dr. Jones fights with the urge, the perennial urge, to turn away, to not look. To never know. He straightens his back and puts both feet on the floor and without thinking, leans forward ever so slightly.

"Hers. He can't, I don't . . . he . . . he . . ."

What? What does he know?

The room closes its eyes. David buries his face in his hands and begins to shake. The clock on the wall stops.

"He closed the door. He closed it, he shut . . ."

And then?

"He was choking. He walked away—dead."

That's when he died.

"He should have stayed with her. She's dead. He killed her. She was good. He should have died . . . he's bad, too bad to die."

He couldn't bear it. Seeing his mother like that. He was a boy, wasn't he? He lived because he felt he needed to be punished.

"He wasn't done with blood."

More, there was more blood. What are you remembering, David?

"More blood. So much blood. He couldn't get away. It was all over him. He shut the door."

And he never opened it.

"So much blood."

Blood drips from the clock. And the horror that cannot be washed away sits down between the two men. Their eyes are vacant, stunned. They are suspended somewhere between the room and the garage where the car is still running, and the blood is still moist on her cheek.

Chapter 9

On a Wednesday morning, David's mother left the beauty parlor and drove slowly through the leafy neighborhoods toward home. Her hair was done beautifully, like Audrey Hepburn's, and her nails were perfectly manicured. She wore her favorite dress, a cotton one with large red tulips on a gold background.

Admiring her freshly painted fingernails which matched the ruby red of the tulips on her dress, she drove the new Plymouth down the street to her empty house, into the two-car garage, and parked it in the middle. She got out of the car, leaving the engine running, closed the garage door, locked it, and got back in the car. Settled in the seat, she shut the door, rolled down the windows and took a slow, deep breath. Then she gazed at her fingernails as if admiring the first rose in bloom. A sigh slipped from her lips and the fingers of her left hand rose slowly to stroke her cheek. With tenderness, she dug her nails into that same flesh until blood covered her cheek and the color of her skin matched the polish of her nails and the tulips on her dress. She turned and looked at her face in the rearview mirror. Satisfied, she lay down on the bench seat of the Plymouth wagon, pulled her knees up to her chest, and closed her eyes.

He was nine years old. He left school that afternoon and walked home slowly. It wasn't unusual for him to find the house empty or discover his mother asleep on the couch, an empty glass on the coffee table. He put his backpack on a chair in the dining room and walked into the kitchen. There, near the fridge, the eerie feeling waited for him. Though the house was quiet, he had the odd sensation that she was there, somewhere. Maybe in bed.

Then he heard a rumble coming from the garage. The boy walked to the door, opened it, and saw the Plymouth parked in the middle of the garage, the engine running. He walked down the steps toward the car, and the eerie feeling followed, turning to nausea as a strange smell spread into his stomach and head. He coughed, covered his mouth, looked through the passenger window, and saw her. Her knees were tucked up like a child napping and one arm was folded under her head as a pillow. She looked comfortable. Her face was without expression despite the blood covering her cheek. He stared at her. She did not move. He coughed again, worse this time, and felt dizzy and weak. He turned, gagging now, and hurried up the stairs to the door to the kitchen. At the door he hesitated and turned for a brief look, but all he could see were tulips and gold.

■ ■ ■

David found himself in the park near his school, sitting on the seat of a tall swing set. He wasn't sure how he got there or why. He sat alone, his back slumped. His feet scuffed the dry dirt, covering his shoes in dust. In time he pushed away from the ground and began to rise in the air, hesitantly at first, then with more and more will behind his efforts. The swing and his young body climbed the steps of space and soared toward the sky. It was the closest he ever came to being rocked.

The upward flight and the downward glide, both of which came to a brief but soothing pause at the conclusion of the arc, brought some ease to his heart. In that hallowed realm, detached from beginnings and endings, David held tight to the chains in his hands. The dread, the fear, the bewilderment, the image of his mother napping, and most of all, the scent of a motherless world, all of it, vacated his body like vapor.

He swung back and forth, back and forth, and the movement put him into a trance. He dreamed of letting go of the iron chains. He saw himself gliding through space. For an instant, he disappeared altogether. He didn't mind. When he came back, he saw himself tumbling to the dusty dirt. He saw his body land headfirst, break into pieces, and lay there, still. Just as his mother lay in the Plymouth. He felt nothing at the sight of his body broken and motionless on the dry ground.

As he began a downward arc, David made the first decision of his life in a motherless world. It was a decision made without thought or desire. He held tight to the chains and aligned himself with the movement of the swing through space and its indifference for up or down, back and forth. A surprising lightness came over him.

At that moment, David exited the exhausting world of yes and no and entered a thin line. A narrow realm of being and nonbeing. This new life, this flat line, the renunciation of all that is soft and sensual, of all caring—especially caring—made it possible to turn away. He turned his back on life and his inner world and in doing so created what nothing else could: a dimension for memory within the narrowed space of his existence. And in that empty, lonely chamber, unbeknownst to him, he preserved the feeling of his mother's presence.

Chapter 10

Hour #15

The room is confused. Confusion turns to worry. David Chase is not there. The minutes pass. Dr. Jones looks at his watch; he looks out the window and sees a squirrel run across the power line. The squirrel stops short, looks about, and scampers on. Dr. Jones stands and walks to the window. He admonishes himself for thinking of tulips and blood. But it does not stop the anxiety building in his chest, nor the doubt; had he pushed David Chase too hard, too fast? Had he driven him over the edge? There is a knock at the door—the room flinches.

David, you're here, come in. I was worried—you're usually so prompt.

"Did you think I finally jumped?"

Well, no, I . . .

"Sure you did. Why wouldn't you? You're close."

Close?

"I'm done."

Done? You want to stop coming?

"You want to make me a person. You want me to feel. That's wrong."

Why is that wrong?

"I've told you. I am nothing. I deserve nothing. Why don't you get that?"

Why do you come?

"I don't know. I was told to. But I'm done."

It must have frightened you last hour to get so close to that little boy inside. To see the blood, to feel something. I understand if you want to run, David.

"What blood?"

You made it all go away since then. You made him go away too, exiled, as though he never existed.

"Nothing is real. You should know that."

Where is he now?

"I told you. You don't listen."

I'd like to talk with him.

"You can't."

I'd like to know about those people who died. They must have been important to him. I'd like to help him with the blood. Perhaps wash it off his hands. If he'll let me . . .

"No! Get away! You're trying to eat me! Get away!"

Why are you so afraid of him?

"He's a monster. He wants to suck the blood out of me. He wants to devour me. Got to get out—get out of here. Out."

Why would he want to kill you? He's a little boy. He is you.

"He's not me. He's not my little boy. He's a thief, a murderer, he's no one's little boy. No one wants him. Look at him, he's a wretched leech, a cannibal. Get him away from me before he sucks all my blood out."

David bolts out of his chair for the door. The door braces. The room pleads with him to stay.

Stay, David, don't run, she can't hurt you now. Stay, sit down, this will pass. I'll make sure you are safe. Stay.

"I can't. Don't you see what's happening to me? I'm going insane."

The many emotions inside your psyche are trying to release. They want to be freed. The little boy who experienced the horror of finding his mother in the garage is trying to speak. I want to hear him and understand what he has to say. And his pain, I want to understand his pain. I trust him.

"No. No, I can't. You can't. This is bad."

David stops and leans his head against the door and moans. Moans turn to sobs of anguish. The door accepts the weight of him like a mother as the torment of his soul cries out. Dr. Jones listens to the scream from hell. He resists the temptation to leave, to wander off somewhere pain does not rule. And he stays and admits to himself that he cares for this person, that he aches for him.

David's breathing slows. He turns and pauses before returning to his seat. He sits and looks at the floor and slowly lifts his head to look at the man sitting across the room. It is the first time. He sees the red cheeks and the moist eyes and turns his head to look back at the door, confused by the feeling in his chest.

I'm glad you stayed, David.

"I don't understand that. I don't understand what's happening."

I think you're coming back to life.

"Why would I do that? That's stupid, nothing but pain."

Maybe there's more. Maybe there's caring, and this thing called love.

"Love?"

The man in the chocolate chair nods. And smiles. The word

reverberates through David's body, but it is the smile that is too much to take in. He looks to the wall behind Dr. Jones for refuge and for the first time notices a painting over his shoulder. It is a simple painting of various shapes and colors. The colors are vivid but soft. They cause him to forget about himself for a moment.

From his seat David watches the chocolate chair across the room turn to mud and then back to leather. He looks up at the face gazing at him and sees kindness on that face looking back at him. He receives what he can and turns back to the painting on the wall—it is not a collection of abstract shapes and colors. It is a photo of a sunrise over the desert. At this moment of recognition, the impossible makes its first appearance. It slips unnoticed under the narrow opening between the door and the carpet like a ghost and flies to David's side where it wraps its arms around him like a mother wrapping a woolen shawl around a shivering child. It is the breath of mercy.

Chapter 11

David met Claire at a conference for cardiologists and cardiovascular surgeons in Chicago. He took his seat at the back of the lush, grand ballroom just as Claire was introduced to deliver the Saturday morning keynote address to a group of a thousand mostly white male doctors. As she walked to the podium, he noticed something uncommon about the way she held herself. Poised, deliberate, and without pretense, she moved with a quiet, steady command. At the podium she paused and looked out into the audience intently, taking the temperature of the room. The pause lasted long enough to create a subtle stirring in a room full of people unaccustomed to being observed.

Claire began her talk with the usual greetings and pleasantries. But after giving thanks for the opportunity to speak and a brief introduction of her work as an emergency room heart surgeon and counselor to doctors and surgeons across the country, she paused again, this time to indicate a shift in tone. Under the bright light of the massive crystal chandeliers, she dove into what had become the theme of her challenge to her comrades across the country. "All of us have looked into the naked, beating heart of a human being. Many of us have taken such a heart from its home and held it while not fully grasping the mystery of the life pulsing in the palm of our hand. We have studied and worked long, hard hours to care for the people who put their trust in us, but we have done little to help make their hearts and lives truly vital. The sad truth is we have saved lives but failed people."

With that, Claire looked out at the Saturday morning audience, searching for a sign of recognition. Some held her with a mix of surprise and interest. Many looked down at the day's program, refusing to meet the challenge in her eyes. Her audience, accustomed to flattery, was unsettled by the woman at the podium who dared to question the status quo of their work. These were the best and the brightest, unmarked by failure. Claire sensed a disturbance in the atmosphere, perhaps a crack in the self-congratulatory mood of attendees fresh off a Friday night of fraternal festivities. When a few from the back of the ballroom stood and left, she was sure her opening remarks had struck a nerve.

As Claire continued with her talk, David Chase felt a different discomfort. He wanted nothing to do with the ego-inflating banter of the cardio docs set loose on a forty-eight-hour pass. He had long ago banished any need for the affirmation of others or escape into alcohol for solace. His character was a fixed grid of invulnerability which made the discomfort he felt all the more unexpected. He was confused by Claire's opening message and mystified by his reaction to the person on the stage. It was not the quickened pulse he was used to when a woman caught his attention. Although Claire was attractive, some would say lovely, it was not her appearance that pulled at him. And though David could not have said what was drawing him in, the resonance in Claire's voice, the tone of steadfast compassion, and the sense of an uncommon integrity in her presence made its way into his otherwise impermeable world.

And as it did, an unfamiliar urge to speak with this woman took control of him.

Her voice struck him like the ringing of a bell. His breath caught and he remembered something and tumbled into a dream. A little boy sat on his mother's soft lap listening to the soothing music of her voice near his ear. The spell may have lasted five seconds, it may have lasted five minutes; he was not aware of time and only dimly aware of the strange but pleasing comfort that entered his body.

All of this disappeared as quickly and mysteriously as it appeared. David came back from the spell to hear Claire's hypnotic voice move into the sure-footed closing challenge of her talk.

"We have allowed ourselves to be taken hostage by insurance companies, pharmaceutical companies, and our own desire for comfort and status. We are guilty of putting profits over people. We have become fixers, not healers, prisoners in a heartless economy of disease. We treat the heart as an organ and do not go near the heart as soul. Our work, and I fear our hearts, have become soulless, mechanical. I implore you to lay down your insatiable egos and your devotion to gain, especially the illusory gain of self-importance.

"Devote yourselves instead to the service of well-being and the development of harmony in your patients, the world, and yourselves. Remember the astonishment you felt when you came to understand the intricacies of the heart. Remember the awe you experienced when you first peered into an open chest and stared at a real human heart, beating, pumping, and serving every cell of the body. Go, infect your patients with this state of wonder. Tend to their emotional and spiritual health. See them for what they are, whole people governed by tired and wounded hearts. Introduce yourselves and those who are heartsick to the mystery and awe to be found in simply being alive. Thank you. I wish you peace."

Claire was Midwest Plains. The quiet still of the prairie showed in the calm of her gaze, the pace of her speech. She lived with humility, at peace with the ordinary. Claire was Willa Cather, no pretense, no illusion, steady as the fertile ground under her feet. She had moved to Portland to be near the trees, to bathe in green. And she, too, was a motherless child, taken in with her brother Andrew and loved at the age of four by her Aunt Martha after losing both parents in an auto accident.

Like David Chase, Claire knew the presence of loneliness in a solitary life. She didn't hide from it; she felt it, and she lived in that sorrow from the moment her eyes first opened each morning to a new day. She also lived with yearning. A yearning to be with someone, to feel the closeness she knew with the Douglas fir and cedar trees. But now in her early forties, she felt her faith waning, and drops of despair seeped into her heart as she faced the possibility that her life might always be one of solitary service.

The gathering of doctors and surgeons sat motionless, embarrassed by the truth. Claire took her seat on the stage with the other speakers, most of whom avoided her gaze. Slowly, a few doctors, mostly women, began to applaud, tentatively at first. Then, as more joined in, a momentum grew and swelled until many were standing, applauding with gusto. A great relief filled the room, if only for the moment, from the constant striving and pretense that hounded their lives. They sat back down on the folding chairs under the ballroom's crystal chandeliers, all but oblivious to the closing remarks of the conference coordinator. Such was the strength of Claire's words and person.

David Chase rose from his seat at the conclusion of the morning program and walked to the stage. By then he had quite automatically transformed the strange discomfort in his chest into the familiar intoxication of the hunt that quickened his pace. But the line of women waiting to talk to Claire was long, and as he stood watching her greet each person with warmth and respect, the familiar rush drained from his limbs. As it did, the space in his chest opened ever so slightly. He couldn't identify it then, but in time he would come to realize that in Claire's presence the rigid sculpture of his life could not persist. It would, of its own accord, break down like an old stone wall, slowly, one rock and then another.

When the last of the doctors had hugged Claire and left, David Chase waited on the stage. He stood at an uncomfortable distance looking at her and said nothing. He stuffed his hands in his pants pockets and finally, after an interminable moment of awkward silence, he said hello. Claire returned the greeting, and in the pause that held that simple word, the unfathomable will of destiny took these two unlikely strangers into her arms and embraced them.

. . .

Claire sat by the window of Café Mingo at a table for two. She was waiting for her best friend Julie to join her for dinner and filled the time listening to the bustle in the kitchen of the boutique Italian restaurant. She watched as couples and groups of friends filled the café. The sound of friendly chatter and smell of onions and garlic on the grill helped her ignore the simmering anxiety in her stomach. She crossed her legs and uncrossed them, trying to forget her discomfort by staring out the window at the Friday night traffic of Portlanders filling the sidewalks.

It was unusual for Claire to feel nervous about meeting up with Julie. They'd been best friends since med school at Harvard and Claire trusted her more than anyone in her life. It certainly wasn't because Julie was late; that was a given for someone who booked every hour of her calendar the way Julie did. Claire wasn't sure why these feelings were showing up on this night but was relieved of the wondering when she saw Julie dart across the street and charge through the door.

"Claire, hello, hello, so sorry to make you wait. Phew! Rick is out of town and the damn babysitter was late again. Time to give her the pink slip!"

Claire stood and the two gave each other a quick but heartfelt hug. "No worries. Here, catch your breath. I took the liberty of ordering you a glass of your favorite. Time to relax and pretend we're normal." Claire looked at the wine rather than at Julie, trying to hide the uneasy look in her eyes. The moment they hugged she realized why anxiety was brewing in her gut. Of course, word had gotten to Julie that she was seeing David Chase, and of course her outspoken friend from Boston would be all over it.

Julie raised her glass and said, "You're a saint, my dear, which is not very normal in these times."

"Saint Claire, wasn't she the sidekick of Frances of Assisi? Pretty good company." Claire tried to laugh off the saint business, but the joke made her even more nervous.

"That's right. You're the modern version, my friend. Except that you're in danger of blowing your well-earned reputation, so before you tell me about how you blew them away in Chicago, how about you tell me about your fling with the Casanova of St. Vincent hospital?"

"Come on, Julie, how about a little catch-up small talk to warm up?"

"No way, honey. Claire, what the hell are you doing seeing that creep? You must know he's a horrible womanizer. The worst. No, he's more than that, he's a fucking sociopath is what he is. He leaves women feeling like trash while he walks away smiling. What is going on with you, Claire? This isn't you—you're steady and rational and good. I don't get it, and I'm getting really freaked for you." Julie stopped her tirade and looked to Claire for a response. She didn't pause for long, and when Claire said nothing, she started in again. This time her big Boston voice was both pleading and commanding. "Tell me you'll stop this, Claire, before you lose yourself and get really hurt."

Claire looked down at her napkin. She looked around the café at the tasteful Italian ceramics, the giant bottles of olive oil and wine at the bar, the photos of Venice and Florence on the walls. She didn't want to talk. She didn't want to be questioned, but she knew it was impossible to avoid Julie's penetrating inquiry. And she knew something inexplicable was happening between her and David Chase. After the pause, knowing she couldn't delay any longer, she turned her gaze back to Julie. "I know, Julie, I know, it seems crazy to me too some of the time. Maybe I'm tired of being rational and good. Come on, Julie, look at me, I'm too much of all that stuff."

"Okay, Claire, be a bad girl, let your hair down, have an affair with a married man, who the fuck cares, but not with him. He's trouble, sweetheart. Real trouble."

"Hey, Julie, come on now, remember our motto."

"What motto?"

"Not everything good is all good, and not everything bad is—"

"Oh, hell, who believes that? There are exceptions, my dear friend-turned-imbecile."

Claire looked down at her hands to avoid the judgment in Julie's eyes she feared she deserved. Her hands were thin and pearl white, a surgeon's hands and fingers. They seemed to her too delicate, too passive. Without thinking, Claire raised her head and looked into Julie's penetrating dark brown eyes, the same eyes she trusted to see into the most confusing medical problems, which now bored into her.

"Besides, Claire, you're good. You really are one of the few good ones. You're an exception to the motto."

"I'm not all here." The words flew out of Claire's mouth before she could edit and revise. They bounced off the atmosphere of Julie's undying affection, causing her friend to blink twice and try to bat them away as though a fly had appeared out of nowhere and was buzzing around her ear.

Claire was lost. She tried to stall by smoothing the tablecloth and sipping her wine. What had she said? What was missing? Fiddling with the spoon didn't help. The unflappable woman from Kansas was lost. Never in her life had Claire felt such confusion. She looked up at her friend and tried to smile.

Julie's face dropped; she stared at Claire, dumbfounded. "You're what?"

"Julie, I'm tired."

"No, that other thing. What do you mean, you're not all here?"

Claire tried to avoid the real meaning of her words. "Something in me is exhausted. I'm trying too hard. I don't know why."

"Tired? Of course you're tired. We're all tired, and most of us aren't working to save the world and our profession like you are, dear."

It was so like Julie to end a sentence with an endearment. Very New England. Claire smiled to herself. Julie was the only person in her life she could confide in.

She sighed a deep sigh and ran a hand through her hair before shaking her head. "It isn't that kind of tired. Tired is probably the wrong word. It's something else. A discontent. An empty feeling, I suppose. Something missing. I'm not all here, Julie. I'm just not connected to all of me. I've always known it, but now I feel it, and I see it in David. I know you think I'm nuts, but we understand each other. And there's more." Claire rubbed her hands together and spoke to the window and the darkening day. "There's something I can't name. Something big. There's a movement, a stirring I haven't felt since I was thirteen when I decided to become a doctor and cure suffering once and for all. But this is deeper and obscure. I can't get a handle on it. All I can say is, something to do with this pull is waking me in the middle of the night in a panic."

"What does this have to do with Dr. Letch?"

"Stop. Please stop." She glared at Julie and surprised herself with her forceful tone.

"Sorry, Claire, I'm sorry. I'm just scared for you. I want to know, go on."

"I don't know, maybe nothing. He just seems to be part of the tide dragging me out. I have dreams, I'm struggling, pulling at the water to get back to shore. I feel helpless, and panicked, and . . ." Tears interrupted Claire, and she hid her face in her hands. She was relieved to hear Julie's voice pulling her back.

"Hey girl, you good? Your face took a deep dive, like you were disappearing on me or something. Have some water. I didn't mean to shake you up. Man, where did you go? The look on your face gave me the shivers."

Claire couldn't answer. She couldn't say for herself. This woman from Kansas felt swept up in a tornado of her own. She had no idea why it involved David Chase. She only knew he had something to do with the force bending the arc of her life. A tectonic shift years in the making that was directing both of them, against their will, into an unknown, uncertain becoming. She recognized something in him that wasn't bad, a solitude. A terrible, lonely solitude that was somehow her own.

"So, what's my diagnosis? Temporary insanity? Delusional hysteria?"

"Let's see, I'm a little rusty on my DSM-5—have you considered an acute motherhood fixation with mixed psychotic features?"

"Always the smart-ass." But the improv diagnosis unnerved her. She felt a knot in her abdomen spasm. Was she unraveling? Slipping into something she couldn't get out of? What was she after?

"Come on, Claire, why not let yourself be like four billion other women on the planet and admit you want a baby? Being a mom will kill you, but it's the best. Maybe you just want to live an ordinary life while you can."

"That's always your go-to, Julie. Can't you be more original?"

"Original sin, sister, original sin."

"Yeah, right, that's me, Madam Illicit. What can I tell you? It's all so strange. The most bizarre of all are the dreams. So many dreams. Kansas girls don't dream, you know. And they are chaotic—everything is chaos, upside down, Alice in Wonderland without the wonder. And blood. Blood everywhere. But you know the most bizarre thing about it, Julie? I am calm. Perfectly calm. Spooky calm." And yet her voice raced, and her palms began to sweat.

"You dodged the question, sister. Come on, be straight with me. We'll talk about the blood thing later. Damn."

"What? What dodge?"

"You know. The baby, the baby you've been yearning for all these years."

"Oh, yeah, the baby. The baby." Claire's voice trailed off, and with that the full flow of desire flooded her mind. Tears followed, bathing her cheeks—a lotion of acceptance. She did not stop them, and she could not have. She did not cover her face. This was not a dream.

Julie took Claire's hands in hers. She held them tenderly, and her voice filled with a new warmth. "Oh, Claire, honey, I'm so sorry, I shouldn't have judged you, or him. Please forgive me. You will be the best mom, the best."

The two friends looked at one another anew. Their eyes glowed even as a shudder passed between them signaling a mutual astonishment with the opening that took place. They leaned over the table, oblivious to those around them, and disappeared into the rapidly unfolding life carrying Claire forth. Their arms made a bridge across the red checkered tablecloth, and a dozen translucent angles, each no larger than a speck of dust, danced across the bridge of friendship and flew to Claire's ears, where they perched just in time to hear her exclaim wholeheartedly to Julie, "Yes, yes! I want to be a mother, I do, more than anything. I want a baby, Julie! I want a baby! I've been afraid to say it out loud."

Now they were both sobbing and laughing and wanting to sing and shout to the angels who flew off into the mystery to spread the word. Both women turned and looked around the room to see if anyone was applauding. At that moment, their suave waiter came to the table and asked, "Can I get you ladies anything else?" His question, and the irony of its serving, broke the spell, and the two best friends, in the same breath, let out a belly laugh that shook the table and said, "No thanks, we're good."

Chapter 12

The irony of his name was not lost on David Chase. From an early age, and certainly from puberty on, he was teased about it. The adolescent taunts were obvious enough. "What are you chasing down tonight, big fella?" These were easy volleys to hit back at his buddies who admired the tenacity of his pursuits. Though he was tall, all bone, and not especially handsome as a teenager, there was something about him that appealed to young women. Some were searching for a lost soul to rescue; others were drawn by the challenge to open what seemed impenetrable.

During medical school and residency, David Chase earned the admiration of other young docs as he was able to satisfy the requirements of a rigorous program and an equally rigorous sexual agenda. By then, his body and face had matured into the chiseled profile of an ideal man. He pursued and had his way with other residents, staff doctors, supervisors, and nurses. His appetite for sexual safari was unbounded. It led him and his game to stolen moments in X-ray rooms and vacated hospital beds, and, on special occasions, a rendezvous with the catch of the day in the hospital chapel. Many women found the hunt irresistible and were willing to risk rejection for the excitement of being the one to open that granite heart.

The cycle began with pursuit. His adrenaline fed off the scent and the tracking of female interest. He resembled a leopard, studying and moving through the grass toward the desired body, his final approach as sure and fast as the great spotted cat. And David Chase made certain that his catch enjoyed being taken, devoured, and opened to the full glory of the flesh.

The sexual contact was somewhat arousing, and to a degree pleasurable, but he was not in pursuit of the hunger of her mouth, the tenderness of her lips, or the pleading of her tongue. It was not in the movement, the pounding ocean of her body over the land of him. Nor was it the entry into her darkness, or the smell of her beckoning.

It was in the afterglow that he saw what he was looking for. In the moment he saw in a woman's eyes the longing for more of him. When he knew he had successfully ignited the longing for more in his subject, he sensed the ancient yearning of the soul to merge into something bigger than erotic satisfaction. Bigger than love. The longing to disappear into blissful union.

It was that vulnerability, that exquisitely tender openness, that he would turn his back on, knowing that all vulnerability and want, shame and bewilderment, would soon be hers; vacated from the boy trapped in the cage of his heart. Her rejection, her shame, her bewilderment. Not his. And it was then that the woman of the hour would join the many others in learning, as had he, that being one does not mean being with. It means deserted and alone.

David was not driven by lust. Or by power. His life was a quest, a demand upon his psyche. The quest was simple enough, but its execution was as technical as a surgical procedure. It became ritualized and required constant tending, not because it was satisfying, but because it was essential. What was essential was the defeat of yearning: the primal need for another. The defeat of an enemy that would never surrender. A victory that never ended the war.

And so it went, time and time again, the perennial battle in the deep vault of his unconscious mind with a yearning boy who wanted his mother. With that yearning quieted, and the arid flat line restored, David Chase moved through his world convinced that he was master of the chase and had outrun the reach of history. But he was oblivious to the ever-tightening bonds of love that wound around him like chains and even more unaware of the true irony of the chase: namely, that which was chasing him.

■ ■ ■

The chance meeting with Claire in Chicago tipped the axis of his life. They continued to meet by unlikely coincidence it seemed, like Venus and the moon appearing to almost touch on a summer night. Turning down an aisle at the market, their carts nearly colliding. Pulling into the hospital parking lot at the same ungodly hour of dark and silence and sharing an elevator to the cardiac unit on the fifth floor. It became almost comical; they laughed about it, suspicious of a trick fate was playing. They looked to the side, uncomfortable, unsure what to say, how to resist the pull.

Their unlikely chemistry coalesced the night they met over the operating table in an emergency surgery to save the life of a teenage girl whose heart was about to explode from too much meth. Claire was the attendant cardiologist and David the chief surgeon. She stood by the operating table, steady and sure. He walked into the room with an aura of calm and assuredness surrounding him, his body certain, his presence both far away and immediate. Each was masked. Their eyes met, and for a second they stopped, held by the other in an acknowledgment of something big. Something inevitable.

Claire stood with the anesthesiologist near the operating table where the team hurried to prepare the young woman for surgery. She watched David approach the table, his step and measured pace revealing a certain inward concentration as he surveyed the room and took command. As they moved into action, a witnessing part of her mind looked for the cold, predatory man that was his reputation. What she saw was not cold. Dr. David Chase paused. He touched the forearm of the young woman whose life was now in his hands and looked to his team with a seriousness that summoned their best.

. . .

The night did not go well. By the time they opened her, that scarred and ravaged heart was bursting. Blood filled the cavity. It splattered into the air and landed on the girl's face. It covered her cheek and spread down her neck. They could not suction enough or replace enough blood to subdue the damage inflicted by the crystal dagger. In less than thirty minutes, she was gone.

The room went silent, the monitor flat. The women and men of the team stood over her body. Several cried. All of those present stared at the heart that would never beat again. They looked at her white, weathered face and the strands of orange hair edging out of her mask. Some felt an impulse to touch her cheek. But all present felt the shock of the abrupt exit of life. Despite the many years in that room and all the saved lives, beholding death and staring into the face of their helplessness, the operating team shuddered.

Without a word, Dr. David Chase turned and left the operating room. He walked alone down the empty hallway to the changing station and washroom, leaving pools of blood in his wake. He scrubbed his hands mechanically, trying to wash the blood away, but it was everywhere—on his hands, his gown, and in his mind. Slowly the flat line of his inner world grew agitated, and he scrubbed more vigorously until he was cursing the blood and damning the rag for not removing it. As it began to seep into his skin David Chase left the changing station and walked to his office. The image of the orange-haired teenager flashed in his mind. The blood on her cheek took the shape of a spider and crawled up his arm onto his neck. His body shook violently, and he let out a strangled scream. With his right hand he swatted at the spot. The scream and the slap woke him from the spell just as he made it to his office and slumped in the chair by his desk.

Claire followed David and found him sitting with his elbows on his knees and his head in his hands. He lifted his head and looked up at her. He was sweating, and a few remaining drops of blood ran down his forehead and into his eyes. He made no effort to wipe them away. Claire picked up a towel and slowly wiped the blood from his face and forehead. She put a hand on his shoulder with the same tenderness.

David lowered his head again. He let it hang and in a barely audible voice said, "I've never lost someone."

Claire sighed and rubbed his neck. She wondered if she was the first to ever see this side of him. "Oh, David, she was gone before we began. You were heroic in there. So steady."

"Don't say that. I failed her."

"I know how terribly hard it is to lose someone. I'm sorry, David."

Claire let her hand move over his shoulders and back. She felt something spasm and release between his shoulder blades. And then she heard a sound come from him. Not a groan, not a sigh, something guttural. A sound that had been trapped for decades.

David lifted his head for a few seconds, and then it dropped down and again the stale sound escaped into the room. When he looked back at Claire it was with the face of a frightened child.

"David, are you all right? What is it? . . . David?"

"It's not true."

"What isn't true?"

"The tulips."

"The tulips?"

"She was wearing a dress with big red tulips . . . Jesus."

"What, who was wearing the dress?"

"God, her cheek, the blood."

"I'm here, David, what happened?"

"I . . . I never talked. Never."

"What happened?"

"Did I say I never lost someone?"

"You did."

"It's not true. Damn, I never lost someone. It's not true. It's not true, Claire." He said the words as he turned to face her, and there in his crystal-blue eyes was the pain she had sensed from the beginning. In that pain she saw a pleading boy, a stunned and frightened boy.

"Who did you lose? Who was it?"

"She had blood on her cheek. I never told anyone. She was in the car. I walked away. She was lying on the seat with her knees tucked up. I went to the park. I don't remember anything after that."

"Was it your mother? Did your mother take her life?"

"My mother?"

"Yes, was that your mother in the car, lying on the seat?"

"Mother? I wasn't sure what happened to her. She loved that dress. She loved it more than anything. More than anything."

"David, that's terrible."

"The blood on her cheek. Maybe if I hadn't seen the blood on her cheek, I could have saved the girl. Christ, that orange hair. Her swollen face. Jesus, her whole body was exploding."

"That's right, her heart exploded, she couldn't be helped. But she helped you remember and let someone help you. God, all these years you've held this inside."

"I feel dizzy."

"Me too."

"I'm sorry to upset you, Claire."

"No, that's not why I'm dizzy."

"Why then?"

"It can wait."

"No, now, please."

Claire hesitated and withdrew her hand from David's shoulder. She looked away and back at him. "Haven't you wondered what's drawn us together? We're the most unlikely pair."

"Right, your friends think you're nuts, I bet."

"But this says it all. We're both orphans, David. My parents died in a car accident when I was four. We've both suffered enormous loss and somehow we recognize it in each other and are drawn together because no one else gets it like we do."

"Are you saying . . ." But David's voice trailed off and Claire was silent. The crucial piece of the puzzle fit snugly into place, and the two drifters stared into the space that holds past, present, and future. They let it wash over and through their minds as two separate and lonely rivers grew closer to a confluence.

Claire's pager rang, and the two lonely hearts flinched in sync. "Oh dear, I have to go." They stood, and David reached for her. "Don't go, Claire. They can find someone else."

Claire touched his arm. She knew what he was asking and shook her head and said softly but unwaveringly, "No."

No. The word became a sound, and the sound swelled and deepened as though a Chinese gong had been struck.

"No?"

"That's right."

"No is very final."

"No isn't final, David. But it is, no. I need some time to think. This is a lot."

And then, in that instant, something took place that was even stranger and more foreign to his experience. Something so very simple that it shook him from his feet to his forehead.

Claire looked into David's eyes as though she were looking at the story of his life. The warmth of hers met the bewilderment of his. Her gaze resembled a child's complete absorption. She looked into David Chase without prejudice and with a tenderness that deftly, but without force, opened one lock and then another until she saw what she was looking for. And then she said hello from the core of her being.

In his many years of sexual triumph, David Chase had undressed dozens of women. This was the closest he could come to understanding his feeling in that moment. Now Claire, without touching his body, and with his full if unconscious participation, undressed the man still shaking from a single syllable and now undone by a simple hello. He was stunned by the sound of hello and closed his eyes. When they opened again, Claire was there, still looking, and he said hello to her. It was for him the first hello spoken from one soul to another.

In a flash they became inseparable, and the two lonely souls took each other's hands and soared into the mystic.

"David." Claire touched his cheek lightly with her fingertips. "David, I care."

David Chase said nothing. He felt something inside his heart run to the fingertips on his face and lie down in the flower of that touch. But he could not speak.

Claire kissed him on the cheek, turned, and left the room. David watched her leave in a state of astonishment.

And the soul of their daughter, Emily, began to pack her bags for the upcoming journey to the land of incarnation.

Chapter 13

In the dream he enters a room and wants to leave immediately. He looks here and there, in the corners, and behind the door. Even the ceilings. What is he looking for? Why does every space menace him? Every space, threshold and interior, is that garage. It isn't the people; they are ants on the counter. It isn't the women; they will find him. It isn't the conversation; he doesn't listen. And he doesn't pay attention to his restless, darting attention. He waits for repugnance to find him. The drone of the engine. The sight of sleeping blood. He turns and enters that other room, the sterile one. The room that is all his, Surgical Room 5, where he covers his face with a mask and his hands with silicone gloves and his head and body with baby blue pajamas and, surrounded by his loyal crew, he slowly and methodically carves an opening in the chest of someone he barely knows for the distinct honor of peering inside a pulsing human heart. He is looking for something. Looking for a way to keep them alive. All of them.

It is the same frantic search. He hears it beating—the beat grows louder and louder. The sound haunts him, but he cannot find it. He is trapped in a cage. The walls of the cage shake. He cannot escape the sound. He is about to break. There are ivory bars he must break through. The sound is terrible: the sawing, the splitting bone, pulling the cage apart. There is rampaging blood. And there it is, the villain.

He shivers. And then, there is terror, as the urge to crush it spreads through his arms and hands. The terrible urge to make its wretched beating stop and put an end to the pounding and relentless yearning. He takes it in his bare hands and wakes, sobbing and shaking.

Chapter 14

Hour #25

The door is open. The room is open, and light pours in through the old windowpane. It casts a wrinkled reflection on the wall behind David's chair. The light is textured and moving ever so slightly as though in meeting the color of the wall it has turned to liquid.

Hello, David.

David looks surprised. He stumbles to return the greeting and turns away from the warmth in Dr. Jones's eyes.

"I'm dreaming. I don't want to dream."

Tell me your dream.

"I'm in the operating room. I'm holding a heart in my hands. I want to crush it, tear it apart. No instruments, just my hands—they're shaking. There's blood everywhere and it's sticking to me. I can't get it off. It keeps coming. I'm screaming! What's happening to me?"

You are reliving the horror of your mother's death and struggling with the belief that you drove her insane, that she took her life because of you.

"I'm sick, I tear everything apart."

You are a tortured soul.

"Don't pity me."

You're right. Let me say that differently. What you experienced that morning when you found your mother was horrifying. You've

*been trying to shred your heart ever since. I think you took to saving
other people's hearts because you could not save hers, or your own . . .
or the others.*

"Everything is in pieces. The others . . ."

*Yes, the others. I shudder when I think that your daughter was one
of the others. When I imagine the blood—*

"I have to go." David gags, stands abruptly, and turns to the
door. He stops just as suddenly as though seized by an invisible force.
He bends over, his head hanging below his knees.

Stay, stay with me. I'm here. We can do this together.

"I'm—I'm coming apart—I'm coming apart!"

*You probably feel that everything is unraveling, that everything
you built to protect yourself from feeling is failing. And this is the worst
of it, isn't it? Talking about your daughter.*

"He should have jumped and landed on his head."

Something in him wanted to survive, to continue on.

"He should have let go of the chains and broken into pieces."

He felt broken and still wanted to live.

"He was afraid, he didn't want to live. He was no good and a
coward—a disgusting cannibal and too cowardly to kill his rotten
self. He killed them and then he just walked away."

*He thinks that love, his love, is the killer and should be destroyed.
He thinks letting himself love them was nothing but selfish cruelty.*

"He's right."

*Perhaps there was something different about the others, something
compelling him to try. Perhaps there was something bigger than him,
bigger than all of them, that pulled them together despite everything
that tried to keep them apart.*

"I can't do this. I won't feel sorry for myself, I fucking-well won't cry, damn it!"

You've been crying all along, David. You've been crying through the pain you left in others. This is your pain, now. Yours, and theirs. And this is the love that will not die.

"I can't stop. I can't stop, help me, please help . . ."

I'm here with you. Don't fight it. You'll come through.

"What do I do with this? It won't stop. I don't deserve sympathy. Stop looking at me like that. Stop."

It's time you had someone caring for you, David.

"You're stabbing me. Stop, please stop! I can't breathe. I can't!"

Your heart is opening, David. It's your heart. It's what Emily wanted for you.

"No, it isn't. I can't. No. No."

You're not alone.

"Fuck you. I walk out of here and I'm fucking alone, bleeding, and what are you doing, sitting all smug in your chair, another notch on your scalpel."

Don't turn back to anger, David. I don't enjoy your pain.

"Sure you do. Fucking liar."

The room is still as the new moon. David leans forward. The liquid light on the wall has washed away.

"What are you doing?"

I'm crying.

"You're crying? Bullshit, why are you crying?"

Because you are alive. Because you have a heart. Because . . . I remember something.

"What?"

I remember what it is like to die.

"You?" David looks at Dr. Jones intently. His face is different; he looks older and worn. His eyes look heavy and dull.

Yes.

"Tell me."

No, this is your time.

"Yes! Tell me, tell me! If I have to be a person and live in this torture chamber, you have to be a person too. Come on, tell me. How did you die?"

It's funny you call it a torture chamber. It's not funny. It was terrible watching my mother disappear. Every day was a death. I couldn't bear it . . . when she couldn't recognize me, I stopped visiting. Something in me died with her.

David stares at Dr. Jones in disbelief. He shakes his head and rubs his hands. And then in a soft voice he says, "I'm sorry. I am."

Thank you.

"I've never said that to anyone and meant it."

Thank you, David. Maybe you are beginning to care. To come alive.

"I don't remember what it is like to be alive."

This is what it is like. You are remembering, David. You are. And you're helping me remember too.

"Will it always be like this? If it is, I'm done. I can't take it, this pain in my chest, it's crushing me. Am I having a heart attack? This is all too much. And now I have to feel sorry for you. Fuck this. I don't want to be alive if this is what it is."

You're moving through it, David, you are. This is the most difficult time, the worst pain. You'll come through. Yes, you'll go in and out of it, feeling the hurt and fighting it, but life is pulling on you to come out and live. There will be good, too. There will.

Sunlight has moved from the wall to the bark of a tree outside the window. The bark glistens like quicksilver. There is a pause. Within the pause two men look at each other. There is quiet. And the quiet is, for a moment, merciful.

"I don't know, I don't. Why is this happening to me? I didn't ask for this." Just then he thinks of Emily. He hears her prayer once more and groans, overwhelmed by a feeling of complete inadequacy.

What happened just now, David? Something struck you.

"Emily. I heard her prayer."

You gave up on life, David, but you wouldn't give up on Emily.

"Did I kill her too?"

For the first time in his life, David Chase hands the sword of judgment to another. Dr. Ed Jones receives the weighted instrument of condemnation and lays it down. He lays it down and looks at his patient with great tenderness. He sees two pleading eyes, imploring him to pardon his misdeeds, begging for mercy, expecting the sword to fall. Dr. Jones pauses and returns David's gaze with kindness covering his face and then says simply,

No, you did not.

David collapses into the chair. He does not moan, he does not sob; he becomes still and rests. And the air in the room strokes his head. And the man in the chocolate chair closes his eyes.

Chapter 15

"I am the motherfucking wind! I am the goddamn motherfucking wind! I am one motherfucker, the worst goddamn motherfucker this goddamn motherfucking world has known!"

Only Randy Tanner heard the flaming proclamations firing from his mouth. Those in the proximity of his declarations heard nothing but the attacking roar of the Triumph Speed Triple 1250 beneath his legs, slamming down the I-5 corridor from Vancouver to Portland at one hundred miles per hour.

The man who knew nothing of Emily, but in a few minutes would take her from her people and the world, tore down the highway thinking he was headed to a rendezvous with sexual nirvana. He wore no helmet, and his long black hair flew behind him like the mane of a wild stallion. His tongue, white as chalk, shot from his mouth along with a scream that split the surrounding atoms and set off an explosion every bit as violent and terrifying as the sound of a steel girder shattering like a compound fracture.

Randy Tanner attacked the highway, cursing every vehicle and passenger in his way. Drivers who saw him or heard the menacing roar pulled to the side of the road, their trembling hands stuck to the steering wheel. Those who missed his approach gasped and instinctively hit the brakes even as he flew by and left them swallowing the hostile fumes of his exhaust. His sleepless face turned a shade of purple in the wind, and he yelled like a mad demon without the aid of a single breath. His tongue struck wildly at existence and spit its poisonous venom at every particle of creation.

"Out of my way, you miserable motherfuckers, out of my way or I'll run your fat white asses into the motherfucking ground. I am the biggest motherfucking wind you have ever seen; I am the tornado wrecking everything in my way, and I will blow your pathetic shit-eating ass away before you know what the fuck hit your miserable life."

And so it went, at maximum volume, at the speed of insanity, separating the molecules of space faster than the triumph of his mighty will, off to raise his mighty phallus to the outreach of Marissa Leonard's pleading, screaming desire. He rode faster and faster, leaving behind every last trace molecule of pain and torment. Leaving the cry of his emaciated soul in the wake of his murderous proclamations.

■ ■ ■

Randy Tanner's sermon on the mount of his blistering Triumph 1250 continued nonstop over the interstate bridge traversing the wide Columbia River. The grand Columbia meandered on its way to the Pacific, unimpressed by the manic ravings of the young man. And the old steel bridge accepted Randy Tanner, his ravings, and his breakneck accelerations just as it did the weighty cargo of impatient human striving that crossed it every hour of the day.

A windless day allowed the crazed disciple of power and rage to believe he was the wind from the gorge, the solar wind, faster than a speeding bullet, a jet stream, more powerful than a nuclear explosion, more destructive than a rampaging tornado. His self-deluded state was aided by five days of sleepless worship at the foot of his omnipotent God: crystal meth.

But the God of Meth is a lesser god, and neither the commander of Randy Tanner's death march nor the poor man proclaiming himself King of the Winds had any inkling of the real forces moving him and a host of characters toward their rendezvous in Portland at the corner of SE 32nd and Belmont. Those winds lifted him like a feather into the current of their grand desire.

And what was that desire? What possible desire exists that would rob the world of someone as good as Emily? That would shatter her already broken father and leave him for dead on the pavement? What voice beckons the winds of destiny to gust, to shower love and joy, horror and death, like pollen upon the heads of the living? Where is the mercy in this world?

Chapter 16

"David, I want a baby." Claire's voice was soft and tired, but it carried a tone of resolve that David recognized immediately as his wife's formidable will. His stomach turned over.

"What?"

"I want a baby. I want to have a baby now."

"Jesus, I thought we were done with that."

"I was never done, you never started."

David squirmed in his chair and looked out the wide picture window into the day's end. Claire was draped over the leather chair in the study. Her blue surgical scrubs, showing a few light stains from the night's emergency room shift, covered her exhausted body.

"Claire, we're too old—you're almost forty-three and I'll be fifty-two in a month, for God's sake. Shit, I'd be nearly seventy when the kid graduated from high school, if I made it that far."

"You'll make it, David, you're in good health. Besides, maybe our age is a good thing. Maybe we have a lot of things behind us."

David flinched inside. He recognized the generosity in Claire's words and tone as something he didn't deserve. "What about your career? You're a partner in the practice now, what about that? You've worked hard. You can't just walk away from that, can you?"

But Claire ignored the leading question. She heard the plea, the not-so-subtle coercion entering their exchange. They had been married for a year and David's tactics were obvious to her. "I don't care about that. I can always pick it up later if I want to. I really don't care anymore."

"How can you say that? All those years of med school and residency and you are finally able to have this good, incredible life, and you don't care?"

"I want to be a mother."

She said this with such authority that David knew it was done and decided. His hands grew cold, and his life seemed to slip from his grasp.

"Claire, you know you're high risk. Dr. Jeffries said you're at high risk of hemorrhaging. Have you forgotten that? You're nearly forty-three for Christ's sake. Are you willing to risk your life, our life, for this, this fantasy?"

"Yes. And don't call it a fantasy. Don't."

"Christ."

An uneasy pause settled between them and refused to move, like a stubborn dog over a scent.

"David, if I don't try, it won't really be my life. Don't you see how badly I want this?"

"But you're not being reasonable, you're being selfish. What kind of life would your child have if her mother bleeds to death at her birth? Great—a motherless child shrouded by guilt her entire life."

"You don't have to remind me. Do you really think I haven't considered that? Do you think I haven't lain awake all night considering that possibility? Do you? Is it selfish to put my life on the line so another can live? Of course not. You're frightened, you want things to stay the way they are. I understand that. But I'm telling you, David, this is bigger than me. It's bigger than me being fed up with watching stoned-out teenagers walk out of the hospital with babies. It is."

Claire paused while her body sought a place of comfort that allowed for her pain to settle. She shifted in her chair and held her head in her hands. When she lifted her face, her voice faltered and she spoke with less certainty. "I feel—I don't know how to say this—I feel I'm not alone in this. Something is compelling me forward, almost leading me by the arm toward—I don't know what. But I do know that there is more than me wanting this baby. I don't know that you can understand. I'm sure you can't. How could you? I'm sure I don't either, but I feel something real, David, something real wanting life."

David grimaced and looked away. "But we have life, such a good life now. Everything is in place—why turn it all upside down? Why?"

"Because I want more than a good life, David. I want more than comfort and stuff. I want messy, unreasonable, unpredictable life. And love. I want to feel a mother's love. Even if I never see my child's face, even if I bleed to death before I hear my baby cry, I will have known that love at least while I'm pregnant. Besides, what if life with a child—our child—could be better, way better than any life we could make just for ourselves? You and I think about what we stand to lose, no mystery there. But I see the look of happiness and contentment on the faces of new mothers and fathers. Have you seen them walking down the sidewalk holding their child's hand with that beatific look? They can't really believe how good it is, how much they can love another being. Don't you want to know that kind of love?" Claire closed her eyes and let herself be taken by a taste of that love.

"I'm not exactly father material, Claire. And I'm a shitty husband. You know that. You put up with my miserable failings. Why torment yourself further? Why torment me with my pathetic limitations? Why did you pick someone like me, anyway?"

"David, I could ask you the same question. Why pick someone like me? So straight the ruler looks crooked. Always measuring, figuring. The libido of a russet potato. Why?"

The answer was immediate, the emotion sharp. The words flew like a Stealth bomber from the hole in his soul that held everything he tried to hide from himself and the world. "I knew you were the one person who would never leave me."

In that instant, David Chase half expected to look up and see Claire run from the room to pack her bags. But she sat there, as always, steady as an oak. She looked at him with tenderness and said, "Oh, David, I'm sorry. Every friend in my life has told me I'm crazy to be with you, but something other than my brain says I'm not. We look different, but we're not. Two drifters, lonely and lost. Maybe I chose you because I knew you would always leave me. Again and again and never. You and I . . . you and I are stunted. We're stunted. Contained in a can. I want to come out, David. I want to be alive as I can be. This is your chance too, to live for something besides yourself, something bigger. You can, I know you can. You're more than your stupid escapades. You are. There's good in you, packed away. I've seen how you care for your patients when you ready them for surgery, when your face is covered with a mask. You're safe in that room, aren't you? Safe to care and show some tenderness. You could find that in a baby, I know it. I'll help you. This isn't just my destiny, David. It's ours."

A heavy sigh left his lungs. Fog rolled in. Realizing he was losing ground, he tried one last approach, appealing from a dark memory to a mother's fear and guilt. "But Claire, if you die, you'll be leaving your baby with me to raise it. Are you sure you want to do that?"

"Yes, I'm sure. I've spoken with Martha, and she will help you if anything happens to me." That was Claire, always prepared, always practical, even in matters of death.

"You talked to Martha before you talked to me?"

"I did. I needed to know everything was in place before I talked to you. David, this is your time to love. To love something bigger than yourself, your success, and your ridiculous conquests. You can. David, you have it in you, I know you do. Try, just try. This is your chance too."

David heard the resolve in Claire's voice. And then he was gone. Lost in a whirlpool, pulled out of his body, out of time, away from Claire and all emotion until he found himself on the swing, holding tightly to the chains with all his might as the world closed in around him and turned him into a wooden thing, dry and faceless.

Horror flashed through his body at the sight of the boy without a face. It broke the trance and David woke in a sweat to find Claire next to him on the couch, squeezing his hand and imploring him to return to her. "David, what is it? David, dear, come back, I need you." Claire's voice was close to panicked. It was not the first time she had seen him go far away, but never like this. "David, are you all right? Is it your mother? Do you need some water?"

David blinked twice and looked at Claire. He wondered who she was for an instant.

"David, David, are you all right? What happened?"

He looked again to see who was sitting next to him. And then he looked away.

"David, look at me. It's me, Claire!" Her voice was shrill by then, and louder, trying to pull David back.

The last of the trance lifted, and then she was Claire. He was startled, but only for a second. He looked down and then up again at her worried face. It was no longer moving in and out; it reached for him.

"I guess it was another flashback. Jesus. Claire . . . Claire, I'm sorry, I am. You deserve better. You do."

"You haven't had an episode for a while. You were so far away."

"I was? I don't know, it's a blur. What were we talking about?"

"Have you been taking your meds? Didn't Dr. Smith say you really need to take them?"

"I hate them. They make me feel like petrified wood."

"But don't they help you be more . . . "

"Steady. Faithful? Sometimes, for a while. Damn, Claire, everything happened so fast. And now this. I'm not big enough. Why me? Is this your final project for the Mother Teresa fellowship?"

"That's mean."

"Maybe you're being mean, asking this of me."

"I'm asking something of life. I haven't done much of that."

"I'm your first irrational decision and you're about to make another."

Claire sat up and leaned toward David. She threw her hair

back and spoke to him more forcefully than ever, "You are my worst nightmare, David. You leave me over and over and over. How many times do I have to relive being left? How many times do I have to feel unwanted? We're both castaways. I've lived my life thinking if I were good, really good, I'd be happy and feel I was lovable. You've lived yours thinking if you were bad, really bad, unattached, you'd be safe, untouchable. Great. When I met you, I had heard all the stories. Believe me, you didn't catch me by surprise. But I had come to see beyond my well-crafted self, and I saw beyond yours. That night we stood and looked into each other, I saw the fear in you, I saw the terrible loneliness and something else I couldn't be sure of. But now I know what it is. And you do too, I think, or you wouldn't still be here. Maybe you won't allow it, but it's there. And it's the scariest of all."

"What's that?"

"Want."

"Want? Me, afraid of want? I want for nothing."

"Exactly. Well done."

David did his best to convince himself and Claire that he didn't understand. That she was way off base. But what he couldn't deny or refute was a sound murmuring from his depths. He looked at Claire with awe and respect as he had that first night while reeling from the impact of the *no* that was his first *yes*. The first *yes* freely given to him, to all that was hidden, all the dormant want. All the yearning that had frozen and survived, wrapped in a shell of fear like fluid in a cyst.

"Claire?"

"Yes, David?"

"Claire . . . I'm so afraid . . . You know, don't you?"

"I do."

David stood and walked to the picture window across the room. He could barely breathe. He shut his eyelids tight to keep from crying. He looked out at the view of the city and the west ridge and heard, for the first time in his life, the muffled cry of the nine-year-old boy wanting his mother to open her eyes. He heard the soft shape of the word leave his lips and merge with the poisoned air. *Mama.* A moment passed, and another. He saw the lights blinking downtown and heard an owl hoot three times nearby. When he turned, he saw Claire crying. He walked to her and slowly brushed the tears away.

"You're right, Claire."

They sat together then, shoulder to shoulder, and stared silently into the last remnants of a sunset draping the dreamy lavender hills in shades of orange and blood red.

Chapter 17

Emily was a magical child. Plants and animals trusted her like one of their own. Trees bent to touch her. Dogs and cats followed her everywhere. Crows softened their tone in her presence. Butterflies landed on her fingertips and swooned. Roses released more fragrance when she came near. Emily understood what she shouldn't have been able to understand at her age. And her dreams foretold the future.

. . .

Early on an October morning, ten days before Halloween and shortly after Emily's fifth birthday, David left his bed to use the bathroom. As he walked the hall, he heard the usual creaking of aging oak floors. Nearing the bathroom door, he noticed a light on in the family room. Thinking he'd forgotten to turn the lamp off, David entered the room. There on the carpet sat Emily, painting with watercolors.

He had grown accustomed to Emily doing unusual things at unusual hours, and still, each time something like this happened, his pre-ordered world was taken aback.

"Emily?"

"Hi, Daddy."

"What are you doing up so early? It's three in the morning."

"I'm painting the fog. And moons."

David glanced out the window and was surprised to see the air clear of any fog, and in fact, he dimly noticed the light of a full moon illuminating the sidewalks and leafy trees of the neighborhood.

"But Emily, there isn't any fog outside."

"I know, Daddy. I had a dream and I'm painting my dream now."

"Oh. I see."

"See, Daddy? Isn't it beautiful? I just love foggy days, don't you?"

"Well, sure sweetie, I do, but it's so early, you should be sleeping, shouldn't you?"

"Daddy, it was the best dream. I felt so happy I had to paint it right away. It was a special dream, Daddy."

"A special dream?"

"Yeah. It was a grandmother dream, you know, like I have sometimes when grandma comes and visits? Those are my favorite dreams."

"But Grandma Martha is upstairs sleeping, Emily."

"Not that grandma, silly. The great grandma I told you about. Remember?"

"Oh, right. I forgot."

"Daddy, you're funny. How can you forget about Grandma Bu? She's the best."

David watched as his little girl resumed meticulously painting what looked to him like tiny snowflakes—brightly colored shades of yellow and silver with flecks of white and lavender in the centers. Together on the black drawing paper they began to resemble a pillow or drifted snow.

"That's a very nice picture of fog, Em." He tried his best

to support his daughter's creative forays even if he found them bewildering.

"It isn't fog, Daddy."

"What?"

"It isn't fog."

"Oh, I thought you said—"

"I'm painting Bu's hair."

"Bu's hair?"

"Sure. It isn't really fog, Daddy."

"It isn't?"

"No, silly. Bu comes to visit us, especially around Halloween, and she lies down by the river or the pond at the park and her long white hair falls over the *whole* neighborhood *all* the way to school. Bu has very long hair. Isn't it beautiful?"

"I see." But David Chase did not see. He did not see into the world as it appeared to Emily. His world resembled a newspaper while Emily's was a turning kaleidoscope.

What he did see above the drifting snowflakes, though he would not remember having seen them until many years later, were three pink moons, twirling like Van Gogh's stars.

"Emily, did you paint these? They're beautiful, really. But why pink moons? And why three?"

"Of course, I did, silly Daddy. Because, every year on the night the moon is full and closest to us, it's called a pink moon. Don't you know that, Daddy?"

But Emily didn't wait for her father's answer; she went right on talking. "Daddy, isn't it wonderful? It will all be better."

"What will be better?"

"It will all be better, Daddy, Bu said so, and Bu is the wisest person in the whole wide world."

"She is?"

"Oh yes! Do you see all the lines on her face? She is a thousand years old, and she knows everything. That's really old!"

"What will be better, sweetie?"

"The smoke, Daddy. The smoke will go away, and everything will be better. You'll see."

"What smoke?"

"Bu says one day the fog will turn to smoke and cover everything."

"Okay. Well, I'm glad everything will be all right."

"It will, and guess what?"

"What?"

"Bu says that will be the day you love."

"The day I love?"

"Yes, Daddy, isn't that great? It will happen, Daddy, you will learn to love. Bu says so, and Bu knows everything, even the future."

"But Emily, I love you, sweetheart, doesn't Bu know that?

"Oh, sure, Daddy, but I'm easy, you can't help loving your little girl. She's talking about big love, Daddy. Really, really big love."

David felt flummoxed and on the spot. He turned and without a word began walking back to his room, still a bit befuddled by his daughter's pronouncement, when he heard Emily's voice reach for him.

"Daddy, why don't you love?"

" I do love, Em, I love you and Martha—"

"Well, you don't smile. Why don't you smile, Daddy? Doesn't being alive make you smile? Doesn't it make you giggle too?

Sometimes everything is so silly. Like grownups, and the way they are always walking so fast and looking down at the cement, and kind of frowning. Why are grownups like that, Daddy? Why don't they look at the trees and the wind and laugh and smile and jump? I love to jump. Do you?"

"I guess I don't jump much anymore."

"Why not? It's so fun."

"I guess I'm too busy, thinking about work and things."

"You guess a lot, Daddy."

"I guess I do, I mean, you're right, Em. Do I seem unhappy to you?"

"Yep. You look like you need a mommy."

"A mommy?" The familiar feeling of wanting to leave a room took over his legs.

"Yeah, you look like my friends at school who look sad waiting for their mom. Did your mommy love you, Daddy?"

"Of course. All moms love their kids."

"Why don't we have any pictures of her, Daddy? We have lots of pictures of my mommy. I want to see yours."

"Well, sweetie, they all got lost a long time ago. It's a long story."

"Do you have a picture inside your brain, Daddy? I have wonderful pictures of Mommy Claire in mine, and they talk, too. And then there are dreams when Mommy Claire holds me and reads to me and sings songs. She's a really good singer, Daddy. And then there's Bu. She's always visiting and telling me stories."

By this time, David Chase was feeling dizzy and looking for a way to escape. He felt cornered, under a search lamp. Many of his conversations with Emily ended this way or in a state of confusion as his long-lost soul began to stir, recognizing in Emily's questions the missing pieces of the puzzle he wished to remain incomplete.

"Sweetie, I have to get a little more sleep before work, okay? And you should too, you have school today. We'll talk more tonight. Good?" And he began his familiar turn, away from anything that might interfere with maintaining his solitary, upright posture around Emily who, like a baker, was continuously kneading the ball of dough that was his heart.

"But, Daddy, just one more question—"

"Em, I have to sleep. Tonight. And you go to bed too. Now."

As he walked to his room, David listened to Emily putting her paints away, humming a tune to herself. The creaking floorboards were cross with him for leaving so abruptly. The walls glared at him for being short with Emily and turning from her as he did from people he didn't care for. By the time he reached his bed the accusing chorus was in full voice, and he lay there staring into the dark, restless with the feeling that once again he had failed his daughter and himself.

■ ■ ■

There would be many comparable conversations in the years to come that would leave David befuddled and trying to fend off the feeling of inadequacy drenching his flesh like the humidity of a summer day in Houston. One of those talks happened on an afternoon in August when Emily was eight years old. The two had walked to Alberta Street to take in the annual fair and have some ice cream at Salt and Straw. Emily ordered a large bowl of rainbow sherbet and butter pecan and David one scoop of chocolate mint.

Happy together licking their treats, groaning in the delight of one scrumptious taste after another, they watched the parade of weird Portlanders pass by and laughed at the costumes and makeup on display. David watched his daughter's face light up and stretch with joy as her happy mouth greeted each spoonful of rainbows. It was in these moments that he thought of Claire and how she would have delighted in her little girl. Inwardly he recognized how right she was: Emily had crawled up on his lap and into his heart despite his elaborate barricade. She seemed to find all the openings with ease.

David laughed as Emily somehow managed to smile and at the same time consume huge mouthfuls of her favorite food. With one of those globs of goodness only half in, and a rainbow melting over her lip and down her chin, she said to her amused and slightly envious father, "I always eat rainbows first, Daddy."

"I see. Why is that, Em?"

"Because I want rainbows to cover my face."

"Why do you want rainbows all over your face, you silly girl?"

"Because. That way I know I'm near the pot of gold!"

"Ah, the pot of gold. Are you looking for treasure?"

"The treasure is right here, Daddy. Look, butter pecan is the pot of gold!" Emily dipped her pink spoon into the butter pecan and took a huge spoonful of the buttery gold to her mouth. "And now, I shall swallow the gold and it will be inside of me!" She swallowed the gold and beamed a golden smile. Her father shook his head, marveling at his daughter's playful love of nearly everything in life.

His little girl, her golden hair in pigtails with purple ribbons, then turned to her father and asked him her perennial question: "Daddy, why are grownups so serious and unhappy?"

This question always threw David Chase off balance. He wondered if Emily was referring to him. Did he look unhappy? Could she sense the flat line that had him in its grip? "Why do you ask that, Em?"

"Because they usually look worried or upset when no one is looking, and then when they look up and see someone looking at them, their faces get all twisted up trying to smile a big smile. Are grownups always upset?"

"Well, grownups have a lot on their mind and a lot of responsibility."

"What is responsibility?"

"Like work, like making sure their families have what they need, food and clothes. It's like your job—your responsibility is keeping your room picked up, which, by the way, is getting pretty messy, my dear."

"But I like it that way! Then I can hide things and forget about them and then find them and be happy. Besides, it doesn't sound like fun being a grownup. Why is all that more important than trees?"

"People have to earn money to buy food and pay bills."

"What's a bill?"

"A bill is like a letter you get in the mail that tells you what you owe someone for something they did for you."

"You mean people don't do stuff for free because they're your friend?"

"No, it doesn't work that way. You have to pay for help and food and a place to live."

"But what do you pay them? What is money, Daddy, and why

is it more important than being nice to people, and trees . . . and why do people kill trees? That makes me so mad!"

"Sweetie, people don't actually kill trees, they make them into something, like houses, or furniture, or paper. You like paper, don't you?"

"What?" Emily slammed her fist down on the table and glared at her father. "They do too kill trees! I saw them kill one by Audrey's house just the other day. It was a huge, old tree—huge, big, big branches, it was the tallest tree around and they cut it down with those horrible, horrible mean saws and then cut them into more pieces, and then worst of all, Daddy, they pushed them through that terrible grinder thing and turned them into dust, and then ground out the trunk with another awful thing. The poor roots, Daddy, the poor roots, what happens to the roots? Did you know the roots go way, way down in the ground? It's true." Emily looked up at the sky and big tears rolled down her cheeks until the angry bear in her rose up again. "And they killed it! That beautiful tree wasn't hurting anybody, and they just cut it down so it wouldn't drop so many leaves on their stupid patio. I wanted to kick them in the shins and stomp on their toes. Audrey and I cried for an hour. Trees are alive, Daddy, and did you know they talk to each other? They do! I read about it in my book, *The Hidden Life of Trees*. Most things are hidden, Daddy. We can't see most of what's alive, did you know that? It's hidden and tiny and the little, tiny things make the big things work. Why do we kill them? It makes me so sad and mad, and I wanted to go up to those mean men with those stupid helmets on and their terrible saws and I wanted to yell at them and scream at them to stop! 'Stop, Stop! You're killing something beautiful that we love.' But they wouldn't have listened to me, would they? They'd probably laugh at me and tell me to go away before I got hurt. Why don't big people listen to little people? We know a lot of things they don't."

David Chase watched as his daughter's face turned from bright red back to her creamy almond skin color. He watched as the steam coming from her ears let up and the fire in her eyes subsided. He marveled at the passion and intelligence of this little girl and thought of her mother and the first time he saw her shake down an auditorium full of cardiologists. He couldn't help but chuckle at the resemblance.

Emily saw him grin. "What's so funny?"

"You just reminded me of your mother for a second. She could get fired up and angry with grownups too."

"Mommy?"

"Oh, yeah. Your mom was strong, and she would say what she thought to whomever. And she did to me too many times, and she was almost always right."

"Did my mommy like trees?"

"Your mom loved trees. She spent as much time as she could in the woods. She was never happier than on the days she had off so she could go hiking on Mt. Hood. Everything in nature was precious to her. A whole lot of things were precious to her."

"I knew it! I just knew Mommy was my kind of person! I wish I could walk in the forest with her right now! What else was precious to Mommy?" She sat up in her chair and leaned toward her father.

"Oh my, so many things. Little things, like bugs, especially ladybugs, but also praying mantis and beetles."

"Yes! I love the praying mantis. One time I found one and held it on my hand—it was not even an inch long, and it bit me! It hurt! They have strong jaws, you know."

"Your mom wanted to be praying all the time. She wanted to fill every moment with happiness. She loved clouds, like you do, and she loved wind and even warm rain. She loved tree bark and newborn baby leaves in spring. And she really loved books and stories that made her think about things differently and see people and the world better. But do you know what was the most precious of all to your mom?"

"Peaches and cream?"

"Close."

"Rainbow sherbet!"

"Good guess. Give up?"

"Okay, what? Tell me!"

"You."

"Me?" Emily's eyes lit up and twinkled like stars in the sky.

"Yes, you. You were everything."

"Me? More than you or Grandma Martha?"

"Way more. A mom's love is bigger than the biggest tree you've ever seen. Way bigger!"

And Emily's eyes opened wide as the crown of a giant elm. She closed her eyes and tried to imagine a love that big. When she opened them and looked at her father they were brimming with tears. Her face turned an uncharacteristic shade of serious and she asked David, "Daddy, you never talk about your mommy. Did she love you like my mommy loved me?"

With that, the thin line that David Chase lived by tightened and snapped like elastic.

"Daddy, you don't look so good. What's wrong?"

"Nothing, nothing sweetie, I just remembered something I have to take care of at work."

"Daddy, what's wrong? Didn't your mommy love you? I keep wondering because you never smile and you don't laugh much, except at me."

In the long pause that followed, her father's unconscious mind had all the time it needed to slam him with unwanted memories. The familiar bank of fog drifted in. He felt the urge to turn away, to tighten the grip on his heart. He heard his daughter's voice appeal to him from a distance. "Daddy, Daddy, what's wrong?"

But the only one who could answer Emily's question was the boy of nine walking away from the house where his mother lay in the car growing cold. That boy was sealed off from the world, trapped in a tomb, unable to hear Emily's plea, certain that not a living soul knew or cared that he was still alive. It would take Emily's death to shatter the doorway to his tomb. Her death and undying love.

Chapter 18

Randy Tanner spent his twelfth birthday alone in the small fourth-floor apartment his mother rented on the corner of 122nd and Powell. He watched horror movies on cable TV, but he was not afraid. He was too drunk to feel frightened, even when the occasional siren came shrieking by the building.

His mother left him alone from the time he was five years old. At that age he was so frightened of the night and the sound of sirens screaming he would pee his pants and lay in his bed shivering in fear. He was frightened of sounds and shadows most of all, especially the cracking of the floorboards and the little movements of light and shadow that became zombies roaming the night, looking to feed on the quivering souls of children.

At no time, however, was Randy as terrified of the dark, of demons, or flickering shadows as he was when his mother came home with a stranger draped over her body like a wet blanket. He was usually in bed shaking when he heard them come down the hallway to the apartment. It was always the same—the sound of her laughter, loud and hard, and the heavy footsteps of another. Each time, she struggled to find her keys and unlock the door as the stranger pounded on the wall and yelled something like, "Come on baby, let me in, I'm a drunk, horny lover boy ready to pound your meat. Come on baby, let's get it going."

She tried to quiet him, but Randy could tell it was halfhearted as their voices grew even louder nearing the moment of glory. "Shh, you'll wake the boy, be patient, big boy, Mama's gonna give you all you can eat." With that, the door flew open, and the two drunken sex machines stumbled inside, clawing at the clothing that separated them from carnal knowledge.

Randy learned it was best to be in his room when the pair arrived smelling like they'd brought the smoky bar with them. The few times he wasn't, he was greeted by the big man's threatening snarl. They all sounded the same: "What the fuck are you doing here, kid? Get the fuck out of here, you little shit."

And Randy did just that, scampering quickly to the safety of his room, closing the door on his mother's plaintive voice: "Come on, don't be hard on my baby, he's been all alone." But this was the briefest of delays, and by the time Randy was tucked in bed under his blankets, the rowdy couple was in the next room, banging away with the pent-up ferocity of combustible fire.

At those moments, five-year-old Randy met his greatest fear. Greater than the fear of facing zombies coming from the shadows. Greater than the terror of being alone and hearing someone trying to open the door. Nothing was more frightening to the little boy than the screams that came through the walls from the next room, the gasping, pleading voice of his mother. "Oh my God, my God, Jesus, my God—you're killing me baby, you're killing me!"

Once, and only once, Randy went to the rescue of his mother when he heard those words. He crashed through the door yelling, "Mommy, Mommy, I'm here, stop hurting my mommy, you pig." And he went for the intruder with all his love and might, but before the cold, hard fist of the man trying to kill his mother could hit his soft little cheek, Randy saw the dome of his mother's ass lifted into the air beneath the towering length of her murderer and he ran from the room. The image ran with him, and the sound of her scream lodged in his brain and convinced him that the one person in the world who loved him was being ripped to bloody shreds and he was doing nothing to stop it.

He lived in terror from that night until the night of his tenth birthday, when rummaging through the cabinets in search of food, young Randy discovered a bottle above the refrigerator. The bottle contained a cure. It was the genie in the bottle that answered his wish for an end to the stinking fear that haunted him and the humiliating weakness that caused him to hide in his bed. It was that cure, that snake charmer's remedy, that put an end to fear and loneliness and any and all of the dreaded attackers that came for him in the night.

Best of all, by the age of thirteen, the bottle had eliminated forever the last and most difficult of all his nightmarish pursuers: the need for his mother. It had eliminated all wanting for the comfort of a mother's touch and the longing for her smile. From that day on, he was freed to take from the world what he believed to be rightfully his.

Chapter 19

Of all the beauty and mystery of the world that beckoned to Emily, it was wind that captivated and delighted her most of all. She danced with the wind, chased the wind, and let it blow her golden locks across her face and straight back like a flag.

Wind was a living, breathing friend to her. She spoke to it, laughed with it, and sang songs intended for the various moods of her playful companion. Together they made joy out of long-tailed kites, glee out of short-lived bubbles, and suspense out of balsa wood gliders.

When it was not possible to be outdoors, Emily evoked the wind through song. She sang the melodies of her favorite tunes, and as many of the words as her seven-year-old brain could hold. The Beatles gave her the happy feeling she liked most, and it was quite common to hear her humming or singing her favorite song, "All You Need Is Love."

...

Coming down the stairway, Martha could hear Emily's merry voice filling the house. Since moving in after Emily's birth, she had grown dependent on that music. It soothed the hole left by the loss of Claire and Martha's husband of forty years. Without child, Martha filled the same absence when Claire lost her parents. From Auntie to Grandma, Martha assumed the duties of the loving mother with grace and delight.

Sweet Emily reminded Martha so much of Claire that she often felt dizzy and strange, as if she were living in simultaneous times. She laughed out loud at the sight of Emily's young body flying about the living room, bounding from sofa to chair, her arms outstretched like the wings of a swan and her rosy face beaming as if this were the most glorious moment life could offer.

"Well, good morning, my little butterfly!"

"Boop-dee-loop-wah-wah to you, Grandma, but I'm not a butterfly, you know. I am a clarinet!"

"Oh, I see, you are a clarinet, are you?"

"Yes, I am actually, doo-da-badee, I am the wind-music from the clarinet, you see, ooo-bop-dee-boop." And she was off, cartwheeling and tumbling over the carpet and through every chamber of her grandmother's heart. Martha had no children and did not hesitate to join Emily and her father after the tragic day that took Claire from both of them. She happily accepted the role of honorary grandmother in residence and gave of herself to Emily and David in every way she knew how.

"You sound like Ella Fitzgerald to me, dear."

"Oh! That's what Bu said too. You and Bu think alike, Grandma. Come on and do a cartwheel with me, they're fun."

"If I do that, Emily, we won't be walking to the park today!" And the old woman laughed at her granddaughter's eternal faith in possibilities. "You do want to go to the park like we planned, don't you?"

"Oh sure, and then I want to come home and make popcorn

and watch *The Red Balloon.*" A little prankster grin passed over Emily's face and she paused atop the couch. "Can we make popcorn without the lid on again? Please, Grandma?"

Martha chuckled. A few weeks before, she'd forgotten to put the lid on the popper, and before she knew it, Jolly Time corn filled the air, and Emily fell to the floor laughing and catching the falling kernels as they landed. It was easy with Emily; Martha marveled at her acrobatic approach to life and joyful embrace of nearly every situation.

"That was a bit of fun, wasn't it, darling?"

"That was sooo fun, Grandma." The little musical score, the youthful Fitzgerald, jumped from the top of the couch to the cushion of the stuffed chair, simulating the sounds and flight of the liberated popcorn. "Pop, pop, pop, POP-POP-POP-POP-POP!"

"Be careful not to hurt yourself, darling."

"How can the wind get hurt, Grandma? I am the wind; I make music and I tickle everything I touch." And with that, she ran to Martha's side and affectionately tickled her grandmother beneath her ribs.

"Oh my, oh my, that does, stop, oh goodness!" Martha bent over laughing and holding her sides as the hands of the wind gently probed her ribs.

"You see? Wind makes people smile and laugh. I love the wind and I can't wait to watch *The Red Balloon!* Watch me, Grandma, I'm a balloon!" And the movements of an autumn breeze transformed before Martha's eyes into the graceful journey of a balloon floating above the heavy world. So light was her granddaughter's being that Martha thought for a moment Emily had actually drifted up off the floor toward the ceiling. She nearly shouted out, "Look out dear, you'll hit the lamps!" But Martha caught herself and shook her head and thought, *That child. She makes me believe in miracles.*

. . .

Emily and Martha set out on their walk to the park after finishing a light breakfast. Emily skipped her way up the hill, saying hello to the leafy silver maples and chickadees darting among the branches. Martha followed behind as fast as she was able. A little out of breath, she shouted, "Emily, honey, wait for me."

Emily stopped and turned around, shouting, "Here I come, Grandma," and she skipped merrily back down the old, cracked sidewalks of Northeast Portland. When she reached Martha, she circled the old woman three times for good luck and settled into a loopy walk by her side.

"My dear child, you have so much energy. I can't keep up with you."

"That's okay, Grams, I'll walk slower now."

And the two companions walked along the curving streets of the one-hundred-year-old neighborhood and past the assortment of century-old bungalows and three-story Portland homes. They took the route up NE Floral that led directly to the park and were happily chatting away when Emily stopped suddenly and grabbed Martha's hand, exclaiming, "I know, Grandma, let's stop and get Audrey! She can come play at the park and then watch *The Red Balloon* with me! Can we, Grandma?"

"Sure, honey, whatever you like." Martha was a pushover to

any request that began with "Grandma." The title warmed her heart like nothing else.

Emily was in love with *The Red Balloon* and the little boy who played Pascal. "I am going to marry Pascal when I grow up, Grandma, and we are going to have a hundred red balloons!" She said this with great pride and certainty.

"You are?"

"Oh yes! I love balloons, Grandma. I love the way they play with the wind and fly toward the sun. But I especially love the red balloon and the way it follows Pascal around the neighborhood and all the way to school."

"That balloon is a good friend."

"The best friend, like me and Audrey, and me and Pascal, and me and YOU!" And she pulled Martha toward her and gave her a big, big hug.

"You have lots of friends because you are such fun, Emily."

"I have lots of silly friends, but Pascal isn't silly. He seems a little sad. I guess because he lives alone."

"But Emily, Pascal is just a little boy. He couldn't live alone, he's too young. I'm sure he has a mommy and daddy."

"Well, where are his mommy and daddy? And why don't they protect him from all those mean bullies?"

"They must be working, I guess."

"I don't have a mommy, and I don't think Pascal does either. I think she was killed, and his daddy is working, and Pascal is alone. I will marry him, and he will be happy and never by himself again."

Martha winced. "You aren't alone, are you, dear?"

"Oh no, Grandma. I'm never by myself. I have you and Daddy and Bu to keep me company."

"Bu is with you?"

"Sure, you know Bu, she's my great grandmother. She's always with me. Especially at night when you are sleeping."

"Aren't you sleeping?"

"No. I travel in my dreams, usually with Bu. I wish you could come, Grandma. It is sooo fun."

Martha shook her head and stood there astonished by how her granddaughter cartwheeled through life and into places she would never know. "I wish I could too, dear, I wish I could."

Chapter 20

Hour #26

He is all bones. Bones become brittle. And break. They don't talk. They carry the weight of years and heartache without a word. His bones fall into the chair like a pile of sticks.

David, you seem far away.

"Nowhere to go."

What has happened since we last met?

"Happened?"

Yes, you look beaten up. What is it?

"Nothing happens. Nothing."

Tell me what your days are like.

"I don't have days."

What do you do with your time?

"It doesn't matter."

I'd like to know. What did you do this morning before our appointment?

"You don't get it."

You must do something.

"Why?"

Because you're alive.

"I stare at the wall. I shit. I walk in the dark."

What about eating? What do you eat?

"You're trying too hard."

Who do you talk to?

"I don't."

You don't? You don't talk with anyone?

"I haven't talked to anyone but you for, shit, I don't know how long. Years. Why would I?"

Years? I'm the only person you have talked to for years?

"Don't act like you're surprised. And don't make that into your new mission."

Yes, you're right. I'm trying too hard to find you, to make contact like we did last hour. I see you've shut down. You look ragged today. I imagine . . . you're not listening, are you?

The shade is drawn, and David Chase is somewhere on the other side of nowhere, lost in a dream, the making of memory too terrible to allow. David looks to the window for escape. He watches the squirrel on the tightrope. The squirrel is nimble; it pauses now and then as if sensing something and continues on without hesitation across its aerial bridge.

Where do you walk?

"What?" His head jerks, like a spasm.

Where do you walk?

The sun disappears behind a cloud. A shadow fills the room.

"Bridges."

Bridges?

"Yes. I . . . I walk over bridges."

I see. Yes, bridges, yes.

"She loved them. She . . ."

She loved bridges.

"She . . ."

It's hard to talk about her.

"I . . . I . . . I can't."

I understand, you can't talk about her, but you walk the bridges to be with her.

"I walk the walk."

The walk?

"I walk the walk to that place. Every day."

Every day . . .

"I walk over the bridge and decide."

Decide?

"Whether to jump."

Every day?

Dr. Jones stops. He feels the undertow of despair pull him out beyond the point where he can touch bottom. His hands grasp the chocolate arms of his chair. David closes his eyes and enters the day that is night. The room is silent as a church at midnight. Dr. Jones is startled back to the room by what has become the familiar sound of David's voice.

"But I can't. I'm a coward. I should jump, but I can't bear to never see her face again. So I keep walking to be with her bicycle at the spot. It's pink. I sit there and think of how beautiful and happy she was, riding to meet us . . . before . . . before everything ended."

I see.

"She loved the bridges, the towers, the river. She loved it all."

Your daughter loved with all her heart.

"Everything. She loved everything."

She loved you. And you love her.

"No, I don't. I can't. I'm a failure. I've failed her and myself."

There's something to the bridges, a connection, a wanting.

"Stop! Stop . . ."

She's everything to you, David. No wonder you shut down. You let yourself love her.

"Stop. I told you. Why do I have to keep telling you? I don't deserve her love. I don't."

What was it? What did that little boy do that was so bad, so unforgivable? Tell me, I'm here.

"He killed her. He killed his mother and walked away. Everyone dies who gets near him. Even Emily. She never hurt anyone. He's poison. He can't be helped. He can't be forgiven. He's nothing. There. Satisfied?"

His bones are buried underground, by a swing set. They wait to be unearthed. Earthworms crawl over them, caressing and blessing. David swings up and down, back and forth. He likes the motion, the curve through empty space that lasts forever. He soars above the world, above snowbanks, above tulips, above the sounds of shattering glass. And most of all, above blood. The rivers of blood that carve through all the stories of the world. He soars through the arc of time until he can fly, fly into eternal night. And then he lets go and leaves this world of dying.

David, what is it? You went far away.

David's eyes blink furiously as he mumbles, "There is no David. I told you he doesn't exist."

You disappear into nothing.

The swing pauses in midair.

"What did you say?"

I said you disappear into nothing.

"Disappear?"

Yes, you run away. You've retreated since—

"Disappear . . . nothing disappears."

Nothing disappears? What are you saying?

"She said it, Emily. Nothing disappears, silly. That's what she said. Jesus."

She said that? She knew.

"She doesn't disappear. I keep feeling her here. You probably think I'm crazy, but I do."

What if I don't think you're crazy? What if you aren't? What if you are running, running from horror and unbearable pain and you feel her presence anyway?

"I always run away. I'm trying to make everything disappear. Jesus, I'm trying to make me disappear, but the one thing I can't, I won't let happen, is for her to disappear. That's why I don't jump. Why I don't let go of the chains. Oh, Emily, dear Emily . . ."

The walls soften and move closer. Sunlight returns and fills the room. David touches his forearm and strokes it gently. Dr. Jones allows his breath to leave his lungs and looks down at his lap, marveling at what is occurring in the room between him and David Chase. When he lifts his eyes, he sees that David is looking at him. He feels a twinge of fear.

What do you see, David?

"I see you haven't packed your bags yet."

I haven't disappeared.

"You probably want to. You certainly should have—not too late!"

Dr. Jones chuckles. A smile fills the room and lightens the air.

Nope, never too late, is it?

Chapter 21

"Fucking idiot. You are the biggest fucking idiot on the planet. Listen to me, shithead, there ain't no fuckin' God, there ain't no fuckin' purpose, nothing matters, don't you get it?" Words flew out of Randy Tanner's mouth like flames from a rabid dragon.

They fell on Bruce Paul, who twelve hours earlier had taken pity on this man standing in the rain begging for gas money to get him home. A new believer in the word of God, Bruce Paul realized the error in his judgment and regretted ever opening his mouth to offer the Gospel of Truth to this madman. Terrified now, he shrank into the recliner under the assault of Randy Tanner's furry. Bruce Paul saw his foolishness in thinking anyone but Christ himself could save this demented soul, and he began to pray fervently for his.

Randy stood over him, enraged, intent on pounding his Anti-Christ Gospel of Death into the one person in the last ten years who had shown him any kindness. "Nothin' matters in this shithole, fuck, it's all totally random, random bullshit flying everywhere, especially from your stupid fucking trap. Jesus fuck, I can't believe I'm standing here talking to such a goddamn ignorant fuck. Let me tell you something, asshole, there are two types of people living on this goddamn worthless rock, those who fuck, and those who get fucked. That's it, so don't give me no motherfucking crap about God fucking karma and shit. It ain't nothin' but random crap flying around, quarks and fucking little strings and shit and what the fuck are those, fucking neutrinos bombarding your worthless shit factory body while you blow that crap out your ass talking about God and salvation. Christ, if your sorry, son of a bitch, moron ass is born again, I'm taking the first train down to hell and getting laid and watching you go through another shit-eatin' life on this death slab—and I'll be laughing my devil's head off watching the show. You born, you fuck, and you sure as shit die. And that's all there is. Jesus fuck."

Bruce Paul sat shivering in his recliner with his knees pulled up to his chest, dumbfounded that anyone could be so hateful and ignorant of the love of Jesus in the world. Why had he taken pity on such a miserable wretch and given him money? Worse yet, invited him to stay a few nights at his apartment? He was trying to be a good Christian when he offered him shelter and food and a chance to get off the streets of Vancouver for a few days, but this had gone terribly wrong, and now he was beginning to fear what Randy Tanner might do before he could find a polite way to ask him to leave.

"Jesus, Randy, you are one bitter asshole."

Randy paced from one side of the room to the other, snorting, coughing, and kicking any furniture within reach. Hearing Bruce Paul's judgment of him, he stopped abruptly, turned toward him and flashed a menacing look his way that made Bruce shrink deeper into his chair.

"Fucking A, I'm a bitter asshole, and so should any motherfucker who has a goddamn brain bigger than your fucking shrunken prick. Which excludes you, doesn't it, shithead? Why do I waste my time with a fuckhead like you? Walking around talking like you know shit about some fucking God who sent his little shit of an illegitimate faggot son to make this hellhole even more of a fucking disaster than before he got here. If your fucking God is so merciful, why the fuck did he turn every crazy motherfucking crusader loose to rape and burn every godforsaken bitch and fucker they could lay their hands on?"

Randy's tirade came to a sudden halt as he struggled to take in some air. His face was turning a shade of purple, but he continued. "What about that shit, asshole? What about those fucking Christians with the white fucking hoods over their heads fucking lynching every cocksucking nigger they could tie up to a tree? What about that shit? What was your fucking all-powerful God doing while that shit was going down? I'll tell your miserable ass what he was doing, probably beatin' off in the bottom of some black hole with one hand and drinking a bottle of rot gin with the other, that's how fucking ashamed his ass must be of this failure of a creation he fucking threw together. What a miserable fucking loser. Almost as bad as you, shithead."

Five days of meth, fucking, and ranting had whipped Randy Tanner into his best oratory form. He picked up a bottle of Turkey Whiskey. "Well, what the fuck, nothing to say, preacher boy?"

Bruce Paul stared at this man he had known for less than a day. He tried to imagine why he was in the same apartment with such a crazed heretic. Why had he felt sorry for him when they met on the street and Randy T. asked for help? He imagined him burning at a stake. But now he felt frightened of the maniac in his apartment and tried to play dead, like a possum.

"You don't have a goddamn thing to say, do you, asshole? You just fucking lay here all fucking day, thinking about your fucking imaginary God bullshit. When was the last time you got laid, you fucking eunuch? Probably in your last worthless lifetime, if then. That's the problem with you castrated wimps, afraid of every goddamn thing that moves, hiding out in those pathetic fucking fairy tales about some fucking Tyrannosaurus Rex God shit. You're afraid some fucking wild pussy gonna take a bite out of your shriveled-up sorry excuse for a cock and spit it out in the fucking sewer. You're a scared little boy hiding in your goddamn everything is God shit, trying to convince yourself that some almighty daddy wet dream is going to save your ass from those terrifying bitches trying to fuck it. Horseshit. What the fuck am I doing? I'm gonna go get myself laid and praise Allah while that miserable whore is screaming her fucking tits off for more blessings from my divine cock."

Chapter 22

One block before reaching Audrey's house, Emily stopped suddenly. She looked up at Martha with a playful yet serious expression on her face.

"Grams, the air doesn't feel heavy, does it?"

"No, I suppose it doesn't."

"Well, it is. It really is. Daddy told me the air is really heavy. He said it is full of moll . . . moll. . . moll . . . "

"Molecules?"

"Right! Molecules! How did you know that, Grandma?"

"Oh, I don't know, Emily. I suppose I learned it in school."

"We can't see these molecules, can we?"

"No, we certainly can't, dear."

"No. I love invisible stuff, Grandma, don't you? Did you know these molecules carry water? And they bump into each other too, like kids in line at school."

"Yes, they must be a lot like children."

"I think they are invisible tears, the water molecules. I think the air is heavy because the world is sad."

"You do? I mean, it is?"

"Yes, Grandma, haven't you noticed?"

"Well, yes, now that you mention it, I have." With the mere mention of the world's grief, the long list of her own losses lined up in Martha's mind. She did her best to brush them away so as not to disrupt the time with Emily who by now was bounding down the street to Audrey's, squealing her name at the top of her lungs just as Audrey burst out of her front door shouting, "Emmmily!"

The two little girls who would still be best friends when they turned seventeen, who would be inseparable till death did them part, held hands and ran through the heavy air as though it contained not a drop of grief.

They ran to Martha, ran circles around her, leaving a song of joy in their wake, and then took off for the park like a pair of happy puppies.

They dashed to the playground, stopping at the merry-go-round for a spin and the opportunity to whip up the wind and invite their friend to come along and play. They took a few fast spins, holding on tight but leaning back into the arms of the friendly air, brushing against the faces of those delighted molecules.

But it was the swings they were really after, and as the merry-go-round slowed, they jumped off and ran to the swing sets at the edge of the playground. Once saddled, the girls kicked and pulled against inertia and gravity and the silent sadness of the world. They climbed the invisible steps of space, moving pockets of air as their joy parted too many molecules to count and made a barely perceptible breeze. The kind that might go unnoticed were it to brush against the sleeve of a shirt or the back of a hand.

"Wheeeeee! Audreeeeeee!"

"Emileeeeee!"

"You look silly upside down!" Emily shouted as her feet pointed up at the deep blue sky and she leaned back, her long, golden hair dangling over the ground, looking into the beaming face of Audrey ascending the steep slope of space behind her.

"You look very silly tooo," Audrey squealed, but by then the two acrobats were passing each other in flight. They reached out to grab hands, but the speed was too great, and their hands only grazed each other before following into the arc that went up and down and up again.

Martha, out of breath from chasing after them, waved to the girls and settled onto one of the nearby benches. What she saw brought a big smile to her face and a share of relief that the girls were safe. Her wrinkles seemed to relax, and she waved to the girls, shouting, "Hello, my darlings, you are going so high!"

"Grandma, watch, I'm upside down, wheeee!" And Emily leaned back into emptiness, enjoying the sip of vertigo that accompanied her daring pose.

"Why yes, look at you, my dear, you're almost standing on your head!"

Nothing gave Martha satisfaction like these days with Emily and her friend. She smiled at the exuberant little girls and watched as their swings eventually synchronized into a parallel flight pattern resembling the one that would chart their lives for the years to come.

Like inseparable twins, the girls soared happily into space and returned to earth again and again, showing no signs of tiring or boredom. She watched them take each other's hands.

"Emily, this is so fun, I could do this all dayyyyyy, couldn't you?"

"All night, tooooooo!"

They giggled, parting the air with their legs and laughter.

"Except I want to go home and watch *The Red Balloon*."

"You just want to dream about Pascal, don't you? You're in love, aren't you?"

"Yes, I am in love with Pascal, and I'm going to marry him someday," Emily announced with the utmost confidence.

They each laughed wholeheartedly at what was to them a great mystery. They laughed and hung their heads back and lifted their legs and feet and cried for all the world to hear, "Whoa!"

Martha's face glowed at what she saw. What happened next was not possible to see because it occurred between the molecules of space and time: that invisible sky of improbabilities and weightlessness.

Only Audrey heard Emily's invitation: "Let's jump!"

"Jump?"

"Yeah! Come on, let's jump!"

"But we're so high, Em."

"It's okay, Bu will protect us."

"Who's Bu?"

But the answer was lost in the wind the two made, parting air and reality with the faith of their imaginations. Their little hands, made pink by excitement and holding off the forces of gravity, slowly, finger by finger, released their grip on the shiny metal chains, and they jumped.

As their hands went from grasping chains to meeting the warm summer air, their happy spirit bodies lifted from the seats and went sailing feet first, squealing with joy into the waiting body of molecules and light. Those spirits, old as the earth's, darted like hummingbirds into the invisibility of tomorrow. Breathless, the two souls merged into one and in a flash, entered a tunnel of color and sound beyond the river of being and becoming.

Reentry to the physical world was seamless. The girls tumbled gently into the age of fifteen, and Emily's friend, Bu, lay them down in tall grass by the banks of the Metolius River in central Oregon. Their clothes lay close to the riverbank atop a patch of bear grass. Emily and Audrey rolled over and under one another in the soft meadow. The ambling river serenaded the lovely young women and merged with their moans of delight. The wind, down from the mountains, celebrated and joined in the caressing and stroking of flesh so tender and lush. Their lips melted and merged, their tongues bathed one another and searched for love behind earlobes and under blossoming breasts. Those same tongues found their way to the headwaters of the world's great mystery, the heartland of life that beckons with aromas too wonderful for gods and kings, too sensual and bewitching, too luscious and erotic for the notions of I and me to survive. They roped together like silken threads beneath a hot and jealous sun. They became two, then one, then none as the pleasures of earth and fire, water and air wrapped them in a bliss more delicious than nectar from the goddess until the bliss of all time erupted like the old and silenced volcanoes standing before them, and the lava of their love and ecstasy, pouring from every sweating cell, spilled into the red dirt of the riverbank.

Emily and Audrey rolled on their backs and held each other's hand, speechless and overcome with wonder.

Their first words were spoken in unison. "Wow, that was . . . awesome!"

They lay there in wonder for an eternity, speechless and quivering in bliss. Audrey was the first to speak.

"I love you, Em."

"I love you Aud, you're my best friend for life."

"Emily, what just happened? How did we get here?"

"We flew!"

"We flew?"

"Not like birds, but we flew from the swing into the big gap, and voilà, here we are!"

"The big gap?" Audrey looked puzzled, and her happy face turned to a slight frown.

"Yeah, the big yawning gap in the space-time continuum. Wild, isn't it?"

"You mean, we're in two places at once? We just took off like Superman and ended up down the road seven years into the future? Shit, how do we get back?"

"Same way we got here, my love. We just part the molecules and off we go. We'll be home before we hit the ground."

"Jesus, Em, I don't know. How . . . how can all this be real?"

"You mean, all this love and all this beauty, and everything in this crazy bubble of a universe?"

"Yeah, and you and me, and this river that never stops. Do you think we ever stop?"

"No way. Not possible, my gorgeous, sexy friend. Not possible. How could anything as lovely as you disappear? Nope."

"Em, stop. Really, don't you wonder? Aren't you ever afraid?"

"Oh, I wonder plenty, but I'm not afraid, at least not of *this* stopping. Why should it? How could it? No stopping it, Aud. And no stopping me." With that, Emily rolled over on top of Audrey and hungrily kissed her surprised mouth like hers were the most delicious lips in life. The two wrestled in the grass, laughing and mocking the grunts and groans they'd heard grownups make.

Audrey, breathless from wrestling, but intent, as always, on finding something she could understand, even if it exposed doubts waiting to invade the rest of her brain, pushed away first and returned to her questioning. "How can you be so sure, Em? How can you really know?"

"I've known since I was little, Audrey. You know, you remember my Grandma Bu."

"Grandma Bu? Really, you still—"

Emily cut her off. "No, I don't believe, I know. I know her better than anyone in my life, even better than I know you, Audrey. Bu talks to me and sings to me, just like a mother."

"Come on, Emily, you're joking. Right?"

"We dance together, she takes me on trips, it's no joke, Aud. Really." Emily paused. "How do you think we got here?"

"What?"

"How do you think we got here, Audrey? We're not really here."

"Where are we?"

"We're in Portland with my grandma, Martha, flying through the air about halfway between the seat of the swing and the ground."

"What are you saying?"

"I'm saying Bu made sure we got here safe. Bu coaxed the space world into making a canal for us to get here and arranged for this carnal picnic." She brushed the tips of her golden locks across the fresh breasts of her age-old friend. "I know for sure she brought us here and laid us on our bed to play."

"Geez, Em."

"I know what you're thinking. You think I've taken this imaginary friend thing a bit too far. You think I should have outgrown this weird syndrome by now. Maybe I've tipped into some kind of psycho world, right?"

"Well, yeah. What the hell, Em, you have to admit it is pretty weird."

"What I think is weird, Aud, is that people only believe what they can see and hear. That's weird. And blind."

"Well, you're right about that, but what the fuck is this? You want me to believe we're really living in two places at the same time and any second now we're going to crash to the earth like some silly antique space capsule, skin our knees and trot off to Grandma's house to watch some pathetic French movie about some gay-ass kid and his balloon?"

"Hey!"

"Sorry, sorry. What, are you still going to marry that freak, Pascal?"

"Of course. I told you that more than ten years ago, didn't I?"

"Does this mean we're not gay?" Audrey chuckled to herself and gingerly stroked the lower region of Emily's abdomen. "We're not gay, we're not bi, we're not anything, are we, but alive, horny, and full of it."

"Yum, more dessert please, waiter."

And the two embraced and kissed and rolled once more over the flattened grasses beneath them. That afternoon, tourists walking by would imagine local deer bedding down in this spot for the night and take no notice of how strange the world truly is.

After another half hour of timeless, unbearably delicious loving, Audrey put her head on Emily's shoulder. "Why do you like *The Red Balloon* so much, Em?" she whispered.

Emily sighed and whispered back, "Because *The Red Balloon* is my life, Aud, and you are my Pascal until I meet up with him one of these days. *The Red Balloon* is everyone's life, isn't it? You look for a friend and find one and you never want to be apart. You're happy just being with your friend and floating through life wherever the wind takes you, as long as you have love in your heart. But life is sometimes cruel, and you have to suffer to know the greatest love of all. And so, life comes along and stomps on you real hard. It breaks you. But that isn't the end, is it? No! Soon all the balloons take to the sky and come to you and off you go, soaring above the city and the cruelty and even above the mountains where the air is thinnest and only love can survive."

"Wow. Is that what your Bu told you?" But Audrey had already heard the truth in what Emily said, thinking back on two years earlier when her father had left in the middle of the night and never returned, never to be heard from again.

"That's what she told me and that's what she showed me."

"She did?"

"Yep. She showed me all right, most of it. I still have to dream the end, but it won't be long now, the pink moons are coming."

"What does that mean?"

"Oh, never mind."

The girl of many passions kissed the girl of her childhood dream once more on her eager lips, and the love that met between the two took flight and carried that one body of desire back to Laurelhurst

Park. Back to the hard landing on the playground yard, back to skinned knees and breathless giggles and the watchful eye of Martha sitting on the wooden bench with Bu, enjoying the imperceptible touch of Bu's arm around her shoulder.

Audrey hit the ground hardest and got to her feet running. She ran to catch Emily like the wind chases a bird. The conversation and erotic pleasures that had not yet happened would join the other happenings waiting their turn to come into this world.

Slightly bewildered, Audrey looked over her shoulder as if she might see a glimpse of what had taken place but could not be recalled. She ran with all her might up the hill to the home of her friend. Not until life had taken its hard foot to her heart and soul would she remember the conversation with Emily that had not yet happened. Only then would Audrey come to understand the dream that rules the world, the dreamer that rules the dream, and Bu, the strange friend of sweet Emily, within whom and of whom dreamer, dreaming, life, and death abide.

Chapter 23

Hour #30

"I hate you. I should leave and never come back. Fuck you."

Yes, of course you hate me.

"I never asked for this. I don't want it. You must be feeling very smug and satisfied. Another victory. Another cold body pulled out of the morgue. You must have a Christ complex. Yeah, that must be it, a goddamn Christ complex, reveling in the resurrection of another fucking zombie. You're a goddamn sadist." David looks to the door, his face covered with disgust, rage steaming from his nostrils.

Maybe you're right, David. Maybe . . . I wish it wasn't so painful . . .

David grabs the arms of his chair. He is a cat about to pounce.

"Oh, here we go with the name thing again. You think you can seduce me into some pseudo-intimacy thing, some cozy relationship—let's get warm and chummy and talk feelings and, oops, fifty minutes is up, out you go, out into that shithole world. Good luck, sucker. Oh, by the way, that'll be another three hundred bucks—no credit cards."

It freaked you out to open up and need my help in our last hour. It terrifies you to give up control and feel so much, and now you're fighting with everything you have to regain control and shut down your emotions and push me away. If you make me bad, you can run from here back to your dungeon and hide out and never let your inner world or love get close enough again to do you harm.

"Love? What love? You think I love you? You think you can save me from pain? You inflated . . ."

I can't save you from anything. Not from yourself. Least of all love and life. I can be with you, and that boy, and the man who lost something precious, who made the gamble of his life and lost and is now raging against himself and me and something inside that knows he must try again. I can be with you in that.

"In that. You make it sound like a walk in the park . . . fuck, no!"

What? What happened, David?

"The park . . . the park, she loved the park . . ."

David slumps back into his chair. His bones rattle. Rage leaves his body in all directions like air from a balloon. He stares at the man in the chocolate chair.

"She loved it. She spoke to me . . . she was dead, and she spoke . . ."

What did she say, David?

"She was dead, gone—blood everywhere—but she said it, she said . . . Oh God! Fuck this, no! She didn't move, she lay there on me, her blood soaking into me, dead, but she spoke. I can't, not again."

What did she say?

"She said, she said what she always said . . . always . . . 'Daddy, love.' That was the last of her. Then there was only blood. Goddamn blood."

She died in your arms. Your beautiful daughter died in your arms. My God, I, I . . . Oh, David, and she left a prayer for you—

"My chest, it's cracking . . . it's breaking . . . you must understand, I can't do this. I am a wretched, terrible person, a coward and a cheat. I hurt so many, I . . . I . . . can't breathe!"

And with the breaking of his chest, the walls give way and generations of grief flood the room. The faithful room and the trees outside the window and the squirrel on the wire break with him and sob for David and all the suffering of the world's people. The man in the chocolate chair wipes his eyes and hands David a box of tissues. His hand trembles as he pulls a handkerchief from his pocket and says to David ever so tenderly, "I'm sorry, David. I'm so sorry."

Time lets go of its hold on the living. No one can say how long they sit there. The squirrel cocks its head as though contemplating a new thought. The trees bow to the window. And the room, that blessed space, knows to remain still and allow what has taken place to soak into the heart and soul of the two men seated just a few feet apart.

David is the first to speak. He looks at his hands, the hands that have held so many hearts, that held Emily's hand as they walked through the world together. He holds his hands together gently and says as much to himself as to Dr. Jones and the sacred space, "I may be ready. I don't know for what, but I feel different. It's time."

This is your moment, David. Your breakthrough moment. Emily's wish has sprouted in your heart. She knew something about you that you didn't. She knew you were more than the hurt you have caused. Something more essential than what you did to others.

"What did you say?"

You are more than your actions, David. Way more.

"Not much of an existentialist are you, doc?"

No, I failed at Sartre. And nothingness. And neither was she, or her mother.

"Her mother . . . Claire."

What was she like?

"She was one of the good ones. A truly good person."

Tell me more.

"No. Not today."

You've had enough for today.

"Not enough of this. I want to feel. I'm here, I can't believe it. I'm here!"

Yes, that's wonderful, David. You're getting closer and closer to you.

But David does not hear the words. He does not think of the existential lesson. He is immersed, swimming in the truth of himself. He lets it carry him, caress him, and show him the rooms of his heart. Emily waits for him there, her arms reached out, and she whispers, "Daddy, you're here!"

David comes back to the room slowly. He doesn't know it, but he is beaming and wondering to himself how he can ever convey to Dr. Jones what happened. When he looks up, he sees Dr. Jones looking at him intently with a bemused look of delight on his face.

David, you look radiant. What happened?

"I can't tell you. I don't have words—it's astonishing."

Ah, I thought it was something auspicious.

"Astonishing. I wish I could say more."

Your face says everything.

"Will it go away? I felt myself alive with love. I don't want to lose it. Will I?" His eyes plead with Dr. Jones and won't let him go until he hears what he wants to hear.

I don't know, David. Most things come and go and return. There are days the sun doesn't shine, and those can be rough ones, but I do know you'll never be the same. You've found yourself, David. You belong to yourself now. Just listen to your inner voice and your feelings. You'll find your way.

"This can't be happening to me, but it is. It's real. And guess who was waiting for me when I got there?"

Of course, it had to be your Emily.

"My Emily."

The room is mystery, is miracle. It smiles on the two men who have come to care deeply for each other. David is the first to speak.

"I thank you. I'm sorry I treat you so badly. You do matter to me."

Maybe there is something important in me surviving your fury and you discovering I'm still alive.

"That is good. I see what you mean. That must be hard."

It is hard, and it is a privilege to be with you and a part of what we have here.

"A privilege? Seriously? Now I'm really astonished. I really can't believe this is happening. What's next?"

You'll find out. Just be close, listen to your inner voice and your feelings . . . you'll know.

David is no longer a skeleton. The worms have softened the ground. He can move and stretch. He sits up in his chair and straightens his back. His bones crack but do not break. His is now a body of flesh and blood, and that blood circulates through a heart. The walls of the room sway, an easy rolling. They sway to a beat that moves within and beyond the sacred space that holds a door, walls, and the pulsing heartbeat of a life.

Chapter 24

Randy Tanner turned his back with contempt on Bruce Paul, the young apostle of Christian love, and stomped to the door. His body prepared to leave, but his mouth was not finished. It was a flamethrower, a tornado touching down on the miserable failure of Bruce Paul and ripping through the neighborhoods of every childhood memento of heartbreak and fear. The winds of rage blew, and by the time he reached the door, that rage had mushroomed into something larger than even Randy T. could have imagined in his most violent of attacks on the weak and frightened.

Bruce Paul saw the look of murderous hate on Randy's face and screamed, "Oh, my God, my God, Jesus, my God!" Randy T. heard those words, and with all the force of a gusting storm, that rage turned him around and he ran back to the chair where Bruce Paul sat cowering in terror. He grabbed him by the hair, threw him to the ground, and kicked him in the ribs with the pointed steel toe of his boot.

"You worthless piece of shit, nothing and nobody's gonna save your miserable soul today, sucker. This is all you're good for, you motherfucking worthless bag of shit, you're nothing but a fucking punching bag, not worth a damn, and I'm going to fuck you up real good, you pathetic scum."

Randy T. proceeded to kick the defenseless man everywhere he could fit his pointed boot. He kicked him in the ribs, the stomach, the teeth—he kicked out his front teeth and then kicked him in the balls. When Bruce Paul tried to crawl away, he kicked him in the nose and stomped on his head with the metal heel of his motorcycle boots, screaming for all the world to hear, "You worthless bag of shit, you worthless cocksucking bag of shit."

Bruce Paul wailed his impotent scream from beneath the boots of his tormentor. "Stop, you fucking bastard, stop, you're killing me! You're killing me!" He spat teeth and blood as he cried out, but his protests were useless. In fact, the more Bruce Paul yelled those words, the harder Randy Tanner threw the weight of his fury into the body of the trampled man at his feet. The more those words echoed in his ears—"you're killing me, you're killing me"—the greater was his desperation to silence them.

He stomped on the head of that unfortunate man as though he were trying, and failing, to put out a fire. He silenced every terrible, pleading syllable as his own voice took on the characteristics of a perverted chant, repeating over and over and over the single word that shrieked like a frozen scream etched in the sky.

Worthless. Worthless. Worthless. Worthless.

When Randy Tanner believed he had at last crushed the past, he wiped sweat from his brow as if completing a demanding chore. He spat on the bloodied body of Bruce Paul and turned for the door and his appointment with the strange, unimagined crossroads of his future.

Chapter 25

Emily woke on the first day of her eighteenth year as the pale light of dawn was dusting the world of trees and moist grass. She noticed her surroundings brighten as the light of day and the arousal of wakefulness combined to provide body and feeling to the life of the earth.

It was a dream that caused her to open her eyes to the light, a dream that delighted every cell of her body, one that reached deep into her core where she felt utterly loved and protected by Bu and Martha and Claire. Claire often visited in dreams and combed her daughter's hair while singing to her. Before leaving the comforts of her bed, Emily reflected on the dream one last time, anticipating sharing it with Audrey later in the day when they would certainly meet for a birthday celebration. Had it been a different world, had it been a world spared the horrors of death, this is how she would have described the dream to Audrey:

Oh, Audrey, I have to tell you the most wonderful, wonderful dream from this morning. It seemed to go on and on for hours. I want to tell you so you can feel it and be in it with me. Here goes—I am on a beach, a beach like Hug Point at the coast, and everything, everything is alive and swirling and playing and happy. The ocean is the most beautiful purple, like a yummy merlot or the deep, rich purple of the winter violas in my planter. Every single wave is dancing and has a personality like an animal, leaping high in the air, signaling those of us on the beach to come in the water and play. The spray from the surf rises into the air and turns into butterflies, really, Aud, and this magical heaven on earth goes on and on like this. The sea creatures, turtles, seals, baby whales, jellyfish, you name it, are all bobbing up and down on the surface of the ocean, squealing with delight. Starfish are doing cartwheels on the sand. Driftwood has transformed into giant marimbas, and beautiful African tunes are filling the sweet salt air with music. Seashells are dancing, seagulls are gliding upside down, and pelicans are doing spiral patterns above the water like the Navy's Blue Angels! Audrey, it's crazy, can you believe it? Then I run to the water and dive in, and the grape waves catch me and throw me in the air, and I can hear them laughing and I'm laughing too! Big belly laughs. Like I'm completely stoned. And then the wildest thing happens, Aud. Everything, yes, everything, begins to change into everything else. Seals morph into starfish, gulls into Cabernet waves, sand into wind, and wind into sand. I am the sun, the warmth, the music, the hundred-year-old driftwood, the little fiddler crab doing his jig. I am tumbling through one life after another, one form after another, until I am unable to breathe or know what I am or will be next. On and on and on, becoming everything, and finally, back to me, Emily, tumbling onto the soft, baked sand and into the arms of none other than my dear Bu. Bu is glowing. She wraps her long hair around me and sings softly—or was she humming? I don't know. I only remember closing my eyes and allowing the sound of her breath to take me over and a deep peacefulness to enter my breasts and flow to the tips of my toes and the top of my head. Bu hums and rocks me like her baby. And when I open my eyes, I notice the ocean is quieting and the motion settling, and all is peaceful. Can you believe that dream, Aud? I'm completely tingly telling you. It's the best present ever, isn't it? Something auspicious must be in the works, my dear. Something very auspicious.

Emily gazed outside, watching her dream evaporate in the sunlight. Birds landed on the branches of the plum tree near her window: goldfinch, chickadee, and purple finch—a choir of darlings singing happy birthday greetings to their friend. She felt the touch of morning on her cheek and came out of her reverie. That touch was a soft breeze stroking her face, inviting her to join the day. The gentle breeze gusted slightly, took her hand, and helped her out of bed. Several more birds at the feeder peeked inside and wished her a happy birthday. Emily laughed at the tiny chickadees serenading her from their breakfast table. She looked into their beady eyes and smiled at the dab of presence looking back at her. She felt the incredible lightness of their bodies in her hand and wondered if the world felt similarly to the mother of creation holding the entire universe on her fingertip.

Emily had lived without a mother for all but a few seconds of her eighteen years. She walked to her bureau and picked up the gold frame that held the picture of Claire sitting by a creek somewhere in the wilderness and imagined sitting there with her mother, singing and laughing. Holding the frame in both hands, Emily wondered if she looked like Claire when she was eighteen. She couldn't take her eyes off the photo, and though she had looked at it a thousand times, today Claire looked back at her with a special glow. Emily knew the story of their hello and goodbye. She knew and felt her mother's enormous love and sacrifice. Remembering all that, she kissed Claire, thanked her, and promised she would return her love and sacrifice to the world.

Feeling warm and satisfied with the moment, Emily headed to the kitchen to prepare a light breakfast. She picked a grapefruit from the basket, set it on a cutting board, and sliced the cutting knife through the thick yellow skin of her favorite fruit. She watched it sever into two. The sight of the juicy pink fruit made her mouth water. And because her life was a festival of little miracles, she was not surprised that the succulent thirteen sections were already carved and ready to eat. Emily smiled, winked, and said in a soft voice, "Thanks for the birthday present, Bu."

She was sitting at her breakfast table eating spoonful after spoonful of the succulent Florida grapefruit and moaning with delight when the phone rang. It was Audrey.

"Happy birthday, girl! What are you doing at this very moment?"

"I am eating the most deeeelicious pink flamingo grapefruit in history, that's what I'm doing."

"Well, will you tell me why in heaven the most beautiful girl in this crazy old world is eating breakfast alone on her birthday? Huh?"

"I don't know what alone means, Audrey dear. How about you explain that concept for me?"

"Will do, my darling, but how about over breakfast for two at the Utopia Café? My treat, if you don't mind."

"Sure thing, great. Let me finish up the God food and I'll meet you there in half an hour. Good?"

"Good to go. And I better warn you, I look ravishing today!"

"You always do, you sexy thing. Every time we venture out, those helpless boys are falling all over themselves to get an inch closer to you. I'll wear my negligee and maybe give myself half a chance."

The two laughed as only best friends from the beginning of time can. They laughed with eagerness, not knowing their happy rendezvous ensured that Emily's birthday would be her last. Not knowing the day of her death would be the end of life for David and Audrey, and Randy Tanner as well—an end they would relive every day until the pink moon rose for a third time. What waited at the corner of Belmont and SE 32nd was the truly auspicious choreography of four separate lives looped together in ways that only fate and the gods understand, and only mercy can revive.

Chapter 26

Life at the intersection of Belmont and SE 32nd went about its business as usual on that fateful morning in May. The one-hundred-year-old neighborhood welcomed residents and visitors alike with the innocence typical of a beautiful spring morning. Newer construction, including an upscale grocery store with modern apartments above, had replaced some of the old brick buildings, including the stretch of one-story shops on the north side of Belmont opposite the Utopia Café.

It was common to find people of all ages on foot and on bicycles in the neighborhood that time of morning. Outside the Utopia Café, the lineup of steel gray bike racks awaited Emily's arrival with the same innocent expectation as the lively street life met the glory of the morning. Emily rode her hot pink Schwinn from her rooms on SE Division and 24th through the neighborhoods lined with large chestnut trees and pink dogwoods. On this glorious day, she left her helmet in the basket, and true to her free spirit enjoyed the feel of the wind blowing her hair in all directions and over her face.

Emily laughed as she rode, flinging her head this way and that to free the long, flowing hair from her eyes. Feeling the joy of the day fill her soul, she was moved to sing and dropped her voice into the deep, sexy drawl of one of her all-time favorite songs, "Summertime." She sang carefree as a bird riding toward her rendezvous with Audrey at the Utopia. Full with fresh feelings of warmth for her best friend, Emily and her pink Schwinn meandered through the side streets of Southeast Portland and the final moments of her life.

. . .

Audrey walked west on Belmont from her mother's home on the east flank of Mt. Tabor. She left early to enjoy a leisurely walk through the park she'd grown up with; she felt inspired by the awesome view of her city and the knowledge that she lived and played on the slopes of an ancient, extinct volcano.

As she walked over the mounded cinder core now covered with Douglas fir and red cedar, she reveled in thoughts of her years of friendship with Emily: the years in preschool, the five-year-old girls playing with bubbles on the lawn, the fifteen-year-old friends finding erotic adventure at the Metolius River. Audrey thought of her huge love for Emily and could not imagine a day of life without her company. She shuddered to think of losing her best friend. What if she were to fall in love and move away? Or decide on college on the East Coast? She shook those thoughts from her mind as best she could, but they were the type of apprehensive thoughts that had shadowed her since her father disappeared, anxious thoughts that forecast sudden loss and sorrow.

When Audrey turned west onto Belmont from SE 60th she remembered the party shop on the corner of 43rd by the Movie Madness video store. She picked up her pace in the excitement of the moment's inspiration. She already had a present for Emily in her backpack, a book of new poems by Mary Oliver entitled *A Thousand*

Mornings. The two had read Oliver's poems aloud in front of the fireplace on many a winter's night. Emily would love it. But there was something else she would love just as much.

She opened the door to Preston's Party shop and eagerly scanned the walls. A young lady behind the counter greeted her happily. "Hi, can I help you find anything?"

"Hi, I want a red balloon. A big, round red balloon. It has to be really round."

"Hmm. I'm not sure we have anything like you're describing— our balloons are more oval than round. We have these on the wall and our regular helium balloons for parties. Would any of these work?"

"Nope, darn, I need something big and round. Rats."

"I'm sorry. You might try Fred Meyer." The young woman was trying to help, but she was so far off the mark Audrey just shrugged.

"Thanks anyway."

She was turning for the door when the owner of the shop, Mrs. Preston, walked in from the back office. Mrs. Preston was in her late fifties and slightly overweight, a very friendly looking woman who in another story might have owned a tea house in England.

"Couldn't find what you were looking for, dear?"

"No, nothing quite right for what I want." Audrey kept moving.

"She's looking for a big, round balloon. I told her we don't have anything that fits that description."

"No, I don't suppose we do. So sorry, dear, please try us again."

Audrey smiled. She wondered how Mrs. Preston came to be in the party business. She didn't look like the partiers Audrey knew by a long shot. As she reached for the door handle, Mrs. Preston called out to her.

"Wait, dear, wait just a moment, I just remembered something. You wait right there. I'll be back in a jiffy." The Miss Marple look-alike scampered back to the storage room with a determined sense of purpose.

A moment later she came bounding out with a small box in her hands.

"Just as I thought," she said proudly. "I nearly forgot we had this in back. One of our customers special ordered it last year for an exchange student staying with her family. It's a French balloon, if you can believe it. The girl was French, of course. Can't imagine why this one wasn't taken, but lo and behold, here it is, dear."

"Did you say it's French?"

"Why, yes, and if I'm not mistaken, it is big and round, a bit unusual for today's balloons. I'm afraid there is only one, like I said, but it is red. Will that do?"

Audrey was nearly dizzy with glee. How did these things always happen around Emily? She stared hard at Mrs. Preston and wondered if this was a funny wish-fulfilling dream. Maybe odd Mrs. Preston was Emily's friend Bu in disguise.

"Did you say you have one red French balloon, that is big and round?" She repeated her question, dumbfounded, and prepared to wake up to the hoax of a dream.

"That's right. Would you like me to blow it up for you? Dear, are you all right?"

. . .

Audrey walked down SE Belmont with the red balloon trailing behind her. Beside herself with astonishment and glee, she made her way to the Utopia Café, wondering how her plan could have possibly worked out so perfectly and dying to see the look on Emily's face when she laid eyes on the red balloon. The only thing better would have been to meet her Emily with Pascal on her arm and offer him up for the evening's entertainment. She caught herself wondering if she had made up the remarkable event in the party shop. One look at the red balloon on a string above her head assured her she had not, but she shook her head in disbelief nonetheless.

■ ■ ■

As Audrey was making her way, David Chase hurriedly jumped into his black Mercedes in the driveway of his home on Alameda Ridge. The car roared down the street toward a rendezvous with the latest of his many lovers. He drove from the ridge down 32nd Avenue, past Grant High where both Emily and Audrey had bewitched an entire school of boys, past Laurelhurst Park where his memory took its usual unauthorized detour into the earliest days of Emily's life when he and Martha had walked her in the stroller to feed the ducks by the pond and listen to their little girl sing to the happy ducklings.

But David ushered those tender memories to the back seat as he sped into the parking lot at Zupan's Market on Belmont, marveling at the reality of his daughter's eighteenth birthday. They would have dinner that evening, and he would give Emily the only thing she had ever wanted: a trip around the world in eighty days for she and Audrey to fill the gap year they had each chosen to take. Both girls would be ecstatic about the fulfillment of a lifelong dream held since they watched the movie together many years ago.

When David Chase parked his car beneath the brick apartment building above the grocery store on the corner of Belmont and 32nd, he noticed he was perspiring. Had he paid closer attention he would have noticed a ripple of anxiety swirling in his stomach with no explanation attached. He walked through Zupan's, picked up a bunch of fresh-cut flowers for his morning delight, and made for the Belmont side exit as though he were late for a train. Outside the building he turned left toward the Blue Moon jazz club where the leggy blond travel agent was waiting. Barely out of the store, he ran head-on into Audrey.

"Audrey, Jesus, I'm sorry, what are you doing here?" Instinctively, David found himself checking out the body of his daughter's best friend. He felt terrible for noticing the fine curve of her hips and the young breasts pushing through her blouse. Immediately, the image of Claire came to mind, and his shame grew stronger.

"Dr. Chase, hello, wow, I didn't know you ever came to this part of town. Hey, I'm meeting Emily for a late breakfast in a few minutes. Why don't you come say hello?"

"Sure, sure, I'd love to. Where are you meeting? What's with the red balloon? Is that for Em?"

"Don't you remember? *The Red Balloon?* The French movie Emily was crazy about as a kid? I found this down the street in a party shop and guess what? You'll never guess! It's a freaking French balloon! Emily is going to go completely nuts when she sees it. Can you believe it?"

David Chase couldn't believe it. And he couldn't believe how great Audrey looked. And he couldn't stop hating himself for noticing.

"Come on, we're meeting at the Utopia, across the street."

Chapter 27

The blood was drying on Randy Tanner's boots as he flew down Interstate 5 at over one hundred miles an hour. It looked less and less the color of spilled blood the farther he got from Vancouver. Soon it would be indistinguishable from the dirt and grease already spotting his motorcycle boots.

The Triumph roared past one alarmed driver after another. It roared down the highway from the north, over the river, past the racetrack, and within sight of the Rose Garden exit. By now the only trace of what had happened in the apartment with Bruce Paul was his recollection of several heated arguments the day before. The blood was erased from his memory, as was the disfigured head and face of the wayward soul whose only sin was believing in a god.

Now all Randy remembered was the debate over the value of human life. He recalled his words over the din of the engine and felt a surge of arousal hearing the brilliance of his grand oration. He was so taken with himself that he burst into voice, reciting some of his favorite lines for all the world to hear.

"I'm telling you there ain't no goddamn value to nobody's miserable life. Shit, motherfuckin' galaxy is fifty thousand fucking light years wide, asshole. Do you know how many miles that is? One fucking light year is six trillion fucking miles long, so that makes our stinking little no-good galaxy trillions and fucking trillions of miles wide, and this shit-eatin' Milky Way is just one pinprick little runt of over one hundred fucking billion galaxies, and you're going to sit there and tell me you have a cocksuckin' idea of what the hell is going on here? What complete horseshit. Shit, one life don't mean crap, and I'm telling you, you fucking morons, I could run some pretty little girl down on the street with my invincible, fire breathing Triumph and even if she were the fucking daughter of the Queen of England it wouldn't make one goddamn bit of difference in this shithole existence. Do you hear me, world? Not a fucking bit of difference to nobody, sure as hell no punk-ass God sittin' up on no motherfuckin' cloud waving his magic wand."

So enamored was the invincible crystal man with the elucidation of his existential treatise that he flew by the exit for Interstate 84 and had to take the industrial exit and head east on Clay and Hawthorne to pick up his twenty-year-old porn star and part-time nurse's aide at the Laurelhurst nursing home on 60th and Belmont.

"Fuckin' A. Fucking Stumptown. Here's to you, fucking Rose City."

And with that hometown greeting riding a current of spit and hatred, Randy T., his steel-heeled boots scraping the concrete, leaned into the turn onto SE Belmont at 20th Ave. He hit the throttle hard and screamed down the two-lane street in third gear at sixty-five miles per hour, laughing like the CEO of Hell, his left arm raised above his head, his middle finger raised above his fist. His maniacal laughter rose above the ear-piercing tension of the Speed Triple 1250 as he greeted his hometown with all the loathing and contempt of an unrepentant prodigal son.

"Look out, Portland, the fucking wind is here, the fucking biggest wind you've ever seen, and I am going to fuck you up good! Real fucking good!"

Chapter 28

The world knew. The sparkling fresh spring air tried to hold back the pending disaster, but molecules of moisture were no match for the rampaging Triumph. Wind held its breath. Silver maples gasped. Birds covered their eyes with trembling wings. Shrubs shriveled up, and roses dropped their petals. Even the blue sky, the mothering witness of humanity's best and worst, turned a shade of white horror.

Emily rode her bicycle over the warming asphalt, heard the music on her lips and the humming of bicycle wheels turning round and round.

Audrey and David Chase did not know. Crossing Belmont, their only thoughts were of imagining Emily's face when she saw the two of them standing on the sidewalk beneath the waving red balloon.

Randy Tanner knew nothing but the fast train of meth flooding his heart, fueling a murderous hatred for any show of weakness, fear, or worst of all, happiness.

Against his arching desire, Randy T. slowed the snorting dragon beneath him when approaching the cars at the intersection of NE Belmont and 32nd Ave. He slowed and eyed the pedestrians turning to make sense of the furious, menacing roar invading from the west.

David Chase took Audrey's arm as they stepped up to the sidewalk. They didn't notice the cacophony of madness heading their way. Their attention was entirely devoted to scanning the traffic coming up 32nd for a glimpse of the pink Schwinn and its rider.

Emily thanked Claire and Bu for allowing her another birthday in this glorious life.

She approached the corner of Belmont and 32nd and saw Audrey and her father waving, smiling from ear to ear. She took her hand from the handlebar and returned a hearty wave. Her mind had seen but not yet recognized the red balloon dancing in the light breeze above Audrey's shoulder and circling around her father's head. Had she noticed, perhaps she might have detected the worried expression on the face of the balloon and the muffled voice of Pascal pleading, *Arête, mon Cher. Arête!*

Randy Tanner spotted the lovely, flowing wave of golden hair in the midst of what was otherwise a blur of images speeding past. Immediately, he sensed the aura of happiness surrounding the pink bicycle turning right onto Belmont. He sensed vulnerability and went after it like a heat-seeking missile.

"Fuck it, you're mine, bitch."

Before the murderous wheels of the Triumph tore into her flesh and traveled up her spine, Emily was gone. Gone in the space between heartbeats and horrified molecules. Bu came for her and accompanied her soul as it spread into the invisible like a plume of smoke from a candle.

With it, the sky turned an opalescent green and bells rang throughout the solar system. Emily left everything and found everything. Bu escorted her child on celestial winds through the light of this world to the realm of all unions where Claire welcomed her into everlasting love.

The world of air, fire, water, and earth continued to spin. Randy Tanner and his Triumph hit the cement bike rack at forty miles per hour. The Triumph flew end over end, wheel of life over wheel of life, and crashed into the picture window storefront of the Utopia Café, shattering glass inside and out and ending upside down on the windowsill. Randy Tanner flew headfirst through the window and into the plaster wall at the far side of the room. His body lay broken under tables, chairs, and glass. He lay there, a pile of bones, on a world made of improbabilities, laced with tragedy and miracles. Beneath his curtain of hair was an unrecognizable face—still breathing. Its eyes were open and staring far away into the end of one life and the beginning of another.

Emily's body lay in the blood-soaked arms of her father. Audrey choked on the sobs and screams that fought for the right to her breath. She leaned over Emily's body and wailed and pleaded with the gods to undo what had happened. She took her friend's mangled head in her hands and kissed her dear Emily, bloodying her lips on the shredded flesh. The red balloon slipped from her fingers and drifted to the sky.

David Chase did not hear his heart stop beating. His head dangled from his body as though it had been severed. He did not cry, and he did not scream. He held Emily in his arms as a terrible silence came over him. He held her as all light and warmth left the world and his heart broke into a thousand pieces of rock.

Emily was gone. But two words remained in her all but flattened lungs. Bu reached out and touched the tip of Emily's tongue, and to the horror and astonishment of David Chase, those two final words, aided by the last wisp of wind in her body, passed over her lips.

"Daddy . . . love."

Chapter 29

The Last Hour: Hour #33

The room is still. It holds the sorrow of the world in its arms. David is uneasy with the resolve taking root in his mind. He sits in his chair and looks around the room as if trying to commit its features to memory. Wind begins to gather but he does not speak.

You're quiet today, David. What's on your mind?

"I realized something. I listened to that inner voice, and I realized something."

Do you want to tell me?

"No. I don't want to even think it."

Something disturbing?

"More than disturbing. I feel bad again, really bad. Worse than the other ways."

Tell me.

"You'll think I'm terrible."

You won't lose me, David.

"I couldn't handle that."

You've let me become important to you and you are important to me.

"Me, important to you? You're saying that to make me feel good. You don't mean it. Come on, don't do that."

It's true. I mean it.

David lowers his eyes, fighting with the impulse that rejects any good that comes his way. He is squirming inside. Especially today when he feels most unworthy. But he can't deny that he feels better hearing the care in Dr. Jones's voice.

"I've never known a man. No father, no uncle, a few friends but not really."

I'm glad for you that you now have a man on your side, and I'm happy to be that man. You have been very courageous throughout our time together. You've let me in. That's huge.

"Don't forget what a coward I am."

I know that you have stayed with yourself and our work here despite how excruciating it has been.

"It isn't courage. I have to. Emily . . ."

Yes, Emily. For her love, and maybe a bit for you.

"Doubtful. But now, now I have to do something—damn." David's voice catches. "I have to . . . I have to talk to him."

Him? The little boy inside?

"No, I have to talk to that man. The one who killed . . . the one who killed Em."

This is incredible. David, you amaze me, again and again. How did you arrive at this?

"Like I said, it was the inner voice. I think it's been trying to break through for a long time. There's so much hate in me I don't think I can ever love until I do something with it. Get rid of it or make it into something else."

That's real wisdom. But did something happen? Was there a moment or an event that broke through and let the voice come out?

"I guess there was. A girl."

The room turns inside out. David buries his face in his hands. Dr. Jones feels his throat close.

Did you say, a girl?

"Yeah. A girl . . . on the Hawthorne bridge, ready . . . ready to jump, one leg over the railing. Just like I did a thousand times. She may have been Emily's age, or a little older. It was dark. I thought she was a mirage. I reached out to see if she was real and she shrieked and raged at me to go away. I almost fell over. She calmed down after a while and I could see longing in her eyes. She was desperate for someone to talk to. And something happened. Something changed for both of us. I can't explain it. Maybe I'm making it up. What was staggering is that I cared. I was caring for another person. I swore I would never let myself. When she asked if we could meet again the next day, I could tell she felt cared for. She didn't come back. I wasn't surprised, but I knew something had happened between us and it was good."

That's astonishing. I, I don't know if I can talk. Man . . .

"I know, Christ, the look on her face; the fear, the pain—so much pain. Fuck, I can't breathe again. I don't want to care . . . It's too much. Maybe I can feel something for that poor kid, but I sure as fuck don't want to care about that monster, for Christ's sake! Why is Emily doing this to me? Maybe I don't want to love. Maybe I want to just live, do something simple, have a dog, walk in the park. Come on, I'm no saint, this is crazy."

Isn't it obvious? Emily loves you . . . and she wants you to be human, not a saint.

"You know I'm a coward. Okay, I had a nice little opening the other day, but here I am all twisted up again. Full of fear and hate. I'm hopeless."

David stops and looks to escape out the window. The squirrel is sitting on the wire looking back at him, wiggling its nose. David can't help himself; he begins to chuckle and shake his head. Tears join his laughter, and he looks back to Dr. Jones and says, "Your red-tailed co-therapist just broke the spell twitching his stupid nose. I suppose I'm being stupid fighting with Emily and the voice inside my heart. I should be glad I still have one."

Yes, you do, David, and it's growing bigger as we speak.

"She says he needs me, and I need him, to love, to really love. To care. The worst of it is I realize it's true. I have to, I know I have to, and I hate myself for it. How the fuck am I supposed to love the guy who rode over my daughter on his motorcycle with a shit eatin' grin on his fucking face? Why should I help that bastard?"

You don't have to help him. You can't. You show up, be in the room with him, and let something happen.

"I want to kill him."

Of course you do. Of course you hate him. Emily knows you, and she is wise.

"Emily's always done stuff like this. Always. She talks to me now. She seems to know him, it's strange. This isn't just about me. I have to remember that . . ." David looks to the door and clenches his jaw.

What's happening now, David?

"Won't I be betraying her? Wouldn't this be the worst of my many betrayals? Worse than leaving the garage, worse than what I did to Claire?"

Why a betrayal? Emily wants you to meet with him. It's for the sake of love.

"I'm her father. Maybe I was a lousy one, but I'm still her father.

It just feels terribly wrong to chum up to the maniac who offed the most precious person in my world."

Not if it's for love, David, not if it's fulfilling Emily's prayer and your own redemption.

"Redemption? Don't go religious on me. This will put me right back on the bridge. Maybe for the last time. I'm not this big. I'm not. You know I'm not."

I know you are bigger than you can imagine and terrified of being big and loving.

"Scared shitless."

Right. You should be. I would be too.

"You?"

Sure, scared shitless, like you said.

"I thought you would be . . ."

Beyond fear? Hell no, I get nervous just thinking of the state pen. Who doesn't? I'm a human being too. These feelings don't go away. They are real, human emotions. They belong to love. Love is dangerous. And let's face it, men aren't so good at this. We are terrified and refuse to admit it.

"I don't know, am I just doing it for me, to get off the hook? And what if I fail? What if I run? I almost ran away from you."

I'm scarier than he is!

"Don't flatter yourself. Damn, I thought you were all, I don't know, all cured of this kind of torture. Like all centered and clearheaded."

It comes and goes. I'm just another person.

"Damn."

He's probably a lot like you, David. By that I mean he's no doubt experienced trauma of one form or another. Imagine how frightened he must be of you.

"He should be. Fuck you, I don't want to feel sorry for him. He murdered my precious little girl, fuck if I'll feel for him. What? I'm supposed to feel compassion for the psychopath who got off crushing my little girl under his Harley? Fuck you!"

I agree. Fuck me. It's outrageous.

The room says yes. The squirrel stands on its hind legs. Dr. Jones feels a shiver go up his back, and David looks startled as he senses another door opening in his heart. The door to empathy.

"Damn, I never once thought about him."

Only someone like Emily would.

David looks dumbstruck. He looks terrified, like he has run over a child on a bicycle. He begins to calm, to settle into the truth like the girl on the bridge. Again, the doubting mind:

"What if I fail?"

Good. Fail again.

"You won't think badly?"

I will be forever in awe of your failure.

"You're shittin' me."

I shit you not.

"Shall I send you a postcard from prison?"

If you don't, I will be very hurt.

"We can't have that. How do I talk to this monster? I'll probably just scream."

You probably will.

"What good is that?"

You won't know until you do it.

"Great."

Just stay with it. Be yourself. Listen to that voice.

"Which one? I have a thousand and one screaming in my head."

The one that asks the most of you. The one linked to Emily's prayer. The one you are most frightened of. The one you want to run from.

"Are you and Emily in on this together?"

Ha! She has my mobile number. Remember, it's not all up to you—there are two of you, and there is more at work here than we realize. Try to trust the mystery that is pulling you in.

"I can't believe that."

You don't have to believe anything.

"I'm shaking."

Me too.

"Thank you."

You're most welcome, and I thank you.

"What?"

I said, I thank you.

"But why? Why would you thank me?"

Because. Because you and Emily have touched me deeply, and I have remembered much that is so easily forgotten.

"What does that mean?"

It means I feel I have become more of a human being in the course of our meetings, and I thank you for that. I am grateful. When you practice this work for as long as I have, well, it's possible to believe you know more than you do, to lose something of yourself, your tender heart. I feel I have that back because of our time together.

There is a pause. A quieting heard round the world.

"When I see you next, I'll be different . . . I don't know . . ."

I don't either, but I do know that what happens in this room, between us . . .

"Is something else."

Yes, something else.

"What is it? You don't say much or hypnotize me or anything weird."

There's something more than we can see or perceive. A tuning fork, a desire. I realize that now more than ever, in large part because of our work together. It isn't really possible to say what happens and how it works, and it's probably better that way. We'd probably fuck it up if we tried to make a formula for it. Better off remaining a mystery.

"Will it be there in the prison? That tuning fork?"

It will be. I'm confident. You don't have to make it happen, just be truthful and listen.

"I guess it's right to leave crying. I can breathe and cry at the same time now. A miracle."

You're a miracle, David. Go on, send me a postcard.

"Right, 'Having a jolly time on holiday in the Oregon State Prison! Wish you were here. Smiley face.' Seriously, can I write, if I . . . need to . . . you know?"

Please do. Feel free.

"Okay. Here I go. Shit, I don't want to go. I was never this scared going in to take somebody's heart out. I guess that little boy is frightened of being on his own."

He had way too much of that. Now he knows he can lean on people.

"In his world you lean, you fall . . . in the snow . . . it's freezing."

He took some big falls, that boy. But now he has you, you have each other, and you have me.

"Man, I don't know. Do I have you?"

You do, David. You do.

"Goodbye. Thank you for putting up with me. Really, thank you."

And I thank you, David. We are both different people than when we began. Different and more of who we are. I feel very fortunate.

"Okay. There's a door for a reason. Here I go. I'm glad you're alive. Really glad."

Two figures rise and move toward a door. The room bows. The door opens—it yearns to speak.

Four hands reach out; they touch. They hold time and caring, and they release.

One figure walks out the door into the hallway and toward an elevator.

The second figure watches as the other grows smaller and disappears around a corner. He feels a pang, pauses for a moment, and turns back into the room that is a lake. He slowly lowers into a chair the color of chocolate. The man in the chair closes his eyes and dreams.

The other body, the body of David Chase, now a body of flesh and blood, walks out of the building into the light of day. Into a world of joy and sorrow.

PART TWO

NIGHT WITHOUT DAY

I stand before my highest mountain, and before my
longest journey,
And therefore, must I descend deeper than I have
ever before descended.

—Frederick Nietzsche

Chapter 30

Nothing is real. Not the sirens blaring, not the doctor's empathetic face, not the sight of Emily's body covered by a gray sheet, not Audrey sobbing hysterically and pinching her face, not the blood discoloring his skin, not the rays of sunshine streaming through the windows. It has all shattered and collapsed—collapsed in, though there is no inner.

His is not a descent into a dark night of the soul. It is not a retreat or a psychological event; it is a trap door—David falls and vanishes. And it is a beginning, a sentence of solitary confinement, a cell with no lock or door—no entrance and no exit. Hell without flames or burning lakes. Without a devil. An end with no ending—nothing but nothing.

. . .

The medieval army of smoke and dread descended on Portland the afternoon of Emily's death. It blanketed the City of Roses and obscured the sunlight from the west. In a matter of hours, the world lost all color and shape.

In doing so, it made the fate of Emily's dearest friend, the wind, impossible to see. It was several days before the people of Portland came to realize that the wind was shattered by news of the charred forests of Sitka spruce at the coast and the sight of Emily's bloodied body on a sidewalk. The wind, her trusted companion, lay on the hard, baked earth, broken into ten thousand pieces of grief.

Because their ears were plugged with white fangs, they did not hear the absence of its song. Because their eyes were sore from smoke and tired from scanning their phones for bits of self, they did not notice the trees no longer swaying in the arms of the wind. And because skin was no longer an organ of sensual arousal, they were oblivious to the loss of the soothing touch of air gently blessing each hour.

It was the children that made them take notice. Children sat on the brown grass crying, their kites and gliders grounded and lifeless. But they did not sob for balsa wood planes with bent wings or homemade kites with funny faces and meandering tails, and they did not even sob for the end of play; they cried and rubbed their eyes when they saw the wind broken, lying face down on the lawn and caught in the drooping branches of trees.

It was then that others realized the cause of the children's sadness. It was then they felt the paralysis of the air, the play of light subdued, and beautiful spring clouds obscured by smoke. And when they heard the quiet, the alarming quiet of their surroundings closing in around them, panic stirred. Broken sentences fell from their tongues. Space was not still, it was dead: the world was no longer breathing. What was there to breathe? How would they bury the wind? What would cool their arms and necks? They fled indoors covered in sweat.

Chapter 31

David Chase sat by himself at Emily's memorial service. The event room in the old Kennedy elementary school, a charming brick building newly converted into a boutique hotel and restaurant, was packed with friends and neighbors. But David Chase refused their comfort. He left them to cry hot tears over the unimaginable tragedy while he sat in a chair by the exit, prepared to leave the service before its completion and walk by himself to the Lone Fir Cemetery where Emily's ashes would be interred.

Emily had spent most Sunday mornings at the wooded pioneer cemetery delivering flowers to the gravestones of strangers and walking the rows of departed souls, talking to them as though they were sitting on lawn chairs sipping tea, awaiting her visit.

The Russians were her favorite. She paused at each stone, trying to master the sounds of the strange names and wondering what in their lives brought them so far from home to live and die. She made a vow to learn their strange language and read their poets so that when she visited the homeland of Tolstoy and Chekov, she could speak the native tongue.

She felt at home in the cemetery and close to its residents. On special occasions, like her mother's birthday, she visited at midnight and danced with the joyous spirit bodies of her friends to the raucous music of Russian folk dances she played on her phone. It was those festive nights that convinced her she wanted a portion of her ashes buried there so she could listen, sing, and dance into eternity to the joyous fiddles and hypnotic clarinets.

Alone at the cemetery, David stared at the ground and the hole that would hold the urn. He stood there for a short time under the mourning sky, then slipped away and disappeared into smoke and rain.

Chapter 32

The doorbell rang at the home of David Chase on Alameda Street in Northeast Portland. Keith Stone stood at the front door, looking inside for some sign of David. For the past week he had tried to reach him by phone. Now, standing on the front porch, he saw newspapers piled against the siding and mail overflowing in the mailbox but no sign of his friend and client.

The sight of the neglected papers and mail disturbed him. He shifted his feet, anticipating the difficult conversation they needed to have. His stomach growled, not from hunger, but from a concoction of anxiety and dread. Uncertain, he turned to look out over the ridge toward the lifeless city shrouded in smoke. He coughed, shook his head, and pounded on the thick wooden door.

David Chase did not come to the door. He did not hear the doorbell ring or the frustrated fist pounding harder and harder. His attorney listened intently and heard nothing. Before turning to leave, he tried the door handle and found it unlocked. Surprised, Keith Stone hesitated, then opened the grand oak door and peered into the house. The house seemed vacant and silenced.

He gathered the mail and newspapers, opened the door wider, and stepped into the entryway. Half expecting to see his friend hanging from the grand stairway banister towering over the foyer, he entered the house with his eyes half shut. The floorboards creaked and he nearly jumped. His nerves were such a mess that he wanted to leave and cursed himself for this sign of cowardice.

Still hearing no movement in the house, he called out. "David, David, it's Keith. Are you here?" Nothing. "David, where are you, man?"

Keith Stone was a cat ready to spring as his voice searched the absence and came back with nothing. He moved farther into the house, reluctant to trespass but resolved that he must search for David in case his worst fears were true. Just then, Emily's black cat, Ringo, meowed and walked toward him from the kitchen, and though his body tightened, Keith Stone was glad to see some sign of life in what was beginning to feel like a tomb.

David Chase was not in the family room watching TV as he hoped he'd be, and he was not in the den where he did his chart notes. The cat followed behind and looked at him plaintively. The instant their eyes met, Keith Stone knew where to look. With the cat close behind, meowing its approval, he climbed the long stairway to Emily's room.

He took the stairs one by one, feeling with each step the growing fear of finding David dead. The fear persisted as he climbed the stairway, and his well-honed iron will failed to stifle it. Remembering the unfortunate detective in *Psycho* ascending the stairway to horror, he half expected a crazed David Chase to run out from the shadows with a butcher knife raised and insanity covering his face. But he reached the top of the long stairway alive and followed the direction of the eerie silence that pointed to Emily's room at the end of the hallway.

In the room that once held the exuberance of a happy child,

David Chase sat crumpled on a rocker like a discarded bath towel. Keith Stone stared at his friend, uncertain if he was dead or alive, but sickened by what he saw and smelled. It looked as though David had not moved from the rocker since the memorial three days before.

At last, there was movement in David's wrinkled shirt and a slight stirring on his face. The sign of life did little to relieve the tension Keith Stone felt. It seemed cruel to wake him, to drag him back to his misery, but he felt the necessity to bring his friend back. He called his name, tentatively at first and then with more insistence, fearing he would not be able to retrieve him from whatever godforsaken place had taken him prisoner.

"David, David, it's Keith. David, wake up, man, we need to talk." His words fell like lint on wooden shelves. David did not stir. His one friend in the world looked out the window for guidance, but the smoke obscured any signals the trees or clouds might have offered. The temptation to turn and leave pulled at him like a dog on a leash. "David, come on, wake up, wake up!" Agitated, he shook the knee of the man he had admired for so many years. The man who had been, to him, invincible. "David, you need to wake up, man, come on, wake up!"

David Chase labored to lift his crusted eyelids. They quivered and closed, and Keith Stone had to shake him again, this time with irritation and impatience shaping his hands.

David's eyes struggled to complete the long journey to opening fully. His eyelids spasmed, blinking like a flickering light bulb until they finally remained open, staring at the shape before him, straining for focus and recognition. To Keith Stone, he looked like an old, demented man waking from the endless dream of existence with no past and no self.

David Chase squinted and rubbed the sleep from his eyes. "What are you?" he said.

The question and the voice shook Keith Stone to his core. He stared at what was left of his friend. "David, it's me! Keith! We're supposed to meet and talk now. Come on, let me help you up. How long have you been sitting here like this?"

"No, don't touch me! Who are you, what are you doing here? Get out!"

"David, look at me, it's me, Keith, your friend, for God's sake! Keith Stone!"

A flicker of light. A trace of something passed over David's face. "Keith? Keith?"

"Yes. Keith. Keith Stone, your friend. Your lawyer. Look at me, David."

David looked at the large body of his friend. He looked at his face and his shoulders and a flicker of recognition flashed in his eyes. He moaned and said, "Keith." And then he looked around the room, slowly, as though it were still part of a dream. He looked back at Keith Stone and tried to sit up. He moaned again, trying to overcome the stiffness that had taken over his limbs. The rocker swayed and he lost his balance, tossed backward by the transference of his weight. Finally settled, he began to stand. Slowly, wobbling, he made his way to vertical and looked at the man in front of him.

"You can't be here."

"What?"

"You can't be here. Come on."

With that, David Chase moved toward the bedroom door and the stairway. He walked like a ninety-year-old man, taking the stairs one at a time, leaning on the railing. At the foot of the stairway, he paused to take a breath. When he continued, it was as though the man following him had disappeared. When his friend spoke to him, David Chase stopped in his tracks, turned, and eyed him as if he were an intruder. Realizing who it was, he turned his back and said, "What are you doing here?"

"David, we agreed to talk this morning. We have a lot to talk about."

David dropped onto the couch in the family room. He stared at his hands, the amazing hands that had held surgical instruments, lifted a human heart from its private cavity, and placed it on a silver tray to be repaired. The hands that had held Emily's, that had been steady and held fast to things, now trembled like a dog at the vet. He held them out for Keith to see. "My hands are shaking. Look, my hands are shaking."

"I see, they are. They'll calm down soon, David. You've been through a terrible trauma."

"No. No, they're ruined. They aren't . . ." As his voice trailed off, he said something that baffled Keith Stone. Something only the wind would understand. "The chains."

"You what?"

"I let go of the chains." And with that, he looked up at Keith Stone, knowing he could not possibly understand but pleading that he would. "The chains broke, everything broken. Everything ruined. Emily's trees, burning, dying, it's our doing, us, fucking men killing her trees."

"David, listen to me, you can put your life back together. It will take time, but you can, I'll help you. I'll help you get help."

"No help!" He shouted and looked fiercely at Keith. "I have to get out of here. I told you to take care of things. Sell the house. Get rid of everything. I'm going away."

"Where are you going, David? Where will you live?"

"Nowhere."

"Nowhere? Come on, David, talk sense. You want a change, I understand. This is a big house for one, I get it. I have rentals . . ."

"No. You don't get it. No rentals. No house. No life."

"But where will you live, what will you do?"

"Nothing."

"You need a place to stay, David. You can't live on the streets— you wouldn't last a week. Come on, be sensible."

"Shut up."

"Okay, okay, I'm sorry. Look, there is the room in the warehouse Paula bought for her business. The foreman stayed there for a while. It's terribly dark, dirty, and depressing, but maybe we could clean . . ."

"Perfect. Don't clean it. Just take me there and sell the house. Sell everything except what's in Emily's room."

"David—"

"No! Don't try to talk sense with me, Keith! Just do it. Please, just do it . . . please . . ." David's voice trailed off into the vacant mind of the house. Both men buried their faces in their hands and leaned into a future without a past or a present, unable to look at one another or the devastation that surrounded them.

. . .

Keith Stone left the home of David Chase deeply troubled. He tried to imagine what it would do to him if he were to lose either his daughter or son in such a horrific way. But his mind disobeyed, and as he drove away in his Mercedes, the last moments of his visit with David came back to him. He saw himself standing at the broad mahogany door to the den, begging David to call his doctor and make an appointment. The helpless tone in his voice disturbed him, but not like the chilling memory of looking into the eyes of a man who was not a threat to take his life because he was already gone. David was gone, and his eyes were as empty as the warehouse he would soon inhabit.

Despite David's insistence, Keith Stone knew he would have the room cleaned and stocked with essentials, knowing full well it was filthy after being left to rats and spiders for the past several years. But otherwise, as his attorney, he would do as David Chase instructed him. He would sell the house and all his possessions and put all the proceeds in a trust. He would have Emily's things, her books and drawings, her skirts and shirts and funny hats, her CDs and DVDs, all of it, boxed and put in storage for someone to claim in the future. There seemed little hope that David would be that person.

And with those thoughts pressing against his forehead, nausea took over his body and made him feel it was no longer his. It was the body of dread. He wished he could put it into storage and take the nausea and dread to the toxic waste dump and deposit them in the incinerator. As he drove over the Fremont Bridge, he saw the terrible smoke blanketing his city. He could barely see the arch that towered over the bridge. The Pink Lady, Portland's tallest building and typically the jewel of the morning skyline, stood in that eerie light like a homeless ghost as smoke thickened and crawled up the top half of her body.

The sky turned a sickly yellow and gray. Cars and trucks hurried east and west as fast as traffic and smoke would allow, and Keith Stone felt the fear all Portlanders had come to know: the fear the smoke might never leave.

Chapter 33

Year One

David Chase was a refugee from the country of himself. Despised. Exiled from the land of being.

He did not leave the room in the warehouse. He did not feel the air. He spoke to no one, and no one spoke to him. His only visitors were two nightmares. They came, gusts of hot wind off the desert floor, and left, leaving his body in the cold, shaking like a child too long in the snow. They came often enough to haunt both sleeping and waking.

In the first nightmare, he enters an empty room. Confused, he looks here and there, in the corners and behind the door. The silence is menacing. And then the room begins to collapse inward. Slowly, the walls, floor, and ceiling move in on him. Space shrinks, making a droning sound that grows louder and louder until it seems it will break his eardrums. The dream shifts. He is in another room, the sterile one. The room that is all his: Surgical Room 5. His face is covered with a blue mask, but his hands are bare. He slowly and methodically carves an opening in the chest of someone he does not recognize. And there it is, staring back at him, the yearning organ, the pump house of humanity, throbbing, pulsing, faster and faster, pounding out beats he cannot bear nor stop. His hands begin to tremble. He takes that heart in his hands, intent on silencing its dreadful want. But as he readies to crush it, his hands stop shaking and the heart begins to weep. Its tears rinse the blood from his naked hands and the sobbing muscle turns into the face of his mother. There is no blood on her cheek, and her eyes reach tenderly for his. He wakes sweating and shaking.

The second dream is brief but no less terrifying. Emily's face appears. She does not smile. Her eyes are closed. For little more than an instant her image flickers—there, not there—in and out of existence: a seizure of presence. Then she is gone. Gone. And the dreamer is gone. Perhaps falling. Perhaps not. Nowhere to fall. Nothing to hold.

He wakes, screaming her name.

Chapter 34

Year Two

The room was near the foot of the Hawthorne Bridge. In the second year of captivity the bridge called for him. It knew his name and it knew his heart. Day and night it waited for him.

David Chase hid for an entire year. He hid in the room without light. The longer he stayed in his cell, the greater the pull of the bridge. He felt the pull but would not answer. What did it want?

On a Monday morning in late March, toward the end of his second year of exile, he left the warehouse and walked toward the bridge. Over four inches of wet spring snow, he trudged to the gallows, a condemned man walking. His footprints melted as he walked.

It took him nearly an hour to walk five blocks. His legs were weak. Fear had replaced muscle. He got within sight of the massive bridge and froze. He heard the bridge call his name and felt its pull. David Chase turned abruptly and retraced his footsteps uphill through the slush and back to the warehouse.

. . .

It was long before sunrise on a Sunday morning one month later. The bridge was empty. From the safety of the east side entrance to the bridge, David looked at the green rafters, at the two towers that rose like church steeples over the river. Just then the bells rang, stoplights on the bridge flashed, and the striped gates made their slow descent to the horizontal. Moments later, the truss began its slow climb to make room for a passing boat.

David waited and watched the tugboat amble upriver, pushing its cargo. When it had passed and the giant green truss completed its descent, he continued walking. He followed the curving ramp to the sidewalk shared by bicycles and pedestrians. The bells were still ringing when he faced the pathway over the bridge. The city stood before him. He could not tell if the lights in the tall buildings were welcoming or forbidding. But he kept walking.

Halfway there, the bells quieted, the gates began the climb back to vertical, and David faced an open walkway. He hesitated and then began the walk he had feared but known he must make. It was his first step into the world. A journey of a thousand miles to a pink bicycle, now a monument on a sidewalk outside a café. He would make the pilgrimage there every day for a year, searching for the person his daughter believed in and listening for her prayer.

Chapter 35

Year Three

In the beginning, to the workers on the warehouse graveyard shift, he was invisible. These were faceless men, familiar with being nothing but shadows. To them, David Chase was just another patch of darkness in the forest of night.

But in time, they noticed that this shadow moved differently. It walked slowly, as if its only care was to disappear into the infinite dark. They recognized it as the shadow of utter defeat and trembled with fear that it was one of their own, one of theirs gone missing that no one had missed. They felt defeat in their muscles and took to naming him to tame the anxious thought that he was the ghost of their future: run-down and defeated by work.

The men called him Broken Top. When they realized he was older than their fathers, they renamed him Broken Pop. He became an amusement that passed the time. Rumors abounded. The boss's ex-con brother. A homeless stowaway. An old-time hobo who missed the train. A Jeffrey Epstein figure hiding from the Feds. Like all shadows, David Chase was an easy target for the frightening and unwanted devils of the mind.

They arrived at midnight. Theirs was a place of black on black: a cave even bats would not enter, a place of mold and fluorescent lights that flickered, and in flickering highlighted the darkness surrounding them. They poked at the dark—they teased it, they mocked it, they tried to tame it. But they could not escape it. They moved like ants, loading and unloading boxed goods into vaults that ran deep. Vaults that would end up on the back of trucks that in the light of day left this shadow world for the bright world of commerce.

. . .

David Chase did not see the men on the platform. His senses were dormant. He knew nothing of their speculations. He left his building around four every morning and began the ritual walk. He was the shadow that walked through shadows looking for an end. There were mornings he thought he had found that end beneath the massive shadow of the Hawthorn Bridge. Big as an aircraft carrier, it loomed over a half dozen blocks of the warehouse district on the east bank of the river.

The workers called it "the shadow of death." There was little traffic crossing the Hawthorne Bridge at that hour, and yet even one car or truck made thunder over his head. It shook the rafters like cattle lumbering across steel grids on their way to slaughter.

Had his senses been awake, he would have turned back. He would have retreated to his room where the only sound was dead silence. But they were not. David Chase moved from the dark toward more darkness without sensation. No sound, no smell, nothing entered or left: his was a walled city in decay.

Each day was both the last and the next. He rose before the sun and walked the streets and bridges of Portland. Every day he walked the same route, at the same pace, with the same indifference to wind and rain, heat and cold. He walked past the warehouse but did not see the workers peering at him from the mouth of their cave. He did not hear their voices change cadence when he walked by. He did not notice the snickering laughter trailing him down the street toward the bridge.

Each day, he walked to 32nd and Belmont as though in a dream. It was a blur, a death march. In two hours, he arrived at the corner where the pink bicycle waited for him, chained to a pole in memory of Emily. Each day, he saw the pink wreck and woke from his sleepwalk with a start. A silent gasp. His mind spasmed with each sighting. Each day, David Chase sat on the sidewalk by the skeleton of the rusty Schwinn, his hand on the pink frame.

As he sat, he dreamed with his eyes open. In the dream, the world was intact, and the three bonded souls stood on the sidewalk celebrating Emily's birthday and marveling at the red balloon floating above her beaming face. They delighted in her joy, hearing her praise Audrey's uncommon good taste, and hugged one another as though love was truly all there was. The party on the corner of Belmont and 32nd filled the world. Love was all, until Emily's fingers let go of the string and the red balloon floated up and away toward the wires overhead where it became entangled and popped.

It was the sound heard round the world. And each day, it awakened David Chase from his reverie. The dream was over. He cried out like a child stung by a wasp. His eyes flickered and squinted. He looked up at the high voltage wires and back to the pink bicycle and ever so softly whispered her name.

∎ ∎ ∎

With methodical repetition, step by step, he made that journey every morning. Only one thing stopped him. At the summit of the Hawthorne bridge, he paused. There, he leaned against the worn railing, bent at the waist, and stared into the muddy river that moved so slowly it seemed in accord with the end of time. The end of his time. Condemnation flooded his mind and demanded that he jump. It was the only impulse that moved the flat line of his soul and the only voice that called his name. It pursued him mercilessly.

He survived the battle of wills not because of any wish to live nor any fear of dying, but because of a terror that he might never again see the image of Emily in his mind or hear the song of her voice whispering in his heart.

Otherwise, he was dead to the world and dead to his body. He was a cold, fallen log, spat out by the ocean, decaying on the shore. Any current of life, desire, or expectation had ceased to move through his veins. His skin was dry. His blood was thick as sap from a tree. The one thing that mattered to David Chase was holding fast to the image in his mind of Emily. He fought to retain that image. He fought like a man with emphysema gasping for air. But his struggle was more like a cramp than a desire for life, more like a seizure than love, though love was guilty of taking his life. And this too, this flickering memory of her face, this gasp of love, was a torment as well: the razor's edge of the only life left in him.

．．．

And that became his life. Every morning was the same. On many of those mornings he found one leg draped over the railing of the Hawthorne Bridge, stuck like a broken branch caught on the limbs of its mother tree. His emaciated body teetered on the edge of the end. Had the wind chosen in those moments to stretch her flowing arms to the north, he would have fallen like a dry leaf in October. He would have fallen without making a sound, without a last protest or a final appeal for forgiveness. A dead man falling to his death. Not a soul would have heard the splash. Not a soul would have gasped and cried out. His life would have ended as he wished it to end, alone, in a vacuum.

But wind, the dearest of Emily's earthly friends, did not blow; it did not howl. It took mercy on the shadow figure on the edge. It turned to the south and gently coaxed David off the railing and back to the walkway where he resumed the long, solitary march with himself, trying to remember, trying to forget, trying to feel the life of his daughter. But the strongest feeling, the one that followed David Chase where shadows could not, was that of failure. His failure to love.

Chapter 36

In time the workers noticed, with surprise, a seed of respect growing in their chests for the stranger who appeared to be fading away. They found themselves looking forward to four in the morning when the narrow figure emerged from the black curtain and walked their way. Occasionally they raised their hands to wave, nearly saluting him as he walked by, his eyes and head lowered, his footsteps silent on the pavement.

On breaks they speculated as to the destination of his travels, never imagining his route was the same every day. It was with a bit of affection that they renamed him Gulliver and made up stories about his life and travels. They dreamed for him of secret romantic meetings in the dark with forbidden loves. They became his hope.

But David Chase was oblivious to the growing attachment the men of the warehouse made with him. Time did not alter his myopic view. Had he known, he would not have cared. He went weeks and sometimes months without speaking a word to anyone but Dr. Jones, whom he saw sporadically. He went even longer without looking into the eyes of another human being. Not an embrace. Not a handshake. Not even a casual brush of a jacket passing a stranger on the sidewalk. He went untouched.

Avoiding all contact was easy because Keith Stone arranged

for a weekly delivery of food and basic supplies to the cell above the warehouse. Without it he would have faded into the plaster-coated walls. As it was, he ate crackers, peanut butter, and cereal and drank protein drinks. Never a hot meal. And only enough to give him the energy to walk the walk each morning. The diet was salty enough that more than once one of the warehouse rats found its way to his bunk, and David woke feeling a rough tongue licking his lips. But he didn't care. He brushed it away like a mosquito. Not even repulsion could live in his body.

Besides the family of rats, he shared his cell with cobwebs and spiders. The daddy longlegs owned the ten-foot ceilings. They roamed the cosmic dust of the web network like *Star Wars* figures patrolling the outer reaches of the cosmos. The room itself was barely twice the size of a prison cell. Against the far wall was a single bunk, and on the opposite wall were a small sink, a stained toilet, and a corner shower with no curtain. The walls were crumbling plaster, a faded navy blue, and the floor wall-to-wall concrete. By the window was a card table and a straight-backed chair. What passed as a kitchen was a small cabinet containing a few dishes and a hot plate. On the floor next to the cabinet stood a mini-fridge, big enough for a half gallon of milk, two jugs of bottled water, some protein drinks, and a loaf of bread. The cell had running water, but it barely got warm and trickled out like water from a pinched garden hose. It carried rust from the hundred-year-old pipes and smelled like iron deposits.

None of it mattered to David Chase. The weather meant nothing to him. He was indifferent to the flow of clouds and sunshine. Even the occasional snowstorm did not move him. Only the walk mattered: the ritual return to the corner of Belmont and SE 32nd where a faithful pink bicycle waited for him. On the sidewalk next to the bicycle, growing from a crack in the cement, a solitary dandelion had found a place to live on the spot where Emily died.

Chapter 37

The workers saw him coming that morning. They paused as he drew near. Something was different, but they couldn't say what. They checked their watches to see if the time was off. When it read four o'clock as always, one wondered out loud if it was the humidity in the air that made the morning feel different. Soon the workers blamed the feeling on concern for the shrinking shadow walking by. One of them, Neal, spoke for all the men. "Man, Gulliver's looking skinnier than ever."

Another, trying to dispel his growing concern, quipped, "Yeah, if he stands sideways and sticks out his tongue he looks like a damn zipper."

"Where'd you come up with that shit, Freddy? That's bad, real bad."

The men laughed and shook their heads, and then Freddy said, "From my poppa."

"Yeah, bet he got real skinny in the hole."

"Fuck you, Ben."

Before the friction could build, the men saw David step in one of the potholes and fall to his knees. They flinched, and one of them yelled to him, "Hey, Gulliver! Ah, hey, mister, you okay?"

But David didn't answer. They watched as he got to his feet, and though unsteady, he kept walking. The men on the platform watched as the shadow man disappeared into the dark. They could not know that the care they had come to feel for him, even in this slight expression, had found its mark. And neither the good men on the loading dock nor David Chase himself had the slightest notion that he was stumbling toward an encounter on the bridge that would bring him to his knees once again.

. . .

David turned down Salmon Avenue, directly under the long steel ramps of the bridge past the quiet encampment of the destitute. The tenants slept and dreamed of never waking again. Some bodies never made it to the small dome tents that were once pitched on Alpine meadows. Some bodies lay on the pavement, crumpled in a pile like a blanket, looking like they had collapsed just a few steps from the finish line.

He walked on, barely noticing that a flicker of feeling for the suffering world had entered his being, a molecule of the kindness offered by the workers on the dock. A solitary light blue bicycle on the far edge of the junk pile tried to speak to him, to alert him to this moment. But the flash was gone as quickly as a moth passing by.

He kept walking, slower now, as though he did not want to climb the pathway to the bridge, as though forward was just that: a direction with meaning and thereby threatening. As though the darkest hour was upon him, transient and preparing for dawn.

And in that moment, David could not have known that one of the bodies from the encampment was standing near the truss of the Hawthorne Bridge, still upright, preparing for the moment of her great freedom flight. One tired and hopeless body, readying to put an end to the nightmare.

He was upon her before he noticed that she was not just another shadow. Her leg was draped over the railing at the apex of the bridge where the truss performed its vertical lift. She stood just a few feet from the candy-cane-striped gates that lowered to stop traffic.

David Chase paused, shaken by the unexpected encounter. He strained to see if he was imagining what appeared to be a person straddling the railing. It might have been his own shadow waiting for him, asking what he was living for. Daring him to fly. He could not perceive the young woman, roughly Emily's age at the time of her death, standing on the precipice of her own. He wanted to see if he could touch the hallucination or if his hand would disappear into the dark mirage, another sick illusion constructed of decay. He raised his hand to reach out.

"Don't touch me!"

Her scream was so loud, so frightened and menacing, that he lurched backwards. Losing his balance, he had to grab the railing for support to keep from falling for the second time that morning. He steadied himself enough to hear her yell again; this time he did not stumble.

"Get away from me, you dirty fuck. Get the fuck away!"

"You are . . ."

What there was of his voice trailed off and was lost in the mist. She heard nothing but a mumbling old man she assumed to be another lecherous, homeless failure of a human being wanting to molest her. She eyed him carefully. Retaining the menacing tone, she said, "Go on. Keep moving. Get the fuck out of here."

But he stood leaning against the railing, struggling to see the shadow that spoke. Struggling to know if he could believe his eyes and ears.

"I said get lost, you old pervert."

He didn't hear her fury, or fear, or the years of humiliation and running and hiding. She was done with that. She stood there, determined the running would stop, and falling, eternal falling, would be her everything.

He didn't hear her; he only looked. She was the first, the only, person outside of Dr. Jones's office he had looked at for nearly three years. He swore he would never look again. But the hunger to look at a human face took hold of him.

"Stop looking at me," she yelled, not wanting, not daring, to feel that somewhere in her darkened soul she felt a stirring of want: a desire to be seen. "What are you, one of those voyeur creeps? You're disgusting."

David Chase put both hands on the railing now. He looked upriver to the lineup of bridges: the Morrison, the Burnside, the Broadway, and the Fremont. He looked at their wide span connecting the land to the east and west. And then he looked down into the swollen, chalky Willamette, now dark and fertile with the spring melt from Mt. Hood. He leaned on his forearms and said to her in a soft, uneven voice, "I'm sorry."

The words, barely audible, left his mouth and floated lazily, meandering out slowly like a bird's feather making its way to the street from a wire. He watched his words wave as they fell in slow motion to the mountain water below. The water paused and gazed up at the two strange birds as if it wanted to listen in on what was to follow.

David, surprised by the words that had left his tongue, dimly wondered who they were intended for. The girl with one leg in the world and one prepared to reject it found herself stunned by the flickering of a desire to be seen and the crush of the two words she had never once heard in her lifetime.

"What? What did you say?"

"Did I say something?"

"Don't fuck with me, mister."

He paused, trying to recall what he'd said. Trying to reach for the falling feather and bring it back. But it was too far into its magic flight.

"Sorry . . . I think I said, I'm sorry—"

She interrupted him. "For what? You aren't sorry. Why should you be sorry?"

"You're right, I don't know. Men are beasts."

She stood there speechless. The bridge moaned and swayed. The sky showed no sign of dawn's early light. The truth was there to stay.

"I am you." His words fell on the silence like they'd tripped on a stone.

"Me? You are me?" She woke from the daze on fire. "You are a crazy old fuck. Why am I talking to you? Me? You don't know shit about me, damn you, you don't know shit about nothing but your toothless, miserable life. Go on, get out of here. Fuck you." She thought for an instant of pushing him over the bridge. Yes. Let him take the fall for all the bastards who had messed with her. Let him scream, tumbling head over heels into the fall that would never end. Fuck him and his sorry bullshit and that other crap about being seen. Fuck that.

"I've had one leg over," he said.

She didn't want to, but she flinched.

"Hundreds of times."

She didn't want it to, but something in her jaw softened.

David didn't see that, but the river did, and the light breeze nudged him. He looked at her again and without giving it any more thought, moved slightly in her direction.

"No! Don't you dare!" She boosted herself to the top of the railing and grabbed hold of the rusted ladder that dropped six feet to the platform where the candy cane gates were anchored. "Just go, go, get out of here, you can't seduce me, get the fuck away."

He could see her now that she was standing closer to the light bulbs on the railing. He could see her tears, and he could see her fighting those tears back with everything she had left. He looked at her and said nothing. And then he looked at the bridge, at the green skeleton that spanned the river. One hundred years old. Older than both of their ages combined. He wondered how many had come to this very spot. How many had not walked on. He looked at the water moving on, always new, always a new river. Who was the first to ask for help in ending a life? Had the river ever said no? Did it suffer with the exhausted soul seeking refuge in its enveloping waters? He noticed something was different. Something was happening in his brain.

"Why this one?" He had said it out loud. It surprised him.

"What? What are you talking about?"

He said nothing but kept staring into the water. In a few hours, as the sun rose higher over the Cascade Range, it would cast sunbeams onto the slight ripples at the surface and they would sparkle like diamonds fallen from the sky.

"Why?" he said.

"Why what?"

"It's not a long drop."

"Shut up."

"You'll survive."

"Mind your own business and get out of here, old man." She spoke harshly, but her voice had lost its fire and conviction.

"The others are more of a sure thing. Especially the Fremont. You can't go wrong with the Fremont." He was stunned by his words, by the resurgence of a voice, by the strangest of feelings growing slowly but surely in his body: the feeling of caring for a stranger.

And when he looked down to the platform, he could see the stranger was on her knees, holding her face in her hands and crying tears that landed on the silver steel of the platform.

"I wish I could cry." He said those words to her with a respect he had never known. For a second, he wondered what was happening to him. The horizon to the east grew paler with each passing moment. He felt dizzy, but then her voice interrupted his thoughts.

"I hate myself."

"So do I."

She looked up at him and saw the pain in his face. Her breath stopped. She on her knees, he bent and leaning over the railing. The candy cane gate standing at attention, the bridge waking to painful joints, gulls and crows flying swiftly under and over the aging Hawthorne, the northwest corner of the hemisphere turning its scarred face to the mother sun, fog in the hills and the valleys, the men at the warehouse loading and unloading, thinking of Gulliver and their grandparents who loved them, the homeless trying to sleep beneath the relentless roar of the daily pursuit of happiness. Time itself paused and sighed. But it all kept moving.

She was muttering now, between the sobs. "It should be over. When will it end?" She spoke to no one. But when he did not answer, panic surged in her gut. She looked up and did not see him, so she scrambled to her feet and hastily climbed the six rusted rungs of the ladder to the top. There she saw him, seated on the sidewalk, his back against the railing, his legs outstretched and his face looking at the bridge's towers far above.

She was so relieved to see him sitting there she nearly let go of the ladder. She tightened her grip. "What's wrong?" But David Chase did not answer or look at her. "What's wrong, mister, are you sick?"

He looked at her then, and with the help of approaching light, he could see her face clearly for the first time. It met his gaze with concern, and he looked down. When he looked up again, he saw her stepping off the ladder onto the sidewalk where he had first seen her. She stood there, on both feet, and looked at him curiously.

"No, I'm not sick. I'm tired." He said this to the open sky, as much as to her. "I'm tired."

"I tend to wear people out." She said this with a slight grin at the corner of her mouth.

"Oh no. Not you. Not you. I thank you."

"You what?"

"Thank you."

She felt, again, a rush of vertigo. "I'm tired of fighting. You helped me stop for at least a few minutes."

He paused, looking down into the cement. "How are you feeling now?"

"I, I don't really know. All confused, and stupid, but somehow all right. I don't get it."

By now the sky had turned pink to the east. She looked at it with longing and then down again at the strange man on the sidewalk.

"I thought you were going to hurt me."

"I've hurt a lot of people."

"What are you fighting, mister?"

Her question was true, and he felt his body sigh. "Caring."

"Caring?"

"I've walked over this bridge every morning for a year, and every morning I've come to this spot and wanted to jump. Today, even before I saw you, something was different. I don't know what it is. You're the first person I've talked to. I guess I'm in shock. I don't know what's happening."

"You could have kept walking."

"I've walked past so much, ignored so much."

"I hate caring. I hate it." Her voice trailed off into the backwaters of pain as more and more cars sped past into the city.

David looked up at the girl on the bridge and realized she was wearing scraps of discarded clothing. He saw, more clearly than before, the pain etched in her face, her blackened eyes, the terrible loneliness of her years.

"I'm sorry." His eyes grew glassy. "I am." This time it was for her that he felt his heart move.

"I'm sorry." She said this for him, the man seated on the sidewalk. The man who dared to look at her.

They were silent. Time stopped as the lotion of a heartfelt apology washed through their astonished hearts. That astonishment was interrupted as the bells on the bridge began to ring and the lights flashed. David struggled to his feet. The girl looked all around for trouble.

A tugboat pushing a barge headed their way. The barge was loaded with big blocks of broken concrete on its way to be recycled in the cement mill on Ross Island a short distance upriver.

"Can I meet you here again tomorrow?" she asked. Silence answered her. "Well?"

But he had turned to look at the barge as she was looking to him for a yes. Looking at the sun, he considered whether for the first time in years he might choose a different direction. Perhaps he could follow the tugboat upriver to the cement mill and watch it deliver its goods. Maybe continue on to the Oaks Bottom Wildlife Preserve. But the undertow of habit was too strong, and he turned again to the west and his daily death march over the Steel Bridge to the grave site and the morning communion with a pink bicycle.

She was trembling now and cursed herself for it. Need, the enemy of the people, had emerged, and she felt the urge to hit herself, to punish the weakness that had allowed this unforgiveable escape from her jailhouse.

But just then, he turned toward her and nodded. "I'll be here." He nearly smiled. David walked on, and she stood there on the spot where something impossible had happened. She watched him make his way across the bridge, and then he disappeared into the curve of the ramp that led to the boardwalk and the Steel Bridge a half mile upriver.

The tugboat blew its horn and the bells on the truss rang louder, more urgently. The girl on the bridge flinched before turning and walking, nearly running, east in the direction of the rising sun, back to the junk pile that was her dwelling. As she moved past the automobiles and their frustrated inhabitants, she felt a twinge in her belly. She stopped to look over the railing at the cabin of the approaching tugboat and strained to see the dim image of the captain steering his ship upriver under the Hawthorne against the current. Her eyes dropped to the river, now covered with the Milky Way and its billions of sparkling stars come to play on the swells of the Willamette. She watched them sparkle and dance, leaping from one tiny crest to another as each swelling came and went with the pulse of the river. No longer caught on the edge of living and dying, the girl on the bridge disappeared into awe, her suffering overcome by a simple act of kindness and a sense of mercy alive in this world.

Chapter 38

A clear hundred-watt bulb hung from a wire attached to the junction box at the center of the ceiling in his room. There was no fixture to soften its glare. David Chase hated the light. He hated the demand to open his eyes, the insistence on wakefulness. It was a prison guard checking on him, a priest ordering him to give something he could not. But because the bulb was clear, he could see inside to the filament dangling like a loose thread. The quivering light swept him into a trance. Unable to take his eyes from the fragile, silken threads, David fell deeper into the spell, helpless to resist the beckoning voice from the past.

"Daddy, do you know why I love wind more than anything else in the world?"

"No, why is that, Em?"

"Because it's invisible!"

"Invisible?"

"Yes! I love invisible stuff, Daddy! Harry Potter has an invisibility cloak, and he can walk around Hogwarts, and nobody can see him. Isn't that great? Can I get one for my birthday, Daddy? Please?"

"Well, I don't know if Amazon carries invisibility cloaks, Em."

"I've been reading about invisible stuff, Daddy. Did you know most of the universe is invisible? Most of everything is. Even the stuff that helps us make oxygen in our cells, the mito, mito . . ."

"Mitochondria?"

"Right, the mitochondria! Have you ever seen a mitochondria, Daddy? And what about dark matter? I read about that. It's invisible too, and nobody even knows what the heck it is."

"Another mystery. Why are you so excited by what you can't see, Em, when there's so much world you can see?"

"Because grown-ups tell us kids to pay attention to the real world and stop daydreaming when they don't even really look at the world and what's all around them or try to imagine what they can't see. And then they tell us stuff isn't real just because they can't see it. That really makes me mad. What about the crazy neutrinos I just read about that are bombarding us all the time and shooting through our bodies like we aren't even there? That's so crazy, Daddy!"

"It is crazy, you're right. But grown-ups want kids to be able to survive in the real world, Em, to get a job and feed themselves and—"

"Ugh, that is so boring, Daddy. Besides, there's something else invisible that you grown-ups miss."

"What's that?"

"Just the best thing there is, and it's totally invisible. Give up?"

"I do."

"Love, silly. Love is the best! There's a million songs written about love so that proves it!"

"I forgot."

"You always forget, Daddy."

■ ■ ■

David stood fixed to the spot in the middle of the room. The flashbacks were coming more frequently now. He had no control over them, so when one darted through his psyche, he fell backwards into a perplexing state of elation and fear. But this one was different. It was more like a dream or recurring memory he watched with a mix of detachment and pleasure.

He had all but forgotten the young woman on the bridge yesterday and his promise to meet her again today. He hurriedly prepared to leave his room by the usual hour, and in his haste, bumped into the table and nearly stumbled and fell at the door. At the stairway he reached for the railing and tried to steady himself before beginning the descent to the street. A restlessness, nearly an eagerness, to leave his room, to begin, had set in. Begin what, he could not imagine, but he had a dim awareness it had something to do with Emily's message to see the world and something big he had forgotten.

It was Saturday. The warehouses were closed, their huge doors pulled down, the workers gone. As David walked, he felt a strange sensation run up his back. It was an eerie feeling that he was being followed. He turned abruptly but saw no one. Disturbed by the persistence of the sensation, persistence that turned to certainty, David stood there for a moment while his mind turned over, trying to remember something.

After a few minutes of futility, he continued walking toward the bridge. Distracted by his attempts to remember something elusive and wondering what was following behind, he stepped in a puddle left by an overnight shower. The rainwater entered a hole in the front of one shoe and soaked through the sock to his toes. The cold moisture on his foot surprised him, and he realized the sensation pleased him—one foot cold, the other numb. And then he knew what had been lurking in his mind since the encounter with the girl on the bridge: *Now, now I have to do something . . . damn, I wasn't going to cry today . . . I have to, I have to talk to him, the one who killed, the one who killed . . . Em . . .*

David stood there trembling, shaken by the memory of his last meeting with Dr. Jones two months earlier and the realization that he had hidden the resolve to meet with Randy Tanner from his mind. He was disturbed by having banished something so important but somehow fortified by the return of what he knew he must do. That which had been following in the shadows was now his. A slight smile opened. It was an authentic smile. One of the few to grace his face since the morning in the snow with his mother. He smiled to himself and the bewildered boy in the snowbank. And to Emily. Realizing with true clarity his calling, David Chase took long strides toward the bridge and a return to the living.

Chapter 39

By the time David reached the homeless encampment, the feeling in his toes had faded. He slowed as he passed the slumbering township, his eyes open to the pile of debris surrounding the tents. The wheelchairs, the broken bicycle, a rubber tire minus the inner tube, rusted-out hibachis, walkers, collapsing tents, clothes no one would ever wear again, and trash. So much trash. A human landfill.

David stared at the debris. The restlessness grew. From beneath the pile of all he had discarded and left for dead, the pile that lay rotting inside him, something inched its way up toward the damp morning air. It crawled from the debris of his life like a newborn insect looking for air. The sensation caught his attention, though it wasn't until a genuine shred of pity inched its way toward the surface of his life, as though it were blind and its legs weak, that he recognized the feeling.

With every image of the people's plight penetrating his heart, the feeling grew. It grew for the inhabitants of the street village while they slept just a few feet away, dreaming impossible dreams.

And then David saw the graffiti. Everywhere. On the warehouse walls and broken windows, on stop signs, on dumpsters, on old trucks, on sidewalks, on everything that did not move. It was there in bold colors and black and white, printed, scrawled messages in the signatures of the untouchables. It shouted from every corner of Portland, and he heard it—

It shouted. WE ARE HERE! YOU WILL SEE US!

It screamed. YOU CAN'T IGNORE OUR SCREAM!

It protested. YOU DON'T OWN US! YOU DON'T OWN ANYTHING! OUR SIGNATURE IS ALL OVER YOU!

It declared. YOU WON'T ERASE US! YOU CAN PAINT OVER US BUT WE WILL BE BACK!

David staggered up the westbound ramp to the bridge. The graffiti had penetrated and made a tunnel for the germ of pity making its way. He remembered the girl and the encounter at the railing. He wondered if she was sleeping in the camp. He struggled to remember her face, but the event came back to him in pieces, and as it did, he asked himself what had happened between the two of them. He remembered agreeing to meet her again. Why had he said yes? Or did he? What did she want? Did she survive the walk to the east bank? The questions made David dizzy. He took the rail in both hands and leaned in. The old urge to jump raised its head, but when David looked down, he saw the flow of the river moving north to its rendezvous with the Columbia, and it inspired him to keep moving.

He shook his head and continued on up the ramp. His steps met the cement sidewalk and left a clapping sound in his wake. The sound of his shoes hitting the cement echoed in his mind and he felt alone. As he approached the meeting place under the twin towers, he saw the candy cane gates standing at attention, and the bridge, quiet now, stretching to the west side where the city's tallest buildings rose above the streets. He was alone. And he was still alone when he reached the spot where the two had met. She was not there, and she would not be there, but something was: care for her, care for another person.

He stood in that familiar place, the place of decision at the railing, long enough for the sun to absorb the dark from the horizon. There he looked into the gray black of the river, into the great contentment of the sky, and when he did, David felt its vast emptiness surround him. An emptiness he could now touch with his senses and feel within his body. Though the experience was foreign to him, he was not frightened. And then, in a flash, the emptiness was Emily. Inside, outside, gone. Just Emily. Alive. Not smiling, not laughing or singing—still as an oak. The living Emily.

David went down on his knees. He slumped to the cement and leaned against the railing, moaning, unable to stop himself from sobbing. Grief held back for decades cascaded down his face, into his skin, and onto the sidewalk. And when his tears no longer flowed, and when the first of the Canadian geese flew over the bridge, calling the wild to another day, David lifted himself from the concrete and stood upright. He turned toward the City of Roses and paused. In the pause he heard drivers honking their horns in jubilation as they drove into the city. The sky began to sparkle. The smoke was gone.

As was Emily. In her place was sound. The sound of time breathing easily, the sound he understood to mean *now*.

Chapter 40

David took a long look at the remaining length of the Hawthorne bridge and the city lights beyond. His nerves were in full swing, and he felt like a boxer on rubber legs. He steadied himself to walk across the bridge to the west bank of town. A few cars sped over the bridge. Their sound carried in all directions before dying somewhere over the water.

David walked down the ramp leading to the Naito Parkway. He did not wait for the little white man to appear at the crossing before he walked across the four-lane street. From there he made his way to the center of town and Pioneer Courthouse Square. The strength and energy of his legs returned, and he walked with purpose toward a destination other than the pink bicycle.

Arriving at the downtown police station, David stopped and stared at the massive gray building. He swallowed hard and looked at the lineup of police cars parked out front. He noticed the feeling of being followed was gone. He could not feel that his neck and spine had straightened, and his steps were steadier than when he nearly tripped leaving his room at the warehouse.

David opened the massive steel door into the large, vaulted entry. He passed through security and the metal detector and made his way toward what looked like a large reception desk at the rear of the fluorescent room. Seated behind a plexiglass window was the on-duty officer reading a report. David walked up to the window and stood before him.

The officer looked at his watch. It was 5:30 a.m. "Yes, sir," he said. "What can I do for you?"

By then David was dazed. The energy left his legs. Overwhelmed by the high ceiling and cold interior of the station, he said nothing. He was unable to read the name printed on the officer's badge or remember why he had come to this place at all. He looked down at his shoes and the square floor tiles and tried to resist the force that would drive him to his knees again.

"Sir, what brings you in this morning? Is there something I can help you with?"

Sergeant Jacobs had no way of knowing that the man standing before him had not spoken to anyone in the past three years except his attorney, a psychiatrist, and a stranger about to end her life. He might have suspected David was a homeless stray, lost and wandering about the downtown streets. He might have figured he was one of the mentally ill that showed up looking for trouble or a lost fragment of themselves. But the man standing on the other side of the plexiglass shield was more in shock than psychotic, more deeply saddened than paranoid, and an unusual pull from his heart moved Sergeant Paul Jacobs to get this odd man to look at him and talk.

Sergeant Jacobs tried again. "Sir, are you all right? Sir?"

"What?"

"Are you all right, sir? Can I help you?"

David took one step into the groundless space of relatedness when he answered with what he thought might be the right word.

But it was not yet a word. What he pulled from his molded

storeroom of abandoned language was unrecognizable. He looked away to the walls and doors leading to other rooms.

"What did you say, sir? I couldn't make that out." Sergeant Jacobs was now leaning over his desk, his face nearing the glass divider.

Again, the word came out like clay in search of a sculptor.

"Him. Him." David heard the sound that had yet to become a word. He looked to the eyes of the sergeant, pleading for help.

"Him? Who is it, sir? Are you trying to find someone?"

"Gone. My daugh . . ."

"What did you say? Dog? Your dog is gone?"

"My daughter."

"Oh, I see, your daughter is gone. Is that right? Your daughter has gone missing?"

David Chase looked at the sergeant. So many words at once. He looked at the floor, at the specks of sediment in the tile. He was completely lost. His hands trembled and his voice stuttered, but he did his best to communicate to the officer by raising his hands above his shoulders, slowly, as though he were surrendering for a crime committed in his sleep.

"That man," he said to the bewildered officer. "I want to talk to that man."

"Sir, can I get your name?"

"I want to talk with him."

"I don't understand, Mr. . . . can you tell me your name, sir?"

"I must talk to him. How do I talk with that man?"

"Sir, I don't understand. There's someone you want to talk to? Is that right?"

"Emily."

"Emily? Who is Emily? You want to talk with Emily?"

"Emily. Emily is my daughter."

The words were coming out of a deep well. Waterlogged and sputtering.

"So, Emily is your daughter, and you want to speak with her. Is that right? Is she lost?"

It staggered him to hear a stranger speak her name. David looked at the man through the plexiglass barrier. He wondered if the man had a daughter. He looked at his silver blue eyes and his white moustache and thought this man must be a father.

"She is dead."

"Dead?"

"Yes."

The clock on the wall stopped. The father of three girls, with the badge on his shirt and the white moustache above his lip, stopped and looked at the man before him and somehow knew to say nothing.

"I want, I want . . ." David's voice fell to the floor and rolled under the counter like a piece of fruit that falls from a cutting board.

"What is it, sir?" Sergeant Jacobs settled into trying to understand how he could help. "How can I help you?"

"I want, I want to speak with that man . . . that killed my daughter."

A cold shiver ran down Sergeant Jacobs's spine. "You want me to help you find out how you can meet with the man who killed your daughter. Is that right? You want to talk to this man? Is that what you want?"

"Yes."

A sacred, audible hush filled the room.

"Can you?"

Chapter 41

"You what?" Keith Stone sat on the only chair in David's room and stared at what was left of his friend. Incredulous, he said it again: "You what? Are you fucking kidding me? You want to talk to the bastard who offed your daughter? Fuck, David, have you completely lost your mind?"

David winced but managed to utter, "My mind doesn't want this." He paced from the window to the door and back but did not even glance at his inquisitor.

"Oh, I see—your mind doesn't want this. Great, then who or what does? Huh? Tell me that. What the fuck is up with you?" Keith Stone tried to calm himself but failed. He stood and threw the chair down behind him and stormed toward the door.

"I don't know" was all David could say.

"You don't know. Great. This is insanity, David. Really. You want me to write a letter to the State Board of Corrections and ask permission for you to visit that maniac and cozy up to him? You're thinking crazy, David. You've been alone too long in this god-awful room." Keith Stone didn't stop there. He hit David with a barrage of reason and accusation, and the worst punch he could throw: the declaration of betrayal. "How can you even think of such a thing? Fucking visit with her murderer and have some sort of perverted love fest? You'd do that to your daughter's memory?"

David reeled from the blow and slumped to his corner. Keith Stone left the warehouse, declaring himself the winner in a knockout. But he was mistaken. He had overestimated his own powers and underestimated the tidal pull of love that moves a parent every bit as forcefully as the moon moves the ocean.

What Keith Stone did not realize was that his accusation was not the first to broadside David. David's own judgment was merciless. Since the first thought of visiting Randy Tanner in prison, he had pummeled himself with verdicts of his unredeemable guilt. Compared to those beatings, the blow thrown by Keith Stone was nothing.

But there was another force moving the events of David's life that neither man had considered. That force was the power of love to do the impossible, even when the impossible is moving mountains, mountains of history and suffering that shape the lives of generations. That force, once only a whisper from a dying girl's lips, was now the heartbeat of her father's life.

Chapter 42

In a few weeks it was done. Despite his protests, Keith Stone, who had long ago renounced any affiliation to acts of mercy, wrote the letter per David's instructions. He held the response to that letter in his hand as he pounded on David's door. Once inside the warehouse he wasted no time admonishing his friend for what he believed to be self-destructive stupidity.

"So, you're really going to go through with this craziness? You just invite trouble, David. What the hell? It's been three fucking years. When are you going to stop punishing yourself? This is nuts. You really think there's something to be gained by talking to that psychopath? He'll fucking eat you alive. You won't have a chance. Fuck me."

"The warden said yes?"

"Of course the warden said yes. It's a great PR stunt for them. Rehabilitation bullshit."

"You don't believe in much."

"I don't believe in fantasy or stupidity."

"I don't believe in anything, really. That's the trouble with us."

"I believe in plenty. Especially getting the most out of life. You're not responsible for this tragedy, David, and you certainly don't owe that freak anything."

"Getting . . ."

"What?"

The pause was more than he could stand, and Keith Stone was about to blast him again when David muttered the words that stopped them both. Words that made the room hold its breath. Words that the world was desperate to hear.

"Getting . . . always getting . . . it's always about getting more, Keith, never enough. We don't know when to stop."

"Damn it, David . . ."

But David wasn't done. He lifted his head and looked at Keith Stone, his one friend on this earth, and he said to him, "Emily believed in me."

And with that simple phrase Keith Stone was defeated, and he knew it. He shook his head and turned for the door, which did not object to his departure. And for the first time, that room, despite the dust and mold, the cobwebs and spiderwebs, the years of neglect and despair, that solitary room, more a cell than a dwelling, held dignity within its four walls.

PART THREE

THE WICKED AND THE DEAD

No self can survive a real conversation.

—David Whyte

Chapter 43

David left his room at six on a Saturday morning for the Greyhound bus station and the one-way trip to Salem, home of the Oregon State Penitentiary. He walked with purpose but also with fear at his side, the fear that at any moment he might turn and walk back into the world of shadows.

On that balmy morning, he chose his usual route over the Hawthorne Bridge and up the west side esplanade toward the clamoring Steel Bridge. As he approached the grounds of the Portland Saturday Market by the river, he veered off the usual path and through the happy grounds of the market. But David paid no regard to its atmosphere, ignoring the vendors busily setting up their booths and putting out goods for the day. He passed through the marketplace, fixed on making his way under the Burnside Bridge and onto the main street that led to Chinatown.

He paid no attention to his surroundings until he came upon the sisters and brothers of the streets. Some were still sleeping on the sidewalk and in doorways. Others mingled and spoke to their neighbors in muffled tongues. Some were crumpled in a pile that looked like nothing but a discarded sleeping bag with shoes sticking out the end. In some cases, it was impossible to tell the living from the dead.

His eyes were now drawn to suffering. He asked himself if he could love the exhausted souls standing in single file waiting to be fed. David looked at the ragged clothing and especially the shoes, and the holes in the failing canvas. Shoes that no longer protected tender feet, could not protect those feet from the wet and cold or the ache of another hopeless step. He wondered what it took for them to keep going. Could these people love? Something about them gave him courage; he wasn't sure what that was.

Against his will, David peered into the eyes of the men and women standing in line. He could not meet their gazes for long. It made him want to disappear into the line along with them; he felt an urge to join the ranks of the forgotten and unwanted, to throw his anxiety and dread in the street and let it be crushed by passing cars and left to rot at the curbside. He wanted to join the tribe of the invisible, eventually to be swept away like litter from the sidewalk.

The eyes that met his were dull and tired, fearful and colorless. In some he saw a trace of yearning that had somehow survived the furnace, looking out for a shred of kindness. David wondered what these people saw in his eyes. He wondered if the same absence, the same fear met their gaze. And then a jolt of panic shot through his body. He staggered and lost his breath. He forgot his name and the people standing in line, remembering that in forty-eight hours he would be looking into the eyes of Randy Tanner. But what panicked him was the realization that Randy Tanner would be looking into his eyes as well.

Chapter 44

From Burnside, David made his way to the entrance of Chinatown. He passed through the gate guarded by two large dragons mounted atop ornate pedestals. Had he looked up from his troubled thoughts he would have seen, seated on the head of the dragon to his right, a crow with its head cocked to one side.

The crow took flight, following David as he made his way to the bus station. It was large, with extraordinary wings that made wind as it flew ahead, looking to ward off demons and spirits that might be waiting in the shadows to ambush this vulnerable man. Emily would have recognized the benevolence of the crow. She would have instantly known the urgent cawing to be blessings of the dark mother, and she would have thanked the crow for its fierce protectiveness of her father.

David was also an admirer of crows. He admired the stern, unromantic reality, the hard-headed intelligence, and what he considered to be a surgeon's eye. Because of his affinity with black and the coarse fiber of life, a receptive neighborhood in an otherwise battered psyche allowed the blessings of the crow to enter and soothe what had become a nightmare of condemning thoughts shrieking at him like a mad witch spitting curses in his face.

Even with the crow's blessings, the accusations of betrayal were searing. Meeting with the monster who had taken Emily from him was a capital offense, surely the most wretched of his countless betrayals. He was convinced nothing could or should save him from the merciless judgment he deserved.

With each step toward the bus, David's body grew heavier. Lurking beneath the condemnation battering his mind was a growing sense that his trip would be a one-way journey. The certainty that he would not return began to occupy him like an infection of the blood. Death waited for him in the cellblock of the state. Why he did not run, as fast as his aging legs would permit, to the nearest bridge and throw himself into oblivion was the final proof of his unlimited moral failing.

He turned onto NW Broadway and caught sight of the old Union Station. The handsome dark gray stucco building with red brick trim struck a grand profile against the sky. Its tower pointed to something above the large round clock at its summit, a transcendence that prevailed outside the spell of time. The stately presence beckoned like a chapel to travelers bound for that which they had not considered, but was to become a part of their soul's confounding itinerary.

■ ■ ■

David boarded the Greyhound bus for Salem at nine in the morning. He lifted feet cast in cement and a lifetime of guilt that bent his back like a branch after a wet snow. His hair was now white as that snow, and his rigid body gave the impression of a man ten years older.

As he made his way to the back of the bus, a surge of claustrophobia hit, and he turned and looked over his shoulder for an escape. Close to fainting, he collapsed into a seat halfway down the aisle. The world spun upside down and turned in all directions. David did his best to hang on. He grabbed his bag and hugged it close the way a frightened child would grasp a favorite stuffed animal.

Tears welled in his eyes, and he found himself silently pleading for help—and it was immediate. A white light, dazzling and radiant, flashed over his head and descended into the gusting whirlwind of his inner world. The light spread throughout his forehead, down his back, and into his concrete legs wedged into the narrow seat. His arms and fingers, feet and toes tingled and warmed. Unable to open his eyes, David moaned and sobbed as the merciful wave of light bathed him and offered his suffering to an ocean of peace.

. . .

When he returned to normal consciousness, the bus was lumbering down the Willamette Valley on Interstate 5 toward the state capital of Oregon and site of the Oregon State Penitentiary. Despite the touch of grace, David woke to a nightmare of images flashing and dive-bombing from all directions. The blood-soaked body of Emily. The crazed, demonic face of her killer. Audrey shrieking. The murderous siren of the Triumph, and the smell of its fire. The eternal scream of shattered glass. A horrified, shaking hand. The red balloon irretrievably lost and drifting up into the indifferent blue sky.

The hellish collage of that day raced across his mind's eye like swarming killer bees, and neither shutting his eyelids tight nor looking at the pastoral countryside floating by could stop the seesawing battle between the torment of a lifetime and the warmth of the white light. David sat in the vinyl seat-turned-electric chair, besieged by the insurgency, lurching as volts of damnation's fury attacked, helpless to influence the fight between its wrath and the merciful insistence of love. Sweat poured from him. He groaned and his world shrank to the size of a pinhead before consciousness of all possible worlds was lost.

Chapter 45

"Hey, mister, wake up. Come on, wake up, we're in Salem, last stop." The bus driver shook David by the shoulders, but he did not stir.

"Jeez, he's sweating. Just my luck if he had a goddamn heart attack on my shift." The bus driver shook his head and spoke louder: "Hey, mister, wake up!" One of the remaining passengers tried to help him by saying, "He made some terrible sounds, like he was having a nightmare or something. Do you think he's dead?"

"No, he's not dead, I can see him breathing. I better call 9-1-1. Will you wait here with him, sir?"

"Sure, I can do that."

The bus driver turned and walked toward the front of the bus, muttering profanities to himself. As he did, David began to moan and move in his seat. His eyes opened and blinked rapidly. "Wait!" The passenger yelled to the driver. "Wait, he's coming around. Sir? Sir, you okay?"

David struggled to bring himself back. He shook his upper body and tried to stand. The first attempt failed, and he fell back into his seat.

"Not so fast." The passenger took him by the arm and David allowed the help. By now the driver was standing in the aisle watching him try his best to orient and stand.

"Take it easy, mister, we'll help you up." The bus driver joined the passenger, and together they got David to his feet and supported him walking down the aisle toward the front exit.

"Watch out for these steps now," the driver warned.

Once securely on the platform, David attempted a smile. "Thank you," he said, in a voice weakened by the experience on the bus. "Thank you. That must have been some dream I had."

"It must have been—we couldn't wake you up for a while there. We were worried you'd had a heart attack or something. How you doing?" The bus driver, concerned about releasing someone so unstable, looked him over carefully for signs of another collapse.

"I'm okay."

"You sure? Maybe you need a doctor or something. The hospital is nearby."

"No, no. I'm fine."

"You have someone meeting you here? Family or friends?"

"No. No family. Where am I? Where is Mission Street?"

"You're in downtown Salem. Center Street. Mission is where?" The driver looked to the passenger for help.

"Mission Street is that way, south, not far. Where are you going? I can give you a lift."

"No, no thank you. I'll be fine. I don't have far to go. Really."

David gathered his bag, nodded to the two men, and began to walk in the direction the passenger had pointed.

"Hey, where are you going on Mission Street?" the passenger called out.

He turned slowly. "I'm going to the Quality Inn."

"Oh, that's a long walk, mister. It's out at 24th and Mission.

Turn left when you find Mission and keep going. You sure you don't want a ride?"

David didn't answer. He turned and began the long walk to the Quality Inn. He walked slowly, and to the two men watching from the side of the bus, he looked unsteady on his feet. Neither man could say why his emotions were so disturbed by the encounter with this strange man, but each went his separate way feeling an unfamiliar need to watch over David. In their own time, both men turned to check on him and saw that he had disappeared amidst city life in search of Mission Street.

Chapter 46

David's sleep was fitful the first night in Salem. He tossed and turned and kicked the blankets from the bed. He dozed for an hour and got up to use the bathroom, then stared at the ceiling and counted the raindrops pelting the window. Fearful of sleep and finding himself in another terrible dream but afraid not to sleep and be a basket case in the morning, David lay there tormented by his worst nightmare: the encounter with Randy Tanner.

Around two o'clock, he gave up on sleep, got out of bed, and paced. He looked out the window at the fluorescent parking lot. He checked the clock and cursed its passivity. He tried to force the picture of Randy Tanner from his memory. When nothing worked, he took a hot shower and shaved.

Exhausted and without a shred of hope in sleep or refuge of any kind, and least of all in himself, David fell into the chair by the window. He stared at the carpet without blinking and was besieged by the words in the warden's letter to Keith Stone proclaiming Randy Tanner an "exemplary inmate." Those words threw his exhausted body into a rage. He wanted to smash the table lamp against the wall and tear down the motel art and break it over his knee. He stomped the floor and threw himself on the bed kicking and hitting. After a few minutes he stopped, drained of the little energy his body had brought to Salem. Sometime close to his usual waking time of four o'clock, David, released from the tenacious torment of his journey, fell into a deep sleep.

. . .

At last, in sleep, there was peace. The peace that comes with dying. What was dying was tenacious as a forest fire and imperceptible as the movement of the earth. Dr. David Chase was dying, a person grafted onto a broken stem made from unbearable pain. Asleep in his motel room, just a few miles from where Randy Tanner was sleeping, Dr. David Chase rested. And dreamed.

It is early evening at the end of a long workday when he arrives home. The house is large and made of stone. It is floating inches above the ground. He turns the doorknob and is surprised to find it soft, like flesh. Inside, the house is roomy as a castle. The ceiling is three stories high, and the walls are painted a deep, passionate red. Candlelight on the walls gives the room a religious feel. In a large stuffed chair by a roaring fire, Emily is curled up reading Are You My Mother? *She is five years old and completely absorbed in the book. David's heart falls to his knees. Emily senses his presence, looks up from her book, and smiles a smile that would melt a glacier.*

"Daddy, Daddy, you've come!" The little girl bounds out of the chair and runs to her father. "Daddy!"

Emily cries out to David and hurls herself into his arms. David catches his daughter in mid-air, lifts her to his chest, and they hug long and tight.

"My daddy! My daddy! My daddy is home!"

David carries Emily to the big chair by the fire and they sit down together. She is snuggled into his lap, her face buried into his chest. The roar of the fire becomes the voice of a choir, and Hayden's Paukenmesse mass *fills the room.*

Emily looks up at her father and asks, "Are you my mother?"

David is taken aback. "No sweetie, I'm not your mother, I'm your daddy."

"I know, silly. Who is my mother?"

"Your mother is Claire."

"Nope, wrong, guess again."

"Well . . . your mother is Martha?"

"Daddy! Martha is my grandmother, silly Daddy."

"Oh, right, of course."

"Daddy, everything is my mother, everything." Emily wiggles from her daddy's arms and dances around the cavernous room, singing and leaping from couch to chair to the ornate rugs. "The moon is my mother, the sun is my mother, and strawberry ice cream is definitely my mother!"

At times she seems to fly, and indeed, just then, the entire room begins to float upwards like a giant hot air balloon, and the voices of a celestial choir become passionate as the ceiling opens onto a starry night. Next, the walls of the great room fall away and spaciousness surrounds and embraces David. The crackling fire turns to celestial bells. The stars turn into the faces of ten thousand women, old and young women across time and continents, wrapped in the colorful robes of all cultures. Ten thousand mothers, some old and some young, all of them lovely, tough, and strong, not smiling but beaming rivers of warmth that wash over and through his rusty soul. Emily grows larger and larger and flies like an angel to join the women in the sky looking down at her father.

With an abundance of love, they say to him in unison, "Remember, David, love. Love."

■ ■ ■

The dream dissolved and David opened his eyes. A fresh feeling of ease greeted him. Unable to remember where he was, who he was, or what he was doing, he lay in bed and let the dream settle through his mind. To his great surprise, it was effortless. Everything in his life up until that moment had been an effort, an act of his enormous will. An even greater surprise was the joy he felt. A joy inseparable from the sound of the bells lingering from the dream. It was within the music of that spaciousness that David heard again the whispered words of Emily and the galaxy of mothers:

Love.

Chapter 47

It is nearly six. The day is putting on its clothes and stretching to the moon over the horizon. David exits the hotel lobby and heads east on Mission Street toward the rising sun and the state prison. The two-mile walk is straightforward enough: once he turns onto State Street it is a direct twenty blocks to the prison gate.

But the walk becomes increasingly surreal. Something different is happening, something that makes his insides feel like a whirlpool, twirling and pulling him down into a place without any of the usual hitching posts to tie his name to. For a moment David wonders if he is having a stroke. He stops walking and looks for a solid object to hang on to. Is he dying? Losing his mind? Neither of those possibilities would have mattered a few weeks back, but something has shifted inside. Now his life means something.

Just then a pair of crows circle above him, shrieking and cawing with an urgency that brings him out of his delirium. He looks up and smiles at the two Zen priests of the air, wings flapping and mouths chanting one rapid-fire koan after another. They circle and dive like fighter planes, and David can't quite make out if they are angry, trying to warn him, or just trying to pull him out of the psychic quicksand threatening to devour him. He decides that because he has always admired crows, they must be trying to help somehow, but it is still impossible to understand their crackling message carved in the air. And still, in a hidden, tender part of his ear, an ancient sensing hears their verse:

Whatever brought you here
will bring you home
Haw, Haw, Haw

The crows fly off in the direction of the state penitentiary, cawing in the key of laughter as though they have just said the funniest thing ever. David feels a pang of longing as their bodies grow smaller and their voices more distant. He wishes he had one on each shoulder to fortify his resolve, which seems likely to collapse at any moment.

He returns to his private hell, cursing himself for his weakness and wondering how he could possibly live up to Emily's prayer. Though his mind is harsh in allotting punishment for his many failings, the magic of the crows and the afterglow of the morning dream smooth his edges. Soon he begins to feel it is all a dream: the day, this walking, this city, his broken life. Suddenly it dawns on him; someone, something, is dreaming a vast, seamless dream. He is swimming in a dream world flowing in perpetual motion, with no beginning and no end, no center and no perimeter. Emily had, from an early age, called it "The Goo!" Dear Emily. Was she a dream? A dream within a dream? As he walks on, he feels himself disappearing into the gooey goo of it all.

David rides the waves of this dreaming. There are moments when his mind comes forth and lifts its head, like a seal in the surf, and he thinks to himself that life is stranger than he'd ever recognized. He shakes his head in disbelief and walks on, forgetting everything that lies ahead, so mesmerized by the undertow of the dream world carrying him out to sea.

The rasping voice of the crows interrupts the dreamer. He looks up to find himself a hundred yards from the gate of the penitentiary. The sight of the massive structure shocks him. The faucet of fear opens wide. David freezes. His body shrinks two sizes. He is dwarfed by the prison, inadequate and foolish. The confidence that grew over the course of the morning vanishes. Only the call of the crows pulls him forward to the home of the wicked.

The two crows escort David to the gate. They perch atop the roof of the checkpoint and caw at the top of their lungs. One flaps its wings furiously and bends its head forward, stabbing its beak at the air. The other points to the heavens and its deep, rounded chest opens broadly to the world. Together they raise a ruckus that reaches a cacophony of sounds that to the human ear are tortured screams, the laughter of a madman, Sisyphus cursing God, all in one piercing, wailing cry.

David looks up at the birds and marvels at their audacity. He does not hear the guard at the gate ask him what he wants. He is too busy trying to translate the message the black knights shout to the blessed and the damned.

Courage fools, courage, Haw, Haw
The world will soon end! The world will soon end!
CAW, CAW, CAW, CAW

"What is it, sir? What can we help you with?"
David looks everywhere but at the guard speaking to him. He

looks at the faded yellow of the massive building and shudders. He looks at the ground and says, "I'm here to see someone."

"Who are you here to see?"

David does not answer the officer. He reaches into his pocket and pulls out the letter from the superintendent, Dr. Scott, authorizing his visit. The letter is wrinkled and torn at the edges. He opens the folded paper and tries to straighten it out before handing it to the guard.

The crows go berserk, and the guard shouts at them. "Damn crows, get out of here!" The crows laugh at his waving arms. He takes the letter from David and reads it slowly.

"May I see your photo ID?"

"I don't have one."

"You don't have one?"

"No."

Who are you?
Haw, Haw, Haw!

"You can't enter this facility without ID. Do you have any identification in your wallet?"

"I haven't had a wallet for over three years."

"No wallet?"

"No."

"No ID? No wallet?"

"No."

Aah, Aah, Aah

Nothing is real!
Hah, Hah, Hah

"I'm sorry, mister, I can't let you past this point without proper identification. You'll have to—"

"Wait, Sullivan, is that Dr. Chase?" Lieutenant Crawford steps out of the gatehouse and approaches the pair. The crows go crazy.

"Dr. Chase?" The first guard is incredulous and stares at the ragged man standing before him.

"I haven't been a doctor for three years."

"Let me see that letter, Sullivan." The lieutenant steps forward and takes the letter from the officer and reads it carefully.

"This guy's no doctor, Lieutenant. He doesn't even have a damn wallet, much less ID."

"Wait a minute, I forgot, I have an old ID from the hospital. My attorney made me bring it . . . "

Lieutenant Crawford scans the wrinkled letter and announces his verdict. "This is Dr. David Chase from Portland. He's the one we've been expecting."

"This guy?" Corporal Sullivan is agitated now. He looks at David with disdain for making him look bad.

"Dr. Chase, the superintendent said to bring you to his office. He wants to speak with you."

Corporal Sullivan looks at the disheveled old man and shakes his head. The crows look at the two prison guards and shake their heads. David looks at the massive building he is about to enter, and a voice inside says *no!* Another voice, neither inside nor outside, says *yes.*

. . .

Doors. A thousand steel doors that only close. Their closing echoes with the sound of fury screaming, "Never!" Those screams make the gravelly screech of the crows sound like a nightingale's song. With every step into this barren tomb David wants to turn and run. With every door that slams behind him, he wants to scream the scream of the damned.

From a distance he hears the tortured voices of men echoing off the walls. The endless walls mock him, sneering. They are bare, stark white plaster layered over plaster. They own this place. Hopeless souls crash against the unyielding world of the walls and fall to the cement defeated in the cold, unmerciful silence.

. . .

By the time he reaches the superintendent's office, David is in pieces. He feels he might vomit. He aches to see something green. To touch something living. There is no exit.

David sits in a chair in the waiting room trying to calm his mind by remembering the ease of the morning. But he fails. Dizzy and weak, he is sagebrush careening down a dusty road, helplessly tossed here and there by hot wind off the desert.

Dr. Scott opens the door to his office and stands there for a second, pausing to scan the territory for danger. After surveying the scene and taking in a quick impression of this most uncommon visitor, Dr. Scott steps into the waiting room and reaches out his hand to David.

"Dr. Chase, I am Adam Scott, superintendent of OSP. Won't you please come in?"

The dream turns bad: the greeting arm turns into a rattlesnake ready to strike. David flinches and draws back against the wall.

Dr. Scott is tall and robust. He could pass for Gary Cooper in his prime playing the town sheriff in a Texas western. His voice echoes the calm, assured voice of the movie icon. "I'm so sorry to startle you, Dr. Chase. Please come in. Can I get you some coffee or water?"

The strong voice of the superintendent breaks the spell.

"Yes, water. Please."

David slowly rises to his feet and takes the hand of the man he has mistaken for a snake. His own hand is weak and trembling while the hand of Dr. Scott is strong and confident. His is the handshake of a man who allows no doubt to enter his world.

"Come in, Dr. Chase, we're happy to have you here. Please have a seat."

"I'm sorry, Mr. Superintendent, I . . ."

"That's quite all right, Dr. Chase. Everyone gets jumpy in this place the first time."

"I see. I suppose so."

Dr. Scott hands David a cup of water and sits down at his desk. He notices the trembling hands of the weathered man and wonders how he ever performed heart surgery.

"Is that better?"

"Thank you," David says. "I feel better. Nerves, I guess. I'll be all right."

"Of course. Like I said, we all get the jitters around here. This is not an ordinary place."

"It reminds me of certain hospitals."

"Really? Isn't that interesting? How long did you practice medicine, Dr. Chase?"

"I'm not a doctor anymore." David's voice is abrupt and detached, and Dr. Scott has difficulty reading him.

"Of course. You're retired."

"I quit."

"You quit?" Dr. Scott finds David's bare, unembellished presentation disquieting. He feels uncharacteristically self-conscious.

"Yes. After that day, I stopped."

"I see. That must have been quite traumatic for you."

"Traumatic?"

"Yes, I mean, well, no one can imagine losing a child, I'm sure, but I can only think it must have been so terrible."

"My name is David."

"David. Right, you prefer to be addressed by your first name then, is that right?"

"I don't know. No one says my name."

"Well, David, we can certainly use whatever name you like. I can call you David when we meet. While you are out in the prison, though, for the sake of discipline and professional propriety, I would like the staff to address you as Dr. Chase. Is that all right with you?"

"I'm not a doctor."

"How about Mr. Chase then?"

"All right."

The superintendent is losing his rhythm. He picks up his pen and legal pad and leans on the big oak desk.

"Well then, David, let's talk about your visits. As I said in my letter, we have the utmost respect for what you have asked of us, and we want to accommodate you in whatever way we can. Our mission at the prison is to make this institution a place of rehabilitation for as many of the prisoners as is possible. What you have requested is very much in keeping with the approach to corrections we are striving to implement. Does that make sense?"

David nods but says nothing.

The superintendent, somewhat unsettled by David's silence, shifts his position in the chair but continues. "It so happens that the prisoner, Mr. Randy Tanner, has made remarkable progress in meeting these goals since his recovery from the injuries suffered at the scene of the crime. And since undergoing treatment for drug addiction, he has been a model inmate and is most agreeable to meeting with you. I believe you'll be quite surprised and impressed with the person he has become. He is a model for other prisoners, a meditation coach and a counselor of sorts. I'm confident you will be able to speak freely with him. We are very pleased to offer this opportunity for both of you to heal, David, and we believe that this will be a novel example of rehabilitation for the rest of the country to take notice of."

Again, David says nothing. Dr. Scott searches David's eyes and is uncomfortable meeting his gaze. In over twenty-five years of service with corrections, he has looked into the eyes of killers and rapists, judges and lawyers, and not flinched. In fact, he takes pride in his capacity to be steady, even when staring into the face of evil. Why he would feel shaken now, in the company of such a strange and broken man, is a mystery to him.

The superintendent leans back in his chair. "Perhaps I'm talking too much about our program. We are very proud of what we are accomplishing here. Before I go on to explain some of the ground rules of the visits, for instance the number and frequency of your visits with Mr. Tanner, why don't we talk about you, and what your goals are in having these conversations?"

But David's mind is lost in the oak that gave its life to become the superintendent's desk. It is the first sign of life he has seen since entering this concrete tomb. He fades into the grain of the wood and the color, a soothing, warm, honey brown.

"Mr. Chase? Are you all right?"

"What?"

"Are you all right? You look, well . . ."

"I'm sorry, I was thinking about my daughter."

"I see. Of course. It must be very emotional for you to be here."

"Yes. Yes, it is." David looks out the window to the blue.

"It was a terrible thing that happened, and I hope that visiting with the prisoner will bring you some peace. But if you feel you're not up to it, I completely understand. We can always delay until you're ready."

"No, no! Please, no delay, no delay."

"Are you sure you can manage this?"

"No, I mean yes, I don't know, but I'm as ready as I'll ever be. I can do it. Emily believes in me."

"I'm sure she does, David. All right then, we'll proceed, but if at any time you want to stop, please just say so."

"Thank you." His eyes leave the blue and land like a moth on the gray of the superintendent's watchful eyes. For a second, they seem like another concrete door, but when they moisten, nearly imperceptibly, David has a glimpse into the future of sorrow that will paint those eyes the color of rain. He nearly smiles.

"What do you hope will come of these visits, Mr. Chase?"

"I don't know." He is taken aback by the arrival of the word hope. It is something he had never considered. "I really don't."

"What motivated you to come here and talk with Mr. Tanner?"

"I don't know if I can talk." His head drops.

"I see. There must be something you have thought about that you want to say or hear."

"My daughter."

"What's that?"

David hears his voice quiver. He looks for a place to hide. He searches the blue face of the sky outside the window for strength. "My daughter asked me to love."

"I see. So, you have come here to find love in your heart for your daughter's killer?"

A long pause follows. A pause that fills the room and fills the two men sitting together in a building full of pain, locked doors, bars, and walls, and all that can be called profane. Enough hatred resides within those walls to dry up the oceans of the earth. And only the honey brown oak and the blue sky are witness now to the audacity of love daring to grow from this ground.

David is silent, and in that silence he looks for one drop of courage, just a drop. But he looks like a fighter who will not leave his corner at the sound of the bell.

"Mr. Chase, I'm not sure you're up to this. What you are proposing is . . . I'm not sure of the word, but it is, well, courageous and requires strength."

"I have no courage."

"I'm sure there is no shame in saying this is too much of an undertaking. Have you sought counsel from a minister or therapist?"

The back door opens an inch. David rushes to shut it. "No. No."

"You're not religious?"

"No! I mean, no, I'm not leaving. I have no hope and I have no courage and I'm . . . I'm not . . . I am a father. That is all I have."

Silence comes to rest in the well-fortified heart of the superintendent. He looks down at his desk and then, to his surprise, at his hands and fingernails. Something about the little wrinkles on the skin above his knuckles comforts him. He looks up at David Chase and smiles in a way that is rare for him to do in this office. With a warmth he did not expect would ever find his voice, and against his better judgment, he speaks. "I respect you very much, David, I really do. Your daughter would be very proud of her father right now. I hope your visits with Mr. Tanner are helpful to you and bring you to a place of peace and renewal. Please call me at any time if you need to talk or have questions."

David nods. He searches the face of Dr. Scott to see if he believes in him, but the superintendent has begun to take his leave. "The lieutenant in charge of visitations will brief you on the parameters of your visits." Dr. Scott stands and walks around his desk toward the father seated in a chair. He offers him his hand. "I am quite happy to have met you, David. Good luck to you, sir."

David rises from the wooden chair and accepts the hand of the superintendent. He feels the warm flesh meet his bony hand and says, "Thank you. Thank you."

Dr. Scott watches David open the door and walk out into the reception area. His gray T-shirt is damp with sweat near the spine, and he looks like a man who has spent his life in prison and will never know anything different. A vague discomfort falls over Dr. Scott like a morning shadow falling on a sidewalk. His hand, of its own accord, reaches out and takes hold of what is the only wooden door in the entire prison complex.

Chapter 48

Day 1—Conversation 1

Two guards escort David to the visiting room that at one time served as an interrogation room. In recent years this room has been reserved for special interviews and high-security meetings with inmates. The room is square and roughly twice the size of the cells occupied by prisoners. Its walls are whitewashed. The only window is the two-inch-thick plexiglass window that looks into another room. This one is dark and no larger than a closet. On either side of the plexiglass, shelving serves as a desk that holds a phone the visitor and prisoner communicate through. The guards explain how the phone works, ask David if he has any questions, and when he doesn't answer, they wish him well and turn to the door, certain nothing will come of this.

David stands immobilized, rooted to the floor facing the window some five feet away. He looks like a tree once hit by lightning—charred and splintered. The window is black, and behind the window Randy Tanner sits in his wheelchair looking at a man suffering from a paralysis greater than his own.

The door closes, the sound hanging in space. When space does not move, David feels short of breath and begins to pace. He stops at the wall and hits it with his fist. He turns abruptly, faces the empty room, and expels a muffled scream. He faces the burning in his chest and the weakness in his limbs, but he cannot face the chair, or the phone, or the window. He cannot face the man behind the window. In less than five minutes he calls for the guard to open the door and runs from the room, gasping for air.

He does not see the look of pity on the face of Randy Tanner. Nor does he see Randy Tanner lower his head as if bowing in prayer.

Chapter 49

Day 4—Conversation 2

He has entered a place that does not know wind. In the absence of wind, the sound of dying is all that moves. And the sound of dying is the ceaseless echo of interrogation, of accusation, blasts of damnation hurled against the walls that echo past the end of the world. David lives with that relentless pounding. He knows the condemning judgments that pose as questions: *"What kind of man are you? How could you betray your daughter like this? Why are you still alive?"* There is no wind in this place. How can there be mercy?

. . .

David sits in the chair. His body is turned at an angle to the window. The window is dark, opaque. In order to see Randy Tanner, he must lean across the desk and look for him through the thick slab of plexiglass.

He stares at the floor and then he stares at the phone. He picks up the receiver and lays it on the desk, unable to bring it to his ear. He trembles and turns away. He is sobbing now, crumbling. He hears a giant oak scream in the distance.

Randy Tanner is done waiting. His voice is a flame thrower: "Fuck, man, speak! I got shit to do. Speak!"

David Chase freezes when he hears the voice. When he talks, it is more to himself than to Randy. "No. I . . . I . . . I shouldn't be here."

"Shouldn't be here? Shit, man, you here! Why are you here? Shouldn't be here? Shouldn't nobody be here. Nobody. What you want? Come on, tell me, let me have it."

David puts his hands over his ears and closes his eyes. He does everything in his power to shut out the voice invading his psyche. But he cannot forget who is behind the plexiglass shield. Try as he might, he cannot purge that face from his mind's eye. He says plaintively, "This is wrong."

Randy is all over him in a flash. "Wrong? Shit man, you all tied up in right and wrong. I'll say it for you then. Fuck, this ain't no mystery. You'd fucking love to break through this damned shield and cut my ass up into little pieces—screaming and spittin' on me—screaming and spittin'. Ain't that right? Hell yes. Don't lie to me—we got nothin' to lie about. Tell the truth—it's good for you."

The air leaves David. His chest sinks. "I do."

"Shit yeah, of course you do. You hate my miserable guts and want to murder my rotten ass, right now. Right now. Shove me in a greasy fire to burn and suffer, burn baby, motherfucker, burn. Go ahead, shit, that's nothin', say it. It will do you good, go ahead. I'm the motherfucker that flattened your pretty little baby girl into the cement, ain't I?

A low rattle rises in David. The walls amplify it until it rumbles in his brain. "Shut up."

Randy Tanner laughs. "Shut up? Shut up? Is that all you got, Doc? Shut up? What the fuck, they teach you not to talk nasty in that med school? They teach you not to kill anybody? That little girl ain't worth more to you than some feeble-ass 'shut up'?"

The rumble bursts from David's mouth riding a tidal wave of rage. He is out of his chair, transformed, pounding the glass, looking every bit as crazed as his tormentor in his prime. "Shut up! Shut your ugly fucking mouth, you bastard. You bastard! Damn you! Damn this fucking glass. I'd like to slam this fucking phone down your fucking throat. I'll kill you, I'll fucking kill you, you bastard!"

"Go, Doc, go! Yeah! People are easy to hate and I'm easier than most. Go, baby. Hate me with all you got—I deserve every fuckin' bit you got."

"I said shut up. Shut your miserable voice the fuck up. I never want to hear that voice or see that cocky fucking face ever again, never! Fuck this goddamn glasslet me through! I'll kill—I'll stuff this fucking phone down your ugly throat! You fucking murdered my daughter and laughed! I'll kill you!"

David's words fly on the wings of spit. It hits the plexiglass and explodes into a thousand particles of hatred. Some of it bounces back into David's face.

"Good stuff, Doc! Pound that fucking glass wall, break it, bloody those fucking clean surgeon hands and come get me. Put your bloody hands around my neck and strangle me. Make my fucking eyes pop. Go ahead, kill me, Doc, we know I'm no good."

"Fuck you—fuck you! I'll kill you, I'll kill you! You should die, you should be dead." David pounds his fist into the window and desk. A sound leaves his mouth like the cry of a wounded heron. From outside the door the guards watch the unfolding drama and look at each other nervously and laugh.

Randy's face softens and he says, "Easy, Doc, that's enough. You'll break your hands, man. No more surgery. Enough, you can't break through that shit, I tried."

David's voice weakens, sputters, and falls to the floor into a puddle of failure. "I hate you, I hate you . . . Emily . . . Emily . . . I'm sorry." He buries his head in his hands. He cannot move. It takes everything he has to stand, and when he does, his legs are so weak he fears he will fall. Finally, he steadies himself, turns, and shuffles to the door.

Randy Tanner watches David leave the room. Again, there is pity. But the pity is joined by a glimmer of respect. He whistles to himself and nods, knowing the magic has begun. With a dim feeling of hope, Randy wheels himself from the interrogation room to the guard station and back to his cell.

Chapter 50

Day 7—Conversation 3

Randy waits for David in the small space formerly reserved for the observation of interrogated prisoners. Today a prisoner will sit on either side of the window while the room now invites a conversation neither man can script or predict. Randy feels the calm of someone with nothing left to lose or gain. He has stepped into the mystery many times, with many men far more lost and hateful than this man. He has seen walls crumble and hearts beat once more. Shortly before David walks through the door, Randy thinks of the misery he caused David and feels remorse.

"Hey, look who's back! You got some balls, Doc, some genuine balls."

"Stop. Stop calling me Doc."

"What's wrong with Doc? You're a fuckin' doc, right?"

"I said stop, you son of a bitch."

"Okay, okay, no more Doc, but what the fuck do I call you then?"

"Nothing."

"Nothin'?"

"Nothing. No name, nothing. I have no name, to you."

"Okay, I get it. No name, fine, I get it. You still got balls, no name."

David's face goes blank. He is nowhere; emptiness has swallowed him again. The bright light hanging from the ceiling dims. He might as well be talking to a ghost when he says, "I'm almost gone." A flat voice leaks from David's mouth like air from a tire.

"Sure, you are. You're shakin' and you got nowhere to go. You nowhere man. Look at you, head hanging like you at the end of a rope."

"I am dead. Gone. Nothing else. You killed my daughter, and you ruined me."

"Fuckin' bullshit, man. You ain't ruined, you in prison. That's all, you're in motherfuckin' prison like the rest of us. That's all." Randy is heating up. He looks at David with scorn.

"You talk like a dirty punk."

"Shit yes. You think I'm gonna be in this rat nest and talk like some fuckin' Ivy Leaguer? I'm playing my part. Talkin' trash. There's about a hundred motherfuckers out in the yard that would love to fillet my ass and hang me from my dick. It's the prison game. I know my lines. It don't mean shit."

"I hate it."

"You hate it? Fuck you, you're here in prison and you better face up to it. You in a far worse prison than me, baby. Far worse."

"Fuck off."

"You been in prison your whole fucking life and you just now gettin' it. And you want to think I put you here. That real good shit."

"You killed my daughter, and you don't give a goddamn. You just don't care about anything, you lousy shithead. You ruined me and now you just want to spit on me too."

Randy pauses and takes in the man behind the plexiglass. His features are distorted by the fading ceiling lamp, and he looks as though his face is melting. For a moment Randy feels dizzy, but he soon finds his track.

"You the victim, man. The big righteous victim. Wow, life shit on you, now ain't that front page news! Never happened before, did it? No sir. Fuck, you in prison. This whole fuckin' world is a prison and there ain't nothin' but victims walking the streets and in the yard. Victims everywhere, man. You lookin' at one motherfuckin' victim right here. Yes sir, this is one big victim. Shit, I come into this can strapped to this two-wheel rig. Can't run, can't stand up and defend myself—fuck, I been raped, pissed on, spit on, and worse in this little buggy. But I ain't no victim. Nope, I am one motherfuckin' asshole, but I ain't no victim. And you ain't either. You somethin' else, but you too stupid to know it. You just want to hang on, hang on to being wronged, to losin' everything, no point in livin'. 'I lost it all, I'm the world's first authentic victim.' Shit, you in solitary confinement. You on death row, baby, fuckin' no end."

David is stunned. He leans back in the chair and hangs up the phone. When he picks it up a minute later, he stammers, "You don't know. You don't know anything. About love, about having a daughter who loves you. You—"

Randy is too quick; he is a street talker and does not hesitate to set David straight. "Oh yeah, here we go, right? Here we go with the real shit: 'You wouldn't know about my pain because you never known the kind of love I've known.' Ain't that rich? Man, you got the poor, poor me, pity my privileged white-ass act down. Brother, you got the whole package, don't you? The victim, the no one can understand my pain, the whole sack of shit. Beautiful. You in one tight prison cell, Mr. Shit. I bet you weren't even that great a daddy to that little girl or the old lady. Bet you were out there screwin' all those sweet cunt nurses in between washing your hands and carvin' the hearts out of the chests of those no good, rich motherfuckin' attorneys. Weren't you? Tell the truth. You weren't even around that much for that little girl, were you, Mr. V for Victim?"

David's face turns red with fury. "Fuck you. Fuck you. I'll kill you, you bastard. I'll fucking kill you. Damn you!"

"Well, well, guess we touched a little sore spot there, eh, Mr. V? Couldn't keep your dick in your pants, could you? The world's your fuckin' oyster, right? Well, at least you and me got one thing in common. Make that two. I'm strapped to this chair and you, you in a fuckin' straitjacket. And we both in prison. Now what?"

Randy watches David look everywhere in the room but at him. He feels him reaching a breaking point and wonders if he can survive it. They are on a high wire, and it is a long fall.

When David speaks, his voice is hollow, his words directed at no one. "I don't need this. What am I doing?"

"Oh, you need this, Mr. V. You need me, ain't that a riot? You need my sorry ass, and you know it. I'm your only hope. Ain't that a chuckle? You and me baby, we married. Ha, ha. Ain't that hilarious? What, you gonna run again? Man, all you do is run."

David leaves the room without a word. He walks like a man on his last legs. But Randy sees strength in David's step and takes note. He has seen the backs of many men running from themselves and feels confident David is fleeing, not breaking. He will be back.

Chapter 51

Day 12—Conversation 4

David is missing. He doesn't leave his hotel for three days. He sleeps most of the day and spends the dark hours sitting in a chair, staring out at the parking lot, afraid to dream. He does not change his clothes or eat. His thoughts are chaotic and brittle. From time to time the image of Randy Tanner darts into his mind like a wasp. When that happens, he gasps as though only then remembering where he is. On the fourth day David leaves the hotel and walks to the prison. He is accompanied by the crows. They are quiet. Blessed quiet. And within that quiet, the wind whispers *mercy*.

· · ·

"Well, what do you know? The return of Mr. V. Where you been the last few days? Holed up in some hotel room, sleeping on some nice, clean white sheets? They pretty nice?"

"Don't start."

"Don't start? We already started, ain't we? Yep, no beginning, no end. We are talkin' the talk. Nothing but the truth, so help me. Right?"

"I haven't the slightest idea what the truth is."

"Now you really talkin'."

"Why do you talk like a Black man?"

"Why? The black man rules this joint. Never forget that. Not Mr. Polished Superintendent, not those muscle-bound boys in police costumes. Not the Gov. Nobody owns this place but the black man. I pay my respects. Besides, I'm half Black myself. I'm what you call bi-lingual, ain't that fancy? Mama's a white whore and Daddy's a black pimp. Ain't that the All-American family? Hell, man, I got no clue what that makes me, and I like it like that. Keep 'em guessin'. It's all a bunch of bullshit anyway."

"I see."

"You don't see. You only see one thing, and that's your own fuckin' misery. That's your whole damn problem."

"You don't know me."

"Hey, I take one look at you and I know you, plain as day. You a lifer. They all look the same, slumped shoulders, hopeless, gray. Every fucking one. You a lifer. Locked up till you start to rot and they throw your ass away with the trash, maybe in the fuckin' incinerator."

"I'm a skeleton."

"Yes, you are. A worthless skeleton. Flesh eaten away by your own teeth, your own self-pity and rage. I know you, but you don't know you. You just hanging on, hanging on to nothing but death. Thinking about nothin' but the end. You blind and stupid."

Randy isn't finished but he pauses. In the pause he looks at David carefully. He wonders if David likes being a punching bag, thinking he deserves it, if he's playing into some need to be punished. He looks closer and feels something is different about David. His expression hasn't changed since he sat down. He seems resigned, like he's given in to not knowing what to do. His thoughts are interrupted by David's voice. It moves slowly across the distance between them.

"Why do you hammer me like this? Haven't you done enough damage to me?" There is a hint of real curiosity in David's tone. He does not look away when he is done speaking.

"Me, me, me. I'm trying to get through to you, brother. I'm trying to break through your shell. Shit, I'm trying to spring you, set you free. Why else you here? Why you here? You so stupid you think you brought your sorry self here. Don't you? You think it's you that carried that worthless skeleton here. Why you here? To kill me? Shit, sometimes I wish you could. You think you gonna bore through this thick slab of glass and take me out? Shit. You here to forgive me? Hell, no. You ain't forgivin' nobody. What, you here to find love in your heart for that poor bastard that fucked up everything and then broke his fool neck doing some damned Evel Knievel flip through a fucking plate glass window? You're a fool. Whatever brought you here is a whole lot bigger than you and a whole lot bigger than you and me and this shithole world. Whatever you want to call that, it's runnin' the show, and if you're wantin' to leave here feeling good 'cause you forgave me for my sins, you're too late, brother. I been forgiven and then some. This whole game a lot bigger than you know, than you or anyone ever fuckin' dreamed. Damn."

The world stops spinning to see if he is done. The guards look puzzled by his tirade. David does not move. His mind is on someone else.

"She asked me."

"She asked you what?"

"Love. She asked me to love. I can't."

"Shit, man, you can't even look me in the eye. How you gonna love? Why you always looking at your hands and rubbin' 'em? Come on, look at me."

"No. I can't. I don't want to see your face."

"What you afraid of seein', man, your own naked skull? What? Come on, stop playin' with your hands and look at me. I'm right here. Right here."

"If I look at you I'll see her covered in blood. I can't take it, I can't. I have to see her alive . . . I have to."

"Tell me more about this little girl."

"No! No! Stop. You cannot, you cannot—you cannot say her name. You cannot talk about her. Never."

"You're too late, brother."

"What?"

"You're too late. She has come to me."

"What did you say?"

"She came to me and put her hand on my shoulder."

"Stop. Stop fucking with me."

"It is the truth."

David is speechless. Struck by lightning. He pulls at his hair.

A century passes before he says, "It can't be."

"It is."

"I won't talk about her with you. You have no right to ask."

"I am not asking. She is."

"No."

"She says yes."

"You're fucking with me, you bastard. That's all you know how to do is fuck with people. Fuck this. I'm gone."

"Stop! You can't keep running and hiding. You know that. You know what Emily said, this is your time. Come back, sit here. Look at me. Just this once, look at me. Come on, you can, you can."

The room holds its breath. David, for the first time, leans forward and quickly rocks back, a staggered start, rocking back and forth like a schizophrenic on a psych ward. After several false starts he steals a look through the slab of plexiglass at the face of Randy Tanner. A look that comes and goes quick as a heartbeat.

"That's it, there you go. There you go. What do you see? Come on, what?"

"Blood. Nothing but blood and your fiendish grin."

"No, you're not seeing me now. That's the horror, stop looking at the horror. Look at me, right here, today."

"I'd rather look at that spider on the floor. If I look at you . . . if I look at you, if I see you and Emily together, talking, I—I can't stomach that. I'll go insane."

"You won't. Emily won't let you, I won't let you. Come on, ten seconds. Just look."

"But I don't want you to look at me. Maybe that's the worst, you looking at me. Why is that?"

"I get it, yeah, bein' seen, that gets real fuckin' ugly. Okay, I'll look over your shoulder, won't look at you. You can look at this ugly mug all you want, and I won't look at you. Promise."

"This is crazy. You want me to accept you, to see the real you. Fuck that. It's all about you, Randy Tanner, reformed murderer turned ego-maniac guru. I won't do it."

"I don't give a shit about you accepting me. I want your brain to stop seeing blood and death everywhere. Come on, man, where you goin'? Come back here, don't leave." Randy pounds on the window and yells, "David, stop, don't go, don't go!"

David stops at the door but does not turn back to the room. He does not see the plaster on the walls begin to crack and beckon him to stay. The guards look at him with sympathy and encouragement in their eyes. The image of the girl on the bridge flashes, and a bolt of electricity runs up his body from his feet to his head. He nearly smiles thinking of that morning with the girl. Just as suddenly, Emily's voice brushes his ear. He can't tell where it is coming from, but it is so real he jerks his head to look for her. And then he hears it again, softer this time so that in order to hear her he must give it all his attention. And there it is, the whispered prayer—"*Daddy, love.*"

He is trembling now as he turns to make the long walk back to Randy. Emily's words are a fading echo. David feels like he may faint. But he doesn't; something besides fear moves him. He sits down at the window and looks through the chalky plexiglass, through blood raining down on tulips, through the muddy water of the river, and finally when it all parts, he sees the ragged, lovely face of Randy Tanner looking at him with deep care. His vision blurs, but he looks again and there it is once more: care.

David closes his eyes and waits. He doesn't know for what until he hears himself say out loud, "Okay. Okay, I will."

Randy's eyes glisten. He nods his head and smiles.

And the wind whispers *mercy*.

Chapter 52

Day 19—Conversation 5

And the moon goes through its phases. Not even the mighty ocean can resist the pull of its desire. The moon has its way with David. One hour he is a werewolf hungry to tear the world apart. One hour he is radiant, another merged like a new moon with the dark night of the soul. There are openings and closings, and what closes opens. What is old is new, and what is new is old.

The crows tell him not to worry, this is the way, but to David it is bewildering, evidence that he is unfit to fulfill Emily's prayer. He sits across from Randy and laments.

"I'm not big enough."

"You are bigger than you know."

"I'm not. I'm small, too small for this. I can't hold the good. I'm all over the map. In and out. Right now, I'm out. It's exhausting."

"You're not small, man. You wouldn't be here if you were small. You're just afraid, cowering in your corner. What are you so afraid of?"

"Why are you talking like this now?"

"Like what?"

"You're not swearing every other word. What's gotten into you?"

Randy chuckles. "Ha! The wheel has turned. Besides, I told you, man, I'm bilingual, I have many tongues. I play the dialects like an instrument switching keys. That's all."

"What wheel?"

"The wheel turns as it is needed. The wheel of circumstance, necessity, destiny, karma—you can call it a hundred things. I'm a mirror to you, that's all. How could I be anything other than what I was when you arrived? You needed to kill me, right?"

"I still want to. You're still alive and she isn't."

"You want to, but you can't."

"I don't want to look at you."

"I am a mirror."

"No. I want you the other way."

"He is dead."

"What?"

The room spins, and David has nothing left to hold on to. He is dizzy, groping for something to help him stop the spinning.

"You are dying too, man. The old stuff is fighting like hell to hang on, but it knows its days are numbered." A satisfied smile passes over Randy's face. He nods and looks at David tenderly.

"Stop talking like that—it isn't you. Stop! And don't look at me like that. Damn." David turns to the wall, but the wall offers him the same care and acceptance that he cannot bear.

"What is it, man?"

"This is worse. You don't give a shit about me, don't pretend you do."

"You're burning up."

"Stop! You're lying. You're a fucking fake. What are you trying to do? Are you trying to make me crazy? It's not enough you destroyed me—now you want to make me really crazy? Is that it? Fuck you!"

"I'm not doing anything. I'm just here. It's you, you that wants this."

"Shut up! I want this? I don't want this. Fuck this. They warned me about your games, about your fucking head games. Now you're playing all peaceful and kind."

"Of course they did. That's their job."

"This is bullshit, fucking bullshit."

"This is you and me."

"Fuck you. You aren't real."

"Look at me." Randy leans forward and puts the palm of his hand on the plexiglass.

"No! You're disgusting. Sitting in that fucking wheelchair, getting everyone to feel sorry for you and believing you've changed, you're exemplary, some miracle, some fucking spiritual miracle. You're a freak, like Manson, manipulating every stupid idiot in this hellhole into thinking you're fucking 'rehabilitated.' Fuck them. Fuck you. You aren't going to manipulate me into believing you're some kind of saint. Horseshit."

"Don't believe anything."

"Don't worry. I haven't believed anything for years, since you bloodied my whole world. I sure as hell won't believe you."

"You're afraid of what you'll see."

"You don't know me. Stop telling me what I am." David turns his head in disgust. He looks to the floor for guidance, but the floor is mute; all it can offer is something solid, unmovable. David is reeling inside, caught in a flurry of emotions tearing at his flesh like the teeth of a cat. He can't think and he wants to scream and blow this house down. But his mouth is bound and gagged. The scream explodes in his lungs.

Randy removes his hand from the window. He sighs before delivering his punch line.

"You're using her."

"What did you say?"

"You're using your daughter."

"You miserable fuck. You goddamn fuck!"

"It's true. You know it is."

"No, I wouldn't. I wouldn't . . . Emily, dear Emily . . ."

But despite his impotent protest, David knows it is true. He slumps in his chair and the familiar beat of self-reproach pounds on his already battered mind.

"Emily loves you and wants you to live and to love."

"Emily . . . dear God, what am I doing?"

"You are dying in order to love."

"I can't live. It isn't right. I can't live, or love, or anything without her."

"You're afraid to live and you're afraid to love. You're using her to hide."

"What are you saying?"

"You heard me, you're runnin'. On the run your whole life. What the devil are you running from? What is it, man? What the fuck has you so spooked? Come on, man, speak. You got to face yourself. It's the only way. Didn't she say to you, 'nothing disappears, Daddy'? Whatever is chasing you—"

"No, stop! How do you know that?"

"Know what?"

"What she said, about disappearing?"

"I told you, she came to me. She put her hand on my shoulder and comforted me. She told me many things."

"What do you mean she came to you? What is this?"

"Do you want to know?"

"I don't know. No. Yes. Yes."

"She came to me while I was in a coma."

"That's impossible. You are crazy."

"I am nothing."

"You're worse than nothing. You are a murderer, and now you're trying to sound like a mystical nut."

"She told me about the fog and smoke, and the three pink moons, and she told me about *The Red Balloon*."

"No. No, she couldn't, she's dead. Stop." But it is too late. With the last revelation David breaks. The phone falls to the floor and his head falls to the desk and lands on his arms where his face cannot be seen. The tears of a lifetime soak the hair on his forearms, and the wailing that comes from his entire being makes every molecule of air in the room weep. And the wind, the blessed wind, cries *mercy* and brushes over his body.

Randy feels the gust of mercy and closes his eyes in reverence. In silence he thanks Emily and marvels at what has just happened. He knew the storm would return but felt sure it would contain less fury. He does not see David raise his head and look at him, but he feels something penetrate the plexiglass and touch his face. David's words bring him back to the room.

"What else did she tell you?"

"It doesn't matter, David." This is said with genuine kindness, and David feels it.

"You're right, it doesn't. And you're right about me using her to hide. Right now, I don't hate myself so much. I can't quite believe that, or trust it, but I feel something else is in me now, some other feeling I don't know."

"That's beautiful, man, truly beautiful. I feel it with you."

"You were in a coma?"

"For three months."

"Three months? And she came to you?"

"She did."

"She came to you . . . she came to me too. She filled me up, completely."

"I believe you."

A pause takes them over. A pause, not a spell. They sit there, three feet apart, separated by two inches of plexiglass, basking in the treasure that is revealed in such moments. The treasure that cannot be divided.

David speaks then, to Randy, the room, and the wind, his voice calm and sure, not interrupting the pause. "Emily is not dead, is she? She's alive."

Randy smiles. "Your Emily is very much alive, brother. So alive."

"But she's not my Emily, is she? She's our Emily."

"She belongs to the world now."

"And to love, right? She belongs to love."

There is no need for Randy to respond. The pause grows beyond the walls, beyond the prison. They each feel the sweet air of mercy fill their lungs. And had they eyes to see, they would have seen Emily cartwheel through the plexiglass, laughing and singing their praise.

Chapter 53

Day 22—Conversation 6

The ground of being is slippery, and David is not done falling. He no longer falls forever, but when he hits bottom, the ground is hard, bitter; Emily is gone.

Human beings find it impossible to hold the goodness of life for long. Love is the most fleeting of all. A veil every bit as blinding as wildfire smoke covers the eyes of the people. They trip over their own feet and fall again and again.

David arrives at the prison not realizing smoke from his mind is burning his eyes. All he sees is destruction. He cannot name it, but he senses something is incomplete—the wheel has hit a rut in the road.

. . .

"You've been gone for days, why you keep disappearing? Where you been?" David will not speak, and Randy, taken by surprise, pounces. "Oh, I see, here we go with the silent treatment again. I thought we was past that shit. You been sittin' around feeling sorry for your pitiful self? What's up with you wasting time on that? Come on, talk, let's have it, give it to me."

David stares into the ether and says, almost absentmindedly, "You should be dead. You're the one who should be gone."

"You're right about that."

His energy builds and he says to Randy, "You should be going insane."

"Sure, I get it." Randy taunts David; he gives him a smug look and smirks and rolls his eyes to the ceiling for emphasis.

David bites. "Horseshit!" All pretense of indifference is gone. "You don't get it. You don't. You don't know anything, anything. You think you have some great realization, but you don't know shit. You don't know what it's like."

"You're right. Tell me. Tell me about her. Tell me about being a father."

"No! That's just it. You want me to tell you, you want me to tell you all sorts of things. I won't. You tell me something. You tell me you're sorry. You plead for forgiveness. You've said nothing."

"I can tell you that where I live there is no right and wrong, nothing to forgive—and it is so full, so full of joy that to say I'm sorry doesn't make any sense. Come join me there."

"Join you? You don't get it. You come to me. You give me something. You break down and beg for forgiveness. Say you're sorry."

"I am giving you everything."

"Bullshit. You aren't giving shit. You're hiding behind this glass wall and that spiritual crap."

"What would it do for you?"

"Say it."

"I live in the present. You live in a dream."

"Say it. Say you're sorry, damn it, you murdered my daughter. Say it." For the first time David looks Randy Tanner straight in the eye and holds him there. He feels a new strength, a new entitlement.

Randy feels the change in David, the newfound aggression and shift in the balance of power. He likes seeing David take command but is unaccustomed to losing the edge in a confrontation. A flare of anxiety intrudes into his lungs as he tries to regain control of the floor.

"Why? So you can feel bad for another three years? So you can hobble around, returning to that same spot, that same moment where it all ended? Look at you shufflin' around. You can't sit still for one fucking minute. You're possessed."

"No! So I can stop. So I can love."

"There's always a catch. Always one more thing. Give it up! You're so close. Just give it up and you'll find more love than you knew existed, and forgiveness will be as natural as breathing."

But none of this is natural, and the pace of the exchange picks up speed.

"It isn't forgiveness I'm after."

"Surrender, man. Surrender. Everything is right here. You, me, this space, consciousness, brimming with joy for no damn reason—everything, right here. Emily too."

"That's crap, stop with that. And don't tell me we all knew each other in a past life or I'll go ballistic. Just be real with me. Once."

"No past life, only life dreaming."

"I have a knife in my chest, and the only way I can get it out is to know you have one in yours."

"The only thing in my chest is this love."

"Are you a human being? That's what I want to know."

"I am nothing."

"Damn! Do you feel pain?"

Randy hesitates. He is unsure what he should reveal. What would help? His voice drops and he says, "There is pain." The new tone of humility catches David's attention.

"There is pain. What is that? What the hell does that mean?"

Randy has his chance, but he sidesteps it. He can't let down with David just yet. But the moment is close at hand. "That means pain comes through. Pain is there like any number of feelings and sensations appearing and disappearing in awareness."

"But?"

"But that is not me."

"You're impossible." With that, David throws his hands in the air and quits. He knows he can never win. Why is he trying so hard? What is he after, chasing down the impossible? An apology from a pathological liar? David is judging himself a fool when Randy begins to speak. His voice is defensive and a little shaky at first but softens as he reveals to David more and more of what he asked for.

"You want me to say I'm sorry. You want me to break down and cry and beg for forgiveness and be a real human being and list my transgressions. Where should I start? Am I sorry for being left alone every night from the age of five? Am I sorry my mother came home with one asshole worse than the next who would beat the crap out of me if I made a peep when I heard her screaming? Am I sorry I had no dad? Am I sorry I felt like a worthless turd my whole life? Am I sorry for all the meth and shit and all the poor victims of my rage and insanity? I can tell you this: when I came out of the coma after ninety days, I was clean and sober for the first time ever since I was ten years old. The first time. You think that wasn't strange? In the coma your daughter and other beautiful beings showed me what is real. Believe me, it is breathtaking, beyond anything imaginable. Still, when I woke up it was amazing how quickly I forgot all of that. I didn't really, but I was so overwhelmed by the memories of what I had done that I couldn't keep hold of it. And I couldn't forget your daughter and what she'd done for me and what I did to her. And the pain crushed me. Pinned me to the floor."

David hears pain and remorse enter Randy's voice. He feels a person stepping out from behind the camouflage. A person unaccustomed to being heard.

Randy pauses to look closely at David. He senses the sincerity of his presence and continues.

"Do you see these?"

"Tattoos?"

"Look closer. These are scars." Randy pauses, looking with new eyes at the evidence of his self-hatred. He shudders, remembering the blood. "These aren't from bar fights. It's hard to kill yourself in prison. I was on watch. Always somebody watching me. But I tried. Almost pulled it off two or three times. Was I sorry? Did I want to use any drug I could get my hands on to escape? Sorry is a poor word. A real poor word. I kept seeing Emily's face and when I did, my chest broke open like an ice pick had been driven into it. I couldn't get high, I couldn't forget, I couldn't die—no escape, just no possible escape. Day after day of dying. I'm no Christian, but I felt those nails pounded into my flesh, I can tell you that."

David feels the nails too. And he feels a wave of sympathy move before he can stop it. He says nothing, but his face changes, and Randy sees it and breathes easier. He takes a drink of water and continues.

"I don't know how long that went on. And then they put me in the hole 'cause I tried to strangle some guard who looked at me cross-eyed. One hundred days of solitary. That was the end. You have to know that my mind did not believe in help of any kind. And still, one day, inconceivably, I asked for help. And it was there, immediate and complete. Complete. The first time was staggering. It was not forgiveness as we think of it. It was release, transformation from living in a shoebox to being a bird in the open sky. Not, oh, you're okay, but being freed and joining the big, beautiful world. Staggering. More tears came out of me then than during all the suffering of remembering all the evil shit I did."

David's body surges, spontaneously revisiting his own experience of grace. Each man pauses to allow those moments to return and wash their pain away once again. When Randy continues, his voice drops an octave. His eyes, holding a family of tears, reach for David's, and accompanied by the voice of genuine regret, he says, "Yes, I'm sorry, David. When I saw you for the first time I wanted to die again. I could see what I had done to you and realized I had never really taken that in. I feel really bad about that. I do. I think it was Rumi who said something like a human being can't really love until innocence has been betrayed and betrayal turns into trust. I think you and I are building trust. I hope so. I'm sorry the world is what it is. I'm sorry there is pain and carnage and death and endings. I'm sorry for what we do to love and one another. I'm sorry for what I did to you, David. I truly am. Thank you for pushing me to say so."

David closes his eyes. He sits quietly for a moment and looks inward to the strange new feeling brewing in his heart: the presence of peace has moved in. When he comes back to the room he smiles and sees Randy looking at him with an expression of kindness brightening his face. David lifts his hand and places his palm on the plexiglass window. Randy meets him there with his own open hand, and David says to him, "Thank you. Thank you."

These words of thankfulness, though unfamiliar, feel like his. And David is pleased. Randy, unfamiliar with receiving thanks, does so. And he is pleased. The room, a stranger to exchanges of kindness, stands still in wonder.

Chapter 54

Day 25—Conversation 7

It is a new day and a different room that greets them. A room with windows and paintings on the walls. Like all rooms, this one has corners, but they are rounded by arms that reach to welcome and hold all that enters. David and Randy arrive at the same moment, and each responds with surprise to the new scenery.

"Hey, look at us! We must have passed the test. We've been moved to the contact room, baby!" Randy is exuberant. "No more telephones and glass walls. The super has blessed us! We good!"

Unable to resist the irony, David adds, "We've been rehabilitated! We're not the bad boys we thought. The guards are giving us the thumbs up."

The two men look at each other with amusement and uncertainty. Each wonders in his private thoughts, what next? Who will they become in this brave new world? They take their seats and look around at the artwork and out the window at the sunlight filling the world. Can they be comfortable with each other in their new surroundings? Can they tolerate good feelings for each other? David says what is true for both:

"Now what? I'm not sure what to do with this." He laughs a nervous laugh and looks to the blue sky for direction.

"Damned if I know. What do people talk about out there? Sports? The weather?"

"Sports. Sure, the Timbers."

"Timbers?"

"Soccer. Portland is crazy about soccer."

"Fucking Portland."

Silence settles in between them. The two men, synchronized in the moment, shift in their seats. The room says yes.

David breaks the silence. "It's strange, sitting with you here, seeing all of you."

"Yeah, I hate that little box, reminds me of the hole. You don't look as old in the light without that damn plexiglass fucking with your face."

"You're bigger than I imagined. Lots of muscles."

"Oh, yeah, they got lots of iron here, lots. And not just around the ankles. Besides, you put on lots of bulk pushing this baby around all day." With that, Randy pats his wheelchair with affection and purrs, "Love ya, honey."

"And your face, it's not deranged like I thought. It isn't. You look like a regular guy."

"You can thank Miss Emily for that. You sure can."

"She made me feel younger too. She had that effect on people. Hey, what's the hole?"

Randy's face grows pale. David has never seen him at a loss for words, and he immediately feels bad for asking. "You don't have to answer that. Sorry, I shouldn't have asked."

"It's all right, David, it kind of fits that we share the suffering, right? Solitary, man. It's a bad place. You lose your shit there. What little sanity people came in with is gone when they come out. It messes with your head, real bad. Damn."

"I guess I've been in solitary the past three years, living in an empty warehouse with rats and spiders. I went a few years without talking to anyone. Jesus, I lost touch with my own voice. I couldn't talk when I came out. I was almost gone, couldn't think. Everything was gone or atrophied."

Randy's hackles raise in a flash. "Oh, I like that word, atrophied. Fancy word. You learn that in med school wearing gloves to keep them hands clean?"

"What? What's with you? You going to mess with me again?"

"Nah, sorry brother, it's just that even talking about the hole brings out the worst. You ain't been in the hole. Nope, the hole is its very own hell on earth. Just hearin' the word makes me shake. I ain't scared of much, but I sure as hell am scared of that place. I can still hear the brothers screamin'. Damn, they screamin' right now. What's worse is when they stop. The living dead. Nothing worse than the scream of the dead." Randy looks through the window into the torment of the past. He shakes his head and moans loud and long.

"You said the other day I was in solitary."

"Oh yeah, you been in the white man's solitary, but that ain't the hole, brother. No way."

"It sure as hell felt like a hole. A bottomless hole. No exit."

"Now don't start quoting Mr. Jean-Paul on me, David. Let's keep it real, like you said. Let me ask you something. When you was locked up, what did you do all day?"

"Nothing."

"Nothin'? Really? Come on now."

"Well, I stared at the wall a lot."

"And?"

"And I walked every morning in the dark to the place."

"Okay, stop right there—you walked every morning. There you go. You was free to be in the outside, walk the bridge, breathe fresh air. That ain't solitary, baby. Fuck no. And what did you see on that walk? Huh?"

"Lots of run-down buildings, homeless camps."

"Okay, you get what I'm sayin'? You saw stuff, buildings and shit, and you saw people. Homeless people. Can you imagine what it's like to not see a single person for years? There's brothers in the hole for years. They never come out alive. I'm talkin' years. I only got a hundred days and it did me in. Fuck me, years with no contact with nobody, you hear the brothers wailin' and you hear the guards fartin' and cussin' and beatin' off, but you don't see nobody, nobody. You got any idea how you can crave to see a human body? No, you don't. And where did you get your food? Huh, where that come from?"

"It was delivered."

"Delivered?" And with the thought of food delivery Randy breaks into a bitter belly laugh. "Delivered! Ain't that rich. Delivered. Hell, ours was delivered too. On a tray. Looked like gravy train leftovers. Make you puke just smellin' it. But we ate it up. We sure ate it up. They put it on a shelf and slide it through. You don't even see a hand, a fuckin' human hand reach through the door. You get what I'm sayin', what it's like to not see no human hand, or skin? You any idea how much you crave to see some skin? I'm talking any skin, white, brown, purple, shit, just some skin, somethin' soft. Nothin' soft in the hole. Nothin' even close to warm. Shit. Why am I talkin' about this? I'm starting to shake."

Randy doubles over and shakes like a terrified animal. As he shakes, he expels a gut-wrenching sound so vile David nearly freezes. It takes everything he has to reach for Randy's shoulder and say softly, "I'm sorry I asked. I didn't mean to put you through that. I just wanted to know something. I don't know why. I'm sorry to upset you. I really am."

Randy sits up slowly, feeling comforted by David's touch. "Thank you, David. It's bad stuff, man. Not human what they do. Look at me now, I'm a fuckin' mess years later."

"I feel for you and the others. It's a crime they did that to you."

"I think you mean that."

"I do, I really do. You should cry. It's good for you."

"I don't do cryin', man. I don't, not in this joint. No way."

"I didn't cry for sixty years. Now I can't stop. Everything is making me cry, even you, this time we have. And good things, especially good things."

"You breakin' up, man, the walls are tumbling down. You been in your own solitary cell. Hell, your cell ain't no bigger than a phone booth. Remember them? Shit, I got it on once in a fuckin' phone booth. We was horny, it was rainin,' and we couldn't wait to make it back to her place so we just deposited our quarter and did it. Shit, when we was done there must have been a dozen people standing outside cheerin'. Damn. But I digress."

"I did it in an X-ray room. With my supervisor."

"No shit? Those are tiny. Get a good picture, doc?"

"No, and we didn't get a standing ovation like you, but the technician gave us the look when we exited."

The two share a good laugh, like old friends might. It changes the atmosphere and brings them out of the trauma spell that was pulling them down the drain.

But they weren't done. David brings them back to the mystery of survival. "Solitary, Jesus. What did you do? I mean, how did you make it?"

"I didn't. I broke like everybody else. I wailed and cursed and finally just . . . just stopped . . . blacked out . . . fell through the fuckin' trap door and just kept fallin'." Once again it pulls at him. The trauma that lives on in the body and never leaves. The pain and panic that at any moment can sneak up and drown its victim in feelings that seem sure to never end.

"You don't see no people, no light, no color . . . nothin' but cement walls everywhere you look and inside your own head—walls closin' in, closin' in, creeping up on you till you can't move an inch to save your sanity. Buried alive, man. Buried alive in cement with a little air bubble, just enough to keep you alive and out of your mind tortured every damn minute. Until you're gone. Gone. I'd never recovered if not for Miss Emily. Bless her soul, and Jarvis."

"Jarvis? Who's Jarvis?"

"Jarvis? You gotta know Jarvis. He's death row in San Quentin, man. He's the real thing. A Buddhist. Writes books, teaches meditation and how to live right to the brothers. He's beautiful, truly beautiful. We been talkin' and writin' for a good time now. He taught me most of what I know. Miss Emily saved me, then Jarvis taught me what's what."

"I'm sorry. About the hole."

"You one of the few white men who can come close to understanding what I'm sayin'. I thank you. I do. But . . . but how . . . how did you come back, David? How'd you come back, man? What made it click?"

"It was a girl."

"Emily?"

"No. A girl on the bridge, the Hawthorne. She was Emily's age, maybe older, ready to jump."

"Woah. The moment of truth. What happened?"

"I don't know. Something happened. Something between us. I can't say. It was some sort of connection. I walked that bridge every day, and every day I looked over the railing and thought of jumping. Every day I disappointed myself."

"What stopped you?"

"Emily. I couldn't bear to never see her face again. Selfish to the end, right?"

"No, man, that was love keepin' you in the game. You're not evil, you just afraid to love, that's all."

"I'm afraid of everything, or at least I have been. Not so much right now."

"And the girl?"

"I don't know. Well, I know she didn't jump that morning. She walked east, I walked west. We agreed to meet there the next morning, but she didn't show, or the next morning either. I'll never know. She could be dead. I hope not. There was something about her, something familiar and some sort of gumption left in her. Sad, really sad. But the strange thing is that when I left her and walked to the other side, I felt this brightness in the world, and I guess in me. I knew I could care for someone. That's when I knew it was time to talk to you. The next day I walked straight from there to the police station."

"You're kidding."

"No, I'm not. I walked straight in and said I wanted to talk to you. Kind of. First I stood there and stared at him, Sergeant Jacobs was his name. I stared at him like I expected him to know what I was there for. Pretty strange, looking back on it. You can imagine the look on his face."

"He must have thought he had a real loose one on his hands."

"Yeah, he was right. That's when it all started unraveling. Jesus."

"Damn right. Unraveling and unraveling as we speak. Fuckin' amazing. I've seen it happen dozens of times, but not quite like this. You on the move, David."

"How did I come back? I can't say. I can't. I only know it wasn't me doing it. It was something else. I had nothing left. But something carried me back and lay me down on the shore in the sand. I don't know, but I am thankful. I am."

"Somethin' carryin' you back for sure. You been in the grave for sure. You was broken and now you're blessed."

"I want to say I don't deserve it, but that seems wrong and small now. And I . . . I don't really believe it anymore after everything, after talking with you."

"Good. It's trash talk. Isn't nobody who don't deserve it. Nobody. Mercy on one and all."

"Mercy. That's what it is . . . mercy. I was condemned. No mercy. Condemnation for life. Exiled from life. Deserving . . . shit."

"It's okay, man, cry . . . it's okay, I'm right here with you. Another condemned, no-good brother. I'm with you all the way. That's it, man, I'm crying with you. Can you believe it? It's a big fuckin' tragedy, and you know what? It ain't just you and me. The fuckin' human race needs to stop, just fuckin' stop and cry for a week or two. Man, we make trouble."

"Especially men."

"Well, yeah, we're the worst."

"We're terrible."

"We do bad shit, we do."

"What's wrong with us? Why do we break everything?"

"Don't know, man. I guess we just real scared. Scared of dyin'."

"We're worms in the mud afraid some robin is going to come by and eat us up."

"Lights out. Breakfast of champions."

"Survival of the worst. Not much hope, is there? We never know when to stop. Never enough."

"Just a little bit more. Right? But I tell you, man, there lots of good brothers in here. Lots. And if there's good brothers in a place like this . . . What?" Randy sees David leave. He watches as his face goes blank and something new comes over him, a ghost or a phantom. He leans toward David and says, "What is it, man, what came over you? You took a dive."

"I wish . . . I wish I could talk to my mother. She just popped into my mind now. Why? Doesn't that sound trite? It's always the mother."

"No, man, I talk to my mother all the time. Mothers are at the heart of it all, for better and for worse. But you gotta love 'em. They precious and most of 'em been treated like dirt, bad as anybody, worse maybe, even if they all dolled up fancy, hair done real nice. They in a prison too."

"I think my mother was in solitary."

"Yeah, that kind of solitary make you crazy, real crazy, like slow cookin', you lose everything little by little and don't even know it till it's too late, and then comes the clincher: thinking it's your own damn fault. That's the nail in the coffin, buried alive. I'm sorry for your mom, and my mom. Man, it was too much, too fuckin' much. What happened, man?"

"She killed herself. Shit, I can't talk . . . sorry . . ."

"No, brother, I got all day."

"Ha. You do, don't you?"

"I surely do."

"I don't really want to talk about her, I just want to feel for her. Lately . . . lately I find myself feeling for a lot of people, people I don't know. Everyone I look at, I can see they're up against something big, really big, too big. For her it was too big. She went to sleep spooned up on the front seat of the car in the garage with . . . with the motor on."

"How old was you?"

"Nine or ten, I think."

"Oh, brother, that's rugged, real rugged. I am sorry, David, sorry for you, just a little guy. Shit, that's when I started drinkin'. Pain, pain go the fuck away. My mom drank more than me, drank herself into the grave. Look, now I can't look at you, I'm lookin' everywhere but at you."

"How old were you?"

"Sixteen. Orphaned at sixteen. On the streets, man, hustlin' for everything. My daddy died down the hall, they carved him up good. Mama drowned herself in the booze and yours truly set out to get back at the world. Revenge was the only thing worth livin' for. Mercy."

"Mercy?"

"Yeah, mercy."

"What is it?"

"Who can say, man, who can say? Can't really say what it is. It sure as hell ain't that Christian sugar lollypop people suck on all day. Nope, it ain't that shit. It ain't forgiveness, really, I don't think. I don't know, it's just some sort of huge acceptance, being taken in, fully taken in, beloved, fuckin' beloved, if you can believe that shit. Fuckin' unbelievable. Beloved. Don't that break your ribs? Beloved."

The two men sit together speechless, trying to comprehend, perhaps feel, the touch of mercy. They feel the longing of the soul for that tenderness. But neither can remember it, nor has either ever known in the cells of the body that he is beloved. They stare off into the wild blue sky while their souls search the interior universe for a shred of that love they might have overlooked. They do not find what they are looking for, but to their astonishment, music fills the air. Music, and the luscious voice of mercy singing their names.

Chapter 55

Day 26—Conversation 8

David and Randy sleep peacefully that night. They dream of worlds populated with kindness. Randy's dream takes him to a field of sunflowers. He is wandering in a field of many suns when his mother appears and walks slowly toward him until she stands before her boy. Once there she takes Randy's hands and holds them to her heart. Randy wakes from his dream, spellbound.

. . .

"Look at me," David exclaims. "My eyes are red and swollen. Jesus, I keep crying. I think it's stopped and then here we are again. Wetting the bed for Christ's sake! Sorry, you must be tired of this."

"No sorry, man. No sorry, that cryin', that the real thing. What you expect leavin' off yesterday talking about our mamas and traumas? Of course, we cryin'. Wait a minute, Jesus, I just remembered my dream from this morning. The craziest dream I ever had. I mean crazy. Woke up and couldn't get back to sleep. My mama came to me, man. We was in a field of sunflowers. She came out of the flowers and took my hands and brought them to her heart. Filled me with love, David. Wild!"

"Really? Hey, wait a minute, I dreamed of my mom, too. She

was there just looking at me, really happy to see me. No pain, just joyful, happy to see each other. No wonder I'm crying."

"I don't fucking believe it! We dreamed the same goddamn dream. My mama walked up to me and took my hands in hers. Shit, now I'm gonna lose it. She took my hands and held them to her heart, she did, and I was the happiest fucking kid in the world."

"This is beyond crazy. We're synchronized. We must be dreaming right now. How can this be?"

The new friends sit there together shaking their heads and laughing. Laughing and weeping. Randy cries out, "Mama, Mama," and David echoes him. Goose bumps run down their necks and shoulders to the middle of their backs. They sit in silence marveling at what is feeling more and more like a miracle.

Randy manages to speak. "Man, we speechless. Tongue-tied, happy beyond words."

"I wonder sometimes if it's all a dream. A crazy, mixed-up dream."

"If it is, David, I like this dream. My mama, she looked good, real happy and full of the stuff."

"Mine too. My mom never looked so happy to see me. I'm spinning."

"Ha, you on a merry-go-round! Ain't that fine?"

"So fine, so fine. You know the other astonishing thing?"

"What's that?"

"I have had openings. They're kind of like a dream. Strange, like you leave your body."

"Yeah?" Randy's eyes open wide.

"They seem like lightning. Flashes that seem forever and a second."

"Really?"

"Yeah. I was on the bus on my way down here going crazy with emotions and terrible thoughts. I pretty much fell into a seat, barely hanging on, and I asked for help—haven't done much of that in my life—and instantly this white light flashed, and my body filled with peace."

"You got hit good. Real good. What else?"

"What else?"

"Yeah, other openings, you said you'd had others. Tell me."

"Oh, I can't remember, exactly. It all gets fuzzy. I think one was in a dream, but I'm not sure. I think Emily was in it and everything just opened, and the universe seemed like a baby kangaroo in its mother's pouch."

"That's wild, David."

"And something happened when I was walking over here the first day. I was just walking and suddenly the colors, the colors . . . I can think about Emily and color and all sorts of things and not feel bereft or cheated, just love for her."

"Beautiful man, beautiful. You turned the corner, brother. You in the new frontier."

"Me? Emily and color. Always painting, painting and coloring. She was so in love with color."

"When I was in the coma, she showed me all the colors of the subtle world. Man, it's beauty, real beauty."

"Do you think she'll meet me there?"

"She will, dude. She will. You are toast. Burned to a crisp. The Big G is working your serious soul to the bone, and when your time comes, wow, it will be something else, something else. Emily will be there for you, yes she will. If she was there for a wretch like me, she will surely be there for her daddy."

"Her daddy . . . I hope so. I hope so."

In the time it takes for hope to circle them, Randy's face turns serious. The change in mood is so abrupt it frightens David. But before he can ask what happened, Randy says, "But first, you got to say you're sorry."

"What?"

"You heard me, say you're sorry. Say it."

"To you?"

"To me."

"Not a chance. To you? Fuck you. You fucking . . ." David readies to go after Randy. His teeth are showing and a snarl leaves his mouth.

"Stay in your seat, Doc. You make one move toward me and those guards will be all over us before you get out of your chair, and you'll be on a bus back to Portland for lunch. Be cool, now."

David sits back in his chair, his fists still clenched. "I don't know what got into me. All of a sudden, I saw red."

"You sure did, phew, you was comin' for blood."

"I've been saying I'm sorry for three years."

"No, you haven't. You've been punishing yourself for all those years. Say you're sorry."

David settles. Something takes his hand and brings him calm. "I don't know if I can. Why should I say I'm sorry to you? To you of all people?"

"Because I am you."

"What did you say?"

"I am you."

"Jesus."

"What?"

"That's what I said to her. To the girl on the bridge."

"You was right, too. One being, many faces. Hurt one, hurt 'em all. Simple."

"I was such a bastard to so many people. Especially Claire."

"Who is Claire?"

"Emily's mother. God. I cheated on her. She didn't deserve it. What a monster."

"Hey, you're punishing again. Say you're sorry."

"I'm rotten. I don't deserve forgiveness. I don't deserve to say I'm sorry. I haven't earned the right. What a shit I've been. I'll never forgive myself for what I put her through. She was good. A truly good person, and I hurt her over and over and still she never got rid of me like she should have. Sorry is not enough. I can't. I have to pay for what I've done."

"Come on, that's old script, David. Why you going there now? You're not that special. Sorry to break it to you, but you just aren't. Look around this joint. Shit, look at me, I'm sitting right here with you. This place is full of the world's biggest assholes who have fucked up lots of lives and ended others, and me who killed four on my miserable run, including your beautiful daughter, and we are all saying our regrets and apologies with every fucking breath, and not one of us is forsaken or rejected."

That staggering, impossible truth shakes the room like a tremor of aftershock from a quake. Paintings rattle on the walls, and the air itself trembles in disbelief.

Randy resumes his mission. "But why not accept Claire's love? Or the others?"

"I guess I'm a killer too. I had to kill it. I can't explain it. I just had to kill it."

"Say you're sorry."

"No. Yes, I am so sorry, so sorry, Claire. Claire, I . . . please, I don't know why I was so cruel, I—"

"Say you're sorry. Say it."

"I did!"

"No, you didn't, you're still looking at you. Look at her and say it. Look at Claire. Say it straight to her, give it to her."

"Claire! Claire! What did I do to you? How could I? I am so, so sorry I caused you such pain. Such pain."

"Say you're sorry to love."

"To love?"

"That's right. Say you're sorry to love and to life and mean it."

"I killed that too."

"You did, brother, you did. I did. We did."

"I am sorry. I am. I am." This time David speaks the truth without hanging his head. Without self-loathing. Randy sees the change and lets him know.

"That's it, my man, that's the real thing, a real apology, not the self-pitying bullshit. The real thing. You got there, man. I'm proud of you, real proud."

Randy pauses, but not for long. "We are killers. But we are more than that. We are. And so is love, brother, so is love. Never born, never dies. That's real love. Always waiting for us to stop lyin' and killin' and come on home. Always coaxing us home through our fear and endless stupidity."

"I don't want to destroy anything anymore."

"Okay. Then don't. But you got to love ruthlessly. You got to be afraid every minute and keep lovin'. No easy way. Even the assholes. Gotta love the assholes too."

"The assholes. You and me? Probably have to start with them, us?"

"Right. So, say you're sorry."

"What?"

"Say you're sorry, to me."

"Say I'm sorry to you?"

"Yep."

"You're serious."

"Damn straight I'm serious."

"To you? You want me to say I'm sorry to you? The man who killed my daughter?"

"That's right, say you're sorry to me. The biggest motherfucker you'll ever know. The one who stole your baby girl and ruined your life. Say you're sorry."

"Fuck you."

"Say it."

"No!"

"Come on, I kill you, you kill me. Say it. You're a killer, I'm a killer—you won't meet a soul out there who isn't a fucking killer. We one being, one being, you kill me, you kill everybody, everybody! I kill you, I kill everybody. One being, one love, one life. You kill life, you kill love, you kill it all, every lousy, precious speck."

Randy stops and watches David closely. He can see shame rising in the way David's face twists, trying to find a way to hide. He knows the cost of apology, the searing emotions of an immature conscience, the relentless press of judgment day. He feels for David like a brother and struggles to think of a way to help him release the bonds of love gone bad. As if reading his mind, David looks down at the floor and says, "I can't shake it. So much shame it keeps following me. It'll take the rest of my life to release this."

"I know what you mean, David, I do. Fucking shame sticks like glue. Maybe you think of your mama smiling at you and you'll burn it up. Shame can't survive that kind of love. No way."

David turns in his chair, looking for blue. Too much has changed in him to completely believe the voices of belittlement. He is able to push back now and see how distorted that self-portrait is. Randy has helped; the conversations of the last four weeks have moved mountains. He can't bring himself to apologize to Randy but thinks he can express his gratitude to this strange man he has come to respect.

David turns to Randy and clears his throat, which has already begun to tighten. "There is something. Something here. I don't think I can say it. I don't want to say it out loud, but it is here. I feel something for you. I'm close. You're a real person, and I think I like you. Listen to me stumbling. I must be crazy. Really, really crazy."

"I know, it's all right. I feel it too. Who could have imagined? Tomorrow?"

"Maybe. I have to wait and see. I'm not sure what I'm feeling. Is this what Emily wanted? Am I getting close? First the dream about my mom and then admitting you matter to me. Jesus. What the hell am I doing?"

"You way out past your comfort zone, man. Way out. Love ain't no cozy warm blanket—more like a Kansas twister or somethin' wild like that. Your storm is about to clear, David. I truly believe so. Miss Emily, she smilin' down on you. On us. We blessed, brother, truly blessed, even when it don't feel like it."

David nods. He rises from his chair taller than when he sat down. His back and shoulders straighten and align on their own. He reaches for Randy's hand as he begins to turn his wheelchair for the door. Randy stops and takes David's hand, feels the warmth and vulnerability in that touch. He gives a tender squeeze in return and puts his other hand on top of David's. The two do not speak; their eyes meet and speak for them.

Chapter 56

Day 29—Conversation 9

"Where you been? You said you was comin' the next day. I thought you ran away."

"I'm sorry, I've been sleeping. Couldn't stop sleeping. Dead to the world."

"Man, it's done you good! Look at you, you look twenty years younger, brother, not the beaten man no more. Standing straight, rosy cheeks—man, I don't believe my fuckin' eyes. Did you go get done up with a facial or some shit?"

"Really?"

"Seriously! Where's a mirror? You're standing tall, your eyes are bright and lookin' straight at me. Damn, you've been rehabilitated in prison! Prison done you good."

"Ha. That's a good one. Maybe I should rent a room here and stay a while."

"Good idea, man, good idea. Food ain't too bad. State pays for it—can't beat that."

"You were worried I'd run?"

"I suppose I was. Wouldn't want you to just fuckin' disappear before you get the marchin' orders."

"Marching orders?"

"Yeah, you know, before D-day, as in departure day. Like a proper farewell."

"Oh, I see. For a minute there I thought you were saying something like you've come to care for me, or even need me, like maybe you've been changed by whatever we call this."

"Oh, that shit. Hell, you can't need nobody in this rat hole. Shit, gettin' attached to somebody would be suicide."

"But you said you care about these guys."

"Sure, I care, in a limited way. But I know where the line is. These guys are beautiful people, most of 'em, but sure as shit they could be dead tomorrow or pull a knife or some shit. You can't give too much or you'll be afternoon snack by some spasm of insanity. You can't forget this place is full of animals."

"I think you're as scared as I am."

"Scared? Shit, brother, I faced it all. I ain't scared of these dudes. I just ain't gonna be no fool, you see what I mean?"

"Not them. I think you're scared of me."

"Scared of you? You? You makin' me laugh now. Why I be afraid of some broken-down white doc who stumbled in here lookin' brain dead and needing a shave? Tell me that."

"Because this is different."

"Different? This is the way it is. This is everyday life, you and me, face to face, here today, gone tomorrow."

"Listen to you, all defensive. You're as scared of loving me as I am of loving you."

"Shit, you turn into a psychoanalyst while you was sleepin'?"

"Nope. Just dreaming. I saw your fear and my fear come together.

I'm different—I'm a white, uptight dude. Everything about me is different, except one thing."

"What's that?"

"The love thing. Love is risk, you said it. You're afraid I'll fuck you over."

"Come on, Doc, easy on the reading my mind thing."

"See, there it is, you keep calling me Doc, after I've asked you not to. You keep on reminding me and yourself that I'm this white guy, this white guy in a white coat with a stethoscope around his neck, and don't forget it, because that's where his loyalty is, not with you and sure as shit not with his heart. Who can trust a fucking white man?"

"Well, now you make a good point there, Doc—I mean David. Shit, maybe you make a real good point. Trustin' a white man ain't real smart."

"I don't blame you. I don't trust myself. How do we know I won't go back to Portland, pick up my life, meet a good woman, and forget all about you?"

"We don't. We sure as shit don't. And I wouldn't blame you neither. Why not forget me and this godforsaken place? You should go live your life, man. Live it up, love life, and have a lot of good lovin'."

"But that's it. That's the goddamn temptation and trap. Just another form of love 'em and leave 'em. Thank you very much, Mr. Exemplary Prisoner, I've had a fantastic experience, catch ya later. No, that's the whole problem—the disposable society bullshit. Take off those surgical gloves and throw them away. Next! The white man strikes again. Something has happened here that has changed me.

Maybe it has changed you too. Has it, or am I playing games with myself?"

"No, man, no. You're right. I'm holding back somethin'. Not going all the way. I hate to admit it, but part of me is still that dude thinks nobody ever gonna love this guy. Nobody, much less some rich city doctor who watched me off his daughter. Man, it's there, you right, telling me I am one fuckin' unlovable freak. Damn."

And the wind cried *mercy*.

...

"Now you cryin' again."

"I am."

"Don't want you cryin' for me."

"Too late, asshole."

"Ha. Now that I can take. Mr. Asshole. Randy Tanner, the asshole. That's me."

"Do you like your name?"

"My name? Shit, what kind of question is that?"

"I don't know. I never liked my name and I just realized I kind of like yours."

"You never said my name out loud."

"I know. I'm sorry. It feels wrong. Like if I do it will seal the deal."

"Yeah. I can't quite say yours without doin' the tighten up. What's the word? Intimate, too intimate. Shit, we gonna be intimate? Man, I don't know. Easier to love than be intimate. You know what I'm sayin'?"

"Yep. You can make up love in your head—it's easy to fool

yourself—but intimate, I don't know. You have to lay yourself more open. It's a gamble, not a sure thing. Maybe something you make with somebody. Right?"

"Yeah, that sounds right. No wonder. How the fuck do you do that when all the while there's that little motherfuckin' kid sitting there inside, lurkin' there feelin' like shit, terrified, and no fuckin' way in hell is he gonna be loved, or liked, or gamble on shit but whether or not the bottle of whiskey gonna get him rocked and make it all go away. Damn that kid. That poor fuckin' guy."

"About now someone makes an off-color joke, and we just speed away and bypass all that. Just leave him, that little shit, to rot. Poor fucking lost kid. Why can't we love him?"

"I don't know, man. That there's a tall order. Way tall."

"Maybe that's why we took to each other. Maybe we spotted that kid in one another a mile away and felt some affinity, some sympathy."

"That could be. That could be. Maybe we also spotted somethin' else, like courage."

"I don't know. Not me. Not courage. You, I see it. Huge courage—who you are, what you do. I really respect you, I do."

"Shit, no one ever said nothin' like that to me before. They called me exemplary, but never said the *r* word. Never. Man, that's somethin'. Thank you."

"It's true."

"And you know what? There's another thing, David, you're honest. That's rare. Especially in a white man. Very rare."

"I'm a reforming liar. Lied to everybody, even my patients. Terrible thing is, I didn't even know it half the time. Just automatic.

One hundred percent. Made it all up on the fly. Bullshit everywhere, flying this way and that."

"Not now. You an honest man. You are."

David wipes the tears from his eyes with his shirtsleeves. He wishes he could wipe them away permanently. "Thank you, maybe so. These tears sure as fuck feel honest."

"They tell the truth. Mercy."

"Mercy . . . I wanted to hear myself say it. I like it. What is it? Why is it so comforting to hear you say it?" David said the word silently to himself. It sounded like a church bell ringing in a town square. His body said yes and followed the vibration into the clouds.

"I don't know, man, but I have the same feeling. Comfort. Something relaxes way deep. Way deep. Like you stop holdin' your breath. Ah . . ."

"Yeah, like the hammer isn't waiting to fall."

"The judgment hammer sucks. Delivers one hell of a blow, don't it?"

"There are days it's relentless."

"Won't let up. No mercy."

Randy and David shake their heads in dismay, thinking of the painful moments of no escape from the onslaught of attacks. They recoil even now, hearing the echo of those voices of condemnation.

Grateful to feel accepted sitting with Randy, David says, "It helps to have someone to cry with."

"Yes, it does, yes, it does."

"It's a first for me."

"Me too, brother, me too. Maybe having this time together those voices will ease off." Randy takes a deep breath and sighs a deep, long sigh, like a man shedding the burdens of a lifetime. And then he continues, his voice lighter and brighter. "We into the mystic now, David. Tears of sorrow, tears of joy. Which is which? Don't matter. Surely don't matter, we here in the mystic, that's all."

"What do you mean?"

"Well, I just mean it's a fuckin' mystery, a real fuckin' mystery. Somethin' is happenin', and you ain't makin' it happen and I ain't makin' it happen, but it sure as fuck is happenin'. Somethin' big, some force right here in this room, right here between us. I read about it, but I never been part of it like this."

"But why do you call it mystic? What's the mystical thing?"

"Because, brother, it so big. So big. You can feel it, man, can't you? Right? Sure, it's bringin' us home to the source, you and me, two undeserving motherfuckers like us, accepted, fuckin' accepted and brought in even though we all know we is unacceptable, totally unacceptable. Damn if that ain't the mystery."

David scratches his head. He looks puzzled, lost, and says to Randy, "I don't get it. I don't get the mystical thing. I can't even accept forgiveness. But even though my mind is fighting it, I seem to have forgiven you. It's crazy. I didn't do anything, I don't think. I didn't wake up one morning and decide it, you know, all that choice bullshit. But it's happened. I'm different. I don't hate you."

"That's what I'm sayin', it's a mystery, goddamn mysterious how somethin' bigger than our sorry, petty self is at work. And it's more than forgiveness. Much more. It's mercy, it's bein' fully, completely embraced, held like a motherfuckin' newborn. Shit, that more than a dude can take in."

Several minutes pass as both men try their best to understand, to take in this most unlikely reality. Each is left bewildered in his own way, having never felt belonging. Face-to-face with that which is beyond understanding, they look like two little boys sitting on the front steps of their house, dumbfounded by the world.

David speaks in a halting voice. "I've never been able to accept stuff. I've spent my life running away, resisting the truth. Hell, I worked on about three thousand hearts fighting to fix them and fight off death for a while. I'm not sure I can accept this. It's too good, it can't last. I don't know, here I am feeling like I'll fail at this too."

"Must be why they call it mercy, man. Mercy. Everything fails, this body, our dreams, our best intentions, and love, don't forget love—we fail miserably at love. Breaks your fuckin' heart over and over. I guess that's the whole fuckin' trip, we big enough to sense this mystical somethin', this great love, but we can't reach it. Fuck, we can't even name the goddamn thing. But sure as shit, we return, we make the round trip, it brings us into its fold, and we can't comprehend it, but that don't matter. We are accepted and loved no matter what. In the meantime, it seems we go on doin' stupid shit and thinkin' we in control. What a fuckin' joke that is. What a fuckin' joke." Randy laughs and slaps his knee. But the laughter is short-lived as his words catch up with him and he feels remorse pile up in his chest.

"Right, everything I thought, everything I thought was in my control seems like the biggest lie of all. How could I fool myself so completely? How do I know I'm not still doing it? It seems impossible. Maybe I'm just making this up too. I don't think so, but how do I know?"

"Man, you overthinkin' it now. Over the top. You know because we doin' this together, you and me and the force. You know, and I know, because you can feel it. Right? You feel somethin' in your heart you ain't makin' up. Right? And you know it because you and me and this room are different now. We different, and we didn't make it happen by ourselves. No way. We just a couple of hopeless assholes—how we gonna make this happen? Oh yeah, it real, just that now your big white brain winding up the doubt wheel. Startin' to spin the doubt. Here it comes."

"It's true. I hate it. Emily amazed me all the time with how doubt-free she was. So beautiful. She jumped from the chair to the couch, squealing all the way, and when she missed and tumbled, she laughed even harder. Once she said to me there are no mistakes. You can imagine what my head did with that one."

"Oh yeah, I can see it now in that bubble over your head. Why you cryin'?"

"Because I can think of her and not feel sad. I can see something besides tragedy. I can feel her life and joy . . . and maybe . . . maybe, I'm feeling mercy. Maybe."

"That there is beautiful, Doc, sorry, David, truly beautiful."

"What? What happened? Your face fell like you saw a ghost or something."

"I want to feel that for my mama."

"Oh, your mama." David hears the tenderness in Randy's voice. He feels the intimacy of the moment grow deeper when Randy looks up at him with thanks brimming from his eyes.

"Yeah, ever since that dream, I can't stop thinkin' of her. How beautiful and kind she looked in that field with those sunflowers.

And when she touched me, man, I melted, completely melted, felt so good. Shit, I don't remember her touching me except to whip my ass with that fuckin' hairbrush. Sometimes I would have been glad to be beaten. Any kind of touch would have been better than her cold shoulder."

The memory of his mother turning her back on him and leaving the house flashes in David's mind and he shudders. Trying to get away from that cold front, he says to Randy, "Tell me more. What's going on with you and your mama?"

"Mama. It's easier to say your name than my mama's. I'm watchin' you and I see you lovin' your baby girl and takin' her in, all the way in, and I realize I ain't doin' that. I ain't. I forgive my mama, but I ain't takin' her in. I got a lot of work to do here still, brother, a lot of work. I thought I was all good with Mama, but I ain't. You helped me see that, David. Thank you. Damn, I'm sorry, Mama, I'm truly sorry."

"Your face is different. I've never seen it without some anger. It looks relaxed, kind of peaceful."

"Me peaceful? Now that's a miracle, a fuckin' miracle."

"That's it, isn't it? Taking in the good. Taking in the love. I get a little hung up on the taking part. I've been such a taker, never giving. How about receiving, how about we call it receiving?"

"Call it whatever you like, David. I'm swimmin' in the realization. Swimmin'."

"Sure, I get it. We could both use a good soak in that water. I thought I just had to come down here and talk with you and it would all be done. I'd be cured. What a fantasy that was. This is more like a beginning, isn't it? More like a start, a fresh start—but lots of work ahead to really live it in the world. To really bring this kind of care to my life."

"Looks like it's ongoing, man. A never-ending dance. Man, and I thought I had arrived. Just another doorway, but I think we may be close, real close to something beautiful."

"I hope so, I really do."

Randy undoes the brakes on his wheels and puts on his gloves, preparing to leave. David watches him and sees that Randy is slower than usual. He looks bothered by something, and for the first time David can recall, insecure, hesitant.

"Hey, what's up?" he asks, not sure he wants to open up something just as they are leaving.

"There is one more thing, David."

"Uh-oh, what's that?"

A small voice crawled out of the little boy Randy. "I wish . . . I wish you'd say my name, man."

"Oh, Jesus, I'm sorry . . . I want to, I try sometimes, and I just can't turn the page. I'm really sorry. I don't mean to hurt you. It's just got me, as if I'm holding on to that last branch. I don't know why. I am sorry."

"Okay. I get you. It's all right, we got plenty. More than that, we got lots of plenty. I . . . I just wanted to say it, you know, just get it out. Besides, ha, you said it, you said, 'I'm sorry!'"

"Wow! I did. I said it without thinking or fretting. Holy cow, I said it. I'm sorry it took me so long. I am. And thanks. I'm glad you told me about your mama, I am. That helps me realize how much

I have to reconcile with my mom. One thing at a time. Okay, see you tomorrow."

"See you tomorrow, brother."

"Are we going to hug?"

"Not allowed. Strictly forbidden. I put my hand on my heart."

"I put my hand on my heart."

"It is good."

"It is."

Chapter 57

Day 30—Conversation 10

"Hi." David's greeting is relaxed and comes with a genuine smile.

"David, you lookin' good, my man. Real good."

"You are too. You still have that peaceful look. Have you been talking to your mama and taking in her love?"

"Little by little, brother. Breath by breath. I'm tryin' and she's willin'. We showin' up."

"That's so fine. Never too late, even for us assholes."

"Ha, that's right, never too late. Open the door and there it is. There it is. Now even my mama cryin'. Never thought I'd see the day. Never."

"My mom is close. She's smiling."

"That's good, man, real good. Ain't we the lucky ones? Damn."

"We are, we definitely are, but I feel melancholy today. I don't know why, but I do. My mind is trying to dream. Maybe my mood is a leftover."

"Some people say you can dream your life."

"No, this is an actual dream, when I'm sleeping. I don't know if I really have the dream and I can't remember, or if somehow the dream is trying to happen, or maybe it is happening, but I can't quite get there."

"Wild."

"Well, interesting that you say that, because in a strange way it does feel wild, or big. It feels like everything inside the dream is, I don't know, swelling, or trying to."

"Like the space wants to open?"

"Maybe. Yeah, something like that. Like it wants to go from nothing to something but can't quite. Or maybe I can't quite open up enough to let it be."

"You've had this dream more than once?"

"Many times. More than half a dozen."

"Maybe you're pregnant." A grin spreads across Randy's face. He winks and chuckles to himself.

"Pregnant?"

"Yeah, pregnant, you know, about to give birth."

"Wow, I never thought of that. I wondered if I was trying to dream someone else's dream and it hasn't quite lined up yet. Something like that. But pregnant?"

"Why not? Kinda fits, don't it? You about to be born again, as they say. Born again, brother—get down on your knees and praise the Lord. Ha, how about that, one of us busy dyin' and one of us born again into this crazy old world. Man, how about that?"

"You look like you'd jump up and start dancing if you could, kind of like Emily dancing in the living room."

"I can still boogie in this buggy, you watch." And Randy's body from his waist up begins to roll and swing to the music of the spheres. His head bobs and his hands raise above his head waving to the sky.

"Ha, look at you, twist and shout, do the monkey." David gets to his feet and does the twist without the shout, although his body is so stiff the twist is more like a half turn.

"Come on, David, shake it, let it roll, baby, roll. Yeah, just like that. Every particle is dancing the dance, whirling and diving, becoming and dissolving. Wow. And what did that guy Rilke say? The whole shebang 'is shuddering with joy!' Shuddering with joy. Hallelujah, born again!"

"Shuddering with joy. I've been shuddering with dread." With that, David sits down quickly, and lets out a gust of air.

"That you have, but that dread is fallin' away."

"I guess it is."

"Yeah, it is. Staggering, baby."

The music returns to the spheres and both men lean back and close their eyes to take in the staggering possibility of happiness. David's melancholy burns off like morning clouds and though his body is stiff, it softens into the moment's goodness.

Randy's deep, warm voice breaks the spell. It seems to come from far away, a carrier pigeon delivering a message. David opens his eyes and is surprised to see Randy's face turned serious and intense.

"I was dreamin' last night too, David."

"Oh, yeah? What was your dream?"

"You ready?"

"Uh-oh, sounds serious."

"Emily came to me last night."

"She did?"

"Yep, in a dream."

"Really? What was it?"

"Lots of like wind chimes, beautiful sounds, and this real tender feeling in my chest. I couldn't see her, but she spoke to me. It was her voice."

"I'm a jealous guy. I can see it—you look serious but at ease. Man, what I'd give to hear her voice."

"Maybe she was singing. I don't know."

"I may have to hate you again."

"Ha. I know, I'm sorry, you'll have your dream. It's coming, that's for sure. She's with you, you just can't hear her yet. You will, you will."

"I do wake up feeling pretty darn good these days, peaceful and almost content. That's why the melancholy surprised me this morning. You think she's talking to me in my sleep? No way."

"Sure do. Absolutely!"

"Jesus. What did she say?"

"To you?"

"No, no, to you . . ."

"Ready, David?"

"Probably not."

"Time for you to go."

"What?" David hears the whistle blow and sits upright in his chair.

"She said, you should go home now."

"Now? Today, just like that?"

"That's what she said."

"I don't know."

"Maybe you do know. What, you gonna stay here forever?"

"Well, no, I . . . I guess not. I had thought in a while I might go home, but this is so abrupt."

"Things change on a dime, man. She gave us a full moon together."

"Has it been thirty days?"

"A full moon. The whole cycle. You and me, gabbin' away, a couple of old farts making shit up while the moon watched and took off her clothes. Ha."

"Geez, I don't know. We were really getting humming, weren't we?"

"We have it going, Doc, we really do. You're a new person, look at you, fuckin' amazing. You should get yourself a new suit. Truly."

"You look pretty good yourself, and how about that, you can call me Doc and I don't want to kill you. Fucking hard to believe."

"Fuck is right. Fuck is the only word that does it all justice, right? Fuck. Fuck says it all—the awe, the beauty, the outrage, the amazement, the protest. Fuck just covers everything, don't it? Maybe you can still fuck, man. Maybe you can still have some good lovin' before you're done. What do you think?"

"I think I want an ice cream cone."

"I'm talking divine, erotic love and you're talking ice cream cones? Man, you got a long way to go."

"I'm afraid. I have no idea how to make love with a woman. None. The thought of it makes me shake. Brings back terrible memories. Not ready for that by a long shot."

"All right, all right. Of course, you scared and don't know nothin' about really bein' with a woman. I see you tremblin' now. I get that for sure. But you ain't alone. Not alone at all. You'll have help. Just get on your surfboard and ride that motherfuckin' wave of fear. Ride it! Ride it! What else do you want?"

"I want a dog."

"A dog? Man, I don't get you. You can have cosmic love and you want to suck on a scoop of ice cream and pick up some puppy dog's poop. Man."

"Dogs are magic. Emily wanted a dog so badly and I never got one for her. Too much work, I said. What an idiot."

"Don't start with the punishing, David."

"You sound like somebody's father. Hell, I'm old enough to be your grandfather."

"I'm old enough to be your little boy."

"What an odd pair."

"A couple of genuine freaks."

They were glad to have a laugh, a break, no matter how brief, from the message hanging in the air.

"You can have the mystic stuff. I'm not big enough for all that. Besides, Emily taught me it's all right here in the little things if it's anywhere. I want an ordinary, tactile, gritty, sensual, erotic life. I've been walking the thin line so long. I want to breathe the air and feel hot and cold. Stuff like that."

"I get it. I get it. Sounds like the real thing, man, the genuine juice. Besides, I can't argue with Miss Emily. She knows her shit."

"I want to listen to a woman's voice. I want to listen in the dark."

"Oh, yeah, I can hear her now."

"I can't just say sorry. I've got some making up to do. Some sweet talking. I'm going to have to give a little and see if this big bad life will give me a little kiss."

"I imagine she'll give you one big wet one!"

"Not so fast."

"One big wet French kiss!"

"I just want a smile. And I want to care for someone. Really care, day after day. I don't know if I can."

"I hear you, brother. I do, that's beautiful. It gonna happen, I know it."

"Thanks. You'll be out someday. What do you want?"

"No, I ain't getting out. Not this dude. This is home sweet home, this is. Nope, I won't get out. They won't let go of me."

"But I thought you only got twenty years. Besides, you are the model prisoner. They have to let you out. I'll testify at your hearing."

"You would?"

"I would."

"Wow. That is very kind, David. Damn, that is so kind. I can't talk, can you believe it? Me, speechless?"

"You aren't speechless, Randy, your eyes are saying everything."

"Did you just say my name?"

"I did? I did! And I didn't even plan it, it just flew out. Holy cow!"

"Ah, holy, holy, that's the best gift, brother, the best."

"Maybe I can care. And I can care for you. I can write letters to the warden—he thinks I'm big time. It will make a great story for him to retire on."

"Yeah, he would dig that, he would. But I don't want you to, and it will never happen. They won't let me go. They don't know how to let people go. I got twenty for killing Emily, but you're forgetting the others. I got life sentences stacked up like pancakes. Anyway, the whole thing is way too political. They'll never let a villain like me back out into society. I'm a menace, remember?"

"You deserve to be free."

"Come on, man, I thought we had an understanding. I'm as free as a bird. I have everything and now I have you."

"But—"

"No buts. You leave and go kiss the sky, like Jimi said. Go kiss the sky and taste the world and maybe even find yourself an old lady. An old, old lady."

"Very funny."

"Ha. And I got work to do. Lots of brothers in here that need me, that want to find the truth before they rot from the inside. I got lots to keep me busy. Beautiful souls here, man, truly beautiful."

"Don't forget your mama."

"My mama . . . that's right, I need to sit down and write my mama a letter. I got to learn to, how did you say it? To receive her love. Damn. That gonna take some doin'. But I am lookin' forward to that, I am. I can almost feel her now."

"You've taken me in."

"That I have. And I am grateful. I am."

"I'll write."

"Don't."

"Don't?"

"That's right."

"Why not?"

"Don't look back. This is a warm-up for you. Don't look back. Get out there and groove."

"Bullshit. This is it. Right here in this rock, this, between us, whatever it is, this conversation, it's bigger than us, it's made me over. It's . . ."

"Magic?"

"Yes, kind of like that. I can't really put it into words, but I'm different. We're friends, right?"

"That we are, David, good friends. Emily is happy."

"Do you think so?"

"Oh yeah. Real happy. She's dancing and singing."

"That would be the best. I could die at peace if that were true."

"It's nothing but the truth, David."

"But I can come see you, right?"

"Best not to. Just go live, make some friends, have some ice cream. Just remember me like this. What we are now. Friends."

"I don't get it. Why not visit?"

"There's another thing."

"What's that?"

"My liver."

"Your liver?"

"Too much bad shit. Meth leaves a stain. Hep C is on the move."

"Oh, Randy."

"You said it."

"Said what?"

"You said my name again. You said my name."

"I didn't even think to. We're naming each other, aren't we?"

"We are indeed. There you go, the last rope is undone. The ship is sailin', we brothers now."

"Brothers. I like that. But I don't want you to die, I don't."

"Thank you, David, thank you. I see you care, and I truly thank you. It's a miracle. But it's coming. Not much time, not much. The big ferry coming for this worthless shit factory. Coming to carry me home. And now I can die in peace."

"Damn, I'm sorry. Nothing they can do? They have good treatments."

"Nothing. Don't want no treatment. Just let me go when the time is right. Just let me go."

"What will happen to you?"

"Me? They'll probably throw me out back with the old shoes. Let the microbes dine on me for a time."

"Stop."

"Oh, they have some old fire-snorting incinerator they throw you in if you got no family, flush what's left down the toilet for all I know. Maybe they'll scatter me over the prison garden, make me into fertilizer, bein' as how I've been the model inmate for all these years. Great word ain't it, inmate? Fuck, who cares? I'll be off. I'll be long gone, off to Beulah Land. Amen. Don't look so damn sad, man, and don't fucking cry."

"It's not that."

"What then?"

"I'll come for you."

"What?"

"I'll come for you, for your ashes."

"You will?"

"I will. I'll put you around the grave site with Emily and at Hug Point if that sounds good to you."

"You will?"

"Yes, I will."

"I . . . I . . . Jesus."

"Whoa, steady there, Randy, you'll fall over."

"Man, if I weren't strapped into this buggy, I'd be on my knees now. On my knees! That's where I should be, down on my knees, overwhelmed. You'd really do that for me?"

"It's a promise. Go ahead, cry. Emily always said it's good for the soul."

"Shit, man, I'm overcome, no one, no one ever . . . You'll really come for me? That's the kindest thing ever."

"Yes, I will. One way or another. I may get to Beulah Land before you, you know."

"Damn, this is too much, man. This is harder to take in than Mama's love. Look, now I'm the one who can't look you in the eye. I'm looking at the floor, the ceiling, everywhere but at you. Damn, this a lot to take in, gonna take me some time to take this shit in."

"I know what you mean. This whole time, what's happened between us and inside too, it's astonishing. I don't believe in miracles, but this comes really close. We're both different."

"That we are. And we ain't done—we got a lot of work to do. Hey, maybe I'm not the eternal asshole I been sayin' I am. How 'bout that? Maybe I'm just a regular dude. Wait till I tell the brothers this. Just wait. Randy Tanner, Regular Dude."

"A regular guy, I like that, Randy. Sounds good to me. What a relief."

"Hey, I can look at you again! I'm not crawlin' on the floor lookin' for a crack to hide in."

"I like it when we're just two regular guys looking into each other."

"Two dudes trying best we can to take it in."

"Mercy."

"That's right."

Randy looked out the window and shook his head. His eyes were glistening when he turned and said to David, "Thank you, David. Thank you."

"You're welcome, Randy. You're welcome and thank you. For everything. We have our lives back, more than ever, I think. Don't you?"

"Yes, I do. I surely do. Listen to me, short on words. Nearly fucking speechless."

"Ha, not for long, I bet. I . . ."

"I know, I know. Ain't no words. It's okay, your face says it all. A lot of love in those eyes, a whole lot of love, David. Hope you're seein' the same in mine."

"It's there, I see it. Let's take it in, best we can, one last time."

"Let's do that, brother, let's do that. Man, this ain't easy."

"So, this is it?"

"Yeah, this is it. The end, but not really. We'll go on, we're friends, you and me, what an unlikely pair. Fuck, the guards are even cryin'. They been nicer lately."

"We are friends. We are. I've never had a friend, really."

"Me neither, brother. Ain't that crazy? Not a real friend. This is good, real good."

"I don't want to go. Emily said I should?"

"She did. Emily and her lady friends are calling the shots. She said it's time. She said not to worry. She said we are beautiful, can you believe it? The wicked and the dead turned beautiful? How about that shit?"

"Yeah, how about that?"

"You ready to love?"

"I . . . I don't know. Maybe. Maybe."

"I'll be living with this for a while. Letting it sink in. And I thought I came here to help you. Damn. Okay, I'm out. I can't look at you no more. Time to go look at some walls."

"Okay. Damn, this is . . ."

"Hug?"

"What about the guards? Don't want you going to solitary for a hug."

"Fuck the guards. They probably out there huggin' and cryin' anyway. That's good, that's real good. Here's a hug that will last a lifetime. Okay, this is it. You ready?"

"No."

"Yes, you are. Come on now. Here we go, brother. You go your way, I go mine, but we're brothers now, wherever we go. We are. We have each other."

"Goodbye, Randy."

"Goodbye, Doc. Farewell."

"Hey!"

"Sorry, sorry, look at me, suitin' up the armor already. Sorry, David, it's a tough world out there. Okay, here we go, this is the real thing. Love you, brother."

"Love you . . ."

The two men turn and leave. The room shimmers, bursting with love. Mercy follows the two prisoners of war down the hallways and into the freedom of their separate worlds. The prison guards salute Randy and David as they pass; all eyes are red and moist. Mercy washes over them.

PART FOUR

LOVE

I want to love the things
as no one has thought to love them
—Rainer Maria Rilke

We must love one another or die.
—W. H. Auden

Chapter 58

Dear Ma. Damn, that was hard. A simple endearment took me days to write. I spent hours staring at the paper. Dozens of pieces of that paper ended up in the recycling can all crumpled up. I've spent years avoiding you. Years trying to forget you and everything I can't forget. I don't know where to look for you. I don't know where to begin. All I can think to do is call out your name, and maybe you'll come looking for me. Maybe you'll call out my name and we'll find each other. It all feels impossible. Maybe it is, but at least I've started. At least this didn't end up in the trash.

Dear Ma. Did I really call you Ma? That's what I remember, but it sounds odd, and I don't know, too close, too young for what I feel. Can I work up to that? Just call you Mom for now? Maybe for a long time.

I'm learning to love, Mom, I am. Still loosening the grip, but it's happening. I'm not the thin line I was, operating on the world, dissecting the hearts of others. I'm learning to feel for another person, to care. I can love you, and hate you, and be all mixed up about you. But the hardest of all is to need you. That's what is most terrifying.

I'm writing to bring you back, Mom, even if I can't find you. I'm writing to tell you about me, even if I can't find me. Even if you are happier elsewhere. I'm writing to say I'm sorry. I'm sorry because I struggled to begin this letter with an affectionate greeting. I'm sorry that for so many years I told the world I was a motherless child.

Worse than that, I told myself you left because you didn't want me, that you died glad you'd never see me again. It isn't true, is it? You didn't leave, did you? You were taken by a gang of memories and emotions. An old-fashioned gang with switchblades, chains, and bloody teeth. They dragged you off past dark alleys into oblivion. I couldn't watch.

Now I know you didn't want to keep hurting me. You knew the gang of nightmares and terrors was coming for me. Coming to take me away. And you fled to a place you hoped they would follow and leave me alone. I know this, but it's still tough. I see you lying there, I see the blood on your cheek, your soft cheek. Your eyelids are shut. I can't look at tulips.

. . .

Your granddaughter was all love. I can't give you her name. I can't let you have it yet. I'm holding back. You haven't earned it. Listen to me. As she died, she asked me to love. It was easy to love her, though I failed many times. It was insanely hard to love her killer, but I found I could. Can you believe that? Maybe you can. Maybe you were there.

I'm writing to you because you are the last stone in my heart. Because you haven't spoken to me. We haven't met on the bridge and looked into muddy water together. You haven't said you're sorry. You haven't washed the blood from your cheek with tears.

And I haven't said *come in*. I haven't said *please come back, Mom, I need you.*

But I do. I want to feel you with me. I want to bring you with me into this new life. I need your help. I'm shaking.

Chapter 59

Dear Mom, here I am. I'm in my studio apartment in Southeast Portland, near the Morrison Bridge, sitting at my desk, which is an old card table in the corner of the room. There are two nice windows in the room to look out at the Willamette River that flows north toward the Columbia. I'm looking for a place to buy, a modest place to drop anchor. I'm done with the pretentious upper-class houses I used to covet. I want a simple bungalow in a neighborhood with big trees and real people for neighbors.

Starting this letter took a lot out of me, and I had to put the pen down for a few days. I didn't know this would be so exhausting. But it's way more than that, isn't it? It's reaching for you, inviting you into my world. What's the word everyone uses now? Vulnerable, that's it. It's being vulnerable. I'm not used to that.

I've been thinking about you. Trying to remember us. I can't dig us up. What I remember is you leaving—the back of your coat. I never knew where you were going, and I don't remember you coming back. I don't remember seeing you smiling, coming toward me. You were always going, leaving me with one stranger after another. Until you left and didn't come back. You left empty spaces where there should be memories, giant holes I fall through. Nothing to catch me.

Why would I want you back when I never had you? Or did I? I don't know. I just know I feel incomplete, unable to really give myself to life if I'm keeping you out. I want you back. I want you with me. I do. Even though just the thought of you tangles up my insides like a rubber hose. Most of the anger is gone–it's the fear that holds me back. I'm still that little boy inside. I want you here with me so I can show you my life. I'm making a life, Mom, and I want you to be in it. So I'm going to write to you and tell you my stories. Maybe I'll remember some of ours along the way. Maybe you'll tell me your stories. I'll try to be brave.

. . .

I arrived back from the prison to my room at the warehouse on SE Ash and went to bed for I don't know how long, at least two days. No, I wasn't in prison; I was visiting someone. I went to see the man who murdered my daughter, and I realized what I always knew but wouldn't face: that I was in prison. It's too long a story for now—just know that the time I spent there changed me and became part of the motivation to seek you out. To open my heart to you.

The exhaustion I felt on my return was more than the grueling fatigue of residency in San Francisco. I suppose it was the exhaustion that comes from all the years of running from myself. It doesn't matter. I slept and slept.

When I finally woke it was dark, but I could tell by the sound of traffic that it was still early evening. I left the building and began searching for the nearest ice cream shop. I don't blame you if you think that's strange. It will make more sense later. I felt my daughter's presence and she prompted me to remember the little gelato place on 28th and Burnside we used to visit on summer nights. I made my way there quick as my feet would take me, and I was so happy when I arrived on that warm August evening.

A long line of ice cream lovers stretched out the door onto the sidewalk. I found my place in line and eyed those sitting outside at the little pink café tables enjoying their scoops of gelato. I couldn't help myself; I looked to see if my little girl was among them. Foolish me. The truth is, I was a little nervous. Isn't that strange? I couldn't remember the sensation of ice cream in my mouth, not even the sensation of cold, sweet, or creamy. All that was lost to me.

By the time I reached the counter to order, I felt about five years old, trembling with glee. Ten containers of fresh, creamy gelato in the cooler looked up at me. Each one was scrumptiously inviting. I was in a daze when the young woman behind the counter, apparently taken by the wide-eyed senior kid, laughed lightly and asked me what I wanted.

To my surprise, I laughed too. "I—I really don't know."

"Well, can I get you a taste of anything?"

"A taste?"

"Sure. Would you like a sample?" And she held up a little pink spoon no larger than a dime.

She probably thought I was an old stoner because I just gazed at that little pink spoon for what felt like at least a minute. I didn't say "wow" or anything really stupid, but she did have to interrupt my reverie to attend to other customers. Finally, she asked me if I needed a more time to think about it. But then I landed on the one I knew was for me.

"Can I have a taste of the orange creamsicle?"

"Of course."

Thoughts of summer days, baseball, and dry, dusty fields with brown grass and clover floated into my mind like a lazy summer cloud. I remembered my buddies, Mark and Doug, and the long afternoons highlighted by the arrival of the Good Humor truck and its familiar jingle. Nearly every day I went for the orange creamsicle, and here I was again, about to dive into my favorite summer delight.

My hands were trembling when I took the tiny pink spoon from her fingers. I must have looked pretty odd standing there, gazing at the orange gelato as though I had found the golden egg.

I stepped aside for others to place their orders and brought the spoon of orange creamsicle and the quivering anticipation of the moment to my mouth. The dancing taste buds were ready for the party . . . and it was sensational. Better than I dreamed. Time stopped. I swooned like Judy Garland in the garden after her first kiss.

I was so taken by the experience of dissolving into the universe of cool, creamy orange, and by the very new feeling of satisfaction, of *enough*, that I had no awareness of leaving the gelato shop, and it did not occur to me to go back for a scoop on a cone. I certainly didn't notice the servers' reactions, but I imagine their commentary went something like, "Those old hippies! You gotta love 'em."

That's about how it went those months after returning from the prison. Every day, sometimes twice or three times a day, I went back to Staccato Gelato—for orange creamsicle, tiramisu, black raspberry, peppermint, chocolate mint, triple chocolate. I learned to eat one, then two, and even three scoops of ice cream at a sitting, and each serving was as yummy and transcendent as the last. Many of those days I thought of you, Mom, and wondered what it would be like to sit at one of those pink tables with you. Did we ever have ice cream together? Why can't I remember? The only cold I can't forget is standing in the snow watching you run away screaming.

•••

It took nine months to find my new home, Mom. In that time my senses opened and the world became enchanting. It is mystifying to me how my state of mind could have changed so radically. But it did, and I took my seat on the magic carpet and rode it where it led. And where it led this wayward drifter was the greatest and most delicious surprise of all. I want to tell you all about it, Mom. I want you to be part of my world. Do you want to? Will you?

•••

I moved into a modest old Portland bungalow at 2739 SE Buford, only two blocks off SE Clinton, in mid-October. It's a cozy, unassuming place, built around 1930, surrounded by huge ash and maple trees that shade the house. Inside, large windows let in the morning light that makes it through the trees. There's a brick fireplace in the living room with built-in bookcases on either side. The floors are old Siberian oak, common for the time, stained a nice honey brown. The interior needs painting, but no hurry on that. It's a bit daunting getting down to the basement. The steps are so steep, I have to hold on to the railings with both hands. That makes carrying laundry up or down a challenge, but at least it has an old-fashioned laundry chute to drop my dirty clothes. The first time I stepped inside I felt the warmth and love of the place and knew it wanted me, and I wanted to be there. Five weeks later I moved in.

I'm embarrassed to tell you that the first night at the house I was awakened at midnight by, of all things, a wet dream, accompanied by a raucous thunderstorm and downpour. Imagine a seventy-three-year-old man, who hasn't had an erection for over three years, shaken from his sleep by the likes of that! I felt for a second like it was the big earthquake or a heart attack, and then like I was sixteen again. When my body stopped shaking and came to a rest, and the storm passed, I laughed and thought it was all truly auspicious. I went back to sleep knowing this house was charmed and I was lucky to be here.

I probably shouldn't be telling you about my nocturnal surprise, should I? But then I figure you probably aren't offended by anything where you are. Besides, I want you to know everything. I want you to know me, is more like it. It's time.

Believe me, sex was the last thing on my mind. I had no libido or interest of any kind. None. In fact, when memories of sexual encounters did show up, I felt ashamed for the way I had treated women. But I am encouraged and surprised by the sense of remorse that is beginning to take the place of shame. I feel like I want to apologize to every woman I pass on the sidewalk. Not to ask for forgiveness, but to recognize the trespasses. I want to give something of myself to the women I hurt and offended. I'm afraid I don't know how. Why are men like this?

I hope you're not disappointed in me. I must sound childish and superficial to you. This is love? Wet dreams and a pink spoon dipped in Italian ice cream? Really? I wouldn't blame you. I find myself saying the same things in my head. I could be fooling myself, but try to understand, I woke up in a coffin. I needed to revive myself and find a feeling of innocence and delight in the world, a feeling of belonging to this life. Then maybe I can grow up and love.

I realized this at the prison. There's so much to tell you about Randy and what happened there. I'll get to that later. But it was there, of all places, I learned that falling in love with the green, fertile world was the best way to begin to make it up to you, and to me, and to the life you gave me. There are times now when it feels like I'm close to you, when I'm close to life. I worry this sounds like some elaborate glorification of me and you'll think badly of me. What I really fear is that you'll turn your back on me. Maybe I'm saying too much, too soon. I don't know. Please don't run away. I couldn't take that.

■ ■ ■

It hasn't been an easy entry into the world after so many years of exile in a straitjacket, when cold surgical instruments were my only sensations. There are hours when my body aches and feels like it's coming apart. But I feel I have to love the world to really love its people. And you. And it seems to me a sensual life is the best way to get out of my way, to make sure my anxieties don't hold me back or trick me into thinking I can do this in my head. Does this make sense?

It isn't about ice cream. It's about having a body and senses. So many years of feeling nothing, Mom. Can you understand? You won't believe this, but even the sexual compulsion was lifeless and empty. My body was not mine. Now I'm waking up. Coming back to life. I can feel something. I am discovering the earth. The autumn light, the fall colors, the crisp air, the hour of blue. And the smells, Mom, the smell of decaying pine needles. Mom, I never knew. I never knew.

Please understand, I'm not saying I am having exalted epiphanies. It's that these experiences are new to me. You left me in the snow to freeze. You left the car running for me to choke on. What else could I do but die with you? I'm waking up from a coma. Do you understand? Do you?

I'm just saying I can feel something, and the earth and its glory are astonishing. I am getting a glimmer of Emily's world. Wait a minute! I just said her name. I gave you her name, Mom, your granddaughter, Emily. This is working!

There's something else. Something I had written off as a vestige of childhood innocence. Something I now feel replacing the small and petty me. That something is awe. There were times I felt close to it when I carved open a chest and took a beating heart in my hands. Believe it or not, there were instances when everything stopped and the immensity shook me. It must have been a nanosecond. Was life always trying to get in? Will I let it in now? I think so. I think I am. But there is so much doubt. Maybe talking to you will help make it real. Maybe turning to you will help me trust. Maybe there are too many questions to ever know. Maybe I'm playing games with myself. Is it foolish for a seventy-three-year-old man to think he can feel alive again? Will I be even more afraid when I do?

There's so much to tell you, Mom. So much to remember. So much that feels like a dream. Someone else's dream. I have the odd sense that by telling you about me, your son, I'll remember you, my mother, and all this will feel more real, more mine. Ours. Alive.

I'm still alive. That is the most unlikely story. Or it was, until now. I have a story to tell you—are you listening?

Chapter 60

Here we go, Mom, into the big story. Into the impossible, the fulfillment of Emily's prayer. This is the unlikely story of love, written by your son in his own hand, in his own voice. Listen to me, Mom, I wasn't done when I said goodbye to Randy Tanner at the prison. I had to shape that love. I had to shape it into an everyday life in a world that makes it hard to love, that tempts us every day to give up, to stop caring, to stop giving. I know now what Emily meant when she said, "Daddy, love." She led me by my hand to the threshold, but I have to walk through that door. You're part of that story, Mom. A big part. Come sit by me while I tell it to you. Let me introduce you to someone.

. . .

A family of crows woke me from the deepest, most refreshing sleep that first morning of my life at the Clinton Street bungalow. Knowing my bodyguards were close brought a smile to my face.

My house is empty. The furniture, artwork, and household necessities from the Alameda house are long gone. The storage Keith Stone put them in disposed of everything when I never paid my bill or replied to their letters. Before moving into the new house,

I bought a new bed, a chair, some cooking pans and dishes, a few towels, and one floor lamp. I have next to nothing that is mine.

I like it. I have learned to like living simply, and the absence of things doesn't bother me. There are some things I want, and I'm making a list to help keep me focused. First on the list is a dog. I don't want to be alone anymore. Everywhere I walk in Portland, dogs show up, tongues hanging out, tails wagging, and eyes happily engaging in conversation with anyone willing. They must be angels. I don't have a particular breed in mind, though I'm not sure I can handle a large dog at my age. I just want a smart, friendly dog to play with and take care of. A deep desire to care for another living creature has moved into my heart. Is that what a mom feels?

The house has a small backyard with a little brick patio. It is fenced, although the fence is old, weathered, and badly in need of repair. The space seems just right for a small dog to play. I need a chair to sit in to throw the ball, and maybe a table. The backyard faces south and will be warm and good for sitting in the sun on summer days. It will also be good for planting a rose bush or two, which is the second item on my list. Did you know Portland is "The City of Roses"? They're everywhere. Won't it be great to have two or three roses to enjoy? Didn't you have some roses in our backyard? I vaguely remember seeing you outside picking a bouquet. Did you? It seems to me that roses are a great metaphor for capturing the mystery of emerging life. I think I'll love watching the slow growth of the buds—such loveliness at the end of those hard and thorny stems. And of course, the fragrance. I often think I'd like to die like the bumblebees I see expired in the perfumed embrace of a fully opened bloom.

■ ■ ■

With these thoughts in mind, I wandered into the backyard through the French door by the kitchen. The sun was already warming the chilled autumn air and flooding the area with late October light. I was thinking how perfect this spot would be to sit and read, and how the roses would love the direct sunlight, when I heard a voice coming from over the fence of the neighboring yard.

At first, I couldn't make out who was talking, Mom, but as I moved closer it was possible to make out a muffled but delighted voice. That voice turned to laughter and a gleeful burst of surprise, followed by bemused words of encouragement: "Oh, my, yes, there you go, there you go, ha, well done, dear ones, well done. You have a lovely breakfast, won't you? Go get those nasty little aphids. Eat 'em up! Wee! Fly my dear ones, fly where you will!"

I peered over the fence and saw a woman in a straw hat rising up from deep in the roses. She came up slowly, tall and fit-looking, although she put one hand to her lower back and looked stiff, maybe in pain. Without a thought I blurted, "What are you doing?"

The person in the straw hat made a quick turn and eyed me curiously. In the same familiar and lilted voice I heard a moment before, she said to me, "Oh my, who's there? Ah, it's you! Well, you beat me to it, didn't you? I made you some cookies and was all set to bring them by this morning." And then she took off her hat, wiped the sweat from her forehead, and looked me over head to toe with a big, approving smile.

I nearly blushed and hurried to say, "Why are you on your knees talking to the roses?"

"I'm not talking to the roses, not now anyway. I'm talking to ladybugs, two hundred lovely ladybugs free to roam and do as they please."

"What about the aphids?"

"Oh, those nasty critters? Eat 'em up, girls, eat 'em up! I've got no use for those aphids. Are you worried about them?" She looked at me quizzically and I nearly took a step back.

"Well, no, not exactly. I'm not sure why I said that. I just got a picture of a little green aphid being devoured by a gigantic ladybug and it made me squirm a little."

"Ah, the sensitive type."

"Me? Not really. Maybe I'm remembering the first horror movie I ever went to. I hid under the seat thinking I was about to get eaten up. I never forgot that day."

"Don't worry about a few aphids. They won't know what hit 'em. Besides, you come with me and have a cookie and you'll miss the carnage."

"A cookie?"

"That's right, didn't you hear me say I made you some cookies? Kind of a welcome to the neighborhood present. Come on."

"Oh right, I remember. But I haven't eaten breakfast."

"Perfect. Cookies and milk for breakfast, can't do better than that. Meet me on the front porch."

I felt a little dizzy walking through my house, Mom, and I wasn't sure why. Maybe I was just hungry. I couldn't remember when I'd eaten last, or if I had anything for dinner besides ice cream, and now I was about to start the day with cookies. By the time I reached her porch, the ladybug lady was throwing a small purple and orange tablecloth over a wrought iron table and placing a tray with cookies and milk on it. That's when I realized the dizziness had something to do with her.

"Do you eat cookies and milk for breakfast every morning?"

"Of course not, silly. Only on special days, like today. Usually I eat something like popcorn and a fruit smoothie for breakfast."

"Why is today special?"

"Because of you, of course. And the ladybugs, I suppose, but mostly because of you. Aren't you special?" She winked at me, and a sly, mischievous smile spread across her face. I was so taken by the brightness of that smile and the kindness behind it that the pain in those eyes would only become apparent to me later.

"I don't think so. No, I'm not at all special."

"Oh yes you are. Besides, you're my new neighbor, and that makes you very special to me."

"Well, thanks. Thanks so much."

"Dig in, Doc."

"Doc? Did you call me Doc?"

She paused, taking off her straw hat, and gave me a pensive, penetrating look as though she was reading the history etched in my face. "I did indeed."

"Why?"

"Your hands. That, and I like to observe people and make wild guesses as to who or what they are. Your hands look like the hands of a surgeon. Elementary, my dear . . . what is your name?"

"David."

"Elementary, my dear David. Nothing magic about it. You just have to look closely at the world, and it reveals its secrets quite willingly. Actually, I don't really believe in secrets, do you? It seems to me that people, and the world, are constantly trying to tell everything. Don't you think so, David?"

"No, no I don't. Well, maybe in one way or another, without trying to, I suppose people try to confess."

"Oh, Catholic, are we?"

"Me? No. Heavens no."

She chuckled and said lightheartedly, "Ha, good one, David. Here, have a cookie."

"Thanks."

Some of me wanted to hide, Mom. And some of me wanted more. I have to admit to feeling suddenly captivated by this woman, and at the same time a far-off little voice said, "Why didn't *you* see me, Mom?" But that voice quickly faded because I was so taken by the brilliant white hair that fell to her shoulders.

"Of course. They're homemade, fresh out of the oven this morning. You like?"

I took a bite and swooned. I'm sure I looked like a six-year-old with chocolate on his lips and a goofy smile on his mouth. Still chewing and moaning in delight, I managed to say, "My God, they're unbelievable. What are these?"

"Double fudge chocolate chip. Aren't you glad you're not a ladybug?"

"Yes! Jesus, Mary, and Joseph, these are sinfully good."

"Ha, there you go again. Are you sure you're not Catholic? Not a retired priest?"

"Nope, not me. Not by a long shot. You were right—I was a doctor, a surgeon."

"Praise the Lord! I don't know if I could manage living next door to a priest. Mercy. Oh, it's going to be a good day, a wonderful day. It always is when my first hypothesis of the day is on. Have another cookie, David."

"These are incredible. I haven't had a cookie for years."

The expression on her face turned in an instant from pleased to perplexed. "What?"

"I know it's strange, but I haven't had a cookie for over three years. Man, these are as good as the orange creamsicle gelato."

"Ah, you like ice cream?"

"I am crazy about ice cream. But what I mean is that when I had my first ice cream not long ago, it did the same thing."

"What is that?"

"It stopped my mind, and everything was glorious."

"I see. And just now, the double fudge cookies—did they stop your mind?"

"They did! In a flash, and everything went . . ."

"Radiant?"

"Yes! Do you know what I'm talking about?"

"I might."

"You've experienced that opening?"

"With every bite."

"Ha, I like that. Who are you? I don't know your name. And how did you know I was a surgeon? Are you a private eye, or a shrink?"

"Whoa, slow down, neighbor. All in good time. Let's start with the who are you thing. Two different questions, David. Two very different questions, no?"

"You're right about that, but really, what should I call you? I mean, what's your name?"

She gave me that inviting look again, the one that made my heart skip a beat. "My name is Luciana, but you can call me Lucy. That's what my friends call me."

"How did you get from Luciana to Lucy?"

"That's for another time, Doc. What are you going to do with the rest of this glorious morning?"

"I planned on walking out to the Humane Society to look for a dog."

"A dog? Lovely. Come on then, I'll give you a lift. It's way too far to walk. Besides, if you find a dog you fall in love with, you'll want a ride home."

"Really?"

"Sure, let's go. Grab a cookie for the road."

"One thing."

"What's that?"

"Do you like dogs?"

"More than ladybugs. Lots more."

Chapter 61

I am now deeply in love with ice cream, Mom. There isn't a brand I haven't sampled or a shop within a three-mile radius I haven't walked to. What am I doing? Is this my way of making the freezing snow into something good? Turning what is frozen into something soft? Mom, I stood there in the snow for a long time waiting for you to come back. My feet remember the frostbite. I was too little to blame you, but not too little to blame me.

Ice cream has become for me the symbol of all that is sweet in life. All that is delicious and available. A reminder that it is possible to be in this world and not be consumed by the tragic and cruel everyday sufferings. Maybe this sounds childish to you—a seventy-three-year-old man partaking of the sacrament of gelato. Do you think I'll ever grow up, Mom?

But I find a voice inside asking why I'm weeping when there is so much that is sweet all around. I have no answer for that voice, and I have a thousand answers. Ice cream is my favorite reply. Every time I sit down with a cup or a sugar cone in my hand, I think of Emily sitting on my lap and I feel happy. I say thank you to whoever created the likes of coffee Heath Bar crunch, and I vow to get myself an ice-cream maker and produce the very best homemade ice cream east of the Willamette. I think this means I want to make my own life. A good life. Maybe even a loving life. What if that sweetness can extend to you and me, Mom? What if we can come in from the cold? Come closer, I won't hurt you.

But first, the dog.

Chapter 62

My head was brimming with excitement by the time I reached Lucy's front door. You probably guessed by now it wasn't just the anticipation of finding a dog that quickened my step. Right? I could already sense that Lucy had a way of charging the atmosphere with her presence, and I liked it.

I paused outside her house and took it in slowly. It was vintage Portland Bungalow like mine and most others in the neighborhood. But Lucy's was distinctive beginning with the house colors: merlot purple with gold trim, and colorful pots of marigolds and geraniums climbing up the stairs to her front door, which was an eye-catching lime green.

This woman has a way of saying to the world, "Here I am, this is me!" I was taking it all in and feeling delight take me in when the door flew open, and Lucy popped out with that joyful smile leading the way.

"Hey mister, let's go find you a dog!" She led me down her pathway to a bright orange convertible in the street.

"Is this your car, Lucy?"

"I didn't steal it, if that's what you're asking." Lucy quickly backtracked. "Sorry, David, I shouldn't be such a smart-ass. We've only just met."

"No, it's fine, it was a dumb question. I just haven't seen one of these for a long time. It's a Karmann Ghia, right?"

"It's a 1971, one of the last years they made them. Isn't she a beauty? Hang on to your hat—it gets windy with the top down."

"I've always loved these great, simple lines."

"Sexy, don't you think?" Lucy looked me in the eye and delivered another suggestive wink as she started up the engine and gave it some gas. Was I imagining this? I can tell you, Mom, I wasn't imagining the swing of her hips when she danced her way to the driver's door. And the quiver in my legs confirmed it. The quiver made it all the way to my vocal cords. A bit flummoxed, I tripped over my tongue trying to speak. "Well, sure, sure it is, very sexy."

"Good. It don't mean a thing if it ain't got that swing. Isn't that right, David?"

"Not a damn thing. How long have you had it?"

"I picked her out on Memorial Day. I named her Gina after Gina Lollobrigida. Now there was one gorgeous, sexy lady."

"She was a knockout."

"So is this little treasure. She's got moves you wouldn't believe for a fifty-year-old buggy. Hey, where's your car, David?"

"I don't own a car."

"No car?"

"Nope, I haven't even sat in a car for I don't know how long. I rode a bus a while ago, but otherwise I walk everywhere."

"You were really going to walk to the Humane Society?"

"Yeah. Really." Lucy took her eyes off the road for a second and turned them on me to see if I was serious. Her look was penetrating, and I hoped she wasn't seeing me as some strange dude and reconsidering her decision.

"That's a long walk, David, a real long walk."

"I'm used to it. I walk ten miles a day, all over town. I love to walk."

"I prefer to drive. Kinda like to go fast, feel the wind in my hair and on my face, you know, get mussed up."

"Walking saved my life."

Lucy turned to me again. Her eyes were softer this time, full of a kind understanding. I had the strong sense that I could be honest with this person—that she had taken many a long walk herself.

"I wondered what did. You're coming out of it, aren't you? You're not just surviving the crash anymore, you're coming out and joining the big show, aren't you?"

"The big show? I like that, yeah, I'm signing up for the big show one more time, maybe the first time. Think I'll try out for the flying trapeze!"

"There you go! With or without the net, neighbor?"

"I think I better start with the net."

"Nets are good, good. Lots of bounce to a net."

"I'm not done falling, I'm sure of that." I was also sure that conversation with Lucy had a way of accelerating into suggestive metaphor. It seemed she was talking and thinking on many levels at once. I felt a little dizzy with excitement and doubt as to whether I could keep up.

"So, the dog is part of the plan? Why do you want a dog? You just moved in."

"I'm not sure. I've never owned a dog. I guess there's something so lovable about dogs, so accepting. And they know how to have fun. But what I really want, yeah, what I really want is to take care of another living being. That's a big part of it, loving and caring for another. Do you know what I mean?"

Lucy nodded. "I do." There was a brief hint of sadness to her voice that lasted only seconds and was gone when she said, "We'll find you a good dog, David."

"So, you like dogs, Lucy?"

"I sure do. I'm crazy about dogs. You didn't meet Henry yet. He's getting a little stiff and not as sociable as he used to be. I left him home so your new friend wouldn't be overstimmed in the back seat. You'll meet him soon. He's a good boy. Usually he's sitting right where you are, with his nose way up in the air surfing the wind and the smells. I hope we can fit your doggie in the car."

"Oh no, we'll walk home."

"Walk! It must be eight miles to home."

"Well, I had those chocolate fudge cookies, remember? I have lots of energy to burn off now. By the way, where are those monster cookies?"

"In the back seat. Let's knock one off before we get there. Oh, I'm so excited! They have some great dogs right now. It will be really hard to pick one, won't it?"

"I suppose. How do you know they have good dogs right now?"

"I visit at least once a week."

"You do?"

"Yeah, I'm a sucker for any kind of dog. Shoot, I can't stay away. I just have to go out and talk to them and reassure the little darlings that somebody loves them and wants to take them home. I scratch their ears and sing songs. Breaks my heart to leave every time, but what can I do?"

I thought that was the kindest thing I'd ever heard of, and I told her so.

"Really?"

"Really. Someone once told me that dogs are angels. Do you think so?"

"They're more than angels, aren't they? They're love pollen, or something like that. Something angels yearn for, I suppose. I don't think of my visits as acts of kindness—I feel like I'm the recipient of kindness. When I visit them, all locked up in those cages, what do they do? They lick my hand, that's what they do, and sometimes they lick my toes. Who's the kind one? Whose heart is in the cage? Whoa, slow down, Lucy. Better stop me, David, before I really launch into it, and you jump out of the car."

"No. I like it, really. I know a lot about cages."

"Hey, we're here. You're saved. Let's go find you a wonderful doggie."

"Make sure I don't walk out with two or three, okay?"

Lucy laughed and gave my hand a squeeze. We laughed together and eagerly bounded out of the car, though something in me was just as eager to keep hold of that hand.

Chapter 63

Two hours later, Mom, I left the Oregon Humane Society with my new friend, Sugar. Sugar is a four-year-old cairn terrier. She is sandy brown with eyes that dance like blinking Christmas lights. If happiness and enthusiasm could be packaged into an oversized loaf of bread, well, that would be Sugar. You'd love her. Here's how it happened.

Lucy and I said hello to all the dogs in the kennel. One by one, she greeted each dog and gave me her take on the personality and temperament: "This little one is really sweet, but kind of nervous. This guy is a great big alpha and proud of it!" She was warm and friendly, personal with every dog, and she made each one, for the time she was with them, feel happy and special. I felt my throat throb.

I thought I'd want a big dog, like a lab or golden retriever, but I began to wonder if this seventy-three-year-old body could manage a seventy-five-pound dog pulling me down the slope of Mt. Tabor. Lucy thought I should get a beagle, like Henry. She went on and on about Henry's virtues and was making a convincing argument when I saw Sugar. Should I say it was love at first sight? What was it about those eyes that made me want to laugh and weep and skip down the street, all at the same time? We looked at more dogs, but I kept looking over my shoulder at Sugar, who was looking at me like I was her long-lost best friend.

Sugar fit just fine on my lap, and I decided to ride home in the Karmann Ghia with Lucy rather than walk the eight miles. She probably would have made the trek as merrily as she jumped into the car and snuggled in for the ride. Lucy chuckled and said, "Sugar, girl, you are going to have the best home you have ever had in your doggie life, and you are gonna love Henry, I just know it." I'm sure Sugar understood every word Lucy said, and she looked at her with those musical eyes as if to say, "I'm ready! Let's go!"

And go we did. Lucy peeled out of the parking lot and made haste for the home front. Sugar alternated between standing on my lap with her paws on the windowsill to let the wind mess with her curly hair and sitting on my lap looking into my eyes. It was obvious from the first that she was made of cheerfulness and love. Occasionally she looked at Lucy and tilted her head to the side as though she was trying to make sense of something.

Lucy took her hand from the wheel and rubbed Sugar's head and assured her, "Sugar girl, we are going to have such fun times!"

At the sound of Lucy's voice Sugar stood on her hind legs and licked my face. She would have done the same to Lucy, but I held her back. What I didn't hold back was this crazy new thing swimming in my body. I think people call it joy, Mom, right? But you can imagine joy and I are only now being introduced. To top it off, I put my hand on Lucy's and gave it a little squeeze, which she returned as if we had been friends for centuries.

By the time we arrived home Sugar was up, paws on the car door, sensing that this was her place in the new world. Her little tail did the jitterbug as she begged to be released to catalogue the assortment of smells calling her name.

We pulled into Lucy's driveway and Sugar was out the door in a flash, running here and there in circles for the pure joy of it. Her little legs were a blur as she dashed about the neighboring lawns making them hers. To my surprise, she answered to her name by coming when I called her, as though she and I were already connected by an invisible string of devotion.

Lucy smiled ear to ear and said, "David, she is such a sweetheart. Just look at how happy she is. Let me get Henry and they can say hello."

Henry bounded out of the house at sixty miles per hour. The two dogs were instant pals. Each sniffed the other's butt and then they began a game of chase that had Lucy and me in stitches. Little Sugar was ecstatic with her new friend and a new front yard to play in. Henry looked like the happiest kid on the block, and I couldn't help noticing a surge of hope inside that maybe Lucy would become my best friend. Maybe hers was the woman's voice I longed to listen to. With that, my mind took me back to the moment I heard Lucy's voice drifting over the rose garden talking to the ladybugs. We met through her voice! I find that very auspicious, Mom. And just as I was marveling in that meeting of only a few hours ago, that silky voice pulled me in once again.

"David, let me get you some lemonade, and then I have some things I really should take care of."

"That sounds great, but if you need to get going, I'm good."

"Not yet, you wait here. I'll be right back."

She was back shortly with a pitcher of lemonade and a tray holding a bowl of peanuts and a few cookies.

"Come on, let's sit on the porch and have a treat while those clowns tear up the front lawn. Can you believe those two?"

I was tempted to say something like "just like you and me," but I chickened out. "Instant pals. Thanks for today, Lucy. That was really very kind of you."

"Oh, it was my pleasure, David. You and Sugar were made for each other. She will bring you such happiness."

"I think she picked me."

"She certainly did. She just reached out and hooked you big time. You were a goner the minute you laid eyes on her."

"I'm not used to that. To acting so spontaneously. It kind of surprised me."

"I like it that you could be moved like that. You must be getting younger!"

"God, I hope so. I've been really old for a while." I scolded myself for saying that and wondered if I was trying to warn her about me.

"Oh dear, that'll suck the joy out of life. Hey, I'm wondering why you named her Sugar. It fits her perfectly."

"That's a long story."

"I see. Never mind, another time. I've got lots to do in what little time is left in the day. And what a great day it is! Look at little Sugar running circles around old Henry. He will sleep well tonight."

"Sugar was my daughter's first stuffed animal."

Lucy turned slowly and looked into me. "David, you don't have to go into it now. It's all right."

"No, I want to tell you. I don't know why. I don't tell many people. Well, actually, that's not true. I've never told a soul."

"Well, how sweet. Thank you, David. Thank you. I will hold that close. She's what hit you hard, isn't she?"

"Yes."

"You lost her, I'm guessing."

"I did. Mostly. I mean, I feel her all the time. She always wanted a puppy. Sugar and she would . . ."

"Sugar and she would have lit up the world. They were made of the same delight, I'll bet."

"You're right. That's what captured me, that . . . that delight, that joy for no reason."

"Will you tell me about her sometime, David?"

"Yeah. That would be good. I think that would be really good, Lucy."

"Oh good. I'll look forward to that. Here, have a drink of lemonade."

Lucy handed me a tall glass of lemonade with ice. Our eyes met and there was an unspoken recognition that our conversation and friendship were headed for deeper waters. We held each other's gaze for a moment while the history of love settled into its new home right there between us. And we settled with it.

Chapter 64

That night, Sugar slept on my bed. She slept curled up beside me; she slept on my chest, at my feet, and even with her nearly weightless little chin on my neck. I can't describe to you how good that felt, Mom. I slept like a baby. When I woke up, I was astounded to see that it was light out and I'd slept till nearly eight: a new personal record.

Sugar's wide-awake, happy face was the first thing I laid eyes on. It was impossible to feel anything but love and loved when Sugar looked at me. Her little body shuddered with joy and anticipation, and she licked my nose as if to say, "You're the best."

Any feelings to the contrary evaporated faster than a drop of water on a hot stove. Years of waking every morning with anxiety and dread in my stomach left me unprepared for the immediacy of the cure that came from waking up to that smile and the love it engendered in me. I think it was nothing out of the ordinary for Sugar. She seemed to live in perpetual joy.

I threw the blanket off and got out of bed to let her out, and she bounded after me, eager to say hello to the great outdoors. For some reason I let her out the front door, maybe thinking it would be more familiar to her after her romp with Henry the day before. Silly me—she could have been comfortable anywhere; the world was her home.

But it was fortuitous that we went out the front because when I opened it, I found an envelope taped to the screen door. The envelope was handcrafted ivory linen, and it hung, as if suspended, like a lazy thought that never seems to leave. On the front was a marking I could not understand. At first, I saw it as a random swoosh, a broad, flowing stroke from a calligraphy brush like you might see on Tibetan scrolls. There was a freedom and joy to the brush mark that looked like a bird feather sweeping by. But when I looked closer, I realized it was this and more. It was a smile, hanging in open space, so personal and yet not exclusively for me, or any one person really, but a mark of well-being that seemed to stretch across the universe.

I know that sounds dramatic, but that's how it struck me. I stood there in my bare feet feeling the moisture from morning dew and the crisp touch of autumn air, but the smile took me somewhere else, somewhere my senses couldn't find.

Looking down at Sugar, I said, "Look at this, someone has left us a letter." She clearly understood the tone of my words. She cocked her head slightly to the right and could have been saying, "Well, aren't you going to open it, silly?"

So I did just that. The envelope was sealed with candle wax. Inside was a note written on linen and a set of car keys. This is what it said:

> Good morning, David.
>
> I'm on my way to Mexico for a couple of weeks. A teenager down the street is taking care of Henry. I told her about you and Sugar so she may stop by for a play date. Her name is Suzie.
>
> Yesterday was such an enjoyable day. I just know you

and I are going to be very good friends. I apologize for not telling you about my trip, but I guess I just got caught up in meeting Sugar and getting to know you a little.

I hope you and Sugar have a great time together while I'm gone. You two are made for each other! I trust you found the key to Gina. She'll be lonely while I'm gone and will need some attention. How about you and Sugar take her for a ride? Top down of course! Have a blast.

See you soon,

Warmly,

Lucy

Warmly? I read that word over and over. I made sure I wasn't making it up. Warmly. What surprised me most was that I could feel it; I could feel warmth coming from my heart and from the letters on the page and from the smile on the envelope.

I read it again: Warmly. I read it over and over, out loud and to myself, and then it hit me hard, right between the eyes. Mom, you left me in the snow. To freeze. And I did. I shivered and stiffened, frozen in place while you ran down the street like a chicken with its head cut off. I'm still thawing out, Mom. Still that stiff little guy someone threw in the snow like an empty can. I don't remember who found me. Where did I end up? I'm still him, Mom, frozen in fear. Did you feel bad for what you did? Did you say I'm sorry a thousand times? Tell me you said it once.

I'm all shook up, Mom, all shook up. I want warmth. I want it. I want to come in from the cold. I want to feel your warmth. Your care. And I want Lucy home. It hasn't been a day and I miss her.

Chapter 65

Sugar and I spent the next days and nights walking the streets of Portland and playing in the yard. We were inseparable. Our favorite walk was up to Mt. Tabor Park. We were looking for uplifting scenery and stimulating trails. Mt. Tabor provided all of that plus a dog park. Some of the trails were steep, leading to the top of the ancient extinct volcano. They provided a nice view of the city and a great downhill run for Sugar to fly down at top speed, those cute little ears pinned back on the sides of her head.

One afternoon, after a romp in the park, we headed home as the sun was beginning its descent over the west hills. We arrived home as the sun was setting and spreading more fall colors over the western skies. Yellow leaves were falling from the silver maples outside the house and beginning to cover the sidewalk and lawn, and I decided to sweep the front steps and sidewalk. Sugar thought that was a particularly good idea, and she swung her little paws at the falling leaves and pounced on the leaves piling up here and there. I couldn't resist playing along and picked up handfuls to throw in the air for her to swat at. She made every effort to catch them but with absolutely no ambition other than the fun of it. I have to say I envy her devotion to fun, Mom. Maybe I'm learning.

I was leaning over, picking up a few sticks, when someone from the sidewalk called to me.

"Dr. Chase?"

At first, I ignored what I'd heard and kept throwing sticks and twigs in the air for Sugar. But that voice kept ringing in my head, and when the speaker repeated her question a second time, something in the call beckoned more than it should have.

"Are you Dr. David Chase?"

A plea in the speaker's voice brought me out of myself. I looked up at the woman standing just ten feet from where I stood. Sugar, sensing something important, looked at our visitor with welcoming curiosity.

"Dr. Chase, it's me, Audrey. Emily's friend."

I dropped the leaves and stared at Audrey for what felt like a very long time. Too long. My head froze. I thought I heard a collision on the road. Sugar ran out to the sidewalk and said hello for me.

"Well, hey there, little cutie. Who are you?"

"Audrey? Audrey, is it you?" By now I was nearly tripping over my feet trying to get to her and hot tears were beginning to make rain. "Audrey!"

We threw our arms around one another, sobbing and laughing. Sugar sat on her haunches and looked up at us quizzically. The two of us held tight and wept.

"Audrey, my God, I can't believe it. It's really you. It's really you!"

"I thought I'd never see you again, Dr. Chase. I thought you were dead or something."

"Almost, yes, very nearly, but I'm still here, for a little longer, I hope. And you, look at you. Here you are, dear, dear Audrey!"

And then I saw the scars, around her ear and down into her neckline. In the same breath a pang of guilt shot through my body.

Dear Audrey, what happened? Why did I desert her, Mom? Did I do what you taught me? Turn my back, run away, and abandon someone in need? My scars don't show—or do they? I found myself feeling ugly and hard to look at and terribly sad for Audrey.

Audrey must have seen my attention stumble on this evidence of her last three years. She knelt by Sugar and said, "Who is this little darling?"

"That's Sugar. She came to live with me a few days ago."

"She's adorable."

"Sugar is one sweet dog, Audrey. I'm a lucky guy."

"Aw, hi, Sugar, are you a sweetie pie?"

Sugar answered in the affirmative, and, happy to see the serious stuff had passed, ran and got some leaves for Audrey to play with.

"Well, thank you very much, Sugar. Here. Go get 'em."

And, of course, Sugar did just that, wiggling with anticipation. Audrey did not disappoint. She tossed the leaves in the air for Sugar to jump after. She was suitably impressed and let Sugar know what a good and talented dog she was.

I was still looking dumbfounded when I said, "Do you live around here, Audrey?"

Audrey glanced up at me but quickly averted her eyes. "I do, about four or five blocks from here. I was just out for a little walk when I saw you. How amazing! How long have you lived here, Dr. Chase?"

"Maybe a week. You get to be my age and you don't pay much attention to those things. Time gets fuzzy. But not long. I think it was just a week ago Friday when I moved in. Feels like longer."

"My gosh, I can't believe it. I usually walk toward the park. I don't know why I came this way today. Isn't that wild?"

"It is. It's wild. I'm so glad you did. Can you come in for a minute? I'll make us some tea or lemonade. Will you?"

"You're sure? I'm not interrupting?"

"No, no, this is fabulous. The leaves will be around for a while, right Sugar?"

Sugar looked befuddled as to why anyone would stop having so much fun, but she quickly dropped her mouthful of leaves and followed us to the door.

We wiped our cheeks dry and went in the house, dizzy with the rush of emotion. The stain of guilt in my gut led the way. I made some tea, and we talked about Sugar and the other dogs at the Humane Society. Luckily, I had found two chairs and a table at a local thrift store during the week. I wanted to have something for Lucy to sit on when she got back, but I want to keep things simple, and this was the best I could do.

I think both of us noticed the carefree joy of our meeting had been replaced with a feeling of some discomfort sitting face-to-face. I was at a loss as to where to begin and probably didn't help ease the awkwardness by sitting there staring at Audrey like she was a friendly ghost. Audrey got us going by asking about the house.

"So, this is your place? You bought it?"

Her question broke my trance and a few clumsy words managed to tumble out. "I did. My new home: House of Sugar's Daddy. Nice décor, don't you think?"

"Lovely. It has great rooms. Really, I love it. I can see you two being very happy here. Even more so with a little furniture."

"You're too kind."

"Thanks for the tea, Dr. Chase. This is a little surreal if you ask me."

"Please, call me David."

"All right. I can't get over running into you like this, David. What would Emily say?"

"Right, what would Emily say? She'd probably do a cartwheel and come up smiling and say something about the mother wanting it this way."

"Nothing seemed to surprise her."

"Yeah, for me it really is surreal, Audrey. So many things seem unreal lately. So dreamlike. And now you appear!"

"It's been a nightmare on my end—a lousy, unending nightmare up until the last year or so. But things are looking up, really looking up. And now this, running into you!" Audrey shook her head in disbelief and took a long drink of tea. She was still avoiding my eyes when I spoke.

"Audrey, I can't tell you how happy I am to see you. You know, I've been thinking of you, and . . . and I've felt so terrible that I disappeared and left you hanging like I did. For a long time I've wanted to tell you how sorry I am, how really sorry."

"It's okay, really."

"No, it isn't. It's not okay at all. I should have been around to help you. I should have stood by you, and I didn't. I was a jerk to you, and I apologize with all my heart. Here, let me get a hanky for you, I don't have any tissue. Here, take this, please."

"I'm sorry, Dr. Chase. I'm sorry, I don't know why seeing you has made me so emotional. Maybe I should go."

"No, please don't go yet. It's okay to cry, really, I feel it too. We probably need to cry together, all these years, all these years."

"No one has ever apologized to me for anything. I don't know what to say. I thought it was all my fault."

"What was your fault?"

"Everything. You disappearing, my father disappearing, my mother drinking herself to death, even Emily dying. I blamed myself for all of it, especially for Emily's death."

"No, Audrey. You had nothing to do with it. Nothing."

"It was my idea to go there. I was the one who bent her arm to go out for breakfast. She didn't really want to."

"But . . ."

"I know, I know, it's crazy thinking, but that's how it was for me. Some days I still believe it. It all happened so fast. I couldn't manage it, couldn't get the blood off my arms. I had to cover it with my blood." With that confession Audrey looked to the floor for a place to hide.

"What?"

"Never mind. You don't need to hear it, it's over."

"I want to know, if you want to tell me. I do."

Her voice lowered to match her face, and I could barely hear her say, "I cut myself. I cut myself to cover her blood with my blood, and to stop the pictures in my head. Did you have pictures?"

"I obliterated everything for a while. Then they came and wouldn't stop."

"I wish I could have. I couldn't. Nothing helped but cutting and other stuff that made everything worse."

"Drugs?"

"Drugs came later. Mostly alcohol and sex, and self-loathing, of course. At least hating myself made me stop thinking of Emily. Until the accident."

"What accident?"

"You saw the scars. Lovely, aren't they?"

"You'll always be lovely, Audrey. The accident didn't change that."

"You're not lovely strung out on Oxycodone. That was the worst. It took me a long time to shake that. That was the worst. God, I wanted to die so bad, but I couldn't do that to Emily. I just couldn't."

"I know. I got to the railing of the Hawthorne Bridge about a thousand times and couldn't get myself to jump. I wish I could say it was for Emily, but I was as selfish as ever. I couldn't bear never seeing her face again."

"Jesus."

"I know. We were long gone, you and I."

We went quiet. Survivors of horror, lost in a whirlwind of memory's scarring, unable to look at one another.

Audrey broke the silence. "I needed you."

Her words landed without malice. "I know, I know. I'm so, so sorry. I hope I can make it up to you. I really want to."

"God, I should be so angry with you, but I can't. It's all used up. On me, and the world and life, on every shitty thing in this god-awful existence. Now, I'm just trying to be thankful. Thankful I looked up and saw you there. Jesus, what if I hadn't?"

"I guess you had to. Just like I had to look up and see Sugar. How did you make it, Audrey? How did you get through?"

"I don't know. I really don't. I nearly didn't. Therapy. NA. Lots of pleading with I don't know what for help. In the end, I really can't say what it was. Was it luck, or time? I don't know, something just gave way eventually. It's a long story. I'm just glad I made it. Even more glad right now."

"Wow, that's amazing."

"I suppose it is. What about you?"

"I went to the dark side of the moon. For three years I saw no one, talked to no one, did nothing but walk over the bridge, past the cemetery, and back to Belmont and 32nd. Every day."

"No."

"Yes. It's true. I'm sorry, but it is."

"You walked to that place? Every day? Christ. How could you? I've never gone near it. Never. What brought you out?"

"I wish I could say. It's mostly a blur, but there was something, something pulling me out. What was it? Grace? I don't know, but I just kept thinking of Emily and what she would want. I failed at that for the longest time. I'm still failing. But I'm learning."

"Me too."

"We can help each other keep learning, Audrey. I know we can."

"Okay. That would be good. I'd better go. My boyfriend is probably worrying about me."

"Great, you have a boyfriend! That's great!"

"It is. He's a good man."

"Wonderful. Can I meet him soon?

"Sure you can. That would be really wonderful. I want him to know you."

"You do? Thank you."

"Maybe you can walk me down the aisle."

"You're getting married? Walk you down the aisle? Me? You don't mean it." I was too stunned to take in Audrey's hesitant request. Too overwhelmed to look at her.

"Maybe I do," was all she said. And the room became quiet. Filled, wall to wall with the sentiment of past, present, and future rolled into one. It was the silence of awe and the uncertainty of worthiness.

We stood and walked to the front door to say goodbye. It was now dark out and it felt like both of us were trying to keep our emotions in check. I don't know about Audrey, but for me it took some effort to restrain what had been stirred up.

As we walked down the steps toward the sidewalk, I reached out for Audrey's arm and asked, "How about if Sugar and I walk you home?" As I did so my conscience flared, and I felt the accusations looming and casting suspicious eyes on my behavior. Was I being seductive again? A lousy lech? But to my relief something in me answered *no*. I felt fatherly and protective of Audrey. And most grateful to feel a big love for her and confidence in a future together.

"Thanks, David, but I'll be fine. I need a little time alone to let this sink in. It's a lot."

"Of course. Come by again soon, will you, Audrey?"

"I will, real soon. I'm so happy."

We stood under a dazzling sky. The black night, studded with diamonds, seemed close enough to touch. Audrey kissed me on the cheek and walked out to the sidewalk where our lives had intersected just an hour before. She turned and said good night to Sugar. Sugar ran to her, and they laughed and hugged one last time. She waved and walked on. Then she stopped, paused, and turned toward me slowly. The space between us became a stillness. Audrey looked up at the stars, and then, in the softest voice that could still be heard, she spoke to me.

"David . . . I'm pregnant."

Chapter 66

Dear Mom, I was so stunned by Audrey's announcement that I couldn't sleep for the longest time. I just sat in my chair with Sugar in my lap, astonished by this crazy turn. Audrey a mother—I couldn't wrap my head around it, but it sure felt good, and a fantasy began to grow that I might be the surrogate grandfather. How about that? This story keeps getting better and better, doesn't it? You're part of it too, you know. You get to come along. We get to do a lot of things over, together. Do you want to? Are you hearing me?

. . .

I fell asleep in the chair and had a terrible dream. It pulled me under like a whirlpool. Here it is: *I am trapped, powerless, and my body is convulsing, trying to escape. Images of Audrey cutting her arms dive at me like rabid bats. Emily's broken body is on top of me; I can't breathe. And then, you are lying there, dissolving into a puddle of blood. I am frantic, going crazy trying to hold on to you. But you are gone. All that's left are tulips laying in blood. I start screaming, "Help me! Where are you, Mom? Why won't you answer? Are you here? Touch me, please touch me!"*

Sugar brought me out of the nightmare. I couldn't tell if it was day or night. If I was alive or dead. Sugar had to work hard to bring me back. She stood over me, licking my face and whimpering softly while my legs stopped kicking and the rest of my body quieted. I got up and paced. The images were leeched to my brain, and an aftershock slammed through. I shook as though the horror of Emily's death was happening all over. As though the nightmare would never end.

I hope you can read this, Mom—my hand is shaking reliving it in the telling. Actually, it's been shaking since the day Emily was murdered. Yes, murdered. Run down by a crazy meth freak. The same man I now have a deep friendship with. Outrageous, right? My hands shake less now, thanks to my pal Sugar.

Sugar and I went to bed and lay down to rest. The memory of the night's meeting with Audrey came back. Finding Audrey was such a joyful surprise; I didn't realize it would awaken the memory of that terrible day. Dear Audrey. She and Emily were inseparable, soulmates. She has suffered so much. I abandoned her. I just disappeared. I want to make it up to her now if I can. I can't believe she would want me to walk her down the aisle after the way I dropped her. As I mused over the miracle of Audrey, a terrible longing for Emily came up. I saw her face beaming with delight for her best friend. My heart could only barely contain the joy and heartbreak of the hour, and I fell asleep with Sugar's little chin on my shoulder.

When I woke up a short time later, I knew the electric storm had passed. My mind was fresh and clear, and though I still felt a little shaky from the dream, a feeling of comfort had moved in. It was early, two or three in the morning. I felt pulled to the dark hour. "Come on, girl, let's go outside." Sugar was at the door before I could throw the blanket off. She turned and gave me the "what a great idea" look. On the way to the door, I picked up a sweatshirt and we went out into the first day of November. Sugar took off, scampering and bouncing with joy, perhaps relieved the mysterious emotional flood had passed.

She was smelling and running at the same time when a particularly attractive aroma seized her olfactory brain by the stem. Suddenly, Sugar took off, abandoning scent and the joy of galloping for something more important. And then I discovered why.

Lucy's voice came drifting my way like a butterfly in August. "Sugar girl! Well, hello, dear Sugar. What are you doing up at this time of night? And where is your daddy, huh? Aw, come here girl."

"Lucy, you're home. You're back early!" My surprise and delight matched Sugar's, and I bounded toward Lucy as fast as my seventy-three-year-old legs would move me.

"David, hello! What a wonderful surprise. Yep, I'm back earlier than expected. Got in about midnight but couldn't sleep. Such a wonderful night, isn't it? Too good to waste sleeping. What are you doing up and outside?"

"I couldn't sleep either. Bad dream, then wide awake."

"Come sit with me." Lucy gave me the same warm smile that was painted on the envelope holding her note when she left. It melted me even more, and I scrambled up the stairs to be closer.

We sat together in the two wooden rocking chairs on her front porch. They looked about as old as the two of us and creaked as they rocked forward and back.

"Why did you come back early, Lucy?"

"Oh, things didn't work out the way I hoped. Complications. Time to work on Plan B."

"Plan B?"

"Never mind, I'll tell you soon enough. So, tell me, how are you and Sugar getting on? Famously, I presume!"

"Sugar is the greatest, Lucy. I feel like I've known her all my life instead of nine days."

"I knew it. She is your dog, David Chase."

"How do you know my last name?"

"Must have seen it on an envelope or something. Did you take Gina for a drive?"

"Once. I was pretty nervous. It's been a long time since I've driven. Sugar came with me as my copilot. We bought ourselves an ice-cream maker."

"Really? How is it?"

"Works like a charm. You want some? I've got some fresh butter pecan."

"Of course I do!"

"How many scoops?"

"Got to have two, one's never enough, is it? Excess is the way to go, don't you think, David?" Lucy gave me that suggestive, playful look I had come to adore, and a shiver went up my back that had nothing to do with the cool November air.

"Yes, absolutely. Two it is. Be right back."

I scampered off and dished up the butter pecan. I felt like a little boy, bouncing with excitement. You would never have guessed that fifty minutes before that, I was shaking and drenched in tears from the nightmare. Sugar sat on Lucy's lap the whole time I was gone, and God knows what she told her about this crazy old guy. I sensed they were in cahoots and loving it.

"Here you go, two scoops of homemade butter pecan with real Georgia pecans."

"Yum. Why, I simply cannot believe my good fortune, David Chase! You are such a gentleman, darlin'. A true gentleman."

"Very good. Very good. Just the right subtlety on the accent."

"Thank you, darlin'."

"And no one has ever accused me of being a gentleman until now, so, I thank *you,* ma'am."

"You're most welcome. Now, how about if you tell me about this dream?" She put her bowl down and fanned her face expectantly. I found the southern accent and the shy fanning of her face irresistible and could barely stay in my seat. It took some effort to answer Lucy's question, and I wasn't sure I wanted to go anywhere near the dream again, especially since Lucy's Georgia flirtation had found its mark.

"The most amazing part of it all was that Sugar helped me escape. She whimpered and licked my face until I woke up."

"Sugar, you *are* an angel! Good girl."

"She seems to have a sixth sense to her. Sometimes it's uncanny."

"They know. They really know, don't they?"

"I don't know. She's my first dog, but she seems tuned into me, and into life, in a way I never expected. Anyway, I don't remember much from the dream, nothing really of the content, just the feelings of terrible fear and sadness. I woke up thinking I was in a sweat, but it was a pool of tears. I was soaked. Then I went back to sleep for a few minutes and woke up feeling much better. Like something soothing had taken place. Strange."

"Not strange. Everyday magic. Your subconscious is active, trying to free you. Wonderful. Really wonderful, David."

"Do you think so? Dreams are so bewildering. I've had a dream trying to come through for a couple of years. It's the strangest thing. I can feel the pressure of a dream building but it never happens. It's like it's waiting or blocked or something."

"It can't get through, not yet, but it will. Someone is trying to help you dream their dream. Someone is dreaming and wants you to dream it as well, or for . . . her."

With that suggestion I popped out of the spell of her southern charm. A bit confused and sorry to leave, I could only mutter, "Her?"

"David, I figure the nightmare and the dream that can't be dreamed are related and probably involve the same person. That much grief can only mean one thing—you lost a child. And only a little girl can crack open a man's heart like yours is. Especially the heart of a surgeon. Elementary."

I was speechless. Dumbfounded. "How . . . how did you do that?"

"I'm sorry, David. I really am."

"Emily, her name is Emily. I want you to know that, Lucy. I do."

"Thank you for that, David. Thank you. I love knowing her name."

Lucy reached out and touched my hand with such tenderness I thought I'd break down right then and there. I held my breath and kept the tears to a few, but the real story is the spark that was lit by her touch. I didn't want her to remove her hand from mine.

"Geez, you're going to make me rain on my ice cream, Lucy."

"Don't do that. This is the best. Scrumptious!"

"You like?"

"I love it. Can you make fudge swirl, and butterscotch?"

"Sure, why not? I can make anything. I got this great book of recipes. Did you ever have orange creamsicle when you were a kid?"

"Of course, who didn't?"

"Right, well, have you had orange creamsicle gelato?"

"At Staccato Gelato?"

"Yes!"

"To die for."

"I just about have it figured out."

"You don't!"

"I do."

The gathering warmth between us held off the chill in the air. We ate ice cream and didn't shiver a bit, warmed as we were by being together again in the dark under a star-studded sky. I noticed Lucy's eyes light up with her last spoonful of butter pecan. She licked her lips, and with a twinkle in her eyes, she leaned toward me and said, "David, I have an idea."

"What's that?"

"Tomorrow is the day of the dead, El Día de los Muertos. Let's dig a hole in your backyard and tomorrow night we'll build a big fire. We can invite the dead to be with us and tell each other our best secrets and our biggest fears. What do you say?"

"I say you scare me."

"Perfect. I like a man who can admit when he's scared."

"Why my yard?"

"Because your yard is the perfect staging spot. You have the overhanging trees and a big opening to the sky. Our fire will have all the room it needs to climb to the heavens. It's very inviting. The spirts won't be able to resist!"

Lucy's excitement was contagious. I found myself thinking of you, Mom. Would your spirit show up? Could the magic of the fire help you and I burn up old hurts and resentments and make something new? With excitement came hope, and a prayer I suppose, or was it a plea laced with fear? Could I handle it? Do I really want something new with you? As if to distract myself, a strange question toppled out of my mouth.

"How old are you, Lucy?"

"David! How rude—didn't your mother teach you manners? I thought you were a gentleman." Lucy's scolding was punctuated by her characteristic mischievous smile, and I was relieved I hadn't offended her.

"Sorry. I don't know why I just needed to know all of a sudden."

"Don't want to be getting involved with a younger woman, eh?"

"Ha, no, that's not it."

"Okay, I'll be seventy-seven in January. Want to leave now?"

"No, no, I don't want to leave, I love this. I'm seventy-three. Going on twenty, or a hundred and twenty, I can't figure it out. It's just that you seem so wise and well-seasoned, but also young and playful. Me, I feel like a kid sometimes, bewildered and scared. This is all so new to me."

"Oh, David, don't make me into some saint. Believe me, I'm not. You'll find out. I'm scared, too. What will we find out about ourselves? It's always chancy, isn't it? Let's just forget about figuring it out and set sail. What about tomorrow night? Want to join me by the fire?"

I didn't tell her that the fire had already been lit, but I did respond with gusto. "I'm in! But I don't have a shovel or wood."

"I've got the shovel and the wood."

"I'll make some fresh ice cream. Fudge swirl."

"Great, I'll bring lemonade. David, will Emily like it?"

"She'll love it. And she'll love you, Lucy."

Lucy smiled like an angel, obviously pleased that Emily had given her approval. Emily, dear Emily. I was so occupied with you, Mom, I wasn't even thinking of Emily. Was that good or bad? What if your spirits meet up? What if you take the same flight to get here? What if I am big enough for this? What then? Why would I be afraid of that? But I think I am. And Lucy's right: trying to figure it out won't get me there. Only one thing will—dive in.

Chapter 67

That afternoon we huffed, and we puffed, and we dug the hole. The ground was dry and hard, but we did it. The hole was two feet deep and three feet across. The dogs took to the hole as if the world's biggest, best bones were buried somewhere under all that dirt. Their little butts poked up from the depths as they dug as fast as their paws could fling the dirt out. Lucy and I had a good laugh watching them go at it. Soon work turned to play, and they were much more interested in sticking their noses in the fresh dirt and flinging it up in the air. Sugar's face turned dark brown, but her glow was undiminished.

Lucy and I moaned and groaned and collapsed into the Adirondack chairs we'd hauled over from her backyard. Henry and Sugar looked up at us with a hint of concern in their eyes. They must have been thinking we were about to expire. We guzzled some lemonade and marveled at a new dimension of aches and pains and laughed at what we must look like to our furry pals. We sat there like two old friends, making fun of the pathetic condition of our nearly worn-out bodies and imagining calling the whole thing off because we'd soon be in traction.

"Who will drive us to the ER, David?"

"My God, did I miss something? I feel like I was stoned in the town square."

"An adulterer, eh?"

I froze and tried to hide it when she said that, but Lucy was too keen an observer. "Oops, hit a nerve, did we?"

"Sorry, kind of an old sore spot."

"Well, we might as well start early. I thought we'd wait for the fire to let it all out, but maybe we need some preliminary prep."

"But we're having so much fun. It feels so good to laugh. I don't want to spoil the fun. Maybe I'll tell you tomorrow night."

"Sorry, the day of the dead is reserved for the main event. The big tamale. We'll laugh again, don't you worry, David Chase. Besides, the moment clearly asked for it. Speak. I'm listening."

I swallowed hard and looked to the dogs for reassurance. At the same time, I was beginning to trust that what Lucy wanted was an honest friend, not a perfect one. I waded in. "I did some awful things. I hurt so many people."

"You got a case of the Big G?"

"Guilt?"

"That would be the one."

"I do. Plenty. Just when I think it's gone and not coming back, there it is in bold."

"Nothing goes away, does it?"

"Somebody else said that to me once. 'Nothing disappears, silly.' I don't get that."

"She was a smart one."

"What? How did you know?"

"It's the little inflection in your voice. Tell me what you did that was so bad, although you probably don't need to."

"I cheated on my wife about a hundred times."

"That many?"

"Well, not that many, but it seemed like it."

"That's how guilty you feel." There was not a hint of judgment in Lucy's voice. She said it as if she were commenting on the temperature. It surprised me that I could tell her and not want to run and hide.

"I guess so. Claire was a really good woman. The kindest, most accepting person I've ever known, and I just shit on her over and over. And all the other women I used and dropped. What a bastard."

"I, me, mine."

"What?"

"You know, men get to have whatever they want, especially doctors and surgeons. It's all yours for the taking, isn't it? I've been around a lot of docs and most of them have that aura, that, you know, 'the world is mine' look."

"I guess surgeons are the worst. Detached. All the pressure, all the worship. Playing God with people's bodies. But I was the worst. I just couldn't stop."

"Were you in love with Claire?"

"I don't think so. Maybe. I respected her, but I couldn't love, or really give until . . ."

"Until she came along?"

"Yeah. I didn't even want a child, but Claire pleaded with me and finally I gave in. Thank God."

"She made you into a human being, didn't she?"

"It took her dying to do that. Isn't that sick?"

"No, David. That isn't sick. It's tragic and terribly sad, but not sick. Really. What is a more powerful teacher than death? Nothing."

"I've been a pretty tough nut to crack. I still don't understand how I could have behaved like that."

"What was your mother like?"

I flinched. I wasn't ready. "Oh no, you're not going to be my therapist and play the mother card. Please, not that."

"I'm your priest, your therapist, your mother. Whatever you want. Let's just say I'm your friend, your best friend. And you're my best friend. We tell each other everything, including the bad stuff. What do you say?"

"I like that, but I'm doing all the talking."

"Oh, my turn's coming. You just wait. You'll get an earful soon enough."

"I'd like to know about you, Lucy. I really would. And I could sure use a best friend."

"Good. Me, too. Then tell me about your mother."

"All right, I'll try. She was a good woman, but really depressed. Too smart for her time and couldn't use it. Somehow, she got trapped and couldn't find a way out. She would get so depressed she wouldn't come out of her room for days and days. And then she went off the deep end. Real deep. And then . . . she put an end to it. I was nine. I found her in the car."

"Oh, dear, that's awful, just awful. You poor dear. And your father?"

"Never knew him. He deserted her before I was born. Still want to be best friends with this nut? Not too late to run."

"Not going anywhere. I'm your neighbor, remember? Besides, why pretend we're not broken and then run into it in the dark and claim we didn't know?"

"Maybe so."

By now Sugar was giving me a curious once-over, wondering, I'm sure, if she needed to come to my rescue again. I wondered myself. This was going fast and deep. And just then, Mom, I realized I'd never told anyone about you other than Randy. Not a single person. Saying it felt strange is an understatement. But I have to say it felt better. Lucy didn't blink, and you somehow seemed free to come out of the shadows and be a part of my life.

"Good solution." I could see Lucy's nimble mind working on something.

"What?"

"Seems like you made women interchangeable. None more important than another, easy in, easy out."

"I guess so."

"Why did you marry Claire?"

"Claire was different. She was so good. So unselfish. I thought maybe she could bring out the good in me. It was like I was daring myself to be close."

"But you couldn't meet the dare."

"Nope. Completely failed. She died giving birth."

"Oh, my."

"She knew there was a strong chance."

"She was going to be a mother no matter what. What desire. I love it."

"That's right."

"What a woman."

"She was that. There's another thing. It just came to me now."

"What is it?"

I hesitated. How much did I dare reveal? There is broken and there is demolished. Could Lucy really accept this back-from-the-dead shadow of a person? I was sure what I was about to tell her would blow the whole thing. But it was too late to turn back. "Women. Not just mother. Women. I think I've always envied women. I never realized it until this moment, but women have always fascinated me, and I think I've resented how close you are to life, and to creation and, I suppose, to love. Even Claire dying seemed to underscore just how profoundly connected women are to everything sacred. Now I get those dreams I had. When I was maybe thirty, I started having this repeating dream that I was surrounded by women, beautiful women, with big, round Renoir bellies and warm, contented smiles. Next to them I felt completely lacking. A nothing. No wonder I had to make them feel worthless. Damn."

"David, I'm so proud of you. I've never met a man who realized that and admitted it to himself. Come closer. I want to hold your hand."

"You do?"

"Yes."

"Why?" But just then I saw the tears welling up in Lucy's eyes. And I noticed how beautiful those eyes were, what a rich, bottomless brown. I wanted to bathe in them.

"Because."

"Because? Lucy, are you a Beatle maniac?"

Lucy winked. "Hold my hand, David."

"Gladly."

"Is your name really Lucy?"

"What gave me away?"

"'You Can Drive My Car' was pretty obvious, no?"

"I just couldn't resist. It was such fun. My mother named me Margaret and I did my best to live with it, you know, out of respect."

"Margaret? You're not a Margaret."

"Thank you. Life gets even harder when your mother doesn't see you. You know that, don't you, David?"

"I do."

"Yes. I tried Maggie for years, when Thatcher came into office, but I just couldn't hack it anymore. I figured the Beatles' 'Lucy in the Sky with Diamonds' fit me pretty good. Don't you?"

"Like a glove."

"Well thank you. Besides, I needed to say goodbye to Maggie, and Margaret, at a certain point in time."

"Why was that?"

"My son, Bobby. I think my Bobby and your Emily would have been best friends too."

"Do you mean . . . ?"

"Leukemia. He was eight. I was an oncologist." Lucy's eyes looked into mine; they pleaded, 'Do you understand?' I leaned in and took hold of both of her hands with more warmth and tenderness than I thought I was capable of.

"Oh, Lucy, dear Lucy, I understand."

"You do, don't you? You're the first. I can't tell you . . ." Lucy's eyes closed and I watched her spirit move inward, softening the scar tissue of unbearable grief. It was our moment. I shut my eyes and felt the outer and the inner worlds come together and become one, and all that is, was still. And when our eyes opened slowly onto the world of twoness, we looked at one another with thanks, knowing we had found ourselves and been found.

Chapter 68

I fell into bed after dinner. Crumbled is more like it. I needed a long, deep sleep to restore me for the next day's event. Sugar jumped up beside me, quick and nimble, as though gravity were a force that worked on others but not her. In only two weeks she had become a master of knowing my moods, and this night she looked into my eyes with such warmth and gentleness that for a moment all that was hard and heavy inside eased and made room for good to fill the cup of me.

Sugar's devotion moves me, Mom. I want to be able to give myself to someone and to live the way she does. I want to give without having to get and to receive without lusting for more. Sugar seems to never be on empty. This dumbfounds me. How is it possible to be full all the time? How is it possible to take that fullness into the world and play and live into every nook and cranny of life and not be emptied or wanting? I wonder if a human being can live that way.

It is the same old question and the same old doubt: will I fail at loving? And what about living? Will I fail at living, too? There's probably no difference. I think that's what did you in, Mom. I think you had a taste of love and life but knew you couldn't really live it the way you wanted. I feel for you, Mom, I do. It's all so sad.

The news of Lucy's loss left me with another big sadness. This one felt immovable. My own seems thin in comparison. Maybe that's not fair; maybe my own unwavering grief spooned up to Lucy's and held it close. When I look at it head on, it feels like one grief, a single river of sorrow running through the center of the world. Everything seems to teeter and totter over accepting this ever-present suffering. When I allow it to move how it wants, pain seems to irrigate something inside. I can feel those waters moistening and feeding my heart. When I fight it, the stone grows and feels fixed in my chest. Is that what happened to you, Mom? I want to know. Maybe psychosis is the bursting of the pipes after a hard freeze.

Where is the mercy? How can so much pain exist? What is worse than losing a child? Or losing a mother? How do people survive such intolerable pain? How did Lucy survive it to be such a lovely person? And she and I each lost one child. What about all the mothers around the world who have lost so many children and husbands? And what about the children who lose their mothers and fathers and walk the earth orphaned, forever searching for ghosts?

How can there be that and Sugar in the same spot? And Emily. What about Emily? Where did her love come from? Who was she, really? Why love this life at all, this life that burns the heart and takes all that is precious and grinds it to dust? Is that what happened to you, Mom? Were you ground to dust? Did you even think of me as your eyes closed for the last time? I don't think you did.

■ ■ ■

My mind raced and struggled with these questions until I fell asleep exhausted and aching. I woke in the morning feeling like I'd lived a dozen lives in my sleep. Maybe my spirit friends were arriving early for the celebration.

Sugar and I set out on our usual morning walk toward Mt. Tabor. I thought I saw candlelight in Lucy's house but decided to let her be and check in when we returned. The morning was magnificent; light the color of an apricot with blushing rose on its cheeks painted the eastern sky. We wound our way through the neighborhoods to the north and east of Clinton. Climbing gently toward the sleeping cinder cone, I stopped in my tracks, overcome with awe by dawn washing over Portland. How had I lived so many years without appreciating this beauty? Did you know beauty, Mom? Maybe it was the tulips, the color. Emily loved color, too.

Sugar trotted along ahead, happy as could be, occasionally looking back at me with her best smile. I'm a little embarrassed to admit how much that smile lights me up. I realize how much I love the silent conversation between the two of us. In fact, I am beginning to feel flashes of what must be happiness. Sometimes for no reason at all. For the first time in my life, I feel lucky to be alive. On the return home, walking down from Mt. Tabor, I even felt a desire to skip, just like I'd seen Emily do hundreds of times. Can you believe what I'm telling you? Are you happy for me, Mom?

The Day of the Dead seemed anything but dead, and though a seventy-three-year-old man looks pretty stupid trying to skip, and though I knew I might fall and break my neck, I gave it a try. I was out of breath before I went half a block. I bent over and held my knees, trying to catch my breath, and between hurried gulps of fresh air said, "Sugar, girl, we are being very silly today, aren't we?" Sugar seemed to agree.

We arrived home around nine, and as we rounded the corner by the house, I saw Audrey attaching an envelope to the front door.

"Hey, Audrey! Hi, wait for us."

"David, hi! I'm so glad to see you, and you too, Sugar. Come here, girl."

Sugar obliged. She knew instinctively that Audrey was someone special, and her little tail did three-sixties to prove it as she ran to Audrey and leapt into her arms.

"Oh, Sugar, you are the best doggie, aren't you?"

"Audrey, I'm so glad to see you. We just had a great walk, didn't we, Sugar? What a glorious morning!"

"That's wonderful. Did you have a good walk, Sugar girl?" Audrey gave Sugar's belly a good rubbing and then looked back at me with hope streaming from her eyes. "I just stopped by to see if you want to come by for dinner tomorrow night. I want you to meet Mark. Can you?"

"Sure I can. I'm not in demand, you know." We both chuckled and then turned with surprise when we heard Lucy chime in from the porch.

"Well, I don't know about that!"

"Lucy! You're up. Come and meet Audrey, Emily's best friend. I ran into Audrey the other night while you were gone, right here in front of the house. We hadn't seen each other for a long, long time. Can you believe it?"

"I can believe just about anything that's happening in your life, David Chase. Hello, Audrey, lovely to meet you. Would you like to come in for tea?"

"Oh, that sounds great, but I have to get home. Mark and I are heading out to see his family in Hood River."

"Audrey and Mark are getting married in . . . when is the wedding?"

"We haven't decided exactly. Sometime in late spring,

depending on how much we want to embarrass ourselves with my big belly."

Lucy's face blossomed with joy. "You're pregnant! Oh, Audrey, that's so wonderful."

The three of us stood under the shade of the giant ash tree in front of my house. It must be a hundred years old at least. Its leaves rustled and swayed while we stood there going on about Audrey's pregnancy. Music filled the air.

"Did David tell you he's going to walk me down the aisle, Lucy?"

"He did not. Oh my gosh, how beautiful."

"Lucy, I just invited David over for dinner tomorrow night. Would you like to join us?"

"That's so sweet of you, dear. I wouldn't want to intrude—you probably have lots to catch up on."

"Oh, it's fine, Lucy, really. I want David to meet Mark, and well, you just seem like you should be there too. Please come. That's okay with you, isn't it, David?"

"Of course, I love it. You'll love Lucy, Audrey, she's the real thing."

"Okay, see you tomorrow night around six?"

"Thank you, Audrey. I'd love to come." As she accepted the invitation, Lucy stepped toward Audrey and gave her a warm, motherly hug. The surrounding trees sighed. We all sighed and basked in our good fortune.

"We'll be there. Should I bring some homemade ice cream, Aud?"

"Please! I might eat it all if I'm in one of those moods."

"I'll make extra, just in case."

Audrey hugged Lucy again and then me. She held on tight, and I could tell her emotions were running over. Mine weren't far behind. I looked at Lucy and she had a tear in her eye too. But this wasn't grief; this was joy. And it seems joy is even more of a challenge. Harder to allow. My insides felt like they were about to burst like a bubble and that would be the end. That seems crazy. Why should happiness and joy be threatening?

"David, I've been so happy since I saw you the other night. I didn't think I could be so happy again. It feels like Emily is close, too. Thank you."

"Audrey, you're the best. I am so proud of you and happy we have each other. It seems like a miracle, all of it. And thanks for inviting Lucy."

Audrey let go and turned toward home. Less than a block away she turned and called, "Be sure to bring Sugar with you. Love you."

Lucy came close and took my hand. "She's beautiful, David, through and through. Will you tell me more about her, maybe tonight?"

"Yeah. It's a hell of a story. She is back from the dead, too. What an incredible young woman. I cannot believe my good fortune. Why is all this good stuff happening to me? Why? I don't get it, but I like it."

"I think you've suffered enough, old man."

"Do you think so?"

"Yep. Come on. Let's have some tea, just you and me."

Lucy took my arm, and we ambled up the walk into her house. The Day of the Dead would have to wait until this evening. For now, it was a perfect morning to fall in love.

Chapter 69

Dear Mom, I once thought falling in love was a fictitious delusion, that of all the grand illusions the human psyche is prone to making up, love at first sight had to be the most insane of all.

Today I see it differently. In fact, I think there has been a misunderstanding all along and what has been taken for love at first sight is something far more mysterious. Instead of seeing it as a romantic fantasy, I see now that the heart stops in its tracks when it recognizes a change in the destiny of the soul. A change that is both completely unpredictable and entirely inevitable. The heart drops when it knows what has come before is done and what lies ahead is calling.

Did you ever fall head over heels, Mom? Did you ever feel the earth move under your feet? Did you ever feel really loved? I don't think you did. I'm sorry. You're probably chuckling, thinking that I fell for Lucy the first time I met her, and this is some sort of intellectual rationalization of what is just a lovely twist of fate, or at worst, a pardonable adolescent resurgence. You could be right—how can two aging silverheads fall in love in a matter of days? But you would also be wrong because meeting Lucy changed everything. I could not have dreamed her up, but once she stepped into my life, it was obvious that this world could not have gone on another day without our friendship being a part of it.

Was it love? Maybe. I took to Lucy instantly; something in the way she laughed and smiled drew me to her when she released the family of ladybugs into the wild of her rose bushes. I immediately felt a big affection and remembered what I'd said to Randy about wanting to listen to a woman's voice. Her voice was music. Not a flute or a single instrument, but an ensemble, a trio or quartet of emotional harmonies. I marveled, throughout our time together, at the complex but lighthearted mix of sorrow and joy that rose in my body as I listened to her free and lucid voice. I could listen to her talk all night, and many times I did just that. We sat well into the silent darkness, talking, reading poetry out loud, telling stories of our rebel days in the sixties, and making up stories of lives we never lived. Our conversation soared across the universe and back. At times I followed her step; on other occasions she followed mine, but we came to be great dance partners, and who was leading whom was irrelevant. We heard the music. Here's an example of a poem Lucy introduced me to at midnight on her front porch. It's a few lines from a poem by Rilke:

> and I still don't know: am I a falcon,
>
> a storm, or a great song?

I guess if Rilke didn't know, it's okay if I don't.

Did you ever read poetry, Mom? Did you ever read it out loud with someone you adored? Did you fall in love and have your heart broken too many times? Is that what turned you into a storm? You were once a great song, weren't you? I hear you singing. Sing, Mama, sing to me.

Of course, it didn't hurt that I found Lucy especially attractive. Even at seventy-seven her body was trim and fit. I figured she could easily take me at arm wrestling. There was something intangible in the way she held herself and moved that drew me to her from the start. Something more than her wild white hair and those mysterious dark pools she gazed at the world through. It was her person, her wholehearted engagement with everything and every moment that knocked me out. That's what I fell for. And I fell hard.

Well, Mom, if this was love, it was also confusion. Was this the love Emily wanted me to know? Was I just doing what I'd always done and making everything revolve around a woman? What about loving the earth? What about existence? And then there's humanity. How the hell does anyone love humanity with the cruelty and butchery that goes on every day? What about loving me, and consciousness, and maybe even love itself? I knew I could love Sugar; that was easy, but I wasn't sure about the rest, and I sure didn't trust myself to really love Lucy the way I knew she deserved. Did I deserve love after everything? Could I accept it? Then there was Audrey. We seemed destined to love and care for each other. It seemed like everything was lining up to say, "Yes, you can, it's not too late."

. . .

Lucy and I went in for tea and talked for a couple of hours while the dogs took a nap by the back door. Her house was just like her personality: colorful artwork on the walls, books everywhere, and big stuffed chairs and a sofa to sink into. We talked and laughed about the dogs and the silly things they do every day. Lucy showed me her collection of Beatles music and some photos and memorabilia she'd picked up over the years. It was all quite light and easy. The mystery of tonight's fire ritual waited for us in the vast unknown, and neither of us was in a hurry to get into anything heavy.

I left before lunch and went home to make the ice cream for the night's celebration. The making of ice cream has become an important ritual in my life. First, there is the gathering of the ingredients: raw, whole milk, rock salt, fresh eggs (lots of them), and exotic chocolates. Then, there is scalding and chilling of the can and dasher, measurement of the ice and rock salt—love that rock salt—and cooking the mixture.

I marvel most at the alchemy of the operation. When it's all mixed together, and the ice and salt are layered properly, the churning begins. Slow at first, clockwise, and picking up speed after the first ten minutes until the handle resists. This one-time resistance means you're on the right track. Then, voilà! Ice cream! Something unimaginably sweet and creamy good has come from ingredients that, on their own, never even hinted at the outcome.

Churning. What better word, what better symbol for the inner process? Every time I turn that handle and feel the action of the ice-cream maker, I feel assured that all the pain, confusion, and hopelessness is being mixed and sculpted into love that is beyond understanding. It's the making, really, not the tasting that gets me. Although tasting's a pretty fine payoff.

For the night's celebration I prepared David's Decidedly Dense Double Dark Chocolate Fudge. It turned out perfectly, and I was so excited to give it to Lucy. Maybe it sounds funny to eat ice cream outside on a chilled November night, but to us it felt just right.

In just a short time, my feelings for Lucy had grown big. Still, I worried about helping her with her grief over her son. Would I be able to comfort her? Could I be genuinely empathetic with a woman? With you? I'm feeling it; I feel for the misery you must have known, Mom. I do. Can you feel it? Are we connected? You and me? Us, together. Ah.

Having finished the ice cream, I lay down with Sugar for a short nap so we'd be fresh for the party. As she snuggled up to me, I said to her, "Sugar, how did I ever get so lucky? Tonight is going to be quite a night, girl."

Sugar looked at me with doggie sympathy, as if to say, "You have no idea."

Chapter 70

It was dark when we woke. I should say, when I woke. Sugar was already awake and ready to go. I lay in bed a little longer, wondering what the night would bring, when I heard a few crows returning home from their day's work, cawing and clamoring in the treetops. Hearing their call, I relaxed. I felt confident they would watch me closely and bring me back in a snap if I drifted away.

As I slipped my shoes on, I heard a stirring in the backyard. It was Lucy, scurrying about with branches and twigs in her arms. Her movements were sure and swift, and her arms held their cargo tenderly, as if it were alive and precious. She wore a black hooded jellaba like the people of North Africa wear in the winter. In fact, she was entirely dressed in black including tall boots and something, maybe a scarf around her head.

The way she moved and lay the branches down made me quiver with fear and excitement. I rushed to my closet, threw on a black sweatshirt, and slipped out the back door.

"Hi, you look, bewitching—in a beautiful way." I laughed a little anxiously, and Lucy must have sensed it. Surrounded by the black of night and the full hood of the jellaba, and that enchanting white hair falling to her shoulders like lightning, she took on the radiance of the wild and looked at me with an electric intensity. I nearly took a step backwards, but her voice met me with kindness and reassurance:

"I am a witch, a good witch. Don't worry, I won't put an evil spell on you!"

"Phew, I wasn't sure."

"Ha, maybe you want me to! Wouldn't that be a treat? I think I will put a spell on you. A friendly spell that will protect and prepare us both for whatever comes tonight."

"Protect from what?"

"You never know, my dear. You never know on El Día de los Muertos. One must be respectful and prepared. That's another reason we're building the fire in your yard."

"I've been wondering about that. Your place feels more charmed and inviting."

"Because the crows live here, David, and they will warn and protect us from anything we can't handle."

"I was just thinking the same thing. I love crows."

Lucy lifted her head from arranging the wood and gave me that "tell me more" look.

I continued. "They're fearless. And defiant and smart. I used to hate them and plot to do them in when they did their four a.m. wake-up routine. But after Emily died, they were the only living creatures I could relate to. I learned to listen to their conversations, and when I went to the prison, I definitely felt they were on my side."

"Excellent! Very auspicious, David Chase! We are in for a good, good night. Help me get the rest of the wood. All this wood came from right here in the neighborhood. I've been gathering it for a year. It's fallen limbs and dead wood—silver maple, red oak, and magnificent old elm—left to decompose. I pick it up whenever I'm out walking. We have enough for one very fine fire."

"That's beautiful, Lucy. Well-seasoned dead. I love it."

"Yeah, this wood will crackle and burn and call out to any spirits in the hood that want to visit. The fire will signal to the stars that we are here and welcoming any and all forms of grace. By the way, we've been blessed—did you look up and see the night sky? One of those spectacular, clear nights in November and a new moon at that. We are going places tonight, baby."

I hadn't noticed the stars; I was transfixed by Lucy and the fire in her eyes. I smiled and told Lucy, "You're glowing." What I didn't say was how sexy she looked in her black witch's robes. Something was gathering in the treetops—a growing force, a meeting of the erotic and the mystical, and the coming of the dead.

Lucy must have read my mind. She looked up from the firepit where she was arranging the twigs and branches and let her eyes sink into mine. For a moment nothing moved, and a breathless wind spun us into another orbit. "You are aglow yourself, David, glowing like a full moon."

I wondered if I was too old to blush, but apparently I wasn't. I didn't want Lucy to see, so I bent down and picked up some branches to stack by the firepit. "I love fire. Where are the paper and matches?"

"We're going au naturel tonight. All original stuff. I dried moss over the summer and brought back some flint from Mt. Hood. A witch's fire has to snap, crackle, and pop!"

She looked up at me and winked. Her eyes were already on fire and something in me shivered, both wanting to retreat and wanting to go closer. She was the fire I wanted to be near.

"We're just about ready, David. The crows are gonna love this. And so are we. Love will be roaring tonight!"

The branches were neatly stacked like a teepee about three feet high. They rested on top of a huge mound of dry moss. Lucy had collected enough wood to burn all night and it lay beside the firepit. I carried the Adirondack chairs in and placed them a few feet from the pit. Close enough to be warm, and far enough to be free of smoke and sparks.

A slight breeze circulated through the neighborhood. It seemed the perfect night to welcome the dead back to earth. I wasn't sure what I expected or what I really believed about all this spirit stuff, but I was intrigued and anxious about what might happen between Lucy and me. She must have read my mind.

"Are you nervous?" she asked.

I had made it my vow to always be honest with Lucy, and tonight it was easy to be true to that. "Yeah, I am a little nervous. Are you?"

"Sure, and that's a good sign. We're on to something."

"On to what?"

"Who knows? Let's light the fire and find out."

"We're off!"

"I've been practicing with this flint all summer. Hope I can get the spark tonight. Here we go."

Lucy's practice paid off. She struck the two pieces of flint together and instantly sparks flew from the edges, took to the moss, and blackened it. Smoke began to rise, and as it did, Lucy started humming low, deep notes. The hum seemed to merge with the cloud of smoke rising from the moss and guide it toward the open sky. At the same time, she fanned the small embers forming at the tips of the moss. It looked like a large mound of fibrous hair atop the head of a buried but breathing giant. It was to this presence and to the wide-open vastness reaching from eternity to our little spot on the ground that she spoke.

"Mother of all that breathes and moves, we live in the radiance of your body and owe the spark of our being to your abundant generosity. Please light our little fire with the flame of your love and open us to the truth of ourselves and your presence. We honor you and those that have found their way back to your full embrace. We ask that you reveal yourself in whatever form you desire and give us the courage to offer ourselves to your love and to our beloved friends and family whose spirits we welcome tonight."

I was speechless. Lucy's invocation kept resonating and filling the silence that followed her words. A longing to be in that full embrace rose from my depths and settled in.

Lucy was silent. She gazed into the heart of the fire, which was beginning to crackle and rise.

"Now we must feed our dear fire like the pagans did and as it is still done in India. Here, take these herbs and throw them in, and when you do, say something sweet under your breath. This bowl is our eucalyptus, this is coriander, this one sage. Do lots of sage, will you? Here are fenugreek and mustard seeds—they'll put some snap, crackle, and pop into the mix. I'll pour the oils in. The Hindus use all sorts of oils but I'm a coconut nut, so here goes."

Soon, not only was the backyard illuminated by huge flames leaping for the heavens, but the most intoxicating aroma flooded the surrounding space. I half expected the crows to fall out of the treetops. Henry and Sugar ran around the fire, barking. After a time of circling the flames and adding their voices to the prayer of invocation, they quieted and sat near us with their noses turned up, no doubt perceiving sounds and smells not available to us.

Lucy stroked Henry's ears and sang along, ever so softly, with the first of the dead to arrive: her old buddy, John Lennon. Her voice was barely audible, which made it all the more alluring, as it blended with the crackling percussion of the fire and the silence of the flames.

Everything came together effortlessly. The dark and the light danced. The dogs lay side by side. And Lucy and I sat in silence, feeling our edges melting as we let the magic of the fire bring us together into one wild and peaceful being with many arms and many mouths. Of those, mine was the first to speak.

"This is good."

"It is." Lucy turned from the fire, looked at me, and said softly, "Still scared, David?"

"No. Well, maybe. I guess I'm always a little scared, but this feels more like awe. This is all so new to me I don't know what to call these feelings."

"Good. An honest man. Fear is a good compass. Did you ever hear what Georgia O'Keeffe said about fear?"

"No."

"She said, 'I've been afraid every day of my life and it never stopped me from doing anything.'"

I stared at Lucy for a moment. She seemed to know so much; I wondered for a second if I could keep up with her. "That scares me, but I like it. Easier said than done, but I like it."

"Right. If fear isn't in you, you're not alive. Who isn't afraid, and sometimes petrified?"

"It's so easy to back away, Lucy. It happens. You back away

without knowing you are, and then you are way back. Especially with love."

"Especially with love. Right. The heart fills with fear instead of blood."

"What are you afraid of, Lucy?"

"Oh dear, that will take all night by itself. Let's see. I'm still afraid of the dark at times. Monsters and stuff. Are you?"

"Sure. Monsters and bad people coming for me. Not so much since Sugar's around. She's my security blanket, you know."

"She's the best. Henry, too. Isn't it silly how fragile we are? Big tough guys during the day and little weenies at night. One crack from the floorboard, and yikes, it's the Boston Strangler!"

"Why are we so jumpy, Lucy? Everything seems constructed to make us feel safe."

"Because there is no safe, David. You can't make the world safe and the more you try, the more you put logs on the fire of fear. No refuge—until you learn that you are one with the big mama. But that is one tough class, and not for sissies."

"You sound like Emily. She always said stuff like that. She thought we adults were pretty silly."

"She is one smart cookie, that Emily. I want to know more about her."

"Sure, but first I want to hear more about what you're afraid of. You seem fearless to me."

"Ha, you've got a lot to learn about me, David. I'm as fearful as the next person—I just happen to be kind of sassy too. I'm afraid of not having the courage to go forward. Like you said, that I'll trick myself into backing off. That scares me. But really, that isn't the scariest."

"What is?"

"Too awful to talk about yet. I'll give you the top three runners up. I told you about courage. Sometimes I feel like Dorothy's friend, the lion, and after all these years, I fear that I'm wrong, and there is no God. Maybe I'm just another old fool grasping at straws. I'm afraid I've been making this spirit stuff up for however many years, me and ten thousand of my best friends who were too chicken to look at the bare facts. But then, I worry I fool myself about all sorts of things. I guess I could say I'm afraid of loving and dying, but I guess that's a given."

Lucy took a deep breath and went on. "Ok, here we go, time to get real. Ready? I'm afraid I'm not pretty anymore. How's that for petty? I wish that wasn't still important. Some things never go away, do they? Your turn."

"Not pretty, you? You're beautiful, Lucy. You are. Everything about you is beautiful."

"Thank you, David. I guess it's the inside that counts. But go on, your turn."

"Well, I feel those things too. Some seem so petty and childish, but they hang on. I fear aging, my brain turning to Gorgonzola crumbs and drool coming out of my mouth. Every day I wake up dreading the decay of my brain. And, of course, dying, except I really don't fear dying like I used to. Once upon a time, I would wake up in the middle of the night in terror of disappearing. Or even worse, buried alive—eternal dying like the guy in *2001 Space Odyssey* who got ejected by Hal and disappeared into never-ending darkness. That can still get me shaking, but it doesn't seem to last long or stick anymore, even though fear finds me every day, and my bones and joints ache like crazy, and I forget why I opened the refrigerator. I'm feeling young inside, and kind of fresh and supple. More so since I met you. There's this buoyancy. It's really amazing to me. I think you and Sugar are responsible for most of it, but I suppose something else is at work. I haven't told you, but I even had a wet dream my first night here. Now that's a fear. I really don't want to live the rest of my life without feeling sexual. Do you?"

"Heavens no! That would be terrible. How could a child of the sixties tolerate such a thing?"

The fire roared its approval, and we shared a good laugh. As if to emphasize the point, I put more wood on the flames and Lucy and I exchanged a knowing, lusting glance.

Lucy touched my arm and gently rubbed her fingers over my skin from my elbow to my fingertips. I nearly came undone. "It's the house, David. You won't be celibate in that house. The couple that rented it before you sang the hallelujah chorus just about every night. I'm telling you, they about brought the house down. Besides, you've got the good fortune of having this old flower child for your best friend and neighbor, so you won't go hungry if you treat me good."

"I'm gonna treat you real good, Lovely Lucy. I'll come kiss the sky and bring you lilies that smell like the Goddess herself." To make the promise real, I stroked the palm of Lucy's hand and watched her swoon with delight.

"Oh, I love it already. Aren't we a couple of oversexed seniors!" Her eyes closed and I could see she was taking in every drop of pleasure from my touch. With her eyes opening and closing like the wings of a moth, Lucy tried to talk. "Yum, I love this, David. We grew up in an amazing time, didn't we? I remember those days so vividly."

"I'm sure I wasn't as adventurous as you were, but I still had my share."

"Tell me the most outrageous thing you did."

"The most outrageous? That's pretty easy. I was a young doc on my way to a fellowship in South Africa—remember when they were doing the first heart transplants? Well, there was this stewardess, a very sexy stewardess on Pan Am, remember them? Something about those Pan Am stewardesses was irresistible. Not that I didn't find just about every female enticing, but she was Danish, blond and gorgeous. We had a spark from the first time our eyes met, and, well, it's a long flight from New York to Johannesburg, and we got it on in the business class bathroom somewhere over the Atlantic."

"You didn't!"

"Oh, we did. Four times!"

"Four times!" Lucy's eyes bulged in amazement. She repeated herself as astonishment took over her entire face. "Four times? My, you have quite the appetite, Dr. Chase! That must take some acrobatics."

"Where there's a will there's a way, and there was plenty of will."

"The pilots must have wondered where the air turbulence came from! My God."

"After the fourth time we came out to a line of people waiting to use the commode."

"Horrors!"

"Yeah, you should have seen the looks on their faces."

"Ooo-whee! I can see them now. Good one. Wish I'd thought of that."

"If I tried it now, they'd have to do an emergency landing to put me in traction."

"Ha, I can just imagine them prying the two of you out of there mounted for life."

We doubled over with a good, deep laugh and had to hold on to the arms of the chairs to keep from falling out. But maybe we wanted to fall out and roll around the grass and howl with pleasure like the couple who primed the atmosphere before my arrival. While our laughter was quieting, I managed to say, "Your turn."

"Okay. Hold on to your hat. And no judging, right?"

"Promise."

"If I remember right, it was 1968, summer of love, of course. I was a student at Berkeley. Where else? I had a good friend who rode a Harley chopper and he let me borrow it for the day. I dropped a tab of windowpane and headed for Big Sur. By the time I got to 101, I had thrown my helmet away and discarded my boots. I was high as Jimi Hendrix at Monterey, and when I got to the highway and the ocean, it was time to disrobe."

"Really?"

"Really. I rode the 101 laid back on that chopper barebacked. Easy riding."

"No top?"

"No top. No bra. No pants. No . . ."

"No, you didn't."

"Easy, now. A girl has some discretion. No worries."

"Wonderful."

"Ecstasy. Me, the wind, sunshine, and a pair of sunglasses. Oh, and a bottom."

"Phew. I was worried the highway patrol might have stopped you."

"They did. A motorcycle cop."

"Oh, dear. Did he arrest you?"

"Nope. Not even a ticket."

"Not even a fine? No kidding. Wait a minute, you didn't?"

"That's right—we did it in the road!"

"Unbelievable. You're amazing, Lovely Lucy. Truly amazing."

"No judging now."

"No, no judging, promise. Just awe. A California State Highway Patrol dude? They were said to be really bad dudes, hated hippies, right? And you did it with a pig, on the road in broad daylight?"

"Are we judging?"

"No, I'm amazed . . ."

"He was black, he was beautiful, and his Johnson was divine. My orgasm didn't stop screaming till well past Hawaii. Probably caused a tsunami in Tahiti. Man, we could have caused the great California earthquake."

"All right, all right, calm down, girl, you're making this old white guy feel kind of wimpy."

"Sorry, guess I got carried away. The fire must be really hot."

"The former tenants must have done it in the backyard."

"They did. I watched them one night. Not bad."

By now the dogs were really beginning to wonder about us. We doubled over again in hysterics, reliving those wild and crazy days of our youth, and the dogs jumped to their feet to rescue us from our temporary insanity. We reassured the little darlings we were just having fun chasing memories the way they chase leaves. They seemed to accept that and lay back down but kept an eye on us just in case.

"You're hysterical, Lucy."

"I'm a bad girl."

"I think I love you."

"Now you're talkin'. And I love you, dear David. I've loved you from the first day."

"That's crazy. Love at first sight. I realized I fell for you just hearing your voice float up from the roses. Before I even saw you. It was music, sweet music."

"Oh David, that is so romantic, I can't resist." And she leaned over and kissed my cheek and gave my earlobe a sexy nibble. "I still remember the look on your face that morning—so open and curious, young and uncertain. Aren't we a couple of lucky ones?"

We paused for a moment in each other's gaze and slowly returned to the soothing dance of the fire. Who knows how long we let ourselves bask in that embrace; our minds were empty and our hearts full. A loud pop brought us out of the reverie and my mind returned to where we were before expressing our love took us by the hand. I wanted to know more about Lucy, so I asked her, "But what are you most afraid of? You said there was one thing that frightened you most."

"Do we have to?"

"Of course not."

"Well, it is one hell of a fire. Maybe we can burn this one up. But how about another warm-up?"

"Sure, whatever you need."

"Okay, but promise you won't laugh at me."

"Promise."

"You're sure? This is kind of stupid and kind of sensitive."

"I get it. No laughing."

"I'm afraid people don't like me."

"You? Not like you?"

"Yep. Are you laughing?"

"No, just surprised. Really surprised. You seem so confident and secure and so incredibly likable."

"I suppose I try hard."

"I tried hard to look normal."

"You probably fooled a lot of people. I know I did. Including me. But there it is, following me, stuck on like a leech. Can't really feel it, can't really feel I'm likeable. Seems so simple. But it isn't. Wish it was. Wish I could befriend myself. Why is it so hard?"

"I liked you before I saw you. Your voice found me, and I couldn't help but like you. You didn't even know I was listening— you weren't trying too hard, you were just being Lovely Lucy and sweet-talking the ladybugs. It was beautiful."

"Thank you, David. I can feel you liking me, and it means so much."

"How could someone like you not be likable?"

"Oh, it's a big story. Too big. You know, being a girl, a smart girl—boys don't like that and lots of girls don't either. So many little things add up. So sad. So many girls don't like themselves. You can't imagine how many."

"I added to it, I'm sure."

"You did. But you didn't make it. It's been thousands of years in the making. Maybe tonight will help. I hope so. You help, David. You really do. So many years trying to prove myself. So many. And never quite getting there. And then lost, not knowing which one of me was really me. That's taken some doing to untangle."

We took a breather to lose ourselves in the fire and remember the years of being lost. Our growing closeness allowed each of us to do so with genuine sympathy. As we did, the crows welcomed the spirits of the dead with a chorus of chanting, and the intensity of the night deepened.

Lucy sensed the change in atmosphere and released my hand. She leaned toward the fire and said, "I better keep going or I'm afraid I'll lose my courage. I can feel her wanting to run."

"Feel who?"

"The little girl who is sure no one likes her. She's sure neither of us will want her after I tell you the really big one. Numero uno nightmare fear."

"Yeah. I've got one to throw in with yours. Let's see if the fire can take our fear and burn it up."

"You're on. But you have to hold my hand and kiss me when I'm done. And you can't tell me I'm wrong to feel this way. Right? And I'll do the same for you. Promise?"

"I will."

"Okay. We'll just hold each other and let the fire do the rest. Good?"

"Real good."

"Maybe you should go first."

"I will if you want."

"No thanks. This is my turn. Be brave, girl."

"I think this fire can take anything." What I meant was I had total faith in Lucy. I hoped she felt it. Even as we moved toward the unknown and a ball of fear began to build in my stomach, I believed in this woman. I looked to the heavens for a sign and then aligned myself with Lucy, leaning toward the fire, and said, "We can do this, Lucy."

"Thanks, David. I hope you're right."

Chapter 71

We barely noticed the autumn breeze slow to nothing. The trees stood over us like watchful parents. Our friends the crows took their positions as guardians of the night, and a sacred quiet waited for Lucy to speak. Even the stars stopped twinkling as stillness prepared the world for what was to come.

"I was a terrible, terrible mother."

"Lucy, I—"

"You can't talk me out of this one. I've done everything—every therapy, hypnosis, and drug—and it won't go away. Hear me out."

"Okay, I'm listening."

"How old were you when Emily was born?"

"Fifty-two."

"I was twenty-five. I knew nothing, except ambition and hunger for experience. I was determined not to be held back by a baby and certain I could do it all, including care for the little bundle in my arms. His father disappeared into a Zendō outside of Tokyo when Bobby was six months old, and my resolve just hardened.

"I loved Bobby. No question about that. I was crazy about him. He slept with me, I breastfed him, we danced to the Beatles and Grateful Dead. It was unbelievably sweet. But I was going to be a doctor. Nothing was going to stop me. So I left Bobby in day cares all over the city. I left him too much. I refused to see his distress. I refused to be deterred. A few friends tried to tell me Bobby looked anxious and sad. My own mother suggested I delay residency for a few years. Shit, I've been over this so many times there's nothing new to say. I fucked up. I just fucked up and Bobby suffered. The doctors told me a million times the leukemia was a genetic mistake. They told me he was doomed from the start, but I wouldn't believe them, no matter how many medical lectures I heard. I blamed myself. And I wouldn't accept any condolences, even from my own mother. I still blame myself to this day. I don't want to die thinking I'm a terrible mother, but I fear there's no escaping it. I'm condemned. This month will be fifty-two years. I've been collecting this wood for over a year waiting for this day, hoping to throw my pain into the fire, hoping Kali or Jesus or some kind of grace could help me. I figured on doing this myself. I didn't figure on you. I don't know how that changes things, but I can tell it does."

Lucy bent over in distress. I wanted so badly to comfort her, so I put my trembling hand on her back and moved it slowly in a circle. But she wasn't ready to be touched; she sat up abruptly and shook her back to remove my hand. I wasn't able to sit with the tension, so I tried another approach.

"Would you like to hear a story, Lucy?"

"Not yet. I can't . . . I can't go all the way . . . I'm trying to clean it up some, trying to . . . Damn! I can't say it, I can't . . ."

"I'm here, Lucy. I'm here. Tell me."

And then it came out. "I killed him . . . I killed Bobby. That's the truth, that's what I live with . . . I killed my beautiful baby boy." And then she wailed and pierced the silence of the dark sky.

I rested my hand on her arm.

Lucy's words and her torment took to the flames and were

devoured. The sound that erupted from the fire was more than an explosion, more than anything I have ever heard. Sugar and Henry jumped to their feet barking; the crows beat their wings and shouted a battle cry. That astounding sound reverberated through the surrounding trees, the crow's nests, through our bones, and into the ground, which took it in and made a home for the cry of the damned. And when it was of the ground, the sound that was the breaking of history's hold morphed into a chorus of women's voices wailing and singing and giving thanks.

And with that, the fire grew quiet and the flames rose and fell, rising into the dead of night and falling into a layer of glowing embers. Lucy took my hand in hers. Night turned to tenderness. Tenderness to warmth. For a time, nothing stirred but our beating hearts and the touch of mercy.

■ ■ ■

This is a long story, isn't it, Mom? Are you staying with me? I think I feel you here, but I'm not sure. What I really hope is that when the explosion erupted, it cleared whatever pain and guilt remains in your soul as it did Lucy's. I mean that with all my heart. When I looked at Lucy after who knows how long of being taken into the fire, all I could see was her face, and it was glowing like the embers at our feet. Sure, there will be aftershocks, waves of sorrow and guilt about Bobby, habits of thought, but it feels to both of us that the power the past has had over her will never be the same. We have been touched by mercy. I pray you felt that touch too, Mom.

. . .

"Tell me your story, David."

"Are you sure? It can wait."

"I'm sure, and thanks for asking. I feel, what? Loved, beloved. These are different tears."

"Me too, Lucy. Really different." I took a deep breath, searching for the right way to tell my story. So much had come out at the prison I wasn't really sure where the emotional pain was living. What I did know is that I wanted to give as much of myself as Lucy had. I wanted to go to my depths and find what would evoke the presence of that transformative energy just as Lucy had. But I wasn't sure if I could; I was still transfixed by what had happened just a few minutes before. I was afraid my story would come out mechanical or sounding rehearsed. I needn't have worried; the fire was still burning and the dead had not yet left for home.

"Emily was killed on her eighteenth birthday. I was on my way to meet one of my several lovers that morning when I ran into Audrey, who was meeting Emily for breakfast. I was such a lousy wretch I even eyed Audrey and took advantage of touching her suggestively when we crossed the street. I hate myself for that. Emily was run over on her bike by a crazed meth freak on a motorcycle. She died in my lap with Audrey by her side trying to hold her here. Her spine was crushed, and we were covered with her blood. Audrey screamed loud enough to be heard by the Gods on Mt. Olympus. I froze—head to toe. Emily was killed instantly, and yet somehow, something allowed her to speak, to empty her lungs with two words, impossible words. She whispered to me, 'Daddy, love.' That was it, Daddy . . . Daddy . . .'"

And I broke. A flash flood of fear and grief cascaded through my body. This time there was no explosion. Only heartache. I fell forward and buried my face in my hands. Lucy did her best to comfort me. She put her hand on my back and gently said my name again and again. I felt her caring for me and it helped, but I wanted to be the one caring for her.

"Shit, I . . . I didn't want to cry, not right now. This is for you."

"You're helping me, David, you are, please don't stop. I can feel now in a different way. Look, I'm crying too. It's heartbreaking, but it's good. Good for both of us."

Lucy's words and the kindness in her voice relaxed me, and the flood began to ease enough for me to continue. "The entire lie that was me ended. I ran and hid for years—from Audrey, from my work, from everything. I lost track of days. I was a dead man walking. I was sure it was my fault and I deserved nothing but damnation."

I paused, interrupted by flashbacks of the warehouse room and the daily death march to the bicycle. An involuntary shudder shook the air around us. It shook something loose in me that allowed me to continue. But first I looked at Lucy to see if she was all right, and there she was, so present and attentive I could hardly believe my eyes. No one ever looked at me like that, but I guess I never let anyone see me in this way.

"One day I met a young woman on the bridge with one leg over the railing, ready to jump. We had some kind of big connection that I think brought both of us out of a trance. I know it woke me. She walked away and I never saw her again, but the fog lifted. In the midst of absolute despair, there was a clearing, and then something invisible took me by the hand and led me to Salem and the state pen to talk to Emily's killer. I bucked and cursed and felt I was betraying Emily in the worst way, but I couldn't shake loose. I went in kicking and screaming and sure that I was again failing my daughter by meeting with the man who murdered her and trying to find something in my heart for him when there was only hate."

"My God, David, I can't fathom this. What you did is, is . . . I'm speechless." Lucy was shaking just imagining me walking into the prison in such an unstable and vulnerable condition. Her face darkened, and she seemed to be feeling something of the fear I experienced that first day walking into the prison.

At that very moment, Sugar jumped onto Lucy's lap and kissed her chin. Lucy cried like a baby and held my little Sugar close. She wept and shrieked when Sugar licked her face. When the love storm calmed, she and her friend turned and looked at me with so much affection.

Despite the emotion of the hour, I smiled at the sight of Lucy being undone by Sugar's caretaking.

"So much for being unlikable," I said. "But Lucy, it wasn't only me—I'm telling you, at least it wasn't only me. I felt as weak as ever. Nothing would have made me feel better than to run to the bus stop and take the next Greyhound back to Portland and my dungeon. Don't you see how weak I am? It wasn't me. A force took me there and kept me there, and a greater force took over as we talked. The wicked and the dead sat face-to-face, and over the course of thirty days, ten meetings, nine conversations, something impossible happened. And that's the beauty of it. The crazy, impossible beauty of it. Not the usual 'I forgive you' bullshit. I couldn't really forgive him. I couldn't. But I could be taken deeper. Deeper into something else. Something not made by us. Don't ask me what or how. But that something drew us, and what was unacceptable was accepted. We became friends—more than friends, really, if that doesn't sound too crazy."

Lucy put her hand on my arm, and I stared into the fire hoping to be consumed. I felt a joy pierce my heart again and again thinking of Randy. I felt him close by. Here with us.

"He's dying, Lucy. I love him. If you can believe it, Randy became my first real friend." I held my breath, and looking to the fire for strength, I asked the unfair and scariest of questions: "Do you think I'm awful to love the man who killed my daughter?"

"I think you're beautiful. And . . . so alive. So very alive."

"Lucy?"

"Yes?"

"Do you feel it? The joy?"

Lucy nodded and kissed my hand. And then we came together for our first kiss. Our lips were tentative; they quivered like leaves in a light breeze, but when they met, when they touched, everything melted; the grief and the fear, even shame couldn't hold its own and crumbled once the yearning of those lips came together. It wasn't a long, passionate kiss; it was a perfect kiss, a seal of love that landed like a butterfly on a flower petal. We slowly drew our heads away and I said to Lucy, "That was my first kiss."

Lucy smiled and said, "It was lovely kiss, David, lovely."

"Lucy, is Bobby here?"

"Yes, he is. My Bobby is right here with us, in the joy."

With that we turned to the fire and gave thanks. Our lives danced in the lavender and green flames while we sat in the quiet. Our hands rested side by side, barely touching, sharing whispered words of wisdom. While we sat there, the fire consumed every last bit of fear and self-hatred in our hearts. We did nothing but allow ourselves to be hollowed out and filled with warmth.

After a time, I leaned over and kissed Lucy on the forehead. The fire had burned away all the edges. I felt truly gentle for the very first time. I whispered to Lucy, "I made us some ice cream. I'll be right back."

Chapter 72

I can love, Mom. I can. I could downplay it and say anyone could love Lucy. But that would be wrong and mean-spirited. I'm in there, in the joy, giving what is in my heart. I worry I might back away, retreat to a safety zone. Maybe I'll find I can't take in so much good. Or I'll find some way to ruin it. I think whatever brought me here won't let me get away with that, at least not for long. It would kill me to hurt Lucy.

I'm still amazed that I could find love in my heart for Randy. What a miracle. But what about a woman? Wouldn't that be even more impossible after all you and I went through? How could I possibly trust a woman after what you did to me, Mom? How? You left me in the snow, you left me to find my way to school, and you left me in the garage, choking. How could you do that to me, your little boy? I still don't understand. Help me understand. But that was you. Sick, tragic, lovable you. I'm sorry for you and us. Are you sorry? Can't you do something to let me know? Come to me in a dream? Talk to me? Am I supposed to do this by myself? I need you, Mom. I don't want to be angry any longer. I don't. But don't leave me here alone. Don't ever do that again.

■ ■ ■

When I returned, Lucy was sitting closer to the fire petting the dogs. I had the impression that her entire being was at peace. I was a bit envious but so happy for Lucy and Bobby. "You look so peaceful, Lucy." I said this softly, trying to meet her with the same spirit. I haven't known peacefulness, so I wasn't sure I could pull it off, but I must have done okay because she turned from the fire and looked at me with an expression that was new. Her entire face and body were so at ease and content I nearly dropped the ice cream.

I have to admit to feeling a little uneasy, so I put the ice cream down on my chair and added sticks and branches to the fire. Henry and Sugar asked for something to chew on and were very happy when I handed each of them a juicy hunk of maple.

"Here you go. Have some ice cream. It's straight from the gods. I think you'll like it."

Lucy brought the spoon to her mouth slowly, enjoying the anticipation of the first taste. Once it was in her mouth, she closed her eyes and let out a moan of sensual delight. The sound that came from her body, I have to say, was more than a little arousing. I thought of trying to hide it but gave in to the moment and let my adoration and excitement show.

"Yum. Oh my gosh, this is fantastic! So creamy. Did you really make this, David?"

"Yum is right. And you look positively yummy as well, Lovely Lucy. Positively delicious. And, oh yes, I did make it. Specially for you and this occasion. And for Bobby and Emily. Imagine their chocolate-smeared faces."

"Why, you look stunningly bright and sexy yourself, David

Chase. Aren't we feeling the juice?" She paused and bathed me in her desire, and without touching, we were lovers.

Effortlessly, we moved in sync back to faces painted in chocolate. "Those were great days. Once I gave Bobby some paints and paper and suggested we make self-portraits. He was four, I think. I got the paints out and was putting paper on the easel, and when I turned around, he was painting his face and arms. We laughed and laughed and then I painted mine too."

"What a kick. Emily was always painting. She adored color and seemed to flow effortlessly with the creative spirit."

"You must have loved that."

"I did and I didn't. I couldn't appreciate it. It seemed strange to me. I went along with her artwork and dancing, but I didn't get it at all. She seemed like she came from a different planet. Now I can see it was me that was strange. But that's changing, thanks to you. You're alive like Emily was, Lucy."

"We're bringing each other back to life, David. We are. God, this is incredible chocolate, David. Are there seconds?"

"Sure, eat it up. It's best fresh."

"Hey, I've got an idea. Let's read some poems. It's the perfect mood, don't you think?"

"Well sure, I guess. I'm not much of a poetry guy."

"Oh, you probably haven't read the right stuff. You are going to love Rumi and the gang. Here, let me run and get my book. I'll read one to you right now."

Lucy disappeared into the dark. My body was tingling by now, my heart full of joy. This was all feeling too good to be true.

Was it all a dream? Who was this new guy emerging by the hour? I don't recognize myself, Mom. It's like the magician keeps pulling more and more scarves from the hat that is me! Sometimes it's unnerving. The fire kept on, warm and comforting despite having no answers to my questions. Were you the fire? Was that warmth your presence?

Lucy was gone longer than I expected, and when she came out, she was struggling with two objects, one under each arm.

"What do you have there?"

"Cots. Camping cots from the co-op. We're sleeping out tonight under the Milky Way, you and me and the dogs. This night is not ready to end. Here, you set up the cots. I'll get the sleeping bags. Are you game?"

"I'm in."

"Good. I'll be right back."

She was much quicker this time and came back laughing with two stuff sacks under her arms.

"What's so funny?"

"I was thinking about the first time we met and the ladybugs. What if they get cold and come inside our bags? They might tickle."

"You're pretty silly, and that's a compliment."

"I'm a funny old bird. Here, get your bag and make yourself comfy."

We fluffed the bags and climbed in. The dogs immediately jumped up on the cots and made themselves at home. Lucy got out a pocket flashlight and settled in to read.

"You're in for a treat, David. One Rumi poem and you'll be

a goner. Hold on, I think I need to be quiet now. Let's just be still for a while and take this in."

"Of course, no rush."

It was a sacred pause. The flames of our fire danced in the silence to the music of a magic flute. And the quiet—the quiet entered the cells of our bodies and the surrounding molecules of space. We were perfectly still. Empty and full.

"Okay, I'm ready now. Here we go." Lucy began to read, one beautiful poem after another; her voice was a breeze coming off the ocean, caressing our earthly bodies. I took it in like sand receiving foamy surf. And then she read a line that made us pause:

This we have now is not imagination

And she read it again. "It isn't, is it, David? We aren't dreaming, are we?"

"We aren't, this is it, Lucy, we're living and loving. It's the real thing!"

Lucy sighed and closed her eyes. When she opened them, her voice changed. It was quiet, like she was reading a prayer:

When grapes turn to wine, they're wanting this

Lucy rolled over on her side and said softly, "This we have now, is not imagination . . . when grapes turn to wine, they're really wanting this." She looked at me knowingly and sighed.

"So beautiful . . . this we have now . . . this we have now."

My mind couldn't wrap around that line, but it sure put me in an altered state. I was speechless.

"Isn't it? And what a beautiful evening."

"How are you, Lucy?"

"I'm feeling like a pretty good mother. And a very happy woman. How are you, David?"

"I couldn't be better. This is the best night of my life."

"Do you think all the dead are home by now, David?"

"Look at all the streetlamps up there. They should be able to find their way."

"We're finding our way, aren't we?"

"Yes, we are, Lucy. We're on our way home."

Chapter 73

The first raindrop fell on my forehead. The second on top of the first. It was a warm, nearly silent rain that began shortly after sunrise. I woke easily and was immediately taken by the scent in the air and the music of the falling rain. Despite the beauty of the hour, I couldn't help but feel the world was a touch sad this morning knowing another year would pass before the dead would bless the earth with their return.

Henry and Sugar were sleeping under Lucy's cot, stretched out and dry, showing every sign of intending to sleep in. Lucy was covered with a thin layer of gold leaves that had fallen overnight from the maples lining the yard. If I listened closely, I could hear her soft breath moving in and out under the percussion of droplets arriving on our lonely planet.

I felt fresh and light. That line from Rumi danced in my head, *when grapes turn to wine, they're really wanting this.* This, wonderful this. I wondered what Rumi might write when waking to such a delicious, soft shower. As I was musing about the poetry of raindrops and gazing at Lucy, she opened her eyes quiet as a moth opening its wings.

She smiled sleepily and took in a long, deep breath. "It smells so good." She took another slow, full breath. "Ah, the aroma of living and dying."

I wanted to know what Lucy was experiencing, so I tried it myself—one full breath through the nose, taking in all I could, feasting on the aroma of a light rain bathing dry, fertile mother earth. "Yum. That's intoxicating."

Lucy put her hand on my cheek and whispered, "What else could human beings want?"

"Nice. Thank you, Rumi. And I just have to say, you look lovely."

"Oh, good, I want you to feel good when you look at me. You know what? I actually feel lovely this morning. I had the best dream, David."

"You did?"

"Yes. It was so good. I want to tell you all about it."

"Please do."

"Where are the dogs?"

"Underneath your cot, dry and sound asleep."

"Oh good. Aren't they precious?"

"They are. They're good buds."

"I love that. They're best friends like us."

"I love that, too."

"Bobby came to me. He came and snuggled up on my lap. I can't tell you how precious that was. I could feel the weight of his little body and feel his warm breath on my neck."

"Oh, Lucy, that is wonderful! I'm so happy for you. You gave everything of yourself last night and this is your return. Lovely Lucy."

"Thank you, David. I owe it all to you. You have saved me from my torment."

"I think the fire and the spirits had more to do with it than this guy."

"But it was you—they couldn't make it happen without you. And I certainly couldn't have done it alone. Your kindness and presence was the difference, and I am so grateful. My Bobby came to me. He said, 'I love you, Mommy,' and talked about his forays in the garden. Bobby loved insects and bugs. He made a habit of finding every beetle he could. I guess he really was his mother's child. When he got sick and had to stay indoors, he missed his friends the spiders and beetles the most. When he knew he was dying he said, 'Mommy, who will take care of all the bugs?' David, I can feel Bobby's life again. It is throbbing inside me. I am so happy. Thank you."

"I'm happy for you, Lucy, really happy. I can imagine Bobby and Emily having a blast together."

"Oh, me too. Wouldn't they be wonderful friends? Just like us and the dogs."

With the sound of our voices the dogs were up and shaking the night's sleep off their bristly hair. Sugar jumped up on my cot and snuggled in, and Henry did the same, with a little more effort to get to his mama.

"Well, there you are, you rascals. Good morning, furry ones." Lucy beamed and reached for my hand. "David, I'm so happy to wake up by you. Thank you for being here with me. You are precious."

"I feel the same about you, Lucy. I'm overwhelmed by our good fortune. Here we are, side by side. We found each other. Unbelievable. But if you want to really thank me, how about making me some bacon for breakfast? I'm starving."

"You're on, plus I'll throw in some blueberry pancakes. I froze some yummy blueberries this summer. You'll love them. Let's go!"

Lucy jumped off her cot, grabbed the sleeping bags and took

off for her house. I followed behind at a slower pace, carrying the cots and enjoying the raindrops falling on my head. The dogs were startled by her departure, but they bounced up and ran after Lucy to the back door. A peaceful rain continued to fall, and the spot that held the energy of fire and spirits returned without objection to its natural state. But as we made our way, I had the distinct feeling that not all the spirits had left the premises. There was a subtle buzz in the air, and I was struck by the silence of the crows perched overhead. They resembled monks lost in contemplation.

Chapter 74

Dear Mom, I can now trust that it was that same merciful force that took you home and offered you peace. I trust that you did not suffer eternal torment. This is a great relief to me. I want you to know that I have been touched by that same mercy. It is unfathomable, but I feel it. What's most surprising is that I am talking to you. Reaching for you. There are days I feel you here with me. Days when the guilt and the need to get away from you are gone, and so is the terror that I will never find you. And there are days you are gone; you've turned your back on me again. Those are the worst, Mom. How could you do that to me? Do you know how that feels?

At least now my life doesn't come to a crashing stop. I go on living and sometimes finding you in the little, ordinary stuff of life. Like Lucy with her ladybugs. I like that. And then you're back and we're together. It makes me dizzy, but I like it when you're near me, when we can discover the world together. Lately, I've been stopping to look at the sky. It's amazing! Did you ever see the sky, Mom? Did you ever lay down under the stars and look up at the Milky Way? Did you ever feel overcome with awe and wonder? And what about wind? Did you let the wind caress your face and blow your hair back like a horse's mane? Did you? Was it pure delight? Did you ever spread your arms and let the wind carry you to the heavens?

Do you know the air is heavy? Really heavy. Twenty-five million tons per square mile across the planet. That adds up to over five thousand million, million tons of the stuff hanging around. But this body of air is a restless one, and because the heat from the sun is not equitably delivered to all corners of the earth, big differences in air pressure develop. Before you know it you have this massive game of chase between low-pressure and high-pressure systems and what amounts to an eternally futile struggle for balance. It's crazy. In fact, it is an endless battle, an archetypal war for supremacy of the airwaves that is the living Bhagavad Gita, the struggle between neighbors and family, the feuding Hatfields and McCoys, the tensions between Brits and Frenchmen, North and South. We call it wind.

In other words, equilibrium is a joke, a myth of gigantic proportions. We say, "Have a nice day." But we live in turbulence. We breathe chaos and walk about more than happy to believe in the trance cooked up by our perceptions. What a beautiful, peaceful day. Let's have a picnic. Until the cyclone blows through town and disrupts our little party. Until the tornado rips our cherished little lies to bits. We have words for these happenings: disaster, calamity, tragedy. As if these events were somehow not supposed to happen in our pastoral world and were somehow mistakes, interruptions of dear old peaceful Mother Nature that will soon be corrected and put to order. I remember a cartoon from *The New Yorker* years back; two hikers are walking down a trail in the wilderness wearing beatific smiles on their faces. Ten feet above on a ridge, two mountain lions are perched, ready to jump. One lion says to the other, "Wait until they say the part about how peaceful it is."

That's the whole story right there. Aren't we good at painting pictures on the wall? We call it weather. How nice. "How's the weather today?" "What's it like outside, dear?" Come on, we're living in a blender! Our eyes are stapled shut! We walk around breathing stardust, neutrinos piercing our bodies, utterly dependent on trillions and trillions of marine organisms to regulate the carbon levels in the atmosphere so we don't choke and turn to burned toast. And still, we walk around sermonizing about our sacred fantasies like independence and choosing the life we want. This is the real American dream. The stubborn innocence and entitlement. Please, the world is burning because of us. The trees, plants, and our kids are choking because of us. Stop, look around—the beloved wind is us. The weather? It is us. This self we think we are, this composed, together, mature, and grown-up self, is the best fiction ever. The forces that move and shape and create and destroy and erode and grow the world are not dormant or quelled, they are not out there in the big bad world. No, they are you, and me, and to think we should be one person and stable, or done changing, or capable of holding our world steady to do what we tell it to is, well, lunacy. And aren't we beautiful as we are? Aren't we just as Emily showed us? We're weather systems! Dancing and jumping, laughing and crying with the same rising and falling internal barometer as is on the wall. Aren't we just as wild and fresh as the wind off the Pacific? Just as uncontainable and unpredictable? Isn't that music? Isn't that lovely? Aren't we really like balloons, held by such a thin membrane, so thin but seemingly intact, but aren't we ever so permeable, as much as the sand that welcomes surf? Isn't the world constantly penetrating and making love with our insides and wanting to touch what can't be seen? Our flesh is porous, we must remember; it breathes in and out and is like a little tent surrounding so much space inside, so much abiding space within, and all the weather, the storms, the clouds, the floods and rainbows, the tornadoes and gentle breezes—isn't it all us, the same wondrous dance of a starry night, the dance of the innocent, happy child that in one moment breaks your heart open with love and in the next tears down the castles you have built? Nothing remains; the ocean clears the deck: what should we love? What can we? What speck of stardust brought love to earth? Which drop of rain carried love in its arms on its way to form a cloud? How can it be that we are so confused? There is so much fog. Will it ever lift?

Why am I ranting like this? Is it a disguise? A thunderstorm of anger I don't dare drop on you? I keep the little boy inside gagged. I keep rage locked up. I don't want to kill you again. Will I ever be secure?

We are together, now. Mostly. Will it last? Will it crumble like everything else?

Mom, you were swept away by a twister. Swept up and spit out. Weren't you? What molested you? Someone left you unprotected, right? Something turned you against yourself. Made you feel unlovable. Even with me. Something broke your mind into pieces. My dear Mom. I'm sorry I left you there alone in the garage. I am. I'm here now, talking to you. I feel you. I want to wash the blood off your cheek. I want to take you from the car and carry you into the house and lay you on the couch. Cover you with a blanket. Hold your hand and tell you the story of your granddaughter. Spread your ashes with hers. I will bring you to us and to Lucy. You aren't lost anymore. I'm back.

Chapter 75

"You like?" It was a leading question. Lucy looked at me with great expectation written all over her face. I could feel how much she wanted to please me, and I was pleased. More than pleased.

"Yum. I love it. This is the best bacon ever. And the blueberries are out of this world good. You've got the touch, Lucy."

"Ah, the way to a man's heart."

"You're finding them all. You are, indeed, every pathway."

"Oh boy! Every one?" The suggestive tone was not lost on me. How could it be? Lovely Lucy gave me the eye while her tongue slid slowly from her mouth, taking its sweet time to lick the maple syrup from her lips. Lovely Lucy, sexy Lucy. She knew how to get to me, and I made it clear she had found her mark.

"Every one, Lovely Lucy, every one. Can you hear me purring?"

"Ooh, I like that sound. Music to my ears. Sweet music."

Our playful, enticing moment was interrupted by a pleading yap from Sugar. She must have been smelling the bacon because she had that "please feed me" look all over her face.

"Poor Sugar, you must be starving. I don't think I remembered to feed you last night, did I?" She gave me an affirmative bark as I stood up to get her some food.

Lucy chimed in with, "She can have some of Henry's food, David. He won't mind, will you, Henry?" Henry lifted his head from the floor as if to ask what all the fuss was about. Lucy popped up to get the food, but I interrupted her.

"Thanks, Lucy, but Sugar is on a special diet. I'll go get some kibble and bring it back. It will just take a minute. Don't go anywhere!" And Sugar and I took off for home through the back door, on the run. I wanted to get back to our arousing breakfast as soon as possible.

As I left, Lucy's silky voice followed me down the path and touched my neck. "Don't be long. *Everything* is warm."

But it was more than a minute. At the front door I saw that I hadn't brought in the mail for a few days, and it was bulging out of the mailbox. I took it in and meant to casually toss it on the counter, but out of habit I glanced at a few of the envelopes at the top of the pile and noticed one of them with a return address from the Oregon State Penitentiary. My stomach dropped through the floor—this could be only one thing. It was hard to open the envelope; my hands were shaking so much. When I read the first words of the letter, my worst fears were confirmed: *We regret to inform you*—I stopped right there and sat down at the table and stared at the wall. I really don't know how long I sat there. I just remember saying his name once out loud in a voice I'm not sure even Sugar could hear. "Randy . . ." There were no tears. No regrets, just a deep feeling of respect and thankfulness.

Sugar and I gathered her bowl and kibble and headed back to Lucy's. By now she was at the sink cleaning up. She looked up with an uncertain look on her face and asked, "What took you so long . . ." and then she stopped abruptly. "David, what is it? Your face is gray. Come here, love, what's wrong?"

Lucy looked more than concerned. I sank into her arms and that's when it hit me even harder: Randy Tanner, gone. Heaviness moved in and dropped anchor, and the world turned slowly away from center.

"David, what is it?"

"It's Randy, Randy Tanner, the one from prison . . . I don't think I've even told you his name . . ." I couldn't finish. It was quicksand.

Lucy's face was racked with pain as though the loss was hers. She came for me and took me in her arms and held me tight. We stood there locked together, breathing together; neither of us said a word. I came back from the shock slowly and let my arms drop. Lucy took my hands and said, "David, I'm so sorry. What can I do to help?"

Her voice was warm and tender, and the look in her eyes conveyed incredible sympathy. Everything combined to make me feel a little dizzy and at a loss as to what might help. Even the word *help* sounded foreign to my ear, and I felt the old aversion to any kind of need rise up. But then it came to me; I remembered my promise to Randy.

"You can come to Salem with me. I have to pick up his ashes and bring them home. I promised him."

"Wow. You promised Randy you'd come for him? That's so generous and loving, David. You really care for him in a big way. Of course, I'll drive you down. But can you tell me more about what happened between you and Randy? If you're up to it?"

"I don't know. I need to walk. Can we walk?"

"Yes, of course. Let's do that. We can clean up later."

"I want to take you on my old walk. I don't know why, I just do. It's long—are you up for that? We could shorten it."

"Let's do it. I'll be fine."

"Why don't we drive to my old room and walk from there?"

"Perfect. Coming, doggies?"

. . .

Jesus, Mom, the losses, they keep piling up. They never stop. Layer after layer after layer. I knew this was coming and it's still crushing. It won't stop, will it? Emily was wrong; things do disappear. He's gone. You and I have something going now, but maybe it's a thread that could break at any time and then, poof, you're gone, maybe forever. Nice fantasy, buddy. Fuck. Maybe that kid in me was right and it's better to shut down than to feel this. What if he takes over again and I can't stop him? Who could blame him? The pain is worse every time. And what about Lucy? She's 77, Mom. What if something goes haywire with her body and she's gone tomorrow? That would be too much. I'd be done. I read once that death is an arrow shot into the sky at birth and you don't know when it will land. There's an arrow in my heart, Mom.

. . .

Sugar and Henry were ready in a flash. They raced to the door and watched every move we made. The four of us climbed into Gina and sped off to the warehouse. How long had it been since I moved? I couldn't remember for sure; it felt like ages. I have memories of those years at Ash Street, but they hover like a bad dream. Like something made up, or a thought that is fading from existence.

Lucy drove and I tried to tell her about my time with Randy at the prison. "I can't explain it. He was a good man. A person. I hated him. I didn't have to try. I was so full of hatred. But it was hard for me to get it out, like if I did, something would end, and so I held on tight. Randy wasn't having it. He encouraged me, no, he provoked me into spilling my guts. I broke and screamed, and he never flinched. I threw thunder and lightning and damnation at him, and he met me head on, accepting everything, no reactions, no surprise; he just stepped into the guilt and surrendered to my rage. What finished me off was when he told me Emily had come to him while he was in a coma after the big crash. That did me in. He knew things about her he couldn't have known unless what he was telling me was the truth. Jesus, I can't tell you what happened, Lucy, I wish I could. We just started talking honestly after that, and over the next few weeks, Christ, I came to learn about his life, his suffering. The more he became a real person, the more I was able to care for him, even love him and learn something about opening. I don't know how it happened."

"David, that's extraordinary. Just amazing. Please, tell me more."

"Well, I barely told you anything, but the truth is, I don't remember much, except for this strange feeling that we were held, somehow, in the palm of something hugely gentle and kind. Some sort of presence. I guess it was mercy, in person. No one deserves such mercifulness, but there it was anyway. Why? It won't tell me. I was trying to love, like Emily asked me, but it was impossible. I couldn't—I just couldn't until we talked, and that presence arrived and started to shape things. I'm sorry, I know this doesn't make sense. I don't want to say it was magic, but I don't know what else to call it. After a month we were family. Despite myself, I love him, and I think he loves me."

"Oh, my dear David, thank you, thank you for bringing me into this. This feels sacred. You two deserve a peace prize."

I looked out the window and said to her, in a voice I did not recognize as my own, "Thanks, but I feel like a tree fell on me. Then again, I feel weightless. You're the only person I've told."

"You are fulfilling your dear Emily's prayer, David. You truly are."

I couldn't believe my ears. My head swiveled toward Lucy, and I said tentatively, " You really think so?"

"No doubt, my dear friend, no doubt."

We were silent the rest of the drive, both of us lost in the dream of the impossible that had come to be. In no time we arrived at Ash Street and piled out of the Gia with the dogs close behind.

"This is it, eh? This is where you holed up for those years?"

"This is it. This is the place. Every morning at four, I walked out that door and went to the river."

"Which one is yours?"

"You can't see it from here. It's around back."

"Okay, lead the way, mister."

"I'll take you on the route I walked the morning the fog lifted. That's when everything changed."

"What happened?"

"Come on, I'll show you."

We walked the back streets together, past the warehouses and industrial buildings, past the homeless camps that had grown in size in the short time since I left. We passed the graffiti plastered to the surface of everything in sight.

"You walked through here at four in the morning, David? Man, what was that like? This place is turning me inside out."

"It was dark. Nothing. I was a dead man walking, like they say. It was all rote, just walking and going on. Just continuing."

"No fear?"

"Oh no. I would have welcomed being run over by a truck or getting beaten. No, fear was nonexistent. The only thing coming close to fear was the worry I might forget Emily's face. That was it."

We continued beneath the skeleton of the bridge and up the ramp to the walkway. The surroundings were more familiar to me than I thought they would be, and still, this world felt surreal and frightening. I shuddered, trying to fend off the memories, and had to take Lucy's hand to know that I was not back in that life.

"I remember that fear. I couldn't bear to have pictures of Bobby around, but I couldn't trust I would remember his features."

"I know, kind of a silly fear, but it was all we had, I suppose, and losing that would have killed me for sure."

The bridge loomed above us. We stood there transfixed, spellbound as though we could see into the past and the events that took place not far from where we stood. I wanted to turn back and forget, but Lucy gave me a tug, and we walked up the ramp onto the bridge and toward the massive green towers.

"I've never walked this bridge, David. It's beautiful and kind of majestic." Lucy stopped and stared at the structure. "This is awesome. You walked here every day? There is a very intense feeling here. Do you feel it, David?"

"Oh yeah, I stopped here every morning and put my leg over

that railing and decided whether to jump or not. I better keep walking or I may faint. Come on."

Lucy took my arm, and we followed the dogs the rest of the way to the towers.

Sugar and Henry must have sensed our arrival at a special place. They stopped in their tracks abruptly and went into high gear sniffing the area under the towers, and I put my hand on the railing. I was experiencing time vertigo. Everything was the same: the traffic, the candy cane gates, the light show on the Willamette's surface. It was all the same, but I was not. Or was I? I started to get lost in my head when Lucy snuggled up close and said, "Hey you, come back, tell me what happened here."

"Sorry, I started to spin out. This is the place where I saw the girl. She was standing right there with one leg over the railing. She was, I don't know, very . . . something. Very much tangled up. Frightened, brave, angry, fragile, the whole mix. I didn't fight her. I mean I didn't try to talk her out of jumping. I think that surprised her and made her pause. Maybe that was when I stopped fighting myself. The next day some force opened my eyes to the brilliance of the city, the river, and the world and catapulted me into a realm I'd never experienced, a big rush of expansiveness. I still shudder when I remember it. I had to hold on to the railing."

"That was love knocking on your door, friend."

"Not any love I've ever known or heard about."

"The church doesn't dare talk about that kind of love. They've probably forgotten all about it. Did you just stand here?"

"I did. I have no idea how long, but eventually it subsided, and

I remembered where I was. The commuters probably thought I was making the big dive."

"I'll bet they were pulling out the video cameras. Then what?"

"I walked to the police station. I knew then it was time to talk to Randy. I had to try to answer Emily."

Lucy looked at me wide-eyed. "You just walked in? What did you say?"

"I think I said, 'I want to talk to him.'"

"That's it?"

"That's it. the policeman looked a little puzzled. God knows what he was thinking."

"I know what he was thinking. 'How did this guy get through security?'"

"It was a remarkable time. The fog lifted and everything began to open up. I felt like I was riding a fast train. Scared the crap out of me."

We leaned against the guardrail of the bridge, watching the Willamette flow effortlessly through the city and on to its rendezvous with the Columbia. Neither of us spoke a word; we just gazed into the unfathomable.

"This feels like a holy place, David. Do you know how fortunate you are?" Lucy put her hand on my back and held it there, and the warmth coming from her hand flowed like the river moving below us.

"I'm beginning to. I am. This is all so astonishing, isn't it? Joy in the midst of all the loss. Being here with you, feeling undeserving and grateful and emotions I can't even name. It's crazy." I stopped talking and my head must have dropped to my chest.

"What is it, David?"

Her voice was so gentle I almost couldn't take it. My body was beginning to dissolve.

"I don't know, Lucy. It's Randy, and what happened to him and me and the two of us. Whenever I think of him, I feel this deep, deep love and loss. How can that be? And why should any of this be happening, this good fortune? Why should I meet you and be standing here? Randy and I seem the least deserving, the most unworthy of people. How is it that we could be touched by this thing, this whatever it is? All this pain, Lucy. More fucking lousy pain than water in that river, endless crazy pain. Crazy. And I added to it. I hate that. I made so much of it, how can I accept all this good now? I don't get it."

"I guess you just have to come back with crazy love. Crazy, crazy, outrageous love. Be an insane lover. Love everything! Especially the little things." Lucy got that wild look on her face that thrilled me and scared me, too.

"I like that. Crazy love. Untamed."

"Don't forget, dangerous. Really dangerous—untamed, un-earned, undeserved. Who could do anything to deserve this? Nobody deserves this. Not the horror and not the love. Worthiness isn't about merit, no way. This is crazy, outrageous love. You and Randy proved it, David. And I'll tell you one more thing, and then I'll shut up."

"What's that?"

"I love you, David Chase. I'm crazy about you."

"You do? You are?"

"I am. Please kiss me."

It must have taken twenty-four hours to span the twelve inches between us, because when our lips came together, the moon rose for a second time and swayed back and forth in the sky like a yo-yo, and time itself forgot where it was going. Lucy and I kissed and then flew in the direction of the moon and kissed the sky, the big, blue, beautiful sky. When we returned to our bodies, my legs were trembling and my heart was doing summersaults. Both of us were breathless. Our lips parted and we rested our foreheads together.

Lucy lifted her head and whispered, "Crazy love."

I responded with "Sweet love."

Lucy's eyes sparkled. "Sexy love."

I melted and gulped. "Vulnerable love."

Lucy shivered and held her shoulders. "Terrifying love!"

"Yikes," I said in a low voice. "Forbidden love."

And then, the entire parade of love's infinite sounds and textures tumbled from our mouths.

"First love."

"Erotic love."

"Puppy love."

"Furious."

"Possessive."

"Desperate."

"Sassy."

"Sensual."

"Dark love."

"Clinging."

"Heartbreaking."

"Enchanting."

"Ecstatic."

"Brittle."

"Needy."

"Evil."

"Intoxicating."

"Romantic love."

"Teen love."

"Blind."

"Heartfelt love."

"Tough love."

"Tragic."

"Lucy, I don't know if I can keep going."

"SCREAMING LOVE!"

"FUCKING LOVE!"

"INNOCENT!"

"OUTRAGEOUS!"

"ETERNAL LOVE!"

"TRUE LOVE!"

With that last pronouncement of true love, we fell into each other's arms, laughing and gasping for breath.

"Phew, good one, David."

"No wonder love is so baffling!"

"And indescribable."

"I love this spot, Lucy. I promised Randy I'd put his ashes with Emily's by the big tree in the park, but I'd really like to bring some of them here and give them to the river."

"I think that's a great idea. This spot is yours. You and that precious girl broke the cycle of death right here. It feels like a sacred spot to me too; your opening, Randy's ashes, and our second knockout kiss. Not bad."

"Lucy, let's get Randy's ashes tomorrow afternoon. We'll make a road trip of it!"

"Sounds good to me. Hey, don't we have to get ready to go to Audrey's?"

"Geez, I totally forgot. Thanks, we better head back. Sorry Sugar, time to go home. Come on, let's go."

We paused before leaving and turned to the river and the sky and the present flowing so easily, seamless as light filling space, no beginning, no end, effortlessly appearing and moving like a ballerina from one form to another into the future.

Chapter 76

We made it home in time to take a short nap. It was a hard sleep. I felt like I'd gone to the bottom of the lake where there is no light, no life. Somewhere beyond dark. When I came to the surface, the doorbell was ringing and Lucy was waiting outside. I must have looked hungover because when I opened the door Lucy laughed and said, "Where have you been, mister?"

"Seven leagues under."

"Well, you better get dressed before I tackle you and we're late for Audrey's. Come on."

The idea of being tackled by Lucy was hard to resist. "Hmm, let me think about that . . ."

Lucy gave me a boot and I got dressed quickly. As we walked in the chilly air to Audrey and Mark's apartment, Lucy took my arm and moved in close.

"David, why does Audrey have all those nasty scars on her neck?"

"She told me they are from a motorcycle accident."

"Oh, yes. Poor girl, that's terrible."

"She had a miserable time after Emily's death. Miserable. Besides the scarring on her neck, she told me she cut her arms. It was so horrific, Lucy, so horrific. She and Emily were inseparable. They were more than best friends or sisters. There was something so beautiful about their bond. I should have been there for her. I was experienced at shutting down. I just went dead. Audrey couldn't."

"She still needs you, David, and now you're ready. Maybe you can say something to her."

"I have. We talked the night we ran into each other while you were gone. I did my best to apologize, but you're right, we'll need to talk more. I'm just so happy she made it. You'll love getting to know her, Lucy. She's high spirited like you. And now she's going to have a baby and a husband. I really want to be there for them and help in any way I can. When you stop and think about what has happened and what is happening now, with Audrey and Mark, and you and me, man, it makes your head spin, doesn't it? This is uncanny."

"Uncanny love. I like it. Yeah, it makes you wonder. But listen, David, we're just a block away and I want to know, does Audrey know about Randy?"

"About the visits?"

"Yes."

"No. No one knows but you."

"Are you going to tell her?"

"I want to. It doesn't seem right to keep that from her, and maybe it would help her like it did me. What do you think?"

"I'm not sure. It's very far out, very intense. I wonder if she can handle it. Maybe she'll be furious with you."

"Do you think so? You could be right; she always had a way of flaring quickly. I guess I'd better be cautious, maybe save that for down the road."

"Maybe, or try to read her mood, watch for signs and openings, you know?"

"How do I figure that out? I'm not too good at that sort of thing. And how do I tell her who I am without letting her in on those conversations? She's nearly twenty-two years old— should I be protecting her at that age?"

"But how stable is she? Those cut marks. Her pregnancy. She's barely out of adolescence, David. Let's feel into it. I'll help you, and we can give each other a look, some kind of signal."

I gave Lucy the look of love and tried on my most playful, seductive voice. "How about I squeeze your thigh under the table? Once for yes, twice for no, three times for let's go home and fool around."

"Yum, better not go for three on the thigh, I might start to swoon. And let's see, how about I casually put my tongue in your ear if I agree?"

"Good one, they'll never catch on. Should we have a dress rehearsal under this streetlamp?"

"Why David, are you proposing to cop a feel? You rascal, you."

We stopped there, under the streetlamp, under a crescent moon, in full view of the world. Lucy folded her leg around mine like a snake on a limb. My hand stroked the small of her back, and when I leaned in to touch her thigh, her mouth climbed up my ear and her tongue glided in. We both shivered.

"Good warm-up, partner," I whispered.

"I'd say we're ready, but what if I fall off my chair when you touch me?"

"I'll catch you, love. I'll be right there, and I'll catch you."

"Ah, my darlin'."

Chapter 77

I don't know if Audrey or Mark noticed the mischievous smiles on our faces when we arrived. More than likely, they thought we were long past that sort of thing and interpreted the gleam in our eyes as friendly companionship, not the gathering lust of a tropical system close to unleashing its erotic powers.

We walked in holding hands and the evening sailed away on the wind of our mutual happiness in coming together. The opening conversation was typical of any dinner party: compliments about the house, in this case the apartment, which was a small two bedroom, but cozy and warmly decorated. There were the questions about how we spent our day, which we could only answer in the most indirect of ways, and, of course, more exclamations about the baby and the condition of the mother-to-be. They were already proud parents basking in good fortune. The necessary biographical inquiries were in order, and soon a rough sketch took shape that each of us could make sense of.

Lucy was gracious and funny in her self-portrait, and it seemed to me that Audrey took to her immediately. Mark was less forthcoming, and, I thought, not so comfortable with the standard "getting to know you" line of questions. A few times he looked at Audrey for help, but otherwise he put himself into the casual exchange of pleasantries as best he could. Audrey looked especially happy. She glowed like an expectant mom and seemed perfectly at ease with the innocent delight of a first-time mother. Often her gaze fell on me, as though I had resurrected from the dead, which I had, and perhaps because she felt closer to Emily with me around.

Dinner was delicious and vintage Portland, pasta with veggies, salad with raspberry vinaigrette dressing, and fresh bread from Grand Central Bakery. It was over dessert and coffee that we detoured from safe and pleasant storytelling into territory that altered the pH of the room. It was Audrey who opened the gate and let the horses out.

"David, I've got to tell you about this amazing thing I discovered. I figured out what Emily was talking about all those years. Remember how she went on about Bu and her lady friends, and we never knew what she was talking about? Well, I figured it out. Look at this."

She handed me a thick paperback. I read the title out loud: *Awakening Shakti: The Transformative Power of the Goddesses of Yoga.* Audrey's excitement was palpable. Clearly, she was looking for a response from me that would validate her discovery.

I beamed. "Wow, Audrey! So this explains Emily's lady friends?"

"It does. You won't believe it. It goes through every one of the Hindu goddesses and tells their story and virtues. Even the old lady, remember her, the one with the long white hair? She's in there too!"

"Really? Bu?" I looked at Lucy and was surprised to see her smiling and nodding her head.

Audrey's excitement was building to a fever pitch. "Really! Her name is Dhumavati. Dumi for short. She hangs out with crows."

My back shivered all the way to my head. "Crows? I like her already if she loves crows."

"That's the book by Sally Kempton, isn't it?" Lucy asked.

Audrey was impressed. "You know this book, Lucy?"

"I do. It was a favorite of mine when it came out. I still have it on my desk. It's a treasure. Are you reading it now, Audrey?"

"I just started. I love it—it's so Emily. My gosh, I can't believe you know this stuff. She's a definite keeper, David."

I looked at Lucy with great admiration and said, "I'm dumbfounded."

Lucy took the floor. "I knew Sally a little in the late seventies. She was a swami then, and we studied with the same Indian guru. Her name was Durgananda, and she was one of the smartest and most articulate of the westerners who became monks. I think Sally was a really successful journalist in New York when she took up yoga."

"You had a guru?"

I couldn't tell if Audrey was impressed or disapproving, but I could tell Mark was not happy with this revelation. His eyes could have burned a hole in the carpet. Either Lucy didn't notice his face turn red, or she decided Audrey's curiosity was more important. In any event, she continued.

"I did, for many years. Thousands of us joined the organization and studied with him. It was remarkable. Sally was a monk for close to thirty years, I think, until she left and went out on her own to teach. That's when she started elaborating on the goddesses and their energies. Emily must have been so gifted and open to the presence of these forces that she didn't need to read the book. It must have been a direct experience for her. Amazing. You hear about that happening in India a lot, but not so much here."

"It's true, Lucy. Emily lived in a world I never even dreamed of. I was her best friend, but I'm only now, finally, beginning to understand what made her so special. I can't really express it well, but it's blowing my mind. These goddesses seem so alive. I feel like Emily knew them personally."

"Did you know that she predicted the fog and my breakdown?" I revealed what I thought was just another Emily story, but when I glanced at Mark, I could see he was reaching the boiling point by the way he was rolling his eyes and fidgeting with his empty glass. The temperature in the room had definitely raised a degree or two.

"She did?"

"Yeah, when she was very little, maybe five. She painted it early one morning, with three moons above the smoke and fog, three pink moons, the ones that come once a year when the moon is closest to the earth. She told me it would be all right then. She also laughed and said it wasn't really fog, but the long gray hair of, what was her name, Dumi?" Lucy and Audrey nodded in unison. "Right. Emily called her Bu, like she and this Dumi were pals."

Audrey was near ecstatic. "Wow, really? She knew it was coming over ten years before? This is so incredible. My Emily."

We all paused and didn't speak for a second, taking in the wonder of our Emily and looking at each other in amazement. It was a sweet moment, which made the snarl that came from Mark all the more jarring.

"Stop it! You're making her into a saint. She was just a little girl, not Christ."

Audrey was clearly embarrassed by Mark's outburst. "Mark! What is it? Please, you sound nasty."

"I don't like you, or anyone, anointing people. It isn't right."

"Who's anointing anyone? We're just marveling at Emily's gifts."

"You're right, Mark." I tried to jump in and ease the tension building in the room, but I had the feeling Mark wasn't listening and my words were falling flat. "You're right, Emily was a regular little girl, not some saint. She did what all little girls do—she danced and painted pictures and sang songs. She was very loving and at times had some sort of sixth sense about things that we, I, may have exaggerated into a portrait of her that makes her sound saintly. I'm sorry about that. Sometimes I get carried away, especially with that story about the fog and the three moons." But in the next moment I realized Emily's sainthood was not the real bother to Mark. He was agitated about something far more important to him and, as it turned out, to the rest of us.

"This is all pagan idolatry, this goddess stuff. Bullshit pagan nonsense, made up by primitive people thousands of years ago who didn't know any better and now glorified by modern idiots who like to believe in magic and other fancy stories and are too narcissistic to accept Jesus as their Lord and Savior."

"Mark! Take it easy. You're coming on like a zealot. Calm down."

"I won't calm down, and you shouldn't either. You have to be an apostle for Christ and speak up when the word is being corrupted. This kind of worship of fantasy worlds and spirits is crazy and allows evil a foothold it can exploit, and I'm not going to be quiet about it."

"Can I just explain a little to Lucy and David about your passion, please, so they can understand where you're coming from?"

"Don't apologize for me, Audrey."

"I'm not apologizing. I just want to give them some background, that's all."

"Whatever."

Mark glared at the carpet while Audrey told us how they met in treatment when each of them was a mess and trying to recover control of their lives. Finding Jesus and the church had been pivotal for each in laying down the dependency on drugs, healing from their respective traumas, and dedicating their lives to helping others in the name of Christ. Clearly, we had tripped over a split in their vision of faith that would be a sore spot for their marriage to navigate. When she was finished with her explanation, Mark looked even more perturbed.

"You make it sound like we fell into Christ, like he is some kind of psychological life preserver, Audrey. Like it's just some irrational crutch for us druggies to get by with. Bullshit! It's the word of God, damn it, and this other stuff is self-indulgent perversion. Don't you get that? It's a fucking perversion of the truth."

"But what about our conversations about the Holy Mother, and what about the cover-up of The Eastern Church and the meaning of the Black Madonna? What about that? Isn't that part of the truth that got exiled by the male power structures in the church? You're just ignoring the sacred feminine in the doctrine of love. You can't have love like Jesus talked about without including the mother. Excuse me, us, Lucy. I'm so sorry. We're being very rude. Forgive us, please."

I tried to jump in and help Audrey out. "Audrey, I understand some of what Mark is saying. It feels self-indulgent to me lots of the time, when so many people are suffering and needing help and nearly every dude on the block is running around trying to be spiritual and holier than thou and talking like they have the universe and everything figured out and offering to fulfill every petty desire they can think up. It's really pretty nuts. All I know is that Emily asked me to love, and I'm trying to do that. I'm trying to know what love is."

"There's only one way to know love, David, and that's through Christ." There was nothing casual about this for Mark, and I could see we were headed for trouble. The tension was heated and mounting. I didn't see a way out until Lucy spoke, and the barometer began to fall.

"You know, we're women, Mark, and we can't help but think in terms of mothers and the feminine and elaborate stories of our many children, especially Audrey, who is full with child. Right? We see God in creation, in the incredible diversity of life, and we are overcome with love. But this love is just such a drop of the big love, such a drop, so really, can we possibly grasp the scope of that love? Do any of us have the eyes and ears to see and hear? Human beings seem to be smart enough to sense that something is going on and really stupid enough to not get it, unless someone can put it on stage for us to see and feel, some kind of story we can grasp and relate to. In India they wrote beautiful stories about the divine in the form of male and female, father and mother, but these are just concrete forms people can understand and find in their hearts. But does anyone really think God is a beautiful woman sitting on the biggest lotus blossom in life? No, of course not—these are maps, a tiny candle in the dark. The love of God is too big, too unimaginably and wildly fabulous to be pinned down by the mind. Maybe we can touch a leg or a trunk of the elephant here and there, but the whole elephant? The whole enchilada? Really? No, Mark's right, a whole lot of people are running around talking the talk of knowing the whole truth and nothing but the truth, like they Googled it, or looked it up on Wikipedia or Map Quest. False idols—isn't that what all these concepts are, false idols flying around like bats at sunset? Makes you dizzy. But how else do we talk about it? Should we try? It sounds to me like Emily was overflowing with the spirit of love. I sure wish I could have known her. How else can that love communicate, if not through human figures, and symbols? Isn't it really a fantastic dance of energies and qualities moving in a subtle realm that is beyond our antenna? Oh dear, I'm completely running on at the mouth. I'm so sorry. Sorry, everybody."

The atmosphere stirred and rolled over on its side. I was flabbergasted to see Mark staring at Lucy and smiling. She could charm a rattlesnake. Mark looked at Audrey with a plaintive grin and then he turned to Lucy and said, "I'm the one who should be apologizing, Lucy. What you said was beautiful. Thank you. We get worked up pretty good sometimes. Our faith is so important to us. We found God together and it made everything right. Our treatment would never have stuck without the Lord, and the word is the center of our lives. Sometimes we, I should say, I, get a little carried away. My apologies. Please forgive me."

Lucy, ever the gracious one, smiled at Mark and said softly, "Oh, Mark, it's all right, really. We just got to know you in a big way, thank you. I, for one, admire your passion."

Mark, much subdued, looked down at the remains of his dinner and then at Lucy and said, "You're very kind, Lucy. Very kind. Others have left the table and gone home for less."

"That kind of passion will make you a wonderful father, Mark."

We had avoided a landslide, but not for long.

Audrey looked enormously relieved and said, "I guess we can agree on one thing, though. Isn't it a blessing that the evil monster who killed Emily is dead and gone?" Audrey said this with genuine glee and looked at us expectantly . . . and stepped into a gaping crevasse.

"What? What did I say?"

She saw my face drop. She did not see my heart stop beating.

"David, what's wrong? Didn't you read that he died last week? He's dead. It's over."

Revenge rules the world, and forgiveness? Forgiveness is the most unforgivable of sins.

I looked everywhere but where I should have. Had I looked at Lucy I would have seen the warning lights blinking. I would have realized this was no time to break the news of my time with Randy. It was stupid and impulsive, but I just couldn't thwart what felt like a lava dome building in my chest. Something came over me, and before I knew what I was doing, the truth blurted out.

"Audrey . . . Audrey, I visited Randy Tanner in prison."

Audrey shrieked, "What? No, you didn't! What are you telling me David, what the fuck?"

I shook like a scared dog. "I . . . Randy—"

"Don't say that name, don't you ever say that name!"

Mark's mouth hung open.

I tried again. "Audrey, dear . . ."

"Don't 'dear' me, David. Don't you dare 'dear' me. You went to him? You actually went and saw that murdering bastard?"

"I did."

Audrey shot out of her chair, screaming and pulling her hair. "Get out of here! Get out of my house, you fuck! You pervert! Get the fuck out now!"

Mark stood beside her and tried his best to be steady and calming. "Audrey, honey, please sit down, honey. Let's hear him out. I feel the Holy Spirit here. I know it's crazy, but . . ."

"Fuck the holy spirit! I spent years using razor blades to scrape Emily's blood off my arms, and when that didn't work, more years doping and trying to forget, and this fuck waltzes down to the prison and has a nice little chat and forgiveness party with the son of a bitch that killed my Emily. Fuck that."

"Aud, come here, sit down with me." Mark reached for Audrey's arm, but she swatted him away and continued to rage at me.

"You bastard, David. You've always been a prick, but this is the worst."

"You're right, I have been a no-good prick. And if it matters any, I screamed the same stuff at myself when I knew I was going to see him. I did, and there are days I still do. You can hate me all you want. I won't tell you you're wrong, and if you want me to leave, I will."

"Don't try to manipulate me with understanding, you fucker. Fuck you if you think that bullshit will work."

"No bullshit, Audrey."

"Don't even say my name."

"No bullshit."

"This is too much. Fuck, I thought things were finally settling. How could you, why did you have to tell me this? You're still the same old selfish bastard, aren't you? It's always about you. That's what matters, isn't it? David Chase, the almighty asshole."

"Yep. That's me."

"God, how could Emily come from someone like you?"

"I haven't any idea. Her mother was a truly good person."

"And you fucked her over good, didn't you? I heard about that shit. Goddamn, Emily still loved you. You didn't deserve either of them."

"I didn't. I'm a coward and a cheat. I was even too selfish to kill myself."

"Shut up. I don't want to hear your sob story. Why did you go see him? Why?"

"Why? Right. Why would I betray Emily? Listen, I know how terrible it is. I hated myself, but it had to be done. Do you remember Emily's last words as she died in our arms? Did you hear her plea? I did. And it rang in my ears like a big old bell going off next to my head, and her plea, her prayer would not stop. It still does. The big bang of my existence. Do you remember?"

"No."

"You didn't hear her, did you?"

"No, I didn't hear her—my fucking head was blowing off with ten thousand sirens screaming inside. I didn't hear a damn thing. I don't think you did either. How could you? She was dead as shit. You're making this whole thing up to save your miserable ass. Fuck you."

"Do you want to know what she said?"

"What, go visit my killer and kiss his ass?"

Mark, looking genuinely interested, asked, "What did she say, David?"

"What, Mark, are you going to side with fucking Judas here?"

"Audrey, I'm on your side all the way. You're my love. But there's something here we need to hear. There is. Try."

"Damn, now you've got him hanging on your bullshit story.

Okay, fuck me, what did she say? This better be good, and don't you lie to me, you bastard."

"I won't lie to you."

"You lie to me, and I'll kill you, you fucker, I will."

"You can kill me."

"Go on, what did she say?"

"Daddy, love."

"She said, 'Daddy, love.' With her last goddamn breath, she said, 'Daddy, love'?"

"Yes."

"No. No. I don't believe you. I don't. So, she tells you to love and you hightail it down to Salem and suck his cock and everything is peachy. Aren't you the fucking lover boy?"

"No. I ran. I hid in my little room. I didn't talk to anyone or see anyone. I loved nothing. Nothing. I only stayed alive so I could see her face in my mind. Otherwise, I was dead. Dead. Nothing but fog. When the fog lifted, I remembered her picture and the three moons, and a big rock moved aside. I walked across the Hawthorne Bridge and had an experience of her love, and I knew what I had to do if I was ever going to rid myself of hate and live up to Emily's prayer. So I wrote a letter to the warden, and I took the Greyhound to Salem, and we met. I wanted to kill him more than live. I screamed and cursed and beat against the plexiglass divider, and he accepted me. I went to kill a monster and I found a person."

Though still standing, Audrey began a slow collapse, and Mark was there to catch her. "Honey, here, let me hold you."

"No, I can't. Mark, what do I do? She would have said something like that. She was that way. I can't take this, I don't know.

It can't be true. It can't. I can't breathe—my chest is exploding."

"Honey, I'm here. I'm here."

"Damn it, David, are you telling me you love him? You love that beast?"

"I hated him with everything, with my entire soul. I hated him and would have spat on him and strangled the life out of him. And he encouraged me."

"He encouraged you. Great. A reformed killer turned masochist."

"Not a masochist. He wanted me to purge myself of every molecule of hate so that I could love."

"Oh good, so you want me to believe he was in on this with Emily? You're too much. Get the fuck out of here!"

"He was."

"He was. Fuck me."

"Emily came to him. She came and put her hand on his shoulder when he was in a coma. He knew her and what was at stake. That's when I broke. And began to surrender."

And so did Audrey. In that moment she broke and fell into Mark and buried her face in his shoulder, sobbing like a little girl. She broke, but not all the way. Mark helped her to her chair, and we all sat in silence, worried about Audrey and what would follow.

We had started to relax when Audrey's voice erupted again, and we were startled into fear. This was not the voice of rage at me and life, this was the worst of all voices, the one Lucy and I were all too familiar with: the voice of self-condemnation.

"Emily. Emily! God help me. I can't take it, Mark. I can't take it in. I can't. Emily was my, my everything. Everything. I killed her. She shouldn't be dead. She shouldn't."

"Audrey, my love, you didn't kill her. You didn't."

"I did. I made her come meet me. She wouldn't be dead if I hadn't insisted. I—"

I interrupted, and with everything I had within, said this: "Audrey, Audrey, I know, I know what you feel. I feel the same, but look at me, look at me, Audrey. Emily isn't dead. Did you hear me? Emily isn't dead. She's alive!"

And then, she broke, all the way through, and sobbed and wailed and smiled. And understood. "Emily, my dear Emily, you could never, ever, disappear, could you?" Audrey wailed with joy. She put her arms around Mark and kissed him all over his face. She jumped up from her chair and threw herself at me.

"David, David, I'm so sorry. I said such terrible things to you. Please forgive me. I just couldn't stop myself."

"It's all right, Audrey, really, it's all right. Everything you said is true. I love you. We can lay it down now. We'll all help each other. It's time."

Audrey turned and walked to Lucy and said, "I'm so sorry, Lucy. You must think I'm a terrible person. Please forgive me."

Lucy took Audrey's hands in hers and said ever-so-kindly from one mother to another, "I have nothing but admiration for you, Audrey. Don't you worry—we're going to be very good friends." And the past and future mothers embraced while Mark and I looked at each other and wiped away tears of sorrow and joy.

Chapter 78

My life is a dream, Mom. And Lucy and I are dreaming the dream together, this big love, this big crazy love. Emily must have known this love all along. She rode it like a kite on currents of air over the ocean. I am new to it and drinking in the love like a man coming off the desert. I'm riding the Magic Carpet, as Randy would say. That being said, it isn't all smooth sailing, is it? There are some bumpy air currents out there. Like last night, with Audrey and Mark. Now that was some heavy turbulence. But we made it through something that had to be. Audrey and I had to have that moment, and we hung on for dear life and came through. Maybe Emily and Bu were there keeping the ship from capsizing. What next? What is waiting in the wings to upend everything and make something new? Stay tuned, Mom. I love telling you my story. It's also the story of you and me, isn't it? You're alive.

...

The next day Lucy and I drove to Salem to pick up Randy's ashes. It was a brisk, bright November day, a few weeks before Thanksgiving, but we drove with the top down anyway. We didn't mind the cold, or the wind blowing our hair back; in fact, we enjoyed the rush of air over our faces and the blasts of cold on our necks.

We were quiet for the first half of the trip, lost in our memories of the evening with Audrey and Mark. Lucy was the first to speak.

"David, I can't stop replaying last night in my mind. What a night. I don't have words for it."

"There aren't words, are there?"

"No, there aren't. It was so huge what happened. And David, you were so steady with Audrey, so caring. Selfless, really. You knocked me out."

"Thanks, Lucy. I wasn't cold or hard?"

"No, you were a rock, but a soft rock. You didn't fight her. You stayed right with her. You were awesome. Truly. It made me trust you all the more."

"That makes me happy, really happy. And what about you? The way you spoke to Mark and completely disarmed him without making him mad—that was breathtaking."

"I didn't say too much or sound preachy?"

"No, no, not at all. You were warm and respectful, and every word mattered. And you got through. I didn't think it was possible."

"Oh, good. He's a good soul. I like him. David, what happened with Audrey, in that room . . . it was the same fire as ours. And her explosion was the explosion we heard come from the fire and fly to the air and dive into the ground. The same sound that cleared my torment. The same sound, David."

"Lucy, my God, you're right. You are so right."

With that, quiet returned. And I marveled at how the intensity of the evening, the outrageous love that became hate and turned back into love, had shaken and reshaped me, and I think all of us. I wondered how we survived that eruption and found acceptance and love. I looked over at Lucy, and she seemed deep in contemplation of what I imagined were similar thoughts. When I thought of the four of us saying goodnight, I got goosebumps realizing we were now bonded for life and completely alive with the spirit of Emily.

As Lucy and I drove down the Willamette Valley, I relived some of the anxiety of the first trip to see Randy over a year ago. Could it have been a year? I dimly remembered the bus ride and the driver thinking I'd croaked. Was that me? I hardly recognized that guy. But it was me, and I felt his anxiety return. But this time I was not alone. I turned and looked at Lucy driving Gina, and the anxiety quieted. I could even feel some respect for that guy.

My thoughts came to a screeching halt at the entrance to the penitentiary. It loomed before us like the concrete tomb it is. I froze. Lucy took my hand and held it tight. "This has to be rough for you, David."

"It is. Have you ever been in a place like this?"

"No, I haven't."

"In some ways it feels harder now."

"Of course, you're different."

"I don't feel so different. Boulders feel more alive than this place. They call it 'The Rock.' There are people in there, Lucy. Real people."

"Have you thought about doing something, volunteering in some way? Maybe you could visit and counsel people. Something. You feel a bond."

"I do. Randy did too. He knew they would never let him out, and he accepted that and felt he could do some good with the men inside. What a good man he was." My heart swelled, but a familiar feeling moved in and surrounded me—this place could crush me.

The walls loomed over us, and I prayed the crows would fly in to rescue me, but they did not. I had to walk this walk without them.

"I still get chills when I think of what you and Randy did here, David."

"We did it, somehow. I couldn't have done it myself or in therapy. It had to be the two of us. The conversation changed both of us, really."

"Last night with Audrey was magical, too. I guess the whole of existence is in conversation if we can hear it, and if we can join it, magic happens. Like with us."

"Right now, I feel pretty heavy."

"Your hand is shaking."

"It's this place. You start to feel like once you go in you can never get out. Let's get Randy and take him home."

"I'm with you."

We entered the massive building and found our way to the office of family affairs where we were told we could pick up the urn and any remaining personal items. The officer in charge handed us the basket, and we transferred what there was into a tote bag we'd brought along.

Back in the car we took a closer look at what was in the bag. The urn was not alone. A small white envelope with my name on it was clipped to a paperback Randy had talked about: *Finding Freedom: Writings From Death Row*, written by his friend, Jarvis Jay Masters. I looked at Lucy and held the envelope close to my heart. I shook my head. "There were so many times I wanted to write him. Now he's written me."

"Why didn't you?"

"He told me not to. I think he wanted a clean break, no hanging on. You know what I mean?"

"I do. Very wise. David, let's go somewhere special and read it, unless you want to be alone."

"No, I want you there."

Lucy and I drove slowly out the gate into the ordinary world of everyday living. I didn't look back at the death tomb, but I could hear in my mind the shouts and screams of that first day. I turned cold inside. Lucy's voice brought me out of the spell.

"How about we go to the falls, David? Do you know Silver Creek Falls? They're lovely. I think it's the perfect place to read the letter."

"You know, I've never been there, if you can believe it. Sounds perfect. Get me out of here before that place swallows me. Let's go."

Lucy's Karmann Ghia roared with approval, and we sped off in the direction of the foothills to the east. The late afternoon light was enchanting, and the countryside beckoned with the greens and gold of late autumn in Oregon. Lucy and I sang old Beatles tunes and laughed at our offbeat harmony.

The long and winding road climbed steadily into the hills while the sun began its slow descent. We arrived at the park as the light was dimming but still illuminating the tall Doug fir trees and the top of the waterfalls, which cascaded over ancient rock into green pools a hundred feet below. Few people were on the trail at this hour, and Lucy and I walked mostly by ourselves down the trail to the edge of the falling water and farther down behind the falls in a hollowed-out space dripping with moisture and ferns. The roar was tremendous and primal. It drowned out our thoughts and smoothed out the edges left from the prison. We said nothing and walked slowly back up the steep trail on the other side of the creek and settled, a little out of breath, onto a bench overlooking falls, creek, and pool.

"How are your knees, David?"

"Oh, they hurt, but it's worth it. What a beautiful place. Thanks for bringing us here."

"We did pretty good for a couple of old goats, eh?"

"Pretty damn good. I could use some water, though—my mouth is really dry."

"Here you go—got some right here in my pouch."

We sat for a moment and took in the place and the cool drink. We seemed to be the ears for the conversation between the silence of the forest and the song of falling water. And in a particular way, the joy we felt listening to that marvelous duet was itself a harmony line in the pastoral score of dusk, a harmony line that added to the resonance and immediacy of the sounds of quiet and music coupling as one.

Light was fading into the dark dream of the night woods when I took the letter from my pocket along with my phone and its trusty flashlight and started to read. Lucy snuggled up, and that helped to relax me.

"I'm a little nervous."

"Me too."

"I'd like to read it out loud."

"Perfect."

Lucy moved in closer and put her arm around my shoulder. I felt comforted by her touch but still shaky wondering what Randy's last words would be. "Here we go."

Dear David,

Thank you for everything you are doing for me. I leave this world grateful for you, Emily, and all that we found together. I trust that the great Love fueling this world is within you and guiding your life in a beautiful way.

When you read this, I will be absorbed into that Love. I am at peace and so thankful for the time we spent together. It was an incredible blessing. I thought I was there to help you, but our conversation changed something in me I didn't know was there.

After you left, I had another conversation. This one was with my mother. I wouldn't say I forgave her, and yet, a great sympathy opened for her that I would not have thought possible. And even more surprising, I felt a warm love coming from her spirit directly to me. And I took it in, man, I took it in. Thanks to our talks and the visitations with Emily.

Look, three paragraphs without cursing! Fucking A, I'm cured! That's right mother f#@%$#! Sorry, couldn't resist. You wouldn't want me any other way, would you? (By the way, my writing coach edited this and cleaned it up so my last words would be respectable. You knew I couldn't talk like this, right? Fuck no!)

I hope you like the book. Jarvis is a good man, David. We have become friends over the years through letters. You should write to him and tell him you're a friend of mine. Really, don't be shy. He has so much to give.

So, I can't say that I believe in reincarnation, you know. Won't say it isn't real, but if it is, I'm going to hitchhike to a distant galaxy for my next go-around. Time for a change in scenery. Maybe there's a step up from Homo sapiens I could explore.

Rest assured I have been well cared for and will die peacefully. Five of my brothers have stayed with me and kept vigil night and day. (Special privileges for the "exemplary," brother!) They sing and chant and tell stories so that I can die with ease. When I sleep, a warm, radiant cloud of music lifts me up from my body into a sea of violet. It is breathtakingly beautiful, David. What is there to fear?

Okay. Farewell dear friend. If it is your wish, I will be there when your time comes.

With all my heart,

Randy

Silence leaned into us, and the river paused. Lucy and I sat on the bench and let time lay down in the ferns. Nothing moved but the sacred.

Chapter 79

With darkness filling spaciousness, and spaciousness filling darkness, we stood in the same breath and walked to the car. Our rapport was sure as the moon and ocean.

We put the top up, rolled the windows mostly shut, drove out of the park, and began the long, slow descent down the narrow road to the valley floor.

Fingers from Lucy's free hand crawled over the fingers of my hand, and mine over hers, like baby snakes hungry and tasting, urgent and searching, but certain.

Neither of us knew for sure who said it, or if it was spoken, whose tongue the longing came from. We only knew that every pore and opening of skin and want, every molecule of desire, flooded over our banks, and it was lovely.

We heard yes pulsing in our fingertips; yes, and we felt throbbing in our chests. Our legs grew warm with wanting and more, and the lush cavern of Love invited us into her house and said *stay here, you are my guests, everything you want is here for you, everything.*

Lucy only said one thing on the drive home that night, and I only said one word.

She said, "David, let's spend the night together."

Mom, you know what I said.

Chapter 80

We arrived home to the two happiest dogs in the world. They danced circles around us and sang the "Hallelujah Chorus." And we were every bit as happy to see them. We scratched their ears and rubbed their backs and groaned and said hello again and again.

Sugar and Henry ran out back to relieve themselves, poor dears, and Lucy and I stood by the back door watching them like proud parents.

Lucy leaned into me and said, "Let's build a great big fire in the fireplace and lie down on the rugs together."

"Do you think these bones will break?"

"I don't think so. Come on."

"I'd love to."

We built the base with dry sticks and aged logs from almond trees. Lucy struck the match and lit the paper and turned to give me a smile every bit as warm as the new fire that danced and engulfed the wood. We were immediately warmed. Soon Sugar and Henry showed up and lay down close by, staring into the orange and violet flames.

"Come snuggle up with me, Lucy."

"Let me get a few pillows. I'll be quick as a bunny."

We each let out low, contented moans as we settled in on the pillows and rugs, listening and watching the fire move like a drunken gypsy at midnight. I was aching within a minute but didn't want to move.

"I'm a bony guy."

"You're not the only one. Is it too uncomfortable?"

"No, I'm fine. I should eat more ice cream and put some flesh on these bones."

"Yeah, we should fatten you up."

"Should I go get some?"

"No, don't go, please. I want you near me." There was a different tone to Lucy's voice, more need and something else, something more vulnerable in the way she held on to me.

Several minutes must have passed before Lucy said in her softest voice, "Today was another remarkable day, David. I feel so close to you."

"Me too, Lucy, I'm still pinching myself and hoping I don't wake up and find it was all a dream."

"It isn't a dream, is it, David?"

"It's the real thing, Lovely Lucy. This is not imagination."

Logs fell and sparks flew at the screen. We let the quiet say our names and held each other close. I could feel a serious weather system building in Lucy but decided to give her room to figure out what to do with it. The past few days had given me a renewed feeling of confidence that I could really care for Lucy, no matter what. I lay there, stroking her hair and waiting for her to be ready.

"David."

"Yes, love?"

"There's something I need to talk to you about."

"Go ahead, Lucy, anything."

"I should have told you sooner. I just didn't want to disturb what we have."

"It's okay, Lucy, it really is. Is it Plan B?"

"Plan B?"

"Yeah, when you came back from Mexico you said it was time for Plan B. I've been wondering what that meant. It seemed loaded. What is it, Lucy? What's going on?" Dread was gathering in my lungs. But I was determined to be steady and present for Lucy. I wasn't going to make whatever was coming about me and my feelings.

"David . . . I'm dying."

"What? Oh, Lucy, no. What is it, cancer?"

"Pancreatic, stage four. I'm sorry, David, I should have told you sooner. It was selfish and stupid of me."

"Don't worry, sweetheart. It's all right. Our love feels eternal."

"Oh, David, you're beautiful."

"Besides, I had a feeling."

"You did?"

"I didn't want to think about it, but I noticed you'd lost a little weight, even on a steady diet of my ice cream. And there were a few times you winced bending down to pet the dogs. Your trip to Mexico cut short, I just had a hunch—alternative treatments, maybe? Remember, I used to be a doc."

"Still got your powers of observation intact, eh, Dr. Chase?"

"Enough to know you are the most beautiful woman I've ever known."

"I'm going to blush."

"That just makes you more lovely."

"David, I've refused treatment. No chemo, no radiation."

"I know."

"You know?"

"Lucy, you make it easy to know you. I know you've got to be free. Isn't that from an old Beatles tune?"

"It is. Come here, right now. I need a kiss."

And we did. We kissed like the earth was in its last hour. Warm and luscious, open mouth, sweet lips, it was the kiss of two virgins, the first kiss, the kiss of sunrise. When we stopped, the moon smiled. Our mouths hung open, our eyes closed.

One of us said, "Ah, so nice."

The other said, "Delicious."

It was a kiss to remember. A kiss that dissolves all differences, that makes life and death feel inseparably united. The dread in my lungs couldn't survive that kiss, but something did, and I foolishly asked, "How long do you have, Lucy?" I regretted it immediately and tried to reel it back in. "I'm sorry, Lucy, that was insensitive of me. You don't have to go into that. We have time."

"It's all right, David, I would want to know too. Besides, I kind of want to leave it here for the fire. I'm guessing two, maybe three good months if I'm lucky."

"Damn." I began to wilt, but I didn't want Lucy to have to take care of me, so I gathered myself, took a deep breath and asked, "And then?"

"I've applied for death with dignity."

"Really? Assisted suicide?"

"Really."

"You're a brave soul, Lucy. A brave and wonderful soul."

"You aren't angry with me?"

"Not now. Maybe in the morning, but not now. Surprised? I am. Maybe in shock, tremors of fear, but I feel a deep calm holding it all. I don't know, after the letter, our time together, last night, our time with Audrey, I feel so fortunate and full, so full I can't believe it."

"So do I, David. We're in the midst of something precious."

"I've been mourning our loss for days."

"You have?"

"Yeah, I've been sad, really sad, about the forty or fifty years we didn't have, the kids and grandkids, all the wild and passionate loving. I've been mourning that and watching my mind want to run off with it and be really down and out about what could have been. But then I think of Emily and what she said, and Randy, happy in prison, and I say no, no, keep loving, because Emily didn't say love someone, she said love. Simple. So here we are, so in love, with three or four months instead of thirty or forty years, and the temptation is great, really great, to feel bad about that, really bad, and cheated, but then there is love. I think I'm getting it that the invitation is to keep loving; keep loving even in the face of the horrible, crazy pain and fear; keep loving and don't feel sorry for yourself, and don't turn on life and don't turn on your own heart. Love even when it seems insane and breaks you. This sounds pretty heady right now, and I'm afraid I won't live up to it, but I'm sure going to try, Lucy, for you and for us."

"You're sounding more like Rumi every day. Wouldn't he say to let that love burn up whatever is small and lacking? Just die and let the big love be you. Oh, David, I am such a fortunate woman. You'll be there with me when the time comes, won't you?"

"I'll be there. I'll read to you, sing to you, rub your feet, lie with you, you name it."

"Thank you." Lucy paused and let out a long sigh of relief. She looked at me with such tenderness and put her hand on my face.

"I don't want you to be lonely."

"I have Sugar, and I'm pretty sure I'll have you with me every day."

"Will you take care of Henry?"

"Of course."

"There's something else. I want to give the house to Audrey and Mark."

"Really? Lucy, that is so incredibly kind." The floodgates were preparing to open.

"I don't want you to be lonely, and they have had such a hard time of it."

"They will be overjoyed. Neither of them have parents to help."

"And I have no one, no family to leave my stuff to. I can give a lot away, but I want something more personal. I want to give you my Beatles collection. Good?"

"Me? Your collection? It should be in a museum! I'll treasure it."

"I'm sad I won't meet the little one."

". . . now I'm going to lose it . . . Lucy . . ."

"David, I'm so sorry. But I don't want to cry now. Later, not tonight. Okay?"

"Of course. Whatever you want, Lovely Lucy."

"I have an idea. Aren't your bones about busted? Let's get up and dance, a nice slow dance."

"I'm not sure I can. I've become the wood floor!"

"Come on, old timer, I'll help you up."

The way to vertical was tough. I looked like the crooked man trying to climb a rain chain. Once upright, Lucy turned the lights off and lit candles all around the room.

"Come here, let's dance a slow, tantric dance. I'm going to sing to you, real soft and real slow, and we'll get nice and tender close, but we won't touch. Just stay a finger or two from each other and feel the energy build and build, overflowing with erotic, blissful, yummy energy. And then . . ."

"And then?"

"And then, with fingers trembling, eager and hungry, we undress each other, slow, real slow, button by button, still dancing, moving like summer clouds to the bed, which will be writhing in lust in anticipation of our arrival."

"I'm already dripping."

"Good, me too. Eros is wet."

"Have you done this before?"

"Never. I've been waiting for you."

"Lucy, dear Lucy, don't die." The pain was getting impossibly hard to contain. Lucy took my hands and squeezed them hard.

"Stay with me, David. This is not dying—this is living and loving. I want you. The pain can wait. Let's turn it into ecstasy tonight. What do you say?"

"Right you are. We have plenty of time for crying. Let's start swimming."

"What if we light the pilot light with a kiss?"

Lucy put her arms around my neck and moved into me. Our mouths circled and dipped toward each other, the room, and the candlelight. Our breath moved into slow time over the long, parabolic journey to lips happily finding each other and tongues rolling over and under. We hung there, suspended, like space walkers, and then ever-so-gently drifted apart, but not. Quivering now, but only slightly, we moved, orbiting each other, two moons falling in love, abandoning their planets to circle each other endlessly, endlessly trembling with joy, closer, so close, but not touching, a dervish duet whirling at one mile per hour, whirling but not touching, no gravity, only yearning, sweet, barely bearable yearning, yearning that knows no end, that is the pulse of love that wants nothing but what it is, yearning for the love, the love of song, the love of body and desire, the love, the love . . .

We were not afraid, though we trembled. We were afraid, and we let each other in. We turned, back-to-back, always circling, dark side of the moon to dark side, stranger to stranger no more, circling boundless, sparks shooting up the spine, our arms uplifted and conversing in delight, and a voice from dreaming, an echo from eternity singing, *this is not dying, this is not dying.*

We stood over Lucy's bed, two bodies purring, yet to touch. A billion particles of joy hummed, ready to dance the waltz of the beloved. We dropped all membranes of separateness, button by tender button into a clumsy pile, bidding goodbye to the last possible distance between us. Our clothes fell like rose petals, and we fell like stardust into each other's arms and legs, ears and necks, hands and feet. Like verse falling down the page, slower than the rising moon, we felt every cell gather and move, gather and rejoice, smelling with tongue the plentiful history of this flesh, tasting with being the deliciousness of life, moaning and calling our names—love,

love, oh love, yes love, you, you, sweet you. Waves crashing, stars leaping, prayers answered, water holding water, dream holding light, death smiling and holding life, life breathing lightly, holding death. Love holding all. All holding love.

. . .

We woke in the morning to the sound of a strong wind whipping through the trees, bringing the last golden leaves to their burial ground. Lucy smiled at me, but I knew there was more going on when I saw a teardrop slide down her cheek. Still shaking from a dream, I shed a few tears too.

"What is it, David?"

"A dream. And you, your face, is so warm and tender."

"Will you tell me your dream?"

I hesitated, not sure if I wanted to be the focus right away. But I didn't like saying no to Lucy, so I started in. "I was trying to wade into the ocean, but the surf was rough and kept throwing me back onto the beach. I woke up really frightened."

"You're quite amazing, David Chase, yes you are."

"Why?"

"Hafiz, that's why."

"What?"

"Hafiz of Shiraz, the fourteenth century mystic poet."

"Oh, him." I must have looked as bewildered as I felt because Lucy went on to explain Hafiz, but it didn't erase my interpretation of the dream which was the recurring certainty that I am not up to the tasks facing me. I can't even walk out into the ocean; how can I be enough to help Lucy in her moment of greatest need?

"Yes, oh, him. You dreamed a Hafiz poem. This is incredibly auspicious, David! He wrote a great poem about entering the ocean of God. He thought he was in the ocean and then realized he was just at the water's edge. When he tried to walk in, he was thrown back on the shore over and over. In the end he laments, 'Why did I want this crazy love?' and realizes that opening to love is not without its bruises."

I gaped at her in astonishment and nearly shouted, "Lucy, that's crazy, that's my dream!"

"I know, I'm telling you, it's an omen! You're the next great mystic poet! The next Rumi is lying in my bed, oh my God!"

"Last night I felt so . . . what's the word, incredible? Lousy word, but I've never felt anything like it so it's the best I can do, and now I'm aching like I got run over by a herd of buffalo. I don't want to be a poet, or anything. I want to be with you, Lucy, and you're leaving."

"Oh, David, my dear, dear David, I want to be with you, and I am, with everything I have, everything, but it will be a short life together, a magical, glorious life."

We lay there in each other's arms struck dumb by the magic of our time and the hard blow of fate. "It's so cruel. Isn't it cruel, Lucy? All these years getting ready, and finally we find each other, and poof, gone with the wind. I call that cruel. Who thinks these things up?"

"Whoever it is, I'm glad. I can't stand that it will be so short, but I'm glad. So glad."

"I'll come with you."

"You won't. Audrey needs you, and besides, it's not your time. You aren't done, Mr. Hafiz. You have poems to write and that big love to plunge into."

"I can't swim. I'm chicken. Without you, I'll run, I know myself."

"You will not. Emily won't let you, and besides, that's bull, you didn't run from Randy, and compared to that, me evaporating is a piece of cake. You know that as well as I do."

"I don't know anything. Fuck. Was last night a dream, Lucy? Has it been a dream all along?"

"No, dear, it wasn't a dream. It was the most beautiful night of our lives. It will live forever. It will. You are my dance partner, my prize."

"You just have a thing for older men."

"Hey, mister, I'm your elder, remember?"

"Ha, you're right, you're right. Damn, this hurts. Why not try chemo, Lucy? Why not just give it a shot and see what happens, see if it helps?"

"What? David, stop. Don't do this. You know what chemo does to people—you've seen it as much as I have, and you know they haven't found anything that works with pancreatic. I don't want to fight. I won't. I'm not afraid to die, and I'm not putting me, or you, through that. I'm not."

"I'm sorry, Lucy. I woke up really sad and frightened. We don't have much time, and what we have is so good. This morning I feel small and grabby. I want to hold on tight to everything. I guess I'm afraid of falling into that black hole again."

"Oh, sweetheart, you've lost so much. Here, let me hold you.

Cry as much as you need. I'm kind of glad you aren't all right with me leaving, to tell the truth."

"Are you?"

"Am I? All right with leaving? I ache for us, for so little time. I find myself wondering what it would have been like to be ourselves now in younger bodies. Besides starting forest fires and such, we would have made beautiful babies and a beautiful life. That pains me. And then there's Audrey. How I would have loved watching and helping her be a mom."

I knew better than to keep going, but I couldn't stop myself; I was beginning to feel frantic. "Then why not give it a try? We can go to the best doctors up at Hutchinson. I hear they do miracles."

Lucy pushed me away and for the first time I saw a dragon come out of her. She roared and fire shot from her nostrils. "No! Stop it, David, don't do this! I told you my mind is made up. Don't make this harder than it is, and don't fight me. Don't!"

I shrunk and felt stupid. I also had to admit I liked seeing the ferocious Lucy. She was lightning over the mountains. It woke me up and drove away the fear. "You're right, I'm sorry. I guess I panicked. Thanks for snapping me out of it."

Lucy softened as quickly as she had risen up in fury. She moved closer and stroked my head. "I get it David, I do. I'm scared too, and heartbroken, so heartbroken we have so little time. Come here, hold me, love."

With that we both let loose and soaked the pillows. Our wise old bones absorbed the sorrow as they have every pain that came along over a lifetime. And by this time, we were both plenty bony, especially Lucy, who was busy undoing the flesh that had made so many men happy—the flesh that breathed and sweated and housed a trillion nerves conversing with the vast and immediate world. We cried our hearts out, as they say, but our hearts only grew fuller, full beyond our greatest notions, full but unbounded: a bowl.

"Lucy?"

"Yeah?"

I could tell she was thinking, "Oh no, here we go again." But I was on to something else. Something more playful and perhaps not. "Lucy, did we just have our first fight?"

"Well, I believe we did! Short but not so sweet!"

"A fiery comet in the night sky."

"Like Jackie Gleason and Audrey Meadows in *The Honeymooners*!"

"Perfect. We're not conflict avoidant, are we?"

But Lucy never had the chance to reply. The dogs had had enough of our emotions and jumped on us, licking our tears away and demanding with their tails that we take to the streets for a good round of sniffing. We obliged and threw on some clothes, grabbed jackets, and headed out into the shower of wind, rain, and leaves. Something in the weather and Lucy's temper reminded me of Randy. It was a fond memory, and I immediately wanted to head to the river with his ashes.

"Hey, let's take the ashes to the river."

"Perfect, of course, we almost forgot."

"I'll run and get them."

"I'll get a poem and perfume."

"Let's drive and take the rest to Emily's tree."

"Really?"

"Didn't I tell you? I promised Randy."

"Sweet. This just keeps getting better."

"Meet you at Gina."

The dogs piled in, and the top stayed up. We drove to the Hawthorne Bridge and parked on Main Street by the fire station and the statue of Vera Katz. We must have made a strange procession up the ramp—dogs pulling hard, bicycles passing by, two old-timers, walking slowly, each carrying a bag in one hand and holding a dog leash in the other. Who would have guessed the contents of our holdings? It was a most improbable funeral procession.

By the time we reached the bridge proper, the rain had stopped, and the massive cloudbank was morphing into large autumn clouds with silver linings and broken spaces where blue sky stood by watching.

We were greeted by a great view of the city landscape, the pastel buildings and their backdrop of trees in the western hills. The evergreen of firs and cedars surrounded the urban body with an emerald glow. Even light seemed to open its wings, reflecting off the river's face and cascading upwards into the rollicking rugby game above us.

Lucy and I walked to the center of the bridge and looked north and south, up and down the Willamette, from bridge to bridge and down into the wide arm of water making its way to the Pacific. It felt good to lean into the railing with happiness. I took the urn from my bag and unscrewed the lid.

I looked to Lucy and asked, "Should I say something?"

"Do you want to? I searched for a poem, but I couldn't find the one I was looking for."

"Do you remember what it's about?"

"It's one of my favorite Rumi poems, about identity, about our identity with all, with every molecule and atom, every tree and leaf. Those buildings, the river, the gulls on the water's surface, the gulls in the air, rain and sunlight, the noise of cars zooming by, the sound of Canadian geese trumpeting. There is nothing that is not a part of this life, nothing that is separate from this creation, nothing that is not of this one being. Something like that."

"Wow, that was pretty good. Rumi and Randy would applaud you, I'm sure."

"Why, thank you." Lucy did a mock half bow and came up laughing.

Just then the cosmos broke into the most glorious applause ever. A patch of clouds opened, turning the light into a scintillating silver streak that shimmered and danced and fell upon the river, and the water's rippling movements turned the face of the Willamette into a flowing garland of stars, millions of stars frolicking on the lip of eternity.

"My God, Lucy, it's magical."

"Breathtaking. Let him go, David, give him to the river and the sparkling."

"Here you go, Randy, fly my dear friend, fly, you are free, completely free."

"Wheeeee."

And the ashes fell into the breath of the moment, bobbing and lifting with the wind and falling again like a sine wave, in no hurry whatsoever on their merry journey to the merciful flow of a river happy to take them home. They looked like butterflies fluttering in many directions at once as light caught their edges, flickering on and off, on and off like so many sparkling lives.

"There he goes, David, he's one with all this now, one with the big blue sky and this precious little jewel."

"And one with you and me."

"I brought some flowers to send along." She reached into her bag and pulled out a small bouquet of gold and orange autumn mums. "Here, let's each throw a couple in and say a prayer for his soul and ours and all the lonely people and the mice and crickets and baby spiders too. Here we go!"

We watched the mums chase after Randy's ashes, but I couldn't take my eyes off of Lucy standing there radiant as the light on the water.

"David, this is another perfect moment. We seem to have a lot of them."

"You're magic, Lucy. Pure magic."

"I have an idea."

"What is it?"

"Let's get married!"

"Married? Married!"

"Yeah, let's get married. Right here, right now in this perfect moment. What do you say?"

"I thought you were married to John Lennon."

"Very funny. You're stalling. You don't want to hitch your wagon with mine?"

"Don't play with me, Lucy. Are you serious? You really want to marry me?"

"This is not a game, my love. I want you. I want to die as your wife, and I want us to begin our marriage right now."

"Wow, you mean it, don't you? I've never been proposed to before. Did you ask my mother for my hand?"

"Now who's playing? Don't keep a girl waiting, my darling. You know how fickle we can be."

"Lucy, when Randy and I spoke for the last time, I told him I wanted to listen to a woman's voice. I wanted to hear the melody of the deep feminine, follow it into the quiet and care for it. That first morning in the garden, before I'd even seen you, I felt something move in my chest and in the world. It hasn't stopped moving and I hope it never does."

"Is that a yes?"

"It is."

"Oh good. You may kiss the bride."

"Yum."

This was no ordinary kiss. And it was not the kiss that concludes a traditional wedding service. This was a kiss of recognition, a recognition of mystery and destiny teaming together to unite two souls into one. We kissed. Drivers crossing the bridge honked their horns in celebration. But the wedding had not begun.

"Well, who will give you away, Lucy?"

"The sky. Who will perform the service?"

"The river."

We glanced up at the sky and down to the river and each smiled in agreement.

"I see. Beautiful. And the wind will play the music. Wind was Emily's favorite instrument."

"I love it, David. This is perfect, isn't it? And I have two stems left. I wasn't sure why I didn't throw them in with the others."

"I want Bobby to be my best man."

Lucy was taken by surprise, and she looked at me in disbelief. "Oh, David, you're making the bride cry before we even begin. Thank you, thank you so much. And I would truly love Emily by my side as my maid of honor. May I?"

"Of course. Please, is it okay if the groom cries too?"

"Sure, there won't be a dry eye in the house. We'll cry for all that is not married in this sad world, and we'll cry tears of joy for all that is. Sugar and Henry can be our witnesses—they won't cry, they'll just bark and wag."

"Wait a minute! We don't have rings. You can't get married without rings."

"Oh dear, I hadn't thought of that. I know—our rings will be our words, our beloved words, wrapped around us and holding our devotion to each other like golden hoops. How's that?"

"Sort of like halo hoops?"

"Oh, that's bad! I love it."

"Look, the sun is coming out again!"

"Lovely, David. Okay, I think we're ready. Are you ready?"

"Vows. What about our vows?"

"We're stepping into the unknown. Why make our vows from the known?"

"Hmm, right, we'll improvise, like Rumi coming home after a night of dancing and crazy love with the gang of mystics."

"That's it! Yes, the groundless fountain of being, here we come. How about if I begin with a few lines from Rumi?"

"Great, but let's take ten or fifteen steps back and walk toward each other with Bobby and Emily and meet here and take each other's hands."

"I love this man. I'm weak in the knees."

"Ready?"

"Ready. Scared?"

"First date scared! Happy butterflies!" We smiled like two teenagers approaching each other for a dance. I was trembling but managed to say, "Good, okay, we'll turn and walk fourteen paces, but we can't look back until we reach fourteen. Then let's pause and turn and take each other in from a distance."

"Why fourteen, David?"

"I've just always loved that number. When I was a kid, I was sure it was a magic good luck number. Are you all right with it?"

"Sure, it has a good sound. Let's begin."

We took each other's hands, and the electricity pulsing back and forth was enough to raise our eyebrows. Just then a flock of Canadian geese upriver took to the air and flew in their V formation straight at us and under the bridge, trumpeting in style for the big event. We laughed wholeheartedly, and at exactly the same time we both said, "Now that is a good omen."

With that, we did an about-face and walked off the fourteen paces, paused, and turned to face each other. I smiled and put my hand out for Bobby. Immediately warmth spread over my palm. Lucy put her arm out for Emily and smiled with all her body.

Without signaling, we each took a step toward the other and moved, as slowly as we had danced the night before, closer and closer to our life together. Our eyes never wavered, nor did our hearts. We were sure. When we met, we took each other's hands and proclaimed our everlasting affection.

"I'm crazy about you, Lucy. I love you more than the moon and the stars."

"And I'm nuts about you, David. You are the love of my life."

"We are getting married, world, right here, today!" I couldn't help myself; I felt like shouting to the world and the heavens, and I did.

"Shall I read a little Rumi?"

"Please do. Let's invite Rumi to our wedding."

"Okay, let's see what the old guy has to say. I'm going to read some random lines if that's all right with you?"

"Knock me out, Mr. Rumi. It's my wedding day—knock my socks off!"

Lovers don't finally meet somewhere.
They're in each other all along.

"That's so lovely, Lucy. We are in each other, aren't we? And it seems like we always have been."

"I've been looking for you, David, and now we're here, together."

Lucy threw herself into my arms and held me tight.

"Let's do our vows, or should we call them promises? What should we call them? Vows sound too legal or something."

Lucy had the perfect answer. "Let's call them our sweet nothings.

Let's whisper sweet nothings in each other's ears so only we can hear them. I love any chance I get to whisper in your ear. Yum."

And there it was, that look, that sexy, inviting "I want you" look that bewitched and beguiled my helpless heart. My ears tingled in anticipation.

"Yeah, you and me, and Bobby and Emily, and the water stars. Here we go, Lucy. *I will always be in your tree, no matter what may come.*"

"David, you are sweeter than a fresh strawberry. That is the nicest thing anyone has ever said to me. *I will keep my comrade warm, forever.*"

"*I'll float into the mystic with you.*"

"*David, I will cherish you with every breath I have.*"

"*Lucy, I will give you the truth, always.*"

"*I will see the radiance in you.*"

"*I will listen to your voice sing.*"

"*I will make your favorite ice cream.*"

"*I will make you melt.*"

"*I will always say yes.*"

"*I will never say no.*"

"*I will hold your fears.*"

"*I will dry your tears.*"

"*I will sing to you as you lay dying.*"

"*I will sing to you as you lay dying.*"

"*I will go on living.*"

"*I will go on.*"

"*I will live in Love with you.*"

"I will live and be Love with you."
"I give you my word and my heart."
"I give you my everything."

Silence surrounded the city and moved into the depths. Emily laughed and danced and did cartwheels on the railing. Bobby jumped up and down with the dogs and made the bridge laugh. A crow flew to the top of the green towers.

Haw, Haw, Haw
You may kiss the sky
Kiss the sky! Kiss the Sky!
Haw, Haw, Haw!

Chapter 81

Phew. That was a long one, Mom. But worth it, don't you think? I'm a married man, my new wife is dying, and I'm still happy. Is something wrong with me? Yes, there are moments when it hits me that just as I've found Lucy, I'm about to lose her, and I feel desperate and furious, and I don't know what else. But the strangest thing, Mom, is that it doesn't last. I can't stay mad. It's a flash storm, a summer downpour with thunder and lightning, and then it clears, and I feel overcome with my good fortune. Am I numb? Am I so used to losing what is precious that I no longer blink an eye? I don't think so. This is different. Even as Lucy fades away, our love grows stronger. I'm getting more and more confident that will continue after she leaves. Just like it has with you.

I don't know what my feelings are for you right now. I'm all over the map. That's not new for me. Lucy's easy; you're not. But I think Audrey's fury took some of mine with it when it left. I never thought I'd be alive, and here I am. I'm alive! And you're a part of that life. Isn't it strange that as I'm losing Lucy, I'm finding you? It seems that sorrow and joy are always holding hands. I do wish I had just one memory of you and me holding hands. I'd like to feel your warm hand around mine. When I see mothers and sons walking to school hand in hand, I feel a pang of envy and grief. It must be there. You must have taken my hand. Maybe we walked along listening to the birds sing. Maybe we sang along. Maybe we were happy for a day.

I don't like being full of maybes. We have something now. It's good, even if it gets all mixed up at times. Even if the little boy in me can still feel unwanted. Even if he can think he's unlovable. I feel for him, too. He wasn't a bad kid, was he? And he can join us now, in what we have. You aren't going away again, are you, Mom?

Chapter 82

On Thanksgiving morning, a winter fog settled on the valley floor and covered the area stretching from Eugene to Portland and Portland up the Columbia to Hood River. By mid-afternoon, the sun had burned away the last patches drifting over wetlands.

Lucy and I rose early and took to the fog with an eagerness that resembled the furry little friends at our feet. We loved the fog, as we loved the many things that filled our days now: the reading of poetry by candlelight, holding hands and singing old Beatles tunes, and slow dancing by the fire to the tunes of Nat King Cole.

Laughter followed us everywhere, and so did death. Lucy was noticeably thinner.

By Christmas she was losing strength rapidly. The day after Christmas she stayed in bed and told me she thought we were nearing the time. Strangely, I didn't feel distraught. And Lucy didn't either. Her room was the same warm, welcoming space. Nothing like a funeral parlor. We burned candles nonstop and incense some of the time. I wouldn't call it a happy place, but there was a sense of deep reverence for every breath that was ours.

I sat at the foot of the bed and rubbed her feet. "You're tired, aren't you?"

"I am. I'm very tired. Time for a long winter's nap."

"Are you in pain?"

"No, some discomfort, but nothing terrible."

"You're really fortunate, Lucy."

"I am so fortunate. I want to be awake when I die, David. I want to be here for my death. You know, when I'm asleep I'm awake. It is so amazing."

"Lucy, this is beautiful. You're becoming everything, all the separations are falling away."

"I'm falling in Love. David, the Love . . ."

"I can feel it. The room is humming with it."

"And sometimes Bobby is here. I can't really see his face, but it's him and he's glowing."

"And you are his good mother."

"Yes. Thanks to you."

"I am the lucky one."

"David . . ."

"Yes?"

"Do you think it will go on like this, the dying?"

"I do, Lucy. I think you will have a very easy time of it."

Lucy began to cry softly and held her hands to her face to catch the tears as they fell. "Why is this so emotional? I'm thinking I don't need the drugs. I can let it come. Maybe I can just let myself be taken." I moved from her feet to her side and touched her arm.

"Honey, you are. You are letting yourself become what you really are. You're laying down all the garments and props. I know you can do it the rest of the way."

"Thank you for that. Thank you. I just didn't want one of those terrible, terrible deaths where everything is a fight and I'm in agony and everyone around is tied up in knots. I don't want that, David. I don't."

"You won't have that, my love. I'm sure of it. And if something goes differently, I'll help you. But I'm sure you are going your way, the way you've lived."

"You are such a dear. I know it sounds corny, but I really feel I'm being born into something strangely familiar. And the weirdest part is, I'm not really going anywhere."

"Into the mystic mother. This is it, the mystic sunrise, Lucy. Right there. What a privilege it is for me."

"Are you really all right, David? You'll be all right?"

"I will, Lucy. I'll be all right. I'll miss you like crazy, but I'll be fine. I promise. Don't you worry about a thing. You relax and let that big Love call you home."

"And you'll have Audrey and the baby."

"And Sugar and Henry. And maybe I'll go downtown and hang out with the homeless camps."

"Oh, David, that's wonderful. You'll make a difference, I know you will. And blessed Sugar and Henry. Where are those two?"

"Probably curled up on the couch."

"Speaking of Audrey, isn't she coming over later?"

"She is. Later this afternoon."

"Oh good. I want to rub her belly."

"It's getting pretty big. Somebody's in there getting ready."

"One coming, one going."

"Nothing disappears."

"Nothing disappears. I like that. I'm going to sleep now."

"Sweet dreams, dear one."

"Okay."

Chapter 83

Lucy slept with a slight smile on her face. Her body was shutting down, but she rested peacefully. The air around her sparkled. I sat next to her bed and held her hand. I often closed my eyes and joined her in the quiet, but really, I preferred to look at her loveliness, which, though still as the night sky, moved almost imperceptibly, gliding like a swan on a lake.

One moment she looked like she was kissing, another being kissed, others laughing, others weeping, but always there was the motion within the stillness of her face, rising and falling, rising and falling. It was like looking at a good painting shifting into subtly different expressions. There were moments I felt a slight vertigo, but most of the time I lost myself in the beauty and mystery of her face.

It made me wonder if I could look at your face again, Mom. Maybe I can really see you. More and more memories of us are returning from exile. Isn't that wild? I see your face smiling down at me. Maybe you were tucking me into bed at night. I see that troubled look on your face when you didn't know I was watching. The one I told myself was about me. So troubled. I see your body, exhausted, collapsed on the couch or leaning against a counter. So exhausted. You ran out of fuel, didn't you, Mom? Nothing to go on with. No hope, no will. Nothing. And then there was your face in the car. Blood on the cheek. Eyes closed. What was that expression? What were your last thoughts? Did you think, *At last, finally?* Did you whisper my name? Did you? I heard something. I didn't know what death looked like. I'd only seen a dead squirrel in the street and its eyes were open. Your eyes were closed. You had big blue eyes, didn't you? I'm remembering. They were dazzling at times. I remember now. They lit up when you picked flowers and arranged them. I remember feeling sick when they went dull. I saw you die before you died. It's hard to believe in you, Mom. It's hard to feel you alive in me like I feel Emily. You come and you go. Do I drive you away? Please stay. Stay with me, Mom.

■ ■ ■

There were moments when Lucy's eyes fluttered and opened, and the room was happy to fill with her glow. It took a few minutes for her to orient to the world, but when she did, and when she saw me by her side, she smiled softly and raised her hand to touch my cheek.

"Hello."

"Hello, love." I lived in a state of angst, fearing she might never open her eyes again—those deep pools that took me in and opened onto vistas I found breathtaking. When Lucy did wake and look up at me, my world shifted and began to move again. I felt renewed joy and relief that she was back for a little while longer.

"How long did I sleep?"

"Oh, I think a couple of hours."

"I dreamed something. Not sure what. Oh, it's so close. Oh, I know! I dreamed I was in your dream. You were dreaming something really big, and I was in it. Isn't that a funny one?"

"I guess that makes me your dream man."

"That it does. Come in here, my dream man. Hold me close."

"Here I come." And I dove into bed beside her, and though she was weak and mostly skin and bones, the pleasure of our touch was strong and delightful as ever. Lucy radiated love even on her deathbed, and I absorbed all I could.

"Oh, that's real nice. I like this dream."

"Me too, me too. I don't want this dream to end. Ever."

"Maybe I'll come floating into your dream on a cloud like an old Hollywood musical, wearing a sexy evening gown with a slit up the side. Would you like that?"

"I would love that."

"Okay, I'll order that up first thing when I'm on the other side and you'll know I got there safely."

"That will wake me up, for sure."

"Got to keep my man happy."

"You do that, you do that."

"Good." We hugged and purred contentedly. It was a moment our bodies treasured. A moment to remember.

Lucy stirred after a few minutes of bliss and asked, "When are Audrey and Mark coming?"

"They should be here in half an hour. Are you up to it?"

"As long as they're okay with me in bed. Mark can be kind of, you know."

"I know. They'll be so relieved you're not doing yourself in they'll be good with just about anything."

"Anything, hmm, let's see . . ."

"Don't get too devilish now. We're expecting company, you know."

"Okay, I'll save my best devil stuff for you, mister."

The doorbell rang and we both gave a start. "Whoa, saved by the bell. They're early."

"Oh good. I feel another good nap coming on."

"Hang on, we'll keep it short."

The time it took for me to walk to the front door and welcome Audrey and Mark was all the time Lucy needed to doze and touch for a moment the land of all becoming, that groundless land, no longer calling Lucy, no longer singing her name, but caressing her soul.

I welcomed Audrey and Mark in and made tea while Lucy slept. They both looked shaky sitting on the couch, and as I explained her condition, each leaned into the other for support with pain etched on their faces. Both had come to adore Lucy. The day she told Audrey and Mark she was leaving her house to them, they had crumbled to their knees, overcome with emotion. Neither could imagine such a gift. And now, here in the house that would soon be theirs, they couldn't hold back the emotion, and each sobbed and leaned into the other for comfort. I waited, allowing them room to feel the love and the loss. Audrey was the first to speak through broken sobs. "How much time does she have, David?"

"Not long, a few days, maybe. She's moving smoothly along, not much pain, miraculously. You'll be happy to know she's decided to let nature take its course."

"Oh, thank God! Oh, David, that is the best news. Isn't that wonderful, Mark?"

"It is great, honey, just great. The Lord . . ."

Audrey was quick to reign Mark in. "Hey, easy on 'The Lord' stuff, okay?"

"Right. Sorry."

"It's all right, you two. You can say whatever you want. We don't mind—we know what we all mean."

"How are you, David? How are you holding up?"

I would have gladly told Audrey and Mark how beautiful the time with Lucy was, and how I ached for more time together, but just then we heard Lucy stirring and calling for us.

Lucy was trying to open her eyes when we reached her bedside. There was a different look to her now, a faraway look, as though this world were no longer home. And speaking had taken a sudden turn, requiring much more effort. The three of us had to huddle close to her bed to hear her words.

"David . . . so much love . . ."

"You look like you are swimming in it."

"Yes . . . I am . . . hard to talk . . . so strong . . ."

"Don't work too hard, love, just be, we're good. Audrey and Mark are here to see you. I've told them your plan."

"Audrey . . ."

"Hello, Lucy, you are beautiful." Audrey's face brightened at Lucy's side, but the pain and tears were still on the surface.

"Please . . . hold my hand . . ."

"Of course, I'm here, sweet Lucy." Audrey took Lucy's hand and kissed it. She bent close to her face so Lucy didn't have to strain to speak to her. Mark and I could just barely make out what Lucy was saying, but we could see her dig deep inside to say her last words to the soon-to-be mother.

"Good, it helps if I can feel you . . . you will love being a mother, dear . . . it is so lovely . . . you will be wonderful, I know you will . . . you have the heart for it . . . just trust yourself . . . and don't worry about loving too much . . . Just trust . . . Mark . . ."

Audrey released Lucy's hand and stepped away, wiping her eyes and walking to my side for comfort. I put my arm around her and held her close while Mark kneeled by Lucy's bed. "Yes, Lucy?"

Lucy looked so tired I could hardly bear it. But I saw her grit come forth once more, and that voice I adored rallied to speak. "Mark . . . enjoy your child . . . and you will teach the little one everything . . . understand?"

"I do. Thanks, Lucy."

"End of sermon . . . was it terribly boring, David?"

"It was beautiful, Lucy, really beautiful."

"Good . . . Audrey . . ."

"Yes, Lucy?"

"May I touch the baby?" Lucy didn't wait for an answer; she mustered the strength in her trembling arm and reached toward Audrey's bulging belly.

Audrey smiled sadly and quietly moved back to Lucy's side and said, "Yes, please give our baby your blessing, dear Lucy."

"Ah, so round . . . how lovely . . . thank you . . ."

"Lucy, Mark and I have a question we'd like to ask you and David. Is that okay?"

"Of course, sweetheart . . . and then . . . I may need to rest . . . I'm very tired . . ."

"Sure, well, Mark and I, we were wondering . . ." Audrey choked on her emotions and looked to Mark for help. She caught her breath and tried to continue. "We'd like to ask . . . Mark, I can't

. . . please . . ."

Mark put his hands on Audrey's shoulders and said to us, "Audrey and I love you guys and we would love to name our child after yours. We don't know if it will be a boy or a girl, but either way, we'd like your permission to name our baby Emily or Bobby. Is that all right?"

Lucy turned her head slowly and looked at me and back to Mark and Audrey. "Nothing could make me happier . . ."

"David?"

"Are you kidding? That's incredibly wonderful. I love it."

Audrey burst into tears of joy, sorrow, and laughter. She kissed Lucy on her cheek, then ran to Mark and threw herself into his arms. We were lost in that glow when Lucy's voice called us back.

"Audrey?"

"Yes, Lucy?"

". . . will I be the baby's grandmother?"

We stood there speechless, looking at each other, when Audrey's voice caught again and she nearly shouted with happiness, "Yes you will—you are! Lucy, please, yes, you are Grandma Lucy, isn't she Mark?"

"Yes, Lucy, absolutely! Our baby is blessed. Thank you!"

"Oh good . . . I'll watch over . . . and keep her safe . . ."

Chapter 84

My dear Mom. Our last night together passed slowly. Lucy slept peacefully most of the night and I sat at the bedside holding her hand and reading her favorite poems from Rumi, Machado, and Maya Angelou. Around three in the morning I put on *Tranquility,* music by the East Indian violinist L. Subramaniam. His hauntingly lovely music seemed to emanate directly from ancient caves at the mountainous headwaters of the Ganges. It was the perfect sound to accompany Lucy home, and her breath took to the rhythm without hesitation.

Something in me surrendered as well. A tired version of myself, standing upright, lay down his heavy heart. I could hear the words. They were kind and gentle, more like a mother's touch than a command. *Lay yourself down, dear. Yes, like that, good, yes that's good.* That was you, wasn't it? You, talking to me, soothing me.

I lay myself down into the deep sigh of the violin, into the merciful opening between one breath and another. I lay there with Lucy where differences dissolve, where spaciousness brings one and all into its fold. I could not tell you what happened next. In fact, happening ceased its relentless crashing on the shore, and a peace beyond description put us to bed.

When I woke on the other side of dreaming, Lucy was looking

at me. Her eyes were glistening, and if they could have spoken, they might have said, "You are so beautiful," or "I am so happy," or any number of things you might not expect from the dying. What she did say, from her last thread of being, was this: "*love . . .*"

. . .

Lucy left her body as easily as easing out of a slipper. One breath, another, and then quiet, blessed quiet. The room filled with her still life, that shocking, breathless space the departed leave in their wake. Hers was a beautiful life and a beautiful death.

I wanted to fly after her, but she had vanished in the direction of stillness, and I did not know which trail to take or how to follow. So I lay down next to her lonely body and stroked her hair. It was thin and soft, white as summer clouds. I touched her cheek and thought she might open her eyes one last time. I kissed her hand and marveled at how warm it was.

I tried to sing a song, but I could not. Finally, I gave up and lay my head on her shoulder. I closed my eyes and went searching for the sound of Lucy's voice coming from the garden, speaking encouraging words to the ladybugs. And there it was, still alive, still resonant with this life and all that was Lucy, and all that passed between us. And it was lovely.

. . .

My dear Mom, that was Lucy, my beloved Lucy. As are you, Mom, as are you. Perhaps in the end I will say the same about myself. Beloved. When I woke up from the reverie of Lucy's voice to the absence of her, you were there. Thank you. You are alive to me, Mom. We have each other, at last. I feel your warmth.

Epilogue

Emily Bobbie Stewart was born at sunrise on the morning of June 22 in Audrey and Mark's home. She weighed nine pounds and was twenty-two inches long. Emily took to her mother's body and breast with ease. They melted into each other's lives.

Floating above the bed was a large, round red balloon provided by her grandfather, David Chase, who stood by the bed with Mark, transfixed by the sight of mother and infant. Bobby held the balloon in his delicate fingers, and atop the red balloon, Lucy, Martha, and Claire sat marveling at the beauty of their newborn granddaughter. David's mother sat by the pillow, stroking Audrey's hair and smiling the beatific smile of one who has been to hell and returned. And Sugar and Henry snoozed at the foot of the bed, spooned together, dreaming of their chance to lick the baby's face.

And Emily? Emily flew about the bedroom, gliding from the balloon to the bed, then to the floor, with all the grace of a swan taking off and landing on a pond. She flew to the balloon and kissed the three grandmothers and flew back to the side of the new mother, who held her namesake. Her movements created a light breeze that was Bu laughing while brushing the skin and blessing the soul of the newborn and all her people. Emily took it all in as she had the joyous dream the morning of her last birthday. It was the same unbounded joy, the joy of the world. As love enveloped them all, she looked into her father's heart and found it whole. On a gust of love from the lips of Bu, she flew to David and put her arms around his neck and whispered, "My Daddy, my dear Daddy."

Acknowledgements

Many thanks to John Hohn and Gary Smith for reading the manuscript in its early stages and encouraging me to persevere. Their belief in the book helped me through many tough days. The same goes for the editors at Allegory Editing in Seattle, especially to Christine Pinto who gently guided me through the white water of the developmental edits.

A huge voice of gratitude for the work and person of Jay Jarvis Masters, whose life and writings from death row in San Qentin, opened my mind to the cruelty of solitary confinement. And his compassion freed me to imagine the emotional deadening many men suffer as another form of confinement.

I also want to thank Andrew Durkin at Yellow Bike Press for skillfully and patiently guiding me through the design and publication process.

As always, none of this writing or any other would be what it is without the love and support of my family. You bring out the best in me.

www.ingramcontent.com/pod-product-compliance
Lightning Source LLC
Chambersburg PA
CBHW031435160726
47994CB00005B/1731